RAVES FOR *THE COWBOYS* SERIES!

JAKE

"Only a master craftsman can create so many strong characters and keep them completely individualized."

—*Rendezvous*

WARD

"Few authors write with the fervor of Leigh Greenwood. Once again [Greenwood] has created a tale well worth opening again and again!"

—*Heartland Critiques*

BUCK

"*Buck* is a wonderful Americana Romance!"

—*Affaire de Coeur*

CHET

"*Chet* has it all! Romance and rustlers, gunfighters and greed...romance doesn't get any better than this!"

—*The Literary Times*

SEAN

"This book rivals the best this author has written so far.... Western romance at its finest!"

—*The Literary Times*

PETE

"*Pete* is another stroke on Leigh Greenwood's colorful canvas of the Old West. The plotting is brilliant and the conflict strong."

—*Rendezvous*

DREW

"Sexual tension and endless conflict make for a fast-paced adventure readers will long remember."

—*Rendezvous*

LUKE

"Another winner by Leigh Greenwood!"

—*Romantic Times*

MATT

"*The Cowboys* are keepers, from the first book to the last!"

—*The Literary Times*

LOSING CONTROL

"I never said I didn't want to kiss you." Damn! That was the last thing he should have said. Why was he losing control now?

"Then will you kiss me?"

The logical and safe answer was to go to bed and refuse even to talk about it any longer. Her father wouldn't like it if he knew. His uncle and cousin would run him out of Boston, and Lonnie would shoot him. He would be leaving before long, so a sensible person wouldn't do anything to cause trouble.

But he was tired of being sensible, of following the rules, and getting nowhere. He wanted to kiss her. He'd been thinking about it almost from the time he first saw her.

A Texan's Honor

LEIGH GREENWOOD

LEISURE BOOKS NEW YORK CITY

A LEISURE BOOK®

July 2006

Published by

Dorchester Publishing Co., Inc.
200 Madison Avenue
New York, NY 10016

ISBN 0-8439-5684-4

Printed in the United States of America.

Visit us on the web at www.dorchesterpub.com.

FAMILY GENEALOGY

Jake Maxwell m. Isabelle Davenport 1866
  Eden Maxwell b. 1868

Ward Dillon m. Marina Scott 1861
   Tanner b. 1862
   Mason b. 1869
   Lee b. 1872
   Conway b. 1874
   Webb b. 1875

Buck Hobson (Maxwell) m. Hannah Grossek 1872
   Wesley b. 1874
   Elsa b. 1877

Drew Townsend m. Cole Benton 1874
   Celeste b. 1879
   Christine b. 1881
   Clair b. 1884

Sean O'Ryan m. Pearl Belladonna (Agnes Satterwaite) 1876
   Elise b. 1866 (Pearl's daughter by previous marriage)
   Kevin b. 1877
   Flint b. 1878
   Jason b. 1880

Chet Attmore (Maxwell) m. Melody Jordan 1880
   Jake Maxwell II (Max) b. 1882
   Nick b. 1884

Bret Nolan m. Emily Abercrombie 1881
   Sam b. 1882
   Joseph b. 1884
   Elizabeth b. 1885

Matt Haskins m. Ellen Donovan 1883
     Toby b. 1868 (adopted)
     Hank Hollender b. 1870 (adopted)
     Orin b. 1872 (adopted)
     Noah b. 1878 (adopted)
     Tess b. 1881 (adopted)
     Matthew b. 1885
     Brodie b. 1886

Pete Jernigan m. Anne Thompson 1886
     Mary Anne b. 1888
     Kane b. 1889
     Kent b. 1889

Will Haskins m. Idalou Ellsworth 1886

Luke Attmore m. Valeria Badenburg 1887
     Lucas b. 1888
     Valentine b. 1889

Hawk Maxwell m. Suzette Chatingy 1888

Zeke Maxwell m. Josie Morgan 1888

A
Texan's Honor

Chapter One

Boston, 1881

Bret Nolan approached his uncle Silas Abbott's office with barely concealed anticipation, a smile threatening to banish his habitual frown. He was certain he was being called in for the long-promised but often postponed meeting about the changes Bret had proposed for the company.

He had worked in his mother's family's shipping company, Abbott & Abercrombie, ever since leaving Texas six years ago. During that time he'd carefully studied the inner workings of the transportation industry as the last of the great clipper ships gave way to steam power. He had spent more than a year developing a detailed plan of changes the company needed to make to remain competitive into the twentieth century.

He was doubly excited because the changes would mean bigger roles for him and for his cousin Rupert, who supported him. He wished Rupert were here today, but he was in Providence, Rhode Island, inventorying the contents of Abbott & Abercrombie's warehouses. It was the kind of job that reminded the two men they were poor relations.

"Your uncle said you were to go right in," Silas Abbott's secretary said with a broad smile when Bret entered her office. "He's anxious to see you."

Bret's steps grew lighter. His uncle was *never* anxious to see him. In fact, seeing Bret usually gave him gas. He must have grasped the value of Bret's plan. Finally, he would begin to see his nephew as a valued member of the company, not merely the son of a disinherited sister and her rabble-rousing husband who was thoughtless enough to get himself killed in circumstances that brought unwelcome publicity to the family.

Bret knocked on the door of his uncle's office. The words *Come in* sounded so welcoming, he smiled.

"You wanted to see me, sir."

"Come in and have a seat," his uncle said.

Silas was in such a sunny mood, Bret began to feel uneasy. He felt certain his recommendations were sound, but he'd expected his uncle to argue every point. Silas Abbott liked to think all good ideas were his own. When they weren't, he'd talk in circles, making and discarding suggestions, until he arrived back at the starting point, convinced he had come up with the solution himself.

"How have you been keeping yourself?" Silas asked. "We haven't had a chance to see much of each other lately."

Bret grew even more apprehensive. His uncle *never* wanted anything to do with him, had only hired him because Bret's grandmother had insisted he give Bret a job. Uncle Silas paid Bret barely enough to live on, a measure of his displeasure at having his hand forced.

"I have nothing to complain about," Bret lied. "Working ten hours a day six days a week doesn't leave much time for me to find trouble . . . or it to find me." He could tell from the twitch of his uncle's eyebrows that the remark had angered him, but Bret was tired of seeing his uncle and his son, Joseph, leave the office while he and Rupert still had several hours of work to do. Even the regular staff went home before they did.

"Honest work never hurt anyone," his uncle said. "It's how you get ahead."

But Bret hadn't gotten ahead. Everybody in the office knew he and Rupert could work circles around Joseph, yet Joseph continued to get promoted, with commensurate raises in salary, while Rupert remained a glorified errand boy and Bret an equally exalted clerk. Bret had tried very hard to control the bitterness that burned in his stomach like an acid, but it had become increasingly difficult in the face of Joseph's unwarranted promotions.

"I don't mind. I like the work." Okay, he was lying, but telling the truth wouldn't get him anywhere. This was his chance for a *real* future. It was worth a little white lie.

"Shepherd tells me you've done a very good job," his uncle said. "In fact, he can't seem to stop talking about you."

Unlike Silas, Shepherd wasn't one to withhold praise where it was due.

"I'm glad he thinks I've been helpful."

When he first came from Texas, Bret had had difficulty making meaningless conversation. There was no such thing in the Maxwell household where he'd been raised. Jake was brusque, Isabelle direct, and the other orphans were just waiting for a chance to put somebody down. As long as what they said was fair, Jake and Isabelle let them say pretty much what they thought. They believed all the boys had a right to be heard, that their feelings should be respected as far as possible, and that treatment should be fair. But most of all, they'd loved every one of their eleven adopted kids. The orphans had worked hard, played hard, and occasionally fought hard, but each was a loved and valued part of the family. They knew they belonged.

Bret hadn't expected his mother's family to feel the same way about him, but reality had been a brutal shock. His father's sister had welcomed him back, but she was involved in her causes and was seldom around. Only his grandmother's attention enabled him to keep his tongue between his teeth. She had encouraged him to be patient, said that his hard work and intelligence would pay off someday. Today, he hoped was that day.

"I called you in because I have a very special assignment for you," his uncle said.

"I was hoping we could discuss the suggestions I gave you. It wouldn't take more than a few minutes to—"

"I'm still studying them." Silas tried unsuccessfully to hide his irritation at Bret's interruption.

"I doubt you're aware of it," his uncle went on, "but Ezra Abercrombie had a brother who went West. Samuel was something of an embarrassment to the family, so Ezra was relieved to be rid of him. But apparently their father had a change of heart before he died."

Amos Abercrombie, the ninety-three-year-old only son of one of the founders of Abbott & Abercrombie, had died the previous year and had been buried with all the pomp and recognition the city fathers of Boston could give him.

"It came as quite a surprise to Ezra to learn his father had left a quarter interest in the firm to Samuel in his will."

Bret could see how that would upset his uncle, but he didn't see what it could have to do with him. The

Abercrombies were a proud family who didn't waste time on poor relations. He doubted they'd let him in the door.

"It seems the old renegade has managed to make a fortune in cows somewhere in that godforsaken state of Texas," Silas grumbled. "You ought to know all about that sort of thing."

Bret did know all about *that sort of thing*, and his family never let him forget it. Whenever one of them made any slur about the South or the West, they always turned to him as though he'd been personally responsible for the Civil War as well as anyone wanting to settle west of the Mississippi River. The fact that he would not back down in his admiration for Jake and Isabelle was held to be proof that he was not yet rehabilitated.

"How does that affect me?" Bret asked.

"You can keep twenty-five percent of our company stock from ending up in the hands of some ignorant cowpoke."

Bret had to force down a spurt of anger before he could reply. "How am I supposed to do that?"

"Samuel is dying. He wants this daughter—his only child—to move to Boston. The only problem is the old turncoat has given the girl such a poor image of the Abercrombies, she refuses to budge. The only person she remembers favorably is Joseph, so Samuel wants us to take her in. I want you to bring her to Boston before she gets any foolish ideas about marrying a cowpoke."

Bret wasn't the least bit flattered by this *very special assignment*. His uncle had chosen him to go to Texas because he thought everybody else was too good to be subjected to the rigors of entering a state he was convinced was populated almost entirely by thieves and murderers.

"It's your job to make sure she gets here in an unmarried state. Until she's safely settled in Boston, it's your *only* job."

"I can't force her against her will."

"Who said anything about forcing her?" his uncle asked. "You lived among those people for years. You understand them. If you want me to believe you're smart enough to figure out a better way to run my business, you can begin by delivering that girl without a husband in tow."

"Sons and daughters of *those people* don't always do what their parents want."

"That would serve Samuel right," Silas said with a nasty smile. "*He* never did what anybody wanted, but we can't afford to let those shares go out of the family. You get her here, and I'll find somebody to marry her."

"Who?" She might be heir to a quarter of the company, but Bret couldn't see one of the Abbotts or Abercrombies marrying anybody who hadn't been born into Boston society.

"Samuel has sent his brother several pictures of her over the years. I don't know where he found anyone with a camera in that godforsaken place, but the girl appears to be rather attractive. Joseph is quite taken with her. I admit I'm not pleased at the prospect of a woman of that kind as my daughter-in-law, but we can't allow that twenty-five percent to leave the family."

"I'll have nothing to do with marrying her to Joseph."

"Joseph is capable of handling his own affairs," Silas said. "Your job is to get her here. And don't get any ideas about marrying her yourself." Silas never thought anything he said was insulting. As far as he was concerned, only people like himself had feelings.

"I couldn't marry if I wanted," Bret said. "I don't make enough to support a wife, much less a family."

"Don't despair," Silas said without the slightest hint of sympathy. "Once you work off some of the rough edges you got from spending so many years with horses and cows, you might find a wife. Boston is full of wealthy young women who don't come quite up to the mark and are willing to accept something less in a husband."

Bret wasn't willing to accept *something less* in a wife. "If Joseph is interested in marrying Miss Abercrombie, maybe *he* should go to Texas."

"He wouldn't know how to deal with those people," Silas said. "Besides, I have no intention of letting him marry that girl until she's brought up to our standards. No, it will be much better for you to bring her here. That will give you plenty of opportunity to sing Joseph's praises, let her know how fortunate she is to have attracted the notice of a man of his quality. If you do your job right, by the time she gets here, she'll be ready to fall into Joseph's arms and do anything he asks."

Bret knew he had no choice about going to Texas, yet he wouldn't be a party to talking any woman into marrying his cousin. "If she's spent her whole life on a ranch in Texas, she won't know what to do in a place like this."

"Joseph will take care of that. All you have to do is get her here."

"What if I can't bring her back?"

His uncle's cold stare bored into Bret. "Then don't come back yourself."

"I won't go to Boston," Emily Abercrombie said to her father. "I don't know anybody there. I love the ranch. I don't want to live anywhere else."

"You can't stay here after I'm dead," Sam said to his daughter. "There's nobody to look after you."

"I don't need anybody to look after me," Emily replied. "I've been looking after you ever since Mama died."

Her father had told her nothing about his family that would make her want to have anything to do with them. She'd been to Boston once, when she was eight and her mother had been so sick she went to see special doctors. She'd had ample opportunity to get to know more than she wanted to know about the Abercrombie family. The Abbotts were a little better, especially a cute boy named Joseph, but she was used to almost complete freedom to do as she liked. That would be impossible in Boston, regardless of who she lived with. She couldn't imagine leaving Texas, their ranch, or their house. It was everything she wanted.

"I wouldn't know what to do in Boston," Emily said to her father.

"You could get married and raise a passel of children."

"I don't want a passel of kids to drive me crazy. Think of what I've done to you and multiply that by a half dozen."

Her father returned her smile, reached across the distance that separated them to lay his hand over hers. "I would have welcomed a dozen like you. So would your mother, but she could only have one. I think we got the best."

Emily squeezed her father's hand. "I don't know about that, but you got one who likes getting her own way."

Her father laughed. "Your mother hadn't been dead more than a year before you started changing everything in the house."

Emily's parents had met in Virginia when her fa-

8

ther was studying at the University of Virginia in Charlottesville. They married over the strident objections of both families. When the war broke out, they headed west. Using money he'd made profiteering during the war, Sam had settled in Texas and built a large house, which his wife furnished much like her ancestral home in Virginia.

After her mother's death, Emily had replaced her mother's colorful chintz with subdued leather, delicate porcelain with nearly unbreakable earthenware, and fragile carpets with sturdy rope rugs. Emily thought of the house only as a place to eat and sleep when she wasn't with her horses.

"If I weren't sick or your mother were still alive, I'd never suggest you move to Boston," her father said.

"I wish I could go to my mother's family." That wasn't possible. Her mother's family had lost everything during the war: their home was burned, their land devastated. "I don't see why I have to go anywhere."

"How are you going to find a husband out here?"

"I'm not sure I want a husband."

"Of course, you do. I can't imagine never having been married to your mother."

"You and Mother were special. I promise if I ever find a man like you, I'll marry him."

She didn't want to make things more difficult for her father, but if he wouldn't go to Boston to see doctors, she didn't see why she should go there to find a husband.

"I can't leave you here by yourself. I know you can manage the ranch, and that Lonnie would do anything in his power to help you, but this is tough country. There are rustlers just waiting for me to die so they can run off my herds. You'll be a rich woman. I don't want to think of how many men would be willing to use force to marry you to get your money."

"I can defend myself. You taught me how to use a gun years ago."

"It's not just knowing how to use a gun. Men out here don't respect a woman's right to hold property. Hell, they don't respect *anybody's* right. If you can't keep it by force, you won't keep it."

"I can hire extra help if necessary."

"But could you trust them? You're a beautiful woman, a temptation even to a man of principle. It would be much better to sell the ranch. With your looks and money, you'd have your pick of eligible bachelors."

"I'm not interested in eligible bachelors."

Her father chuckled. "Well, you're going to meet one. Silas Abbott is sending out one of his nephews with orders to escort you back to Boston."

"Did you send for him?"

"All I did was tell your Uncle Ezra I was worried about you and wanted you to go back to Boston. I doubt I would have heard from him if my father hadn't left me a quarter interest in Abbott and Abercrombie."

"You didn't tell me."

"I was going to sell the shares, but I changed my mind when Silas Abbott started putting pressure on me to sell to him. I think he's afraid I'll use my interest to try to get rid of him."

"If they want me to go back, why didn't he send Joseph? At least I liked him."

"Silas would never trust his precious son to the dangers of a land peopled with wild savages, thieves, and murderers. The man who's coming is Bret Nolan. Silas turned his back on the boy's mother when she married a man he didn't like. He's probably hoping Nolan will get lost and never find his way back to Boston, but that's not important. I want you to pay close attention to what he has to say. He knows the Abbotts better than I do."

"I don't care what he or anyone else says. I don't want to go to Boston, so you can tell him not to come."

"I can't. He's on his way to Fort Worth right now."

Bret didn't want to admit it, but the tight bands that had constricted his chest for the last six years had started to loosen as soon as he crossed the border into Texas. As the pine forests of East Texas gave way to the grasslands, he felt his lungs expand to take in deeper and deeper breaths of air. Despite the smoke and cinders from the steam engine, the air smelled cleaner, sweeter. The grass was greener, the sky more blue, the horizon limitless. He'd worked so hard to identify himself with Boston, he'd almost forgotten what Texas was like.

Seeing cows grazing in the billowing grass made him nostalgic for the days when he had chased the ornery beasts, slept under the stars, and cussed when the wind blew grit into the cook pot over the fire. But he'd been his own man back then, trusted by Jake to handle his work without anyone looking over his shoulder.

And when he did head back to the ranch, Isabelle's smile was ample proof he was home and he was wanted there. He would inevitably scrap with Pete and have to fight off Sean afterwards, Zeke would scowl at him and Hawk would virtually ignore him, but nobody hesitated to make a place for him at the table or move over so he could join the circle around the fire. Luke and Chet would place their bedrolls next to his, and Will would bring him steaming coffee as soon as Matt got it ready. Buck treated him like an annoying younger brother, and Drew constantly told him how to behave. But no matter the strains that fractured the orphans along ever-changing lines, he was as much a part of the family as anyone else.

Still, Bret had never been able to forget that his *real* family in Boston had turned its back on his mother, then on him. For as long as he could remember, he'd been filled with an unrelenting need to prove they'd been wrong. At twenty-one, he'd finally packed his bags and left for Boston. Now, six years later, he was back in Texas and was beginning to wonder if he should ever have left. He'd never have guessed he'd feel like he was coming home after a long absence. He had convinced himself he was happy in Boston. Had he been a fool? He'd been shaken badly when his uncle had said not to come back if he couldn't bring Emily Abercrombie with him. Surely he didn't mean he'd turn his back on him, not after he had worked harder than anyone else in the firm. His uncle *had* to recognize his value to the company.

Frustrated, Bret turned his attention to his surroundings. The train was coming in to Fort Worth. Established as an army fort in 1849, it had turned into a thriving commercial town supplying cattlemen and buffalo hunters. He would be met by one of Sam Abercrombie's ranch hands. It was a two-day ride to the ranch. Though he'd rarely been on a horse since leaving Texas, he was looking forward to it.

There wasn't much of interest to look at in Fort Worth, so he tried to wrap his mind around the task ahead—convincing a woman to do something she didn't want to do. Isabelle would have told him it was easier to brand a steer by himself, but Uncle Silas didn't care what people wanted. If they didn't do what *he* wanted, they had to be convinced. Bret told himself he might be making too much of the situation. It was possible Emily Abercrombie *did* want to go to Boston but was afraid. Maybe she thought she wasn't pretty enough, rich enough, smart enough, confident enough to be accepted there. It wouldn't be easy for someone reared in Texas to make the transition to Boston. He'd been trying for years. Without his grandmother's support, he probably wouldn't have made any progress. But he couldn't forget his uncle's parting words.

What if I can't bring her back?

Then don't come back yourself.

It was useless to plague himself with those words. He was relieved when the train came to a halt. A whole tribe of little boys suddenly materialized, competing with each other to carry luggage, to help ladies down from the coaches and across the street to the boardwalk, to recommend the best hotel and the best restaurants. Bret was startled when his suitcase landed at his feet, barely missing his toes.

"Sorry," the porter said without pausing as he tossed one piece of luggage after another from the train. A grimy-faced urchin grabbed up Bret's suitcase.

"Where're you going, mister? I'll take you to the best hotel for two bits."

"I'm being met," Bret replied.

The boy looked Bret up and down. "Probably a good thing. You don't look like you'd last the night by yourself."

Bret had a very good idea of what he looked like to that urchin—just like city slickers had looked to him when he was a kid.

"I'll manage," he told the urchin. "Have you seen any cowhands you didn't know hanging around like they were waiting for someone?"

"Half the people in this town are waiting for someone. Can't you tell me any more about the fellow?"

Kids. Isabelle would have tanned his backside if

he'd talked to her like that. "I'm looking for someone from Sam Abercrombie's ranch. The brand is an interlocking S and A."

"I ain't seen no cowhand with that brand, but I seen a lady ride into town yesterday on a horse wearing that brand."

"Do you have any idea where she went?"

"No, but I know where she is right now. Give me two bits and I'll tell you."

Bret knew he was being hustled, but he just wanted to find the *lady*. He fished a quarter out of his pocket. "Here. If you don't know where she is, I'm taking it back."

"I ain't no cheat," the kid said, backing out of reach as he put the quarter safely in his pocket. "She's standing right over there in front of that dress shop. Where else would you expect a pretty lady to be?"

"You can bring my suitcase," Bret said. "If you're right, I'll give you another quarter."

"Gee, you're some big spender." But the kid grabbed the suitcase and followed Bret. Two other kids rushed up to carry his trunk.

Bret wondered why a woman should be meeting him and what connection she could have to the cowhand who was supposed to be there. Women had a lot of freedom in Texas, but expensively dressed women seldom went out alone, certainly not to meet strange men.

"Excuse me," he said when he reached her. When she turned, he was almost too stunned to speak. She was the most beautiful woman he'd ever seen. "I'm Bret Nolan," he managed to say. "A cowhand from the Sam Abercrombie ranch was supposed to meet me. This kid said he saw you riding a horse wearing the Abercrombie brand. Can you tell me where to find the man?"

The woman appeared to be nearly as surprised as he was. "No, I can't."

"I'm sorry to have bothered you."

"I didn't say I couldn't help you. I'm Emily Abercrombie. I'm not a man, but I've come to meet you."

Chapter Two

Emily hoped she didn't look as shocked as she felt. It wasn't his citified clothing that surprised her, she had expected to see a man dressed liked a tenderfoot. She wasn't even surprised he was tall and good-looking. What she *didn't* expect, and what stunned her, was that she felt an immediate attraction to this man. A tenderfoot. A dude. A man who probably didn't know one end of a horse from another. What could possibly possess her to be attracted to him? Okay, so he was better looking than anybody she knew, but he was still just a man.

"I expected one of your hands," Bret said. "I never thought your father would let you travel this far un-escorted."

He dropped a notch in her estimation. "I don't need an escort, but I came with two—our foreman and one of the hands."

"I wouldn't have let you come at all."

His stock was plummeting so rapidly she'd be immune to him in less than thirty minutes. She raised her chin. "It's a good thing you aren't my father."

"Or your husband."

If he was trying to make her angry at him, he was succeeding. "I came because I wanted to tell you I have no intention of going to Boston."

"And I've been told I won't have a job if I return without you."

"Then it looks like you have a problem."

"I certainly do. And her name is Emily Abercrombie."

It would be foolish to hate somebody she knew so little about, but she didn't like what she knew about Bret Nolan.

"Hey, mister," said one of the dirty urchins who'd followed him, "you gotta pick a hotel. We can't hold this trunk forever."

"If you'll take my advice, you'll get back on the train," Emily said to Bret.

"As much as I'd like to do just that, I can't," Bret said. "Have you picked out a hotel for me, or am I on my own?"

"Follow me." Emily turned and started down Commerce Street. She was tempted to look over her shoulder to see if Mr. Nolan was following, but when she heard the three boys carrying his luggage grumbling that they hoped the hotel wasn't in the next county, she figured he was. She couldn't decide if she was disappointed that he hadn't taken her advice to get back on the train. In general, she'd scorn any man who was spineless, but she didn't know this man and didn't care if he had a spine or not. She only wanted to be left alone.

On the other hand, she hated to see anybody so gutless they wouldn't struggle at least a little bit for what they wanted. Texas wasn't an easy place to live in, and defending cows from disease, wolves, and rustlers just made it harder. If people weren't ready to fight for what they wanted, they didn't survive.

Then there was the puzzling conundrum of her attraction to him. She laid that entirely to the fact that he was tall, handsome, and looked strong enough to handle a longhorn steer by himself. Of course, his looks had to be deceiving. How could any man living in a place like Boston be anything but soft? Still, she hoped he wasn't as bad as she feared. She didn't want to be attracted to a weakling.

"Do we have far to walk?" Mr. Nolan asked.

"Are your shoes pinching already?" It was worse than she thought.

"My shoes are fine, but the boys are going to need help with the trunk if it's much farther."

She turned to see the boys making a great show of struggling with the trunk. All three had assumed the heavy duty, while Bret had taken the suitcase. The boys' expressions of agony made Emily smile. "I believe their groans are intended to arouse your sympathy and cause you to reward them with a larger payment."

"Lady, that's not fair," one urchin exclaimed.

"I already guessed that," Bret said, favoring the boys and Emily with a frown. "I probably know more tricks than they do."

"You ain't planning on cheating us, are you?" the urchin asked.

"I asked how far it was so I'd know if I had enough money to give you a bigger tip."

The change in the boys' demeanor was almost comical. They hoisted the trunk as if it weighed only ounces, their faces transformed by smiles.

"I never thought you'd stiff us, mister," the urchin said. "I can tell a man of character when I see one."

"Stow it," Bret barked. "I know all the lines to use on dudes, tenderfoots, or any other name orphans use to refer to people like me, because I used them myself."

"We ain't orphans," one of the other boys protested. "We got parents," he stated proudly.

"Then don't embarrass them by behaving like street rats."

"Just because I ain't got no parents don't mean I'm a street rat," the first urchin exclaimed.

"I didn't think you were, but a gentleman watches his behavior around a lady. Most importantly, he doesn't tell lies, not even little ones. And that play-acting about the heavy trunk was a lie."

"But I wasn't lying to *her*."

"You lied in her presence. That's what counts."

Emily knew she was staring, but she didn't know what to make of this man. He appeared to be scolding the boys, but she was certain there was a glint of humor in his eyes, even slight admiration for their gumption.

The urchin turned to Emily, raised his head, his face grimy as he looked at her with big brown eyes. "Sorry, ma'am. I didn't mean to tell no fibs. I just thought he was a soft touch. I couldn't help myself."

It was all Emily could do to keep from laughing. His shamefaced expression was masterful.

"I accept your apology," she said with as much gravity as she could muster. "I'm sure you're a very nice young man."

"My pa says he's a young hellion who'll be lucky if someone don't shoot him dead before he's twenty," one of his friends said.

"Shut your trap, you whey-faced brat," the urchin

said. "You've no call to find fault with my character in front of a lady."

"Well, it's what Pa said."

"A fella can change, can't he? I'm going to be a gentleman like this tender—um, I mean fancy dude."

"We're going to the Grand Union Hotel," Emily said. "Why don't you boys go on ahead?"

"Yes, ma'am," the urchin said. "We'll wait outside. They won't let the likes of them two"—he pointed at his two companions—"inside."

"They won't let you in, neither," his friend said.

"They would if I wanted in, but I don't."

And with that he marched off, proud as a peacock, ignoring the slanderous remarks of his friends.

Emily turned to Bret. "Do you always set the cat amongst the pigeons wherever you go?"

"I see no point in not dealing in plain truths."

"Then why did Mr. Abbott choose to send you to Texas?"

"Because he knows I always get the job done."

"Then I'm sorry to be the one to interrupt your string of successes. You could always go back and tell him you couldn't find me. Texas is a big state. It would be easy to lose a female or two."

His answering smile was forced. "But I'm a very determined man. I'd have found you."

Emily turned and headed toward the hotel. "Then you should be grateful I've saved you a lot of time. That'll give me plenty of opportunity to refute all your reasons why I should go to Boston."

He caught up with her. "You haven't heard my reasons yet. You might find them irrefutable."

"And *you* haven't heard my reasons for refuting them. You might find *them* irrefutable."

"Then I expect we're in for a very interesting month."

"A month!" Emily exclaimed as she stopped dead and turned to face him.

"Or year. Whatever it takes."

Even if Mr. Nolan had been as charming as he was attractive, she wouldn't have wanted him around more than a few days. She didn't have time to entertain a man who knew nothing about the West or ranching. He probably thought cows were kept in barns and were tame enough for milking.

"It's my father's house, and he'll determine how long you stay, but I can promise you it won't be as much as a year. I'd say two weeks at most."

"Then I'll have to make sure I've convinced you by then."

"I told you, I'm not going to Boston."

"We'll see."

His unshakable calm infuriated her. He acted as though she didn't have enough intelligence to know her own mind. As though after a few well-chosen words from him, she'd be so overwhelmed by his brilliant arguments, she'd be in a frenzy to pack and leave. Maybe women in Boston kowtowed to their men, but she was a Texan. She didn't jump to obey anybody's orders.

"I've asked for dinner to be served at seven-thirty in a private dining room. You can dine with me and the other men, or make your own arrangements."

"I'll dine with you," he said. "What time will we be leaving tomorrow?"

"Seven o'clock. We have a long two days in the saddle. You do ride, don't you? The train doesn't go to our ranch."

"Can't we take a stagecoach or at least a buckboard?" he asked.

"There is no stagecoach to the ranch, and you'd be bounced to death in a buckboard."

"How about a wagon?"

"You're welcome to take a wagon if you want to spend a week on the trail." This man was pathetic. Didn't he know anything?

"I couldn't go a week without eating."

"If we were to go by wagon, we'd carry our own supplies and cook over an open fire."

"I couldn't ask you to do that for me."

"It's a good thing, because I wouldn't."

Emily didn't know Mr. Nolan, and she admitted she'd started off without a good opinion of him, but she couldn't get over the feeling he was laughing at her. Young, unmarried women were so scarce in Texas, her appearance usually caused young men to start blushing, stammering, and falling over themselves to please. Mr. Nolan appeared completely unaffected by her youth and attractiveness. That irritated her as well as aroused her curiosity. He'd been sent to persuade her to do something against her will. She would have thought he'd try to ingratiate himself with her, or at the very least, try not to make her dislike him. He appeared not to care what she thought.

"We won't have a midday meal tomorrow," she told him. "We'll have breakfast before we leave the hotel. I've made arrangements for dinner and beds with a rancher for tomorrow night. We should be home in time for dinner the second night. Are you sure you can stay in the saddle all day?"

"I'll manage somehow."

She expected he'd be too sore to sit down and too stiff to walk. "You can probably ride in those clothes," she said, thinking it would be a shame to ruin such a nice suit, "but you should see about getting some boots."

22

"I'll see what I can come up with. How long will it take my trunks to arrive?"

Good Lord! She hoped he wasn't a dandy. She shuddered at the thought of him mincing about the ranch trying to keep from getting his clothes dusty or mud on his boots. It would be all she and Lonnie could do to keep the hands from playing tricks on him.

"Lonnie will strap them to a packhorse. You'll need to have them ready a little while before we leave."

"Just let me know the time, and they'll be ready."

He couldn't be very high up in the company if Silas Abbott could spare him for as much as a year. He was probably used to getting up at dawn and working late into the night. She felt sorry for anyone who was treated like that, but she couldn't imagine anyone worse to have as a traveling companion across the Texas plains. She was relieved to reach the hotel and see the three boys waiting outside with Mr. Nolan's trunk and suitcase. A young man who blinked, then stared foolishly when he saw her, jumped to open the hotel door for her.

"Thank you." She gave him a big smile as she passed.

"Be careful," Mr. Nolan said softly. "You don't want to dazzle him so completely that he'll stumble into the street and get run over."

Emily stiffened. There was no mistaking his words or his tone. He believed she was so proud of her looks she couldn't resist flirting with every man she encountered. "I was just trying to show my appreciation."

Much to her chagrin, when she turned around he was telling the boys to bring his trunk and suitcase inside and he'd pay them a dollar each. He had to be crazy. They'd have carried his trunk all the way to Dallas for a dollar.

"The room is reserved in your name," she told him when he followed the boys in. "If you need anything, ask Lonnie. He's our foreman. The clerk will give you his room number. I'll see you tonight." She turned and headed toward the stairs and her room. She wondered how Mr. Abbott thought Mr. Nolan could convince her to go to Boston. So far, Mr. Nolan was a good argument against having anything to do with that city.

She let her hand skim along the banister as she climbed the curving stairway to the second floor. The coolness of the interior of the hotel was a relief from the intensity of the Texas sun. If Mr. Nolan insisted upon wearing his wool suits, he was in for a miserable time. The man seemed angry, unbending, and thoroughly unhappy about being in Texas.

Then why on earth did she still feel attracted to him? She was an intelligent woman. She'd never been foolish about men or fooled by them. She'd liked several in her nineteen years, but she'd never been infatuated with a man. So what on earth could have caused her to be attracted to this surly sourpuss of a dude?

He was unquestionably the most attractive man she knew. She hadn't failed to notice several women turn to stare at him as they passed, but surely she wasn't such a shallow female, she'd fall for a man just because he was handsome.

She reached her room, unlocked the door, and let herself in. She wouldn't think about him until tonight. Once they got to the ranch, she had no intention of being shut up in the ranch house with him any more than necessary. Sending her to Boston was her father's idea. Let him deal with Mr. Bret Nolan.

Bret tipped the boy who tossed Bret's suitcase on the bed and set his trunk against the wall between the door and a large bureau. He was relieved when the door closed behind them, but his privacy didn't do anything to release the painful tension between his shoulders. He didn't know how many kinds of an idiot a man could be at once, but he figured he'd probably set a record. He'd done just about everything he could to make certain Emily wouldn't listen to a word he said.

Neither did he have to pretend he didn't know anything about riding or cooking over a campfire. She'd soon find out he could do all of that, and it would only make her angry at him for deceiving her. And likely to believe that anything he told her about Boston was equally untrue. Was he trying to make sure she *didn't* decide to go to Boston?

He stopped in the act of opening his suitcase. He had no intention of praising his cousin Joseph in an effort to make Emily more willing to marry him, but would he really go as far as *discouraging* Emily from going to Boston when his own job hung in the balance?

He shook his head in dismay at his own actions, opened his suitcase, and began to lay out the clothes he would wear to dinner.

He planned to do everything he could to persuade Emily to go to Boston. He knew Texas was no place for a single woman who was young, beautiful, and rich, but he would make sure she knew what he thought of Cousin Joseph. If she decided to marry him after that, his conscience would be clean.

He unpacked his best navy blue suit and hung it up so the wrinkles would fall out of the wool fabric. He unfolded a sturdy cotton shirt and laid it out on the bed. Both would need to be pressed before tonight. Socks came next. He would have to get his shoes from the trunk, but that could wait. He unpacked a change of underwear. He wanted a bath. The man at the desk had told him hot water was available in a building behind the hotel. This might be the last chance he had to take a hot bath for some time. Sam Abercrombie was very wealthy, but he wouldn't be the first rancher to see no need for baths except in a nearby creek.

He'd shave, too. And make sure he used some of the new French cologne water he'd bought in New York. That thought made him smile. It would probably confirm Emily's opinion that he was a tenderfoot who would be so appalled at the living conditions in Texas he'd turn tail and run back to Boston without making more than a feeble attempt to convince her to go back with him.

He walked over to the window and looked down at the street below. It had been almost six years since he'd been in Texas, but the street looked more familiar to him than those of Boston. It was cut up from the shod hooves of horses, the wheels of wagons and buggies, and the high heels of hundreds of cowhands. A breeze sent dust swirling into the hot, dry air, causing the smell of horse manure to penetrate every building. Women traversed the boardwalk, staring into store windows or hurrying along children trying to do the same. The air was filled with the sound of shouting male voices, the whinny of horses, and the tinny sound of a piano in a nearby saloon.

It sounded so much like San Antonio. It sounded like home. He could almost see Isabelle marching them into the mercantile and announcing to the shocked owner that she wanted to purchase new outfits for all eleven of *her children*. The boys had all pretended indifference to anything as unmasculine as being interested in new clothes, but as orphans they'd often had to wear rags. They'd never had warm winter clothes. They'd each left with a bundle of clothes they jealously guarded. It was a physical sign that for the first time in their lives, someone cared about them.

Bret shook his head to rid himself of memories that tended to give him a heavy heart. His family was in Boston, not in the Texas hill country. He was an adult now, not a scared and angry twelve-year-old who saw the world as his enemy and didn't know how to protect himself except by attacking everyone who came near him. Jake and Isabelle had taught him how to feel safe, how to value his own abilities and accomplishments without having to be better than everyone else. He could stand on his own.

He turned away from the window and his gaze fell on his suit, the white shirt. His brothers would ridicule him for wearing a suit every day and working inside an office in a city. They all lived the kind of life they'd learned while growing up on Jake's ranch. Even Drew, the only girl in the group, was raising horses on her own ranch.

Bret had spent hours talking to Isabelle about her life before her aunt died, when she'd had money and been a part of Savannah society. From the very beginning, he'd intended to go to Boston as soon as he was ready and present himself to his mother's family. They were proud, hard people who had turned their backs on his mother because she didn't conform to what they expected of a member of their family. He'd been determined he would do nothing to give them an excuse to look down on him.

But he'd discovered that merely having grown up in Texas and lived on a ranch was a hurdle he had yet to overcome. There were times when he wondered if he ever would. His looks had garnered plenty of attention from the female members of Boston society, but they were rigidly controlled by their husbands, fathers, brothers, or uncles—men who felt Bret didn't quite measure up to their standards. The very unfinished quality that appealed to women caused the men to question his worthiness to join their inner circle.

He collected his clothes, locked the door behind him, and headed for the wash house. The hotel wasn't large, so it took only a few minutes to reach the end of the hall, descend the back stairs, and come out into an alley between the hotel and a livery stable. The wash house was about a hundred feet to his left. He was surprised when the boy who'd carried his suitcase opened the door to him. "What are you doing here?"

"This is where I work," the boy said, drawing himself up.

"When you're not waylaying strangers and trying to squeeze higher tips out of them."

"It's been right slow lately," the boy explained. "There's not many that wants a bath."

"Well, I do, and I don't want you skimping on the hot water."

"I never," the boy replied indignantly.

"Yes, you would. Now stop pretending to be innocent and tell me your name."

The boy hung his head. "It's Jinx, sir."

"Is that all? What about those parents the other kid said you didn't have?"

"Nobody knows who I belong to. I just turned up one day. People passed me back and forth until I was old enough to take care of myself."

"How old are you?"

"Eight."

Four years younger than Bret was when Isabelle rescued him off the street. "Where do you live?"

"Here."

"In the wash house?"

"It's real warm in winter. Are you going to take a

bath? I can't afford to waste hot water if you ain't gonna use it."

"Yes, I'm going to take a bath. And after I'm done, I want you to take one. You look like you've been dragged through the stockyards backwards."

"The boss don't pay me to take baths."

"I'll pay for it. Now where is the tub?"

"Through that door. There's two pipes leading into the tub, one hot and one cold. You can fix the water to suit yourself."

Bret entered a small room built of rough wood. The floor had been smoothed by thousands of feet. He took his clothes off, folded them, and looked around for soap and towels. He didn't see either. "How am I supposed to wash without soap or dry without a towel?" he called through the door.

"That'll be extra."

"It had better not be too much extra, or you might not live to see your next birthday." He thought he heard Jinx laugh.

"Fifty cents each," Jinx said.

"Fine." Bret opened the door a few inches. "Hand them here."

The soap looked harsh and the towel was rough, but he figured they were the best he was going to get. He stepped into the tub and turned the valve on one pipe. Tepid water came out. Apparently, the tank was on the roof and open to the sun. He turned the valve on the other pipe and water only slightly hotter came out. "Put some extra wood under the boiler," he called out to Jinx.

"Right away, sir," Jinx replied.

Bret's first impulse was to wait until the water got hot, but he could remember washing in icy streams when he was living on the ranch. He could endure a tepid bath.

Twenty minutes later he was relaxing in the tub when his solitude was disturbed by Jinx's voice.

"You still in there?" the boy asked.

"Where else would I be?"

"Nobody's ever stayed in there this long."

"Are you planning to charge me extra?"

"I got another customer who don't want to wait."

Bret reluctantly climbed out of the metal tub and began to dry off. "I'll be out in a few minutes," he said. He put his suit on over the fresh underclothes, put his feet in his shoes without socks, gathered up his clothes and the wet towel, and opened the door.

"You got to pour out your water," Jinx said.

"I'll do it," said an impatient man who appeared to be around forty and was lean and well muscled. "I can't spend all night in this place." He disappeared into the bath without a backward glance.

"That'll be two dollars," Jinx told Bret.

Bret handed him four. "The other two are for you. I want you scrubbed from head to toe and at my hotel room tomorrow morning at six to help me carry down my luggage."

Jinx was staring at the money in his hand. "He won't believe I didn't steal it."

"Who won't believe you didn't steal it?"

"My boss."

"If he has any questions, tell him to see me. Now don't forget. Six o'clock."

"I don't like him," Lonnie said to Emily. "If you'll take my advice, you'll send him straight back to Boston."

"Neither of us has to like him," she said as she checked the table. She wanted to show Mr. Nolan that people in Texas knew just as much about how to set a table as anybody in Boston. "We just have to put up with him until he's convinced I don't mean to leave Texas."

"We ought to be spending our time worrying about the ranch, not babysitting some dude," Lonnie said. "The rustling has gotten worse since your pa got sick."

"Then you should have stayed home."

"Your father wouldn't hear of you traveling alone. Neither would I."

"That's all beside the point now. I don't expect Mr. Nolan will get in our way once we're back at the ranch, so we can devote our full attention to the rustling. I don't want anybody thinking I'm going to allow my father to be robbed blind just because he's sick."

But her father was dying, and she was afraid everybody knew it.

"Do you think he'll show up?" Lonnie asked.

"Mr. Nolan? Sure. He was as cross as a castrated bull by the time he got off the train, but I get the feeling Mr. Nolan doesn't like to fail."

A knock on the door interrupted them.

"If that's Mr. Nolan," she said to Lonnie, "let him in."

She didn't want Mr. Nolan to think she'd been the least bit interested in whether he showed up or not. She heard him and Lonnie exchange greetings, heard his footsteps draw near as he entered the room. But when she turned to greet him, the face she saw nearly took her breath away.

Chapter Three

Bret Nolan had looked good when he got off the train. Now he looked fabulous and smelled just as good. Lonnie was wrinkling his nose, but Emily thought it was wonderful that a handsome man was unafraid of a bath and a little cologne.

"I hope I'm on time," Mr. Nolan said.

"To the minute. You must have been standing outside waiting for the clock to chime." He smiled, and she decided two weeks might not be enough to get used to that.

"Please call me Bret. 'Mr. Nolan' makes me wonder if my boss is looking over my shoulder."

His raven hair was perfectly combed, his cheeks freshly shaved, and his suit recently pressed. His shirt was so crisp and his tie so expertly managed, he looked as if he'd spent an hour getting dressed.

"After the way I behaved this afternoon, I wouldn't have been surprised if you were hoping I didn't show up. I have to apologize for being so badly out of temper."

"I'm sure it was a long journey, and you were tired. In any case, Jem isn't here yet. He's one of my father's cowhands."

As if aware his name had been mentioned, the door opened and Jem entered, looking so uncomfortable in his new suit Emily had to struggle to keep from laughing.

"Sorry I'm late, ma'am," Jem said to Emily, "but I near'bout couldn't figure out how to get these clothes done up proper. I had to get the clerk to show me how to fix this dratted tie."

"Since we're all here, why don't we eat?" Emily didn't think she could hold back her laughter much longer. Jem was a top hand, but his best friend was his horse.

Lonnie took an instant dislike to Bret that grew stronger and more noticeable as the minutes passed at the dinner table. He glared at Bret as though he expected him to attempt to kidnap Emily and carry her off to Boston by force. When he spoke to Bret, he practically growled. Poor Jem was so uncomfortable with his clothes, and eating at a table with settings that confused and terrified him, he was unable to talk at all. He barely managed to eat.

Bret, on the other hand, acted as though there were nothing unusual about the evening.

"You won't believe who was managing the wash house," he said after they'd discussed the weather, the state of recovery in Texas after the end of Reconstruction, the state of the cattle industry, and the smallness of Fort Worth compared to Boston, New York, and Philadelphia. "The urchin who carried my suitcase this afternoon. It turns out his name is Jinx."

"If it's the bath run by that cheating Lugo Cates, he wouldn't get any business if it wasn't one of only two baths in Fort Worth," Lonnie said. "The water's cold even in summer."

"I talked Jinx into heating it up a little."

"How'd you do that?"

"I paid extra."

"He conned you because you're a city slicker," Lonnie said.

"I expect your Lugo Cates will get the money, not Jinx."

"I think it's fine you're so interested in the boy's welfare," Emily said, "but I'd really like to hear your reasons for thinking I should move to Boston."

Having finished his meal, Bret laid his fork on his plate and took a swallow of wine. "No doubt your father has given you more than enough reason."

Jem hadn't touched his wine, instead had eyed it like it was alive and might possibly harm him. Lonnie had taken several swallows, but he couldn't hide a grimace

"My father's reasons are based primarily on emotion." Emily watched Bret over the rim of her own wineglass. "You're a businessman who makes decisions based on logic and pragmatic consideration of the facts. You don't know me, so emotion won't affect your reasoning."

"That's not quite true," Bret said. "It's impossible to look at a lovely woman without feeling emotion."

Emily was aware of a flash of irritation. "I hadn't expected you to be a purveyor of empty flattery."

Something appeared briefly in his eyes, but there wasn't enough light in the room for Emily to read his expression clearly.

"I'm told you're very fond of horses," he said.

"I love my horses."

"Can you look at a particularly beautiful mare or a powerful stallion without feeling any emotion?"

Emily was forced to smile. "I grant you that point. I have the feeling you'd probably be more moved by the sight of a beautiful ship than by me."

"I don't know who's been maligning my character," Bret said, "but you wrong me."

Bret was obviously on his best behavior. It was tempting to forget Boston and enjoy the company of a handsome man who seemed willing to flatter her, but knowing Lonnie was watching her with disapproval and Jem in total bewilderment made that impossible.

"I expect your character is very fine. Since you're neither my father nor a relative, I'm sure you'll see the question from a different perspective."

Bret's smile was faint. "But you have no intention of being swayed by my argument."

She returned his faint smile. "None whatsoever."

Against her will, she was becoming more and more intrigued by this man. He gave every appearance of being intelligent and ambitious, energetic and confident. Yet she was sure he was under a lot of pressure to bring her—or at least her twenty-five percent of the company—safely back to Boston.

Bret pushed his chair away from the table, picked up his wine, and looked at it through the light. "There are several obvious reasons," he began, his gaze still on the wine. "The most obvious is your safety."

"I have a half dozen men to protect me."

"You'll have more domestic servants than that in Boston, and they won't have to contend with thieves and murderers."

"You've got more than enough thieves and murderers in Boston," Lonnie growled.

"Not where Emily would be living. In any case, you'd have the police available if you needed them."

"The boys and I can protect Miss Abercrombie,"

Lonnie said. "We don't need no fancy police, do we, Jem?"

Jem shook his head, but his eyes said he'd lost whatever hold he had on the drift of the argument.

"You would have servants to do the housework, and plenty of free time for yourself," Bret said.

"I can have both right now if I wanted them."

"There's one thing you can't have, no matter how much you want it."

"And what's that?"

"Plenty of female company to go shopping with you and to spend a cold and rainy afternoon in a cozy parlor talking over the latest events."

Was that what he thought she was, a silly female interested in nothing but pretty clothes and pointless gossip? "I have little interest in shopping and none in gossip."

"You misunderstand me," he said.

She could almost feel him smile, like a snake that knew it had its helpless prey cornered. Only he didn't have her cornered, and she would take great pleasure over the next few days making that clear to him.

"My grandmother assures me a woman can never be too careful in the choice of her clothes," Bret said. "She also assures me that a woman of intelligence—a woman such as yourself—appreciates the opportunity to discuss the events of the world around her. We have several newspapers that bring the world to us on a daily basis. Out here, world events can come and go before you even hear of them."

"Your point is well taken," Emily admitted grudgingly, "but I have little need of anything except the most serviceable garments. As for the great events of the world, I'll leave that to the men who are in a position to be familiar with the matters at stake."

Their conversation was halted when two men came

to clear the table. Jem made use of the interruption to excuse himself. Emily poured coffee for herself and Lonnie, but Bret sampled the brandy, found it acceptable, and poured some into his glass.

"Are you ready to resume our discussion?" she asked.

Bret looked surprised. "You know all the advantages as well as I do. Why do you want me to waste the evening naming them?"

"What you choose to think an advantage will give me a better understanding of your character."

He took a sip of brandy. "Why should you be interested in my character?"

"I have to have a good opinion of your character before I can put any confidence in your arguments."

Bret set his brandy down and met her gaze. "I think you're trying to preview all my arguments so you can defend yourself against them."

"I don't have to *defend* myself."

She didn't like it when he smiled as if he had a secret.

"I'll give you one more reason and then I'm done for the evening," Bret said. "You'll have a much wider choice of men when picking your husband, the man who'll become the manager of your property and the father of your children."

"I'm not sure I want to get married."

Bret took a large swallow of brandy. "That would be a great waste."

She supposed he meant it as a compliment, but somehow it felt as if she were a commodity being evaluated for her usefulness in producing children.

"Since you no longer wish to talk about Boston, why don't you tell me something about yourself?"

"I'd much rather you tell me why you're so anxious to stay in Texas."

"I'd rather show you."

Much to her surprise, he swallowed the remainder of his brandy and got to his feet. "Then I'll leave you to rest for the journey tomorrow. Is our departure time still set for seven?"

"Yes."

"Good night, and thank you for a fine dinner."

"He's got his nerve," Lonnie said after the door closed behind Bret.

"I have a feeling he's got a good deal more than that," Emily said. "I think I'll take his advice and go to bed. We have a long day ahead of us."

"He'll be cross-eyed before noon."

"That's what I thought at first, but I have a feeling there's more to Mr. Nolan than we know."

"He's a damned dandy," Lonnie said with a snort. "You saw how he was dressed, and smelling like a whore in August. Sorry, I didn't mean to say that."

"I thought he looked very nice. Smelled nice, too. Still . . ." She didn't know what it was. Maybe it was his quiet confidence, the way his gaze never wavered, the way he always seemed to be one step ahead of her.

She was used to men who were so unsettled by being around an attractive woman, they fell all over themselves to please her. They were an open book. Bret, on the other hand, was a closed book with a lock to make sure she didn't see anything he didn't want her to see.

"After a week at the ranch, he'll be so anxious to get back to Boston he won't care whether you go with him or not." Lonnie grinned as he prepared to go to his room. "I can't wait to see him try to walk after a day in the saddle. He'll probably have to sleep standing up."

As Emily closed the door behind Lonnie, she was surprised to find she wasn't the least bit inclined to smile at the thought of a saddle-sore Bret. She almost hoped he'd prove Lonnie wrong. He was probably a reasonably nice man. Being sent to Texas to convince a reluctant heiress to move to Boston had reduced him to the status of an errand boy, and no man could be expected to like that.

Still, he didn't *act* like an errand boy. Nor did he go out of his way to make himself pleasant. If her father was right and the Abbots and Abercrombies were more concerned about the stock than about her, they would be very angry with him if he returned empty-handed. Bret didn't strike her as a man willing to accept failure.

She left the dining room and climbed the stairs to her room.

As she began to undress, she found herself looking forward to the next few weeks. She had no intention of changing her mind, but it might be interesting to get to know more about Bret. She was more intrigued by him than by any man she'd ever met. She smiled at herself in the mirror. Besides, spending time with a man as handsome as Bret couldn't be all bad.

Bret wasted no time getting to his room. The whole evening had been like a bad play. He undressed and packed his clothes carefully so he wouldn't have to do it in the morning. Once he was sure there was nothing that could cause him to be late, he got into bed. But he didn't go to sleep. He couldn't stop thinking of Emily.

She could say she didn't care about clothes, but her gown had been chosen with an eye for setting her off to her best advantage. There was nothing about it that could have been considered in poor taste, but it was provocative. He wasn't sure whether Jem had been more uncomfortable about his clothes or having to look at his boss's daughter.

Not that Lonnie was unaffected either. But he was so busy being angry at Bret, trying to defend Emily against any imagined insult, he didn't have time to give his full attention to Emily. That was just as well as far as Bret was concerned. He didn't like the idea of Lonnie leering at Emily like it was his right. Not that Bret had been much better at controlling himself. He'd spent the whole evening trying to keep from asking the one question that nearly popped out at least three times.

Why would such a beautiful, intelligent woman want to lock herself away in a dusty corner of Texas with no one but cowhands to keep her company?

Of course, he didn't ask that question. It would set her so firmly against him he'd never convince her to leave. And he had every intention of returning to Boston with Emily Abercrombie at his side. Nor did he intend to return until he had convinced Emily's father to give him the voting rights to his stock. That would be his price for making sure Sam Abercrombie's daughter was safe when he was no longer able to watch over her.

There was, however, one small problem with his plan. He hadn't figured out how to do it.

The knock came before Bret was finished dressing. "Who is it?" he called though the door.

"Jinx," a thin voice answered. "You said I was to be here at six."

Bret opened the door. "You're early." He'd hardly gotten the words out of his mouth before he saw that Jinx was still dirty and had a bruise on his cheek. "You were supposed to take a bath. Did you find it more fun to get in a fight?"

"I didn't get in no fight." Jinx kept his head down. He didn't sound nearly as feisty as he had yesterday.

"Did you slip on the wet floor? Fall down the stairs? Run into a fist?"

"Bastard!" Jinx turned to leave, but Bret grabbed him by the collar, pulled him into the room, and closed the door.

"Okay, I deserve that, but I also deserve the truth. You didn't use my money the way I asked, so I want it back." Bret held out his hand.

"I ain't got it."

"What did you spend it on?"

"I didn't spend it." Jinx looked defiant, but he also looked scared.

"Then what happened to it?"

Jinx dropped his gaze to the floor. "He took it."

"Who took it?"

"Lugo. He said I must have stole it. He said nobody would have given a street rat like me money for a bath."

"Did you give it to him?"

"Do I look stupid?" Jinx demanded. "I ran, but he caught me. He hit me and took it from me."

Bret thought he'd gotten over being angry at the things that had happened to him, but it took only this to make him realize he hadn't forgotten anything at all. "Where does Lugo live?"

"Next to the wash house. He saw you. He said you was too much of a fine swell to even notice the likes of me."

Bret finished dressing. "We're going to his house."

"He's asleep."

"I think I can convince him to wake up."

Jinx looked Bret up and down. "You don't look like you did yesterday. You a Pinkerton or something?"

"No, but you might say I'm incognito."

"What's that?"

"It means I'm trying to look so unlike myself, nobody will know who I am."

"I knew that."

"That's because you're a very smart kid. Now let's go see Lugo. Why aren't you living in an orphanage?"

"I ran away when they tried to lock me up in that place." Jinx backed away from Bret. "You're not taking me there, are you?"

"No. I just wondered why you were living on the streets."

"I'm not living on the street. I got a place to stay," Jinx said proudly.

Bret recalled some of the places he'd slept. The wash house was pretty good by comparison. "What if a family wanted to adopt you?"

"I don't want to be adopted. They'd make me go to school, take baths all the time, come home when it got dark, and put on clean clothes in the morning. It would be worse than being in prison. Besides, nobody would want to adopt me."

Bret thought he detected a note of wistfulness in that last statement. "I know a couple who just might be willing to put up with a brat like you." He tousled Jinx's hair. "You'd have to go to school, take baths, wear clean clothes, and learn to eat at a table, but you'd have a nice place to stay, all the food you could eat, and somebody who'd make sure nobody hurt you or stole from you."

They left the hotel and headed down the street toward the wash house. Jinx's footsteps lagged as they approached Lugo's house.

"How do you know anybody who would take me in?"

"I was an orphan when I was your age."

Jinx stopped in his tracks. "You couldn't be no orphan. You got money and a whole trunk full of fancy clothes."

Bret turned to look at the boy staring up at him,

disbelief and the glimmerings of hope in his eyes. Bret knew if he interfered in this child's life, he had to be prepared to take permanent responsibility for him.

He must have seen dozens of orphans in Boston, yet not one had caused him to take a second look, wonder about their lives, remember his own years as a homeless outcast. Had he been so focused on making a place for himself that he couldn't see anything else, or had he been afraid to see himself in those upturned faces, to remember that his family hadn't wanted him, either? Had being back in Texas unleashed a part of him he'd stored away and tried to forget? He didn't want to believe he'd become so heartless, he couldn't care about kids like Jinx.

"I had no money and only one set of ragged clothes when I was adopted," Bret said. "I was angry at the whole world, mean to other kids, distrusted and disliked everybody, and constantly started fights."

"If I'd been one of those kids, I'd have beat the shit out of you."

"I'm sure they wanted to, but our parents taught us to like and trust each other."

"How'd they do that?"

"By loving us first. After a while, we couldn't help loving them back. And once we did that, it was easy to start liking each other."

"They wouldn't like me."

"Why wouldn't they? I like you."

Jinx couldn't believe that. "Preacher Jones says kids like me are the spawn of the devil."

"I'm sure he would have said the same of me. Now it's time to wake up your boss."

Bret had to knock two times before he got a response.

"Go away," a voice from inside shouted. "Come back when it's daylight."

"I leave town in less than an hour. I have to talk to you now."

Bret got no response.

"It's about beating Jinx and stealing his money. The sheriff might be interested in hearing what happened."

Bret heard a string of curses followed by what sounded like someone stumbling around in the dark. A few moments later the door opened; in it stood a man who exactly fit Bret's image of a person who would beat a helpless child and steal his money. He was unshaved, his hair matted, his clothes dirty and ill-fitted to his fat but muscular body.

"What lies has the little bastard been telling you?" Lugo demanded.

"He said you accused him of stealing the two dollars I gave him, that when he wouldn't give you the money, you beat him and took it from him."

"He's a damned liar." Lugo raised a threatening fist at Jinx, who moved closer to Bret. "Why would a man like you give a street rat money?"

"Why I gave it to him is none of your concern, but I *did* give it to him. I'm here to see that you give it back. And to tell you that if you lay a hand on him again, you'll answer to me."

Fixing his gaze on Bret, Lugo seemed to forget all about Jinx. "Are you threatening me?"

"You can take it like that if you want," Bret said.

"You cowhands are always coming into town thinking you're somebody important." He lumbered toward Bret. "Nobody pushes Lugo Cates around."

"I never met anyone named Nobody. But if he could make you act like a decent human instead of a bully who beats up kids and steals from them, I'd like to shake his hand."

Lugo came down the steps with a roar, apparently

intending to run Bret down. Bret sidestepped, then landed two quick punches in his stomach that doubled the other man over. He followed that assault with an uppercut to the jaw that sent Lugo reeling backward.

"I don't want to fight you," Brett said.

He didn't have a choice. Lugo came at him again, roaring like a maddened bear, depending on his weight, size, and aggressiveness to overwhelm anybody who tried to oppose him. Bret pounded Lugo's body with a series of short, sharp jabs.

"My hobby is boxing," Bret said, dancing away each time before Lugo could move to meet him. "You can either give Jinx his money and promise not to hit him again, or I can batter your face until it looks like a cow carcass after wolves have been at it."

Lugo's answer was another blind charge. Again Bret stepped aside, then battered Lugo's body before he could get his hands on his elusive enemy.

"Stand still and fight, you damned coyote!" Lugo roared.

Bret's answer was a blow to the jaw that sent Lugo staggering backward. Lugo shook his head to clear it, spun around until his gaze focused on Bret, then charged again. The same sequence repeated itself several more times before Lugo staggered and sank to his knees.

"Now will you give Jinx his money?"

Lugo nodded.

"Get it."

Lugo staggered to his feet and finally managed to climb the stairs and go inside. Bret flattened himself against the side of the house and motioned for Jinx to do the same. The boy had barely gotten into position when Lugo came charging out of the house with a gun in his hand. Bret stepped forward and brought his hand down on Lugo's wrist with such force he could hear the sound of bones breaking.

"You'll have to get the money yourself," he said to Jinx over Lugo's moans. He picked up Lugo's gun. "Are you going to leave Jinx alone? You might as well agree. With your wrist like that, you can't really stop me from doing whatever I want."

Lugo's eyes were filled with hate, but pain dulled his features. Bret didn't know how much faith he could put in a promise extracted under these conditions.

"I won't hurt the little bastard as long as he does his work," Lugo said.

"I'll be back through here in a few weeks to check up on both of you." Bret emptied the bullets from Lugo's gun, put them in his pocket, and tossed the firearm into the water tank atop the wash house. "Just in case I don't get back as soon as expected, I plan to explain the situation to the man at the desk in the hotel. I'm also going to leave some money for Jinx. If you touch so much as a single penny, I'll break your other wrist."

"Why do you care about this kid?"

"I was an orphan once. I know what it's like to be beaten and cheated. I don't like it any more now than I did then."

"Are you really coming back?" Jinx stuck close to Bret as they returned to the hotel.

Bret could tell he was scared, but he was also starting to look at Bret with worship in his eyes. "I will definitely be back. And I want you to think about going to stay with those people I told you about."

"Couldn't I stay with you?"

"I live in a single room in a city up North. Jake and

Isabelle have a huge house on a big ranch right here in Texas. You could have your own room."

"Those people might not like me as much as you do."

"I promise they'll love you. Think about it while I'm gone."

"I will if you promise to come back."

Bret hesitated, but he'd already made a commitment to Jinx. He couldn't get out of it now. "I'll come back."

Chapter Four

Emily didn't see Bret when she arrived at the livery stable. Lonnie and Jem had the horses ready, and a cowhand and a dirty little boy were checking the ropes that secured Bret's suitcase and trunk on the packhorse. She should have known that any man who dressed like he did, who seemed accustomed to drinking expensive brandy, and who was part of the Abbott family, would hire someone to do his work for him, but she had expected him to be ready to leave at the appointed time.

She recognized the boy as the one who'd helped with the luggage at the train station, but she wondered where Bret had found that cowhand. His clothes were well-worn but clean, his boots scuffed but recently polished. Even the hat showed signs of long use. But it was the body inside the clothes that drew her attention.

The man was very tall with broad, well-muscled shoulders. He didn't appear to have an ounce of excess fat, his torso tapering down to a narrow waist cinched by a wide leather belt. Worn jeans clung to a rounded bottom and muscled thighs in a way that caused Emily to feel warm. When the man turned and she recognized Bret, the heat turned into a flame.

"What are you doing dressed like that?"

"I didn't think the clothes I wore last night would be particularly comfortable today," Bret explained.

"That didn't mean you had to go out and buy the clothes off some cowhand's back."

There was that smile again, the one she hated, the one that said he knew something she didn't.

"These are my clothes. I thought the way they fit would have told you that."

Emily felt herself blush. "You don't have to check the ropes," she said to cover her confusion. "Nothing Lonnie ties comes loose."

"He tied them himself," Lonnie mumbled.

Okay, it was time to back up before she embarrassed herself beyond any possibility of recovery. "It appears I've misjudged you. Is there anything Lonnie or Jem can help you do before we leave?"

"I don't think so. I've already chosen another horse and saddled it."

"What was wrong with the horse Lonnie picked out?"

"It looked like it was either asleep or near death. It's been a long time since I spent much time on a horse, but as I remember, a mount is supposed to be able to move faster than I can walk."

"I didn't want to pick one that would run away with him," Lonnie said when Emily looked to him for an explanation.

"Can I help you into the saddle?" Bret asked as he came to where Emily was standing next to her horse.

"Lonnie can help me."

"I'm sure he can, but I'd like the chance to show you I'm not completely useless."

She didn't want him to help her. She didn't want to be near him, didn't want him to touch her. She'd thought about him too much last night. Seeing him dressed in clothes that clung to his body like a second skin only made it more difficult to ignore him, to deny she was attracted to him.

"I never thought you were useless."

"You thought I was helpless."

She stood a little straighter. "I thought you'd have trouble fitting in out here, but anybody can see you're not the kind of man who would be helpless."

He looked taken aback. "You surprise me. I thought you'd sized me up as a dandified young man who'd feel lost out of the city."

"I had, but I've realized my mistake. Now, if you're going to help me mount, please do. It's nearly time to leave."

She was prepared to have him hold out his hands so she could step up into the saddle. Instead he put his hands around her waist.

"When I lift you up, throw your leg over."

Emily had never mounted a horse in that fashion and was about to tell him so when she felt herself lifted off the ground. She barely had time to collect her wits and throw her leg over before he settled her in the saddle.

"I don't usually mount that way," she managed to say when she got her breath back.

"I don't like the bottom of a boot touching my hands. No telling where it's been."

She didn't know what to think of him, what was real and what was an act. When she saw the horse he'd chosen led out from the livery stable, she was certain nearly everything he'd done up until now was an act. It didn't surprise her that he swung into the saddle with the effortless grace of long experience or that he had the spirited gelding under control by the time his rear end hit the saddle. What she wanted to know was where he'd learned to do that.

"You're full of surprises."

"I wouldn't be so surprising if you hadn't expected so little."

She didn't intend to change her mind about Boston, but it was time to admit she'd been wrong about Bret. "You're right. I had expected you to be so uncomfortable you'd turn around and run. I should have known Silas Abbott wouldn't send anyone like that. He's too worried I'll marry some cowboy and sell my stock."

"Let's forget what we thought of each other and start over again."

She should have felt embarrassed. Usually she would have been furious at being so completely outmaneuvered, but Bret's smile seemed friendly rather than mocking.

"Okay. It seems only fair. Lonnie and Jem are saddled up. It's time to go."

"You're coming back, ain't you, mister?"

Emily had completely forgotten the dirty little boy. He was standing dangerously close to Bret's horse, looking up at him with a kind of desperation.

"I will come back. Remember, if you need anything, talk to Frank in the hotel."

"I didn't know you had an interest in street kids," Emily said when Jinx disappeared around a corner.

"It's a long story," Bret replied as they threaded their way through the early morning traffic of wagons making deliveries to hotels, mercantiles, warehouses, and saloons.

"It's a long trip," Emily replied.

51

"Then maybe I'll tell it to you."

"I'll hold you to that."

Emily had always wondered why people chose to live in a city. Even though it was barely an hour after sunrise, the streets were already crowded and noisy. The various smells that filled the air—manure, alcohol, human sweat—would only gain strength as the heat rose, until everyone had difficulty taking a deep breath. The buildings were so close together they blocked out all but the sky directly above. There was no room to move, to ride, to feel like you could relax without fear of running over or into someone—or having others do the same to you.

Still, it *was* nice to have several stores where she could buy things that made her feel pretty and feminine. She felt a little self-conscious that the packhorse carrying her suitcases was as heavily burdened as Bret's, but then, remembering the way he'd looked at dinner last night, she wished she'd bought a few more dresses. She didn't want him to think she was unstylish.

She was relieved that the morning air was cool and dry. Her horse felt restless under her. They'd both be happier when they finally left the city and she could let him break into a canter. As hard as it was on her patience, it was necessary to keep to a trot until they cleared the last of the houses that ringed the town. Children were as likely to explode from a side street or yard as a cow was to wander into their path.

"How long has it been since you've been on a horse?" Emily asked. They were riding ahead of Lonnie and Jem, each of whom was leading a packhorse.

"I did a little riding before I left Boston to get used to it again, but it's been almost six years since riding a horse was part of every day."

"Did your family have a house in the country?"

Bret turned to look at her, his expression hard to decipher. "What do you mean by a house in the country?"

"Just what I said. I can't imagine your being able to do more than walk your horse in Boston."

They had moved into a slow canter, a stride that allowed the horses to cover a lot of ground without using too much energy. Bret moved smoothly and effortlessly into the rhythm of his mount's stride. He might not have ridden in a long time, but he was clearly an experienced rider.

"I rent a room a few blocks from where I work. If I have to go somewhere that's too far to walk, I take a cab."

She remembered the cabs from her trip to Boston: smelly, cramped carriages pulled by horses whose iron-shod hooves made a terrible noise on the cobblestones.

"My parents are dead." Bret looked away. "They never had a house in the country."

"I'm sorry." She'd lost her own mother and was facing her father's death, so she thought she would have known how he felt, but he seemed angry rather than bereaved. "Was it recent?"

"My mother died when I was born, my father when I was seven."

It must have been difficult to grow up without parents. "You were lucky to have a family to take care of you."

The look he gave her when he turned to face her was so full of tightly held anger, she nearly recoiled.

"My family didn't want me. I was put in an orphanage."

There were more ways to stumble when talking to this man than holes in a prairie dog town. She pulled her horse to a halt, waved Lonnie and Jem on when they came abreast of her. "I've done nothing but embarrass myself since I met you. I think it's time you told me about yourself. I don't like constantly saying the wrong thing," she added when he didn't respond. "I'm not cruel or insensitive."

Bret's sudden smile was unexpected. "I never thought you were. I'm not angry with you."

"Look, I'm a strong-minded woman who likes to get her way. I'm willing to accept all the difficulties that come with that, but I'm not willing to take the blame for something I didn't do."

"We'd better go," Bret said. "Lonnie will be upset if we lag too far behind."

"I'll ride if you'll talk."

"Okay, but no digging for details."

She'd worry about details later. Right now all she wanted was to know enough about him to keep from making embarrassing comments.

"My mother's family disowned her when she married an idealist who cared more for his causes than her family's approval. They hated the publicity he said was necessary to advance his causes. After my mother died, he went south to agitate against slavery. Seven years later, he was hanged in Texas for helping slaves escape. After my father's death, my uncle refused to take custody of me. The war had started by then, so rather than travel back to Boston, I was put into an orphanage in Texas."

"That must have been awful," Emily said.

"*I* was awful," Bret said. "I was angry at the whole world. I ran away, got into fights, stole, lied, did everything I could to make the people at the orphanage throw me out. They did, and I lived on the streets for over a year before Isabelle found me."

Now she understood what he meant when he said he knew all the tricks of trying to con people. "Who is Isabelle?"

"A wonderful woman who rounded up eleven orphans nobody wanted and gave us a home and all the love we could want."

"She must have been rich to do all that by herself."

Bret chuckled, smiling at what must have been a sweet memory. "She didn't have a penny. She was a teacher who'd been an orphan herself. She was taking us to work for some farmers, but we ended up at Jake's ranch."

He smiled so broadly, she almost asked him what made him so happy.

"You never saw two people go at each other like they did. They were at it, hammer and tongs, practically from dawn to dusk. Jake wanted to turn us into cowhands, but Isabelle insisted we needed love and understanding. Jake got his cowhands, we got love and understanding, and they got married and adopted us. They gave us a home, a feeling of belonging, a sense that no matter what happened, there was a place we'd always be welcome."

Emily couldn't imagine anyone being brave enough—or crazy enough—to adopt eleven orphans.

Bret turned to look at her. "I lived and worked on that ranch for nine years." He urged his horse into a fast canter. "We'd better catch up before Lonnie does permanent damage to his neck looking over his shoulder."

Emily wondered what kind of man she'd come up against. If he had worked on a ranch for nine years, he probably knew more than how to ride. She also wanted to know more about Isabelle, Jake, and the other orphans. She wanted to know why he had left people who loved him for relatives who had turned their backs on him.

Her curiosity was not to be satisfied that day. They stopped several times to give the horses a rest and give themselves a chance to stretch their legs. Bret would unsaddle his horse immediately, find some graze, and stake both his horses while he checked the packhorse to make sure the suitcases were still secure and that there were no creases in the blanket that might cause sores.

"Jake always said if we took care of our horse first, it would take care of us," Bret said when she asked him why he was so careful with his horses. "I used to spend as much as a week away from the ranch by myself."

Bret spent much of the rest of the day telling her about Boston, but it didn't feel as if he was putting pressure on her. He talked about the beauty of the harbor, the museums and theaters, the shops, the beautiful residential areas, even about sailing in the bay.

She noticed the conspicuous absence of the names of any young women. The only people he mentioned with affection were his grandmother and a cousin, Rupert Swithin.

"I never knew either of my grandmothers," Emily said. "Your grandmother sounds nice."

"I had a letter she wrote my father when he was in Virginia, asking him to let me stay with her until he could settle down. I read it over and over until it fell apart," Bret said. "When I finally got the courage to write her, she was happy to hear from me. I'd been content on the Broken Circle ranch, but I always felt like my true home was with my *real* family." He turned to look at her. "Now you know everything. It's your turn at the confessional."

Emily had the feeling she'd seen only a quick overview of the path his life had taken. It seemed impossible that he could be orphaned so tragically, spurned by his family, then leave his adopted family for the very people who had cast him out, without a stronger reason than a single letter from his grand-mother.

"There's hardly anything to tell," she said. "I've spent most of my life in Texas. My mother died when I was nine, and I've been terrorizing my father ever since."

"The strong-minded woman who likes to get her way."

Emily laughed. "Dad would like to keep me a little girl, but I took over the household years ago. I know he's worried about what will happen to me after he dies, but I don't understand why he thinks I'd want to move to Boston and allow a stranger to run my life."

"It's doesn't sound very reasonable when you put it that way."

After a whole day of trying to find a way past his reserve, she felt he might finally be ready to open up a little, but they were approaching Charles and Ida Wren's ranch. As much as she wanted to find out more about him, she would be relieved to get out of the saddle.

"This is where we'll spend the night," she said when the modest ranch house came into view.

"It doesn't look big enough for all of us."

"They have beds for you and me, but Lonnie and Jem will sleep out."

"Do the Wrens have any children?"

"Three boys and two girls."

She could tell he was thinking about something, but he didn't get to mull it over for long. As soon as they came in sight of the house, she heard a yell. Moments later, three children on horseback appeared from behind the house and raced toward them down a well-used trail.

"That's Joey, Buddy, and Clara," Emily said, breaking into a smile. "Charlie Wren used to work for us. The kids were always sneaking up to the house when Ida's back was turned."

"I bet you encouraged them."

There he went with that strange look again.

"It is lonely sometimes living so far from other people."

"I'll remember that when you try to convince me you never get lonely for company."

She thought at first he was teasing her, but his eyes had a faraway look that told her he was thinking about something far removed from her or the three kids racing to meet her, arms flailing, laughter filling the air as they each tried to be the first to reach her. Joey won.

"He always takes the fastest horse," Clara said, pulling her horse up so close to Emily their boots brushed against each other.

"I can't help it if Bounder's faster than Scout," Joey declared.

"Mama said we could sleep out," Buddy said, his eyes wide with excitement.

Emily did her best to listen to all three of them at once. From the way they carried on, you would have thought they hadn't seen her in years. Watching their eager faces as they crowded around reminded her of how much she'd missed them since Charlie had bought his own ranch. They were always so full of energy, excitement about little things, anticipation of any promised treat.

"Are you the man who's going to take Emily to Boston?" Clara asked Bret.

Bret's faraway expression had turned almost sad, but it disappeared the moment Clara spoke to him.

"Does that make me a bad man?" he asked, a teasing smile transforming his face.

"I don't want her to leave," Clara stated.

"Me, neither," Joey and Buddy said in unison.

"Am I going to have to stay awake tonight to keep from getting tied up and dumped in a deep well?" Bret asked.

"Pop would blister our backsides if we did anything like that," Joey said.

"Good. I'm tired and I'm looking forward to sleeping soundly all night."

"You're getting our bed," Buddy said. "Timmy has to sleep with Pop and Mom, but Joey and me get to sleep out with Lonnie and Jem."

"Aren't you afraid of wolves and coyotes?" Bret asked.

"Nobody's afraid of coyotes," Joey said, as though the question was preposterous.

Emily was intrigued to see that in less than a minute, Joey and Buddy were riding on either side of Bret and chattering away like they were old friends. He had them laughing so much, even Clara turned her attention to him. Emily pulled up in front of the ranch house completely deserted by her escorts. Ida came out of the house to meet her.

"Come in out of the heat," she said to Emily before turning to her sons. "Joey, you and Buddy help Lonnie and Jem with the horses. Clara, you watch Becky and Tim while I see to Emily and her guest."

"I'll help with the horses," Bret said. "You wouldn't have to go to all this bother if it weren't for me."

"Charlie would have my head if I let you stable your own horse," Ida said.

"I promise to protect you from Charlie if need be, but I would like to take care of my horses. I'll be living on a ranch for the next while, so I might as well start brushing up on my skills."

Bret dismounted, and before Lonnie could make

his way over, he'd helped Emily dismount. Then he went off to the stables with the boys.

"He's not what I expected," Ida said as she led Emily toward the house. "I don't know when the boys have taken to anybody like that."

"He's not what I expected, either," Emily said, "but I think he has a special gift for boys. When we left Fort Worth, he had an orphan boy begging him not to forget to come back. He's trying to convince the boy to go live with the couple who adopted him."

"I thought he was a nephew of the partner in that company."

"He is, but they abandoned him after his father died."

The two women went into the small parlor and sat down. "I'm surprised he went back to his family," Ida said.

"He hasn't told me why he left Texas, but I mean to find out."

Ida leaned toward her friend and grinned conspiratorially. "I never thought he'd be so handsome. My breath caught in my throat when he rode up."

"You should have seen him when he came to dinner last night. For a moment I thought I might like to go to Boston after all."

The two women laughed. "Listen to us," Ida said, "acting like two silly girls over a handsome man. Charlie would have a fit if he knew."

They enjoyed another good laugh.

"I can't tell you how good it is to see you again," Emily said. "With Dad being sick and trying to send me off to Boston, I haven't had a good laugh in months. And don't *you* tell me I shouldn't stay on that ranch after he dies. We'd never see each other if I went to Boston."

Ida had been like a mother to Emily during the

time her own mother was sick and the first years after her death. Emily had been pleased when a small inheritance enabled Charlie to give up his job as their foreman to buy his own ranch, but she'd sorely missed the company of Ida and the children.

"I do worry about you," Ida said. "I know how lonely it can be out here."

"So do I."

"Of course, if you could convince that handsome young man to stay . . ."

"Don't even think of it," Emily said, covering her mouth to keep from laughing. "He might have grown up in Texas, but you should have seen him last night drinking brandy like he'd been born to it."

"You're rich enough to buy him all the bandy he can drink."

"Ida Wren!" Emily exclaimed. "If I didn't know better, I'd think you were suggesting that I marry him."

"Well, he is mighty attractive."

"I'm not sure I even want a husband, but if I did, I certainly would look for more than a handsome face."

"How about the rest of him?"

Fortunately, Emily was spared having to explain her blushes by the noisy entrance of Bret accompanied by Joey and Buddy.

"Mr. Nolan says he's going to sleep out with us," Joey exclaimed.

"He's got his own bedroll and everything," Buddy added.

"He said he thinks the sorrel mare's colt is going to be faster than Bounder," Joey said.

"Your father will be delighted to hear that," Ida said with a wink at her son. "He thinks the same. But you're not to make Mr. Nolan feel guilty for putting you out of your bed."

"It's something I haven't done in a long time," Bret said. "I used to like it."

The man was continually surprising Emily. He arrived without a hair out of place, then practically encouraged a dirty orphan to attach himself to him. At dinner he acted like an aristocrat, then turned up the next morning dressed like a cowhand. Now when he had a bed to sleep in, he'd decided to sleep out. And where had he found time to buy a bedroll? And why had he done it?

"Now, I know you ladies probably have a lot to catch up on, so I asked the boys to show me around the ranch."

"Wouldn't you like to rest up a bit before supper?"

"I need to stretch my legs after being in the saddle all day." He cast Emily an amused glance. "I wouldn't want to embarrass myself by stumbling over my own feet."

"Supper will be ready in less than an hour."

"Just give me time to wash up."

"What do you make of that?" Ida asked after the door closed behind Bret and her sons.

Chapter Five

An hour later, after Emily had helped Ida and Clara get supper on the table, Emily was still distracted by Ida's question. It seemed the longer she knew Bret, the less she understood about him. She'd come to consider herself something of an expert when it came to men. After all, she'd been surrounded by them all her life. She'd cataloged their strengths, memorized their faults, and worked out their patterns of behavior and the reasoning behind them. Bret didn't fit any of her preconceptions about men.

Her confusion had increased when Bret and Charlie came in for dinner. Charlie fitted perfectly into her schematic for the average male. He was better than most, but he was a Texas cowboy through and through. Now he was acting as if Bret was his best buddy.

"I wish you could stay for a couple of days," he was saying to Bret. "We could ride over the ranch and you could tell me what you think."

"All my experience is in the hill country," Bret said.

"I don't know that I could help much. You don't have all the same grasses and trees here."

How had he had time to learn which grasses grew in this area?

"We have to worry about flash floods. You have to worry about getting enough rain," Bret went on.

"I guess it is different," Charlie said, his enthusiasm undiminished, "but I figure any man who knows as much about horses and cows as you do has to know something about the land."

"Possibly, but I'm sure the ladies would like us to talk about something else. Like the excellent dinner you've prepared," Bret said, turning to Ida.

Ida looked pleased, but said, "How can you compare this with the suppers you have all the time in Boston?"

"You have an exaggerated notion of how much I'm paid if you think I can afford to eat like this every evening."

There was plenty of food on the table—there had to be to feed eleven people—but it was ordinary fare of ham, roasted prairie hen, potatoes, beans, rice with beef gravy, canned peaches, hot bread with plenty of sweet butter, and a blackberry pie for dessert. The coffee was black and hot.

"We eat stuff like this all the time," Joey said. It was clear he didn't see anything special about it.

"My adopted mother couldn't cook at all," Bret said. "She didn't even know you had to soak dried beans before you cook them."

"I know that," Buddy said, "and I'm a boy."

"She's a really good cook now," Bret said, "but she made all the boys learn to cook, too."

"You're not going to do that, are you?" Buddy asked his mother.

She winked at Bret. "I think it's a fine idea." She

looked at her husband, and her smile grew broader. "Then I can sit on the porch and smoke a pipe while you boys get supper ready."

Emily enjoyed listening to Ida and her family tease each other about the kinds of food they'd fix. Her description of the aprons she'd make for the boys, decorated with everything from flowers to bunny rabbits, brought forth howls of protest.

Bret didn't say anything but appeared to enjoy the fun. Every so often, Emily would notice his brows knit. She couldn't tell if the memories brought up by being around the kids were good or bad, but it was clear that they had a profound effect on him.

"Enough foolishness," Ida said after a while. "Mr. Nolan will think we're very silly people."

"I think you're a very happy family," Bret said.

"I hope so. Now if you don't mind, we'd like you to tell us about Boston. It must be exciting to live in a city like that."

Emily got the feeling Bret would rather have talked about the ranch, but he launched into a description of life in Boston that fascinated the children as well as the adults. Much to her surprise, he didn't hesitate to make fun of himself by telling a few funny stories about his first days in the city. She was certain he exaggerated a little, but she only had to see the laughter and excitement in the children's eyes to forgive him.

"That's all for tonight," he said after telling a story about getting an entirely inedible dish because the waitress couldn't understand his Texas drawl. "Maybe I'll tell you some more stories when I come back through."

"When will that be?" Clara asked, her eyes wide with undisguised admiration.

"That depends on Miss Abercrombie," Bret said,

glancing at Emily. "She might get tired of me after a single day."

"She won't," Joey said confidently. "She's crazy about horses, and you know everything about them."

Bret winked at Joey. "You weren't supposed to tell her that. Now she'll expect me to chase cows."

That led to a few more jokes at Bret's expense before Charlie took him off to smoke and talk about the ranch. He sent the boys to make sure all the stock was fed and watered for the night, and told Clara and Becky to help their mother clear the table.

Ida ordered Emily to sit down and enjoy her coffee. She started putting food away while the girls cleared the table. "What do you think of your young man now?"

"Every time I think I know him, he surprises me," Emily said. "I would never have guessed he had a sense of humor."

"I think he's wonderful," Clara pronounced as she spun around, a beatific smile on her face.

"You won't feel so wonderful if you spill those peaches," her mother said as she rescued the bowl from her daughter.

"He makes me laugh," Becky said as she deposited two dirty plates in the dishpan. "I want to live in Boston when I grow up."

Emily got up from her chair. "I'll help your mother with the washing up."

"You don't have to do that," Ida said.

"I can't sit here drinking coffee while you work. Besides, I can't talk in front of the girls. They're certain to repeat the one thing I don't want anybody to know I said."

Ida laughed. "I have to bite my tongue every time Charlie makes me mad. I know one of them will tell him everything I've said, because they tell me everything *he* says."

They both laughed, but Emily sobered quickly. "Do you and Charlie fight?"

"No. If one of us is impatient or tired, we might get snappish."

"But you do love Charlie, don't you?"

Ida washed the dish in her hands, rinsed it with cold water, then laid it on the sideboard. "Why do you ask that? You've known us most of your life."

Emily concentrated on the plate she was drying, then set it on the table. "I can hardly remember Mama when she wasn't sick. I never got the chance to see a normal marriage."

"You don't think my marriage is normal?"

"I was too young, too preoccupied with taking care of the house, and too worried about Dad to think about it. I never remember you and Charlie even getting upset with each other."

"You really didn't pay attention, did you?"

"I guess not."

Ida turned back to the dirty dishes. "You're a young woman now. It's time to be thinking of such things."

"But why am I doing it now? I don't have time to worry about something like that with Dad being sick."

"Being captivated by a man doesn't follow any timetable. In fact, it usually happens at the most inconvenient times."

"I'm not captivated by Bret."

Ida directed a penetrating look at her. "Aren't you?"

"No. I didn't want him here. I told Daddy to tell Mr. Abbott not to send him, but he'd already left Boston by then."

Ida's smile was broad and knowing. "That's not what I'm talking about. Aren't you interested in *him*? The man, not his mission."

"I'm not *interested* in him, but I am curious about him."

Ida laughed. "It could be the same thing."

Emily paused with a serving bowl in her hands. "I probably wouldn't be so curious if I didn't keep making so many mistakes about him. I thought I knew all about men, but he's not like any I've known before."

"I thought I knew all about men, too, when I was your age," Ida said, rubbing hard to remove the berry juice cooked onto the pie pan. "All I had to do was marry one to find out I didn't know anything at all. I love berry pies," she said as she scrubbed, "but I hate having to clean the pan. I was going to cook a peach pie, but the boys found these berries and begged so hard I couldn't say no."

"If I have children, I hope mine are like yours."

"Well, there's one thing you need to learn about men," Ida said, triumphantly prying the last bit of crust from the pan. "They learn early how to look charming and helpless. They also learn that a woman will crawl over burning sand if she thinks a man needs her, and they'll use it against you." She rinsed the pie pan and handed it to Emily.

"I can't imagine Charlie doing that," Emily said, seeing his impish smile in her mind. "And I don't think Bret knows how."

Ida turned to her, a look of amazement on her face. "Are you blind? I've never seen a more masterful display of *charming but helpless* than your Mr. Nolan. The boys think he knows everything. Clara thinks he's wonderful. He's charmed everyone around here, and he had you convinced he was so helpless he couldn't even ride a horse."

"I just made a lot of incorrect assumptions about him."

"You're missing the point. That man knows exactly what he's doing. Nothing he did was accidental. I don't pretend to know what he's like. I get the feeling the real Mr. Nolan is kept carefully out of sight. I do know he's handsome, personable, and he's willing to use his charm to get what he wants."

"You make him sound dangerous."

"I expect he is. The question is, dangerous to whom and in what way?"

Emily respected Ida's opinion, but she didn't see Bret as dangerous. She did agree he revealed very little about himself, but any man who'd seen his father hanged, had been abandoned by his family, been an orphan living on the streets, adopted by strangers, and then tried to force his way into the heart of the family that had rejected him, couldn't afford to let his emotions control him. He would have had to become practically impervious to suffering, his feelings shut down, his sensitivity dulled until nothing had the power to hurt him. A child with no power would have had to learn how to take advantage of the weaknesses of others just to survive.

She didn't believe Bret was a heartless manipulator of everyone around him, using others for his own ends with no concern for their feelings or well-being. Children could sense goodness or evil in a person. Ida's children had taken to Bret just as fast as that orphan in Fort Worth. She didn't know why he was hiding his true self, but she was convinced that somewhere inside that very attractive body was an equally attractive man. The question in her mind was, could she bring him out? And if she could, should she? Whatever lines of defense he'd set up, he must have thought they were necessary. She had no right to breech them, then turn away and leave him vulnerable.

Yet it was hard to think of Bret as being vulnerable. He appeared too strong, too in control of himself.

"Whatever he's really like," Ida said, "everybody seems to like him, especially the children."

"Everybody except Lonnie."

"Lonnie's jealous."

"Why?"

Ida looked at her as if she'd lost her mind. "I'm starting to worry about you. Lonnie's been in love with you since you were fifteen."

"I don't love Lonnie."

"I know that. I expect Lonnie does, too."

Lonnie had worked for her father for ten years. Emily had grown up thinking of him as she did all the men who worked for her father—as nice men who were kind to her because she was a young girl who'd lost her mother. No one had said anything suggestive or done anything inappropriate. She'd tried hard to make sure she didn't do anything that would lead them to think of her in any way except as the boss's daughter. Her father had made it clear that encouraging them in any way would be very unfair to the men.

"Then why would he be in love with me?"

Ida smiled. "Let's get some coffee. It's obvious your education has been neglected. You apparently don't know anything about men."

Ida's look was so sympathetic, so patient—and so superior—Emily felt like arguing, but she accepted the coffee and settled down at the small kitchen table opposite Ida.

"Have you ever heard of the idealized beloved?" she asked.

"Do you mean men who fall in love with someone who is above them?"

"Not quite. The man just thinks the woman is above him, but that's okay because it's necessary to his love of her, his worship of her."

"That doesn't make any sense."

"The woman has to be perfect. Any flaw would ruin the illusion and destroy his love. He might even want her to be unaware of his love. That way he doesn't have to share it. Or prove it."

"Are you saying this is the way Lonnie feels about me?"

"Maybe. He wouldn't want to see you fall in love with anyone else. He'd be jealous, might even fight to drive him away."

"I'm not in love with Bret."

"But you're intrigued by him, and Lonnie sees that as a threat."

"Are you sure of this?"

"No, but I do know Lonnie thinks you're perfect."

Emily shook her head, trying to reject the idea, the responsibility. "I never wanted anything like that to happen. What can I do about it?"

"Nothing except be very careful around Lonnie. He might do something stupid, even dangerous, to attract your attention."

Great. Her father was dying, rustlers were attacking her herds, Bret was trying to convince her to move to Boston, and now she had Lonnie trying to turn her into some kind of goddess.

"Most of all, be careful of your relationship with Bret."

"I don't have a relationship with Bret."

Ida finished her coffee and got up. "Not yet, but you will."

* * *

Bret watched as Joey and Buddy pulled their bedrolls from their hiding place under the bed.

"I really wish you'd sleep in the house," Ida said to him.

"We want him to sleep out with us." Joey hefted his bedroll onto his shoulder.

"I'm sure the last thing Bret wants is to be saddled for the night with two brats," their father said.

"I don't mind," Bret said. "I grew up with two brothers even younger than these two. I ought to feel right at home."

"Come on." Buddy slung his bedroll on his shoulder just like his big brother. "Joey and me have picked out the perfect spot."

"You'd better hope Lonnie and Jem haven't picked out the same spot," Charlie called after them.

"We already told them it was ours." Joey pushed his brother along ahead of him. "We got rocks for a campfire and everything."

"No fires," Charlie ordered.

"The bed will be here in case you can't get to sleep with them around," Ida called to Bret as he followed the boys.

"Let Becky and Tim use it," Bret said. "After a day in the saddle, I'll have no trouble falling asleep."

Bret wasn't sure why he'd decided to sleep out rather than take advantage of the bed. Maybe he was trying to prove he wasn't the tenderfoot Emily thought he was. He suspected he was also trying to prove to himself he wasn't the tenderfoot he was afraid he had become since leaving Texas. During his years on Jake's ranch, he'd taken pride in his physical strength, his ability to do difficult and exhausting jobs. He never stopped trying to keep up with Sean even though Sean was four inches taller and carried fifty more pounds of muscle. He was never as good with horses as Luke or Chet, nor could he ride broncos as well as Matt or Night Hawk. But he could do it all, and he could do it well.

Then he'd moved to Boston, and his life had gone from a physical challenge to a mental one. It had been exciting at first. There was so much to learn, so much to understand, that it was two years before he realized he wasn't happy. That was when he'd let his cousin Rupert talk him into taking up boxing. Except for visits with his grandmother, boxing was all that kept him sane as it became increasingly clear that Silas intended to keep him on the sidelines while he promoted Joseph into a position to take over when he retired.

Over the last year Bret had thrown himself into developing the plan to reorganize the company. After it was done, he'd asked Rupert to look it over and offer suggestions. They'd even discussed it with their grandmother, who'd forced Silas to agree to look at it. He'd thought of the plan as the beginning of his future in Abbott & Abercrombie. But now that he was back in Texas, he wasn't so sure.

The changes had started the moment he'd crossed the state line. They'd continued when he smelled the stench from the Fort Worth cattle pens, when he'd met Jinx, when he'd spent a day astride a horse for the first time in six years. The last six years seemed to drop away.

"This is it," Joey announced proudly. "It's the best spot on the whole ranch."

Actually it was a poor spot. It was flat and relatively free of rocks and thorny plants, but it was along the crest of a ridge which would have exposed them and their campfire to anyone miles away. They would have had no protection from wind or rain, but the boys had a clear view of the ranch on one side and the hills on the other. Nothing obstructed their view of a star-studded sky that seemed to go on forever.

"Put your bedroll in the middle," Buddy said to Bret. "Joey and I will sleep on either side."

"What if I snore?" Bret asked.

"I'll punch you to make you stop," Joey said, laughing.

"Daddy snores." Buddy dropped his bedroll on the ground. "Mama says she has to punch him or she wouldn't get any sleep."

"I'm just kidding," Bret said. "I don't snore, but don't punch me. I might think you're rustlers and go for my gun."

"You're not wearing a gun," Buddy reminded him.

Bret dropped his bedroll on the ground. He untied it, then gave it a kick. It unrolled, and out fell a pistol.

"Gosh!" Buddy exclaimed.

"Have you ever shot any bad men with that?" Joey asked.

"No, but I've scared off a few with my rifle."

"Where's that?" Joey asked.

"In my trunk."

Bret hadn't intended to bring his rifle. He'd even considered leaving his bedroll behind. He wasn't entirely sure why he'd brought either of them. He just knew it didn't feel right being in Texas without them. A better question would be why he'd hung on to all this stuff for six years when he'd never intended to use them again.

"Daddy taught us how to use a rifle for hunting," Joey said, "but he said we didn't need a gun."

"I hope you never do," Bret said. "Now we'd better see about getting to sleep. I don't know about you two, but I'm worn to the bone. I wouldn't want Lon-

nie and Jem to have to tie me to the saddle tomorrow
to keep me from falling off my horse."

The boys insisted that would never happen to Bret.
He entertained them with a couple of funny stories
about his days on Jake's ranch as they undressed and
crawled into their bedrolls. Both boys said they were
too excited to sleep, but barely fifteen minutes had
passed before Bret heard soft, steady breathing coming from each of them.

He lay awake trying to figure out why he felt content to sleep on the ground on the open Texas plain.
The ground was hard, the night too warm, and he had
nothing to shelter him from the weather. On top of all
that, he was wondering if Jinx was okay. He hadn't
given a single thought to Abbott & Abercrombie all
day, but he couldn't stop thinking about Emily.

The trouble was, he wasn't sure of the nature of his
thoughts.

She was a very lovely woman. No man could look at
her without being attracted to her, without memoriz-
ing her smile. He could understand attraction. After
all, he wasn't dead. What he didn't understand was
the feeling that he liked her, too. That kind of appeal
could be dangerous to his future. He'd been sent to
Texas with only one job—to take her back to Boston.
Uncle Silas had made it clear that his future at Abbott
& Abercrombie depended on his being successful.

He'd come to the conclusion that Silas had no intention of implementing his plan or giving him a
more important position in the company. If Bret
somehow managed to gain the voting rights to Sam
Abercrombie's stock, the situation would be different.
Other members of the family were unhappy with the
shrinking dividends. Even his uncle's own mother
thought he was running the company into the

ground. Bret had a plan for gaining the voting rights to Sam's stock, but that brought him up against another problem.

He couldn't in good conscience convince Emily to go back to Boston when he knew Silas would put pressure on her to marry Joseph. The bastard had been writing her for the last couple of years, making her believe he was her only friend in the family. There was no love lost between the cousins, and Bret was certain that Joseph had told her not to trust him. Joseph had an exaggerated opinion of his ability, but he was smart enough to know that Bret and Rupert were threats to his future leadership of the company. Bret had no doubt that Joseph thought Emily was beneath him, but he would marry her if it was to his advantage. He was certain that Joseph would treat Emily very much as his father had treated Bret. And that was something Bret couldn't allow.

Which was something of a dilemma. And at the moment, he had no idea how to solve it.

It would have been a lot easier if he'd been able to think like Silas. Then he wouldn't care about people or the way his actions affected them. Living with Jake and Isabelle had taught him that people could be trusted, that good people didn't do bad things purely to gain an advantage for themselves. They said a man had to be able to look himself in the mirror and not be ashamed.

And at the center of this mess—though she clearly wanted to be anywhere else—was Emily. It couldn't be comfortable to be pressured from both sides to do something she didn't want to do.

He'd been annoyed to find he was attracted to her, but now he was worried because he was starting to feel sorry for her, to like her. That was not a good idea, because he needed to keep a clear head, un-clouded by emotion, if he was to find a way through this tangle. But how was he going to do that when even now he couldn't put her image out of his mind?

Chapter Six

Emily was relieved to be reaching the ranch. She'd spent four of the last six days in the saddle, and she was tired and stiff. She wanted to be in her own home and sleep in her own bed.

"I expect Daddy has been sitting on the front porch since mid-afternoon," she said to Bret. "He's sure that something terrible is going to happen to me."

"He didn't want you going to Fort Worth," Lonnie said, "but he knows Jem and me wouldn't let nothing happen to you."

She and Bret hadn't had much to say to each other today. She could tell he was getting a little saddle-sore, but so was she. Only Lonnie and Jem seemed unaffected by the long trip. Lonnie had made a point of riding closer to her today. After what Ida had told her, Emily watched him closely. She was just as careful to study her own actions toward him, and was disturbed to see intimations of warmth that she hadn't been aware of. And he was much more attracted to her than she'd ever guessed. The looks Bret cast her from time to time signaled that he knew it, too. She wasn't so shallow that she needed the attention of every man she met, but he couldn't know that.

It annoyed her that she cared what he might think. She knew he wasn't fond of Joseph, the only person in Boston she liked or trusted. Joseph had already written her that Bret was jealous of Joseph's success, that he might even try to convince her to marry *him* in order to get his hands on her father's quarter interest in Abbott & Abercrombie. She had no intention of marrying anybody any time soon, most especially not Bret Nolan.

"I'm sure you'll be glad to get out of the saddle," she said to Bret, who was riding on her right.

"I expect his bottom's so sore he'll have trouble sitting down to dinner," Lonnie said on her left.

"It is a bit raw," Bret said with one of his smiles that told her he was about to say something to tease her. "But I'll manage to sit down to the table if the food is as good as Ida Wren's."

"Don't worry," Emily said. "I don't do the cooking."

"That's good to know," Bret said, his smile even broader. "It's been a long time since I had to take a hand in fixing my own supper."

Emily noticed he'd started saying *supper* instead of *dinner*. She wasn't sure what that meant, but she hoped it didn't mean he considered the evening meal in Texas unworthy of the term.

"I don't think that would be a good idea. Bertie doesn't like men in her kitchen."

"A man's got no business in a kitchen except to eat," Lonnie announced.

"It's obvious you didn't grow up in a household of eleven kids," Bret said. "Isabelle did most of the cooking, but we had to set the table and clean up. About the time Eden was born, Jake made us take over all the cooking. Fortunately, Matt knew how to cook, or it would have been pretty bad."

The idea of a group of rough-and-tumble boys learning to set the table and clean up, even cook on occasion, intrigued Emily. Ida's boys would rebel if she so much as mentioned it, and their father would back them up. She couldn't imagine how Isabelle had managed it.

As she drew closer to the ranch house, Emily's father got up from his chair on the porch and started down the steps. She could see his smile of welcome, could sense his relief that she was home safe. She looked at her father closely. Illness had ravaged his body, reducing a big man to a bone-thin frame. He walked slowly and with an effort, but his strength of spirit wouldn't yield to his physical weakness. He greeted his daughter with a smile despite having to lean on the step railing and then a cane for support.

"I'll see you at the house," she said to Bret and Lonnie and kicked her horse into a slow gallop.

"She adores her father," she heard Lonnie say before she got out of hearing range.

She supposed she did adore him. Due to her mother's long illness and early death, her father had been her only parent. No matter how busy he'd been, he always had time for her. She brought her horse to a stop and dismounted. Holding her arms out, she walked into his embrace.

"How's my hardheaded, willful daughter?" he asked.

"Hard head and strong will still intact," she said, giving him a big hug.

"I was hoping Mr. Nolan might soften you up a little."

"You'd be disappointed in me if I became infatuated with a handsome face."

"I'd like to see you infatuated with almost any man's face. It's not normal for a young woman to ignore every man she meets."

Emily grinned. "I confess I haven't exactly ignored this one. He is awfully nice-looking."

Her father's eyebrows rose.

"Don't get your hopes up," she said, laughing. "He's very handsome, but he's just as hardheaded and strong-willed as I am. I'm betting we'll be at each other's throats in a couple of days."

"You promised to listen to him," her father said, some of his enthusiasm waning.

"I only promised to listen. Now smile and act like you're glad to see him. After all, you're the reason he's here."

"I see we're going to have to put our heads together and plot against you," her father said.

When Bret and Lonnie reached the house and dismounted, Emily took her father's arm and turned to meet them. "This is my father, Sam Abercrombie," she said to Bret. "Father, this is Bret Nolan, the man who's supposed to make me believe my future lies in Boston."

"How do you do," Bret said, extending his hand to Emily's father. "I've been looking forward to meeting you. You're quite a legend back in Boston, you know."

"I expect mine is a story they tell little children to scare them into being good," Sam said with a smile as he shook Bret's hand.

"More like to convince younger sons to go out and make something of themselves."

"You're not going to make me believe my brother thinks I'm a success," Sam said.

"Maybe not, but I do," Bret said. "You did what you wanted, and you still inherited your share of the company."

Her father laughed so hard, Emily was worried he'd do himself harm. "I hadn't thought about it like that," Sam said. "By damn, that's enough to keep me in good spirits for at least a month."

"Why don't we go inside," Emily said. "Dad shouldn't be out in the sun too long."

"I'll be in after I see to the horses." Bret turned back to the horses.

"Lonnie can take care of them," Sam said.

"I can't ask him to take care of my horse and bring in my luggage."

"I like him already," Sam said as Bret led his horse to the barn. "I never had a guest take care of his own horse, not even when it *was* his own horse."

"I never expected a city slicker to care about horses, much less know what to do," Emily said as she helped her father up the steps.

"I wonder why Silas sent him. I'd have thought he'd have sent Joseph."

"There you go thinking Joseph wants to marry me. What would he do with a wife like me?"

"Be damned lucky he got you." Sam had difficulty breathing after climbing the steps. "You may not be as rich as some of the Boston girls, but you're a damned fine-looking woman. Besides, you've got backbone and character."

Emily laughed as she held the door open for her father. "When did men start appreciating backbone and character in a woman?"

"When I married your mother," her father said, wheezing. Emily took his arm and guided him to his favorite chair in the great room.

"Don't move until it's time for dinner," she ordered. "I'll be back as soon as I make sure Bret is settled in his room."

"So it's Bret already, is it?"

"What else did you expect? I can hardly argue with him if I'm still calling him *Mister Nolan*."

"You're not going to change, are you?"

"Probably not, but you'll love me anyway." She kissed him on his forehead. "Now I'm home and safe. You're not to worry anymore."

"I can't help worrying about what will happen to you when I'm gone."

"The only reason I'd even consider going to Boston would be so you'd stop worrying. Now rest up. I think you'll enjoy getting to know Bret."

As Emily climbed the stairs to her room, she realized *she* expected to enjoy it, too. Setting aside the fact that he was handsome enough to warm her blood and cause her cheeks to flush, he was an interesting man, full of contradictions and secrets. He was going to set his will against hers—the kind of intellectual contest she enjoyed. She also had the feeling he would surprise her. She wasn't sure how, but something told her it would be a pleasant surprise. None of this made sense, of course, but that was how she felt.

It had been a long trip and she was exhausted, her muscles still felt tight from so many hours in the saddle, but she didn't have time for a bath before dinner. She barely had time to change her clothes and make sure Bret was settled in his room. She supposed she could have left that to Lonnie or Jem, but he was a guest and she was the hostess. Besides, anybody who took such good care of his horses was all right in her book. The fact that he was the best-looking man she'd ever seen didn't hurt, either.

She wondered why Joseph had warned her against him. Bret certainly hadn't done anything to make her think he was interested in attracting her attention, much less winning her affection. It was mortifying to be attracted to a man who seemed uninterested in her. Where was the sport, the challenge, the slight element of fear that things just might get out of control?

He was the first man she'd ever been attracted to. It was probably a good thing she could get this first infatuation—if she could call it that—out of her system on a man who had no interest in her. She would have the experience without the possibility of making the mistake of falling in love.

She was amused and a little out of patience with the foolish thoughts going through her mind. She needed to eat dinner, make sure her father was okay, get a good night's sleep, and get her mind back on her work. Maybe then she could forget about Bret Nolan.

Bret thoroughly enjoyed dinner. The food was excellent, the company even better. Sam Abercrombie was a fascinating man who'd turned his back on family status and fortune, scorned his relatives' opinion, and used their criticism to spur his ambition to prove them wrong. Part of the charm, part of the miracle, was that he didn't think he'd done anything unusual. He'd simply wanted something different and hadn't let anything stand in his way.

Several leaves had been taken out of the dining room table, but it was still too large for three people. The room itself, not to mention the crystal and table settings, were unusual for a ranch some distance from Fort Worth. Joseph and Uncle Silas would never believe this table was as impressive as the one they sat down to each night.

"My daughter's got my rebellious spirit," Sam said. "She's not paying any more attention to me than I paid to my parents."

"I'm not going to sit here and listen to you tell Bret what an undutiful daughter I am," Emily said as she rose from the table. "I'm going to go get my exhausted body ready for bed."

"See, she doesn't give me any respect at all."

Bret could tell from the love-filled look on Sam's face that the father-daughter relationship was entirely to his satisfaction.

"I'll give you one hour," Emily said. "If you're not done by then, I'm coming down and carrying you off to bed. You," she said, directing a severe look at Bret, "are not to let him get worked up. If you do, you'll be on a horse back to Fort Worth before you know what happened to you."

"I promise," Bret said.

Emily kissed her father on the forehead and headed upstairs.

"I love that girl, but she's more than I can handle," Sam said. "One of the reasons I want her to go to Boston is to find a husband who's good enough for her."

"Do you mean one who's strong enough to handle her?"

"No, I don't." The emphasis was impossible to miss. "There's nothing wrong with Emily. She's a lot like me, so why would I think she needs to be handled?"

"I obviously chose the wrong word," Bret said. "Sorry."

"I want her to find a man who can appreciate her strengths, not just be interested in her looks and her money."

"I don't mean to be disrespectful, but you have to realize that men in Boston aren't any different from men anywhere else in the world. Looks and money come first. It takes time for a man to see past that to character. Not many succeed—or want to try."

Sam seemed to shrink a little in his chair. "I should

have sold this ranch after her mother died, but I didn't want to leave Texas. I didn't want to share my little girl or my life with my family. Hell, I don't like my family. Why would I want to live with them?"

"Are they really that bad?" Bret didn't know the Abercrombies well. He wasn't considered on their social level.

"Why do you think I contacted Silas Abbott? I wouldn't send my dog to my brother."

"Then why do you want Emily to go to Boston?"

"Because she can't stay here. She could run this place by herself, but who could she marry? Lonnie?"

"She could move to Fort Worth or Dallas."

"Nothing but cowhands, good-for-nothings, and thieves. I wouldn't send my dog there."

"You know Emily is dead set against going to Boston, don't you?" Bret said.

"I'm sick, not deaf or stupid."

Bret laughed. "I just want you to know it'll be very difficult to change her mind."

Sam gave him a penetrating look. "I get the feeling you're a very capable young man, probably able to convince young women to do things they probably shouldn't do."

"Maybe, but I haven't talked any young woman out of her reputation."

Sam laughed heartily. "I never heard it phrased quite so politely. In my day we said a young woman had disgraced herself."

"I haven't caused one to do that, either."

Sam's gaze narrowed. "Is something wrong with you?"

Now it was Bret's turn to laugh. "I'm perfectly normal, but I'm a poor relation trying to convince my family I won't disgrace them if they let me in the front door," Bret said, hoping he hadn't let the bitterness he felt seep into his voice. "Why would I do something to hurt my own cause?"

Sam's eyes narrowed. "Maybe you've come to Texas to advance your own cause?"

Bret took a moment to taste his brandy. It was very good, quite expensive, but tonight it didn't suit his palate. "My uncle sent me because he thinks I'm the one member of his family who won't be soiled by being in Texas."

"And how do you feel about that?"

"I hate it." Bret hadn't meant to be quite so honest, but Sam wasn't a man to tolerate pretense. "I've worked long hours for Abbott and Abercrombie but have gotten nowhere. When I told Uncle Silas I might not be able to convince Emily to go to Boston, he told me not to come back without her."

"He sounds a lot like my brother."

"So I made up my mind to offer you a deal," Bret said.

"If Silas thinks so little of you, what can you offer me?"

"You want Emily to be where she's safe, but you want someone to look after her to make sure she doesn't marry the wrong man."

Sam wasn't allowed brandy, but at this point he drew the bottle toward himself and took a swallow directly from the bottle. "Go on."

"I will undertake to convince Emily to move to Boston. I'm prepared to stay here for several months if it takes that long."

"Until I'm dead."

Bret hadn't wanted to say that. He was grateful Sam did it for him.

"If I can convince her to go to Boston, I'll see she doesn't marry anyone who will treat her badly. Don't ask me how I'll do that, because I don't know yet."

"And what is this going to cost me? Half my ranch? Half my fortune?"

"Just the right to vote your stock."

Sam pushed the brandy bottle away and leaned forward. "Are you trying to take over the company?"

Bret shook his head. "Uncle Silas has kept me in piddly jobs for six years, but that time has given me a chance to see how the company works. If we don't make some changes, we'll be out of business in ten years."

"I knew the company wasn't making much money, but I didn't think it was that bad."

"I've worked out a plan to restructure the company. My cousin Rupert Swithin—another poor relation—agrees it's what we need to do to survive. Even my grandmother thinks it's a good plan."

"I haven't thought of Elizabeth in years. Is she as independent as she always was?"

"If it hadn't been for her, Uncle Silas wouldn't have given me a job."

"So you're a young rebel who wants to bring down the head lion. Why should I help you?"

"Because I can help *you*."

"And how do you plan to do that?"

Bret laughed. "You can't expect me to give away all my secrets."

Sam slammed his fist down on the table. "I won't have you trying to make Emily fall in love with you just so you can push your way into a job I can't be sure you can handle."

Bret sobered quickly, reined in his temper. "I'm not ready to get married, and I'm not in a position to marry in any case."

"Your position wouldn't matter if you married Emily."

Bret could see that Sam wasn't going to give in

quickly, but he respected the older man for not accept-
ing Bret's word without any validation. "I'm not asking you to commit to anything now. I realize you don't
know anything about me, but you haven't been able to
convince Emily to go to Boston on your own, and you
won't be able to guide her after you're gone. At some
point, you're going to have to trust someone."

"And you think that person ought to be you?"

"As I see it, you have four choices—your brother,
Uncle Silas, Joseph, or me. You have to decide which
one you trust with your daughter's future."

"You think you've got me cornered, don't you?"

"No."

"Don't lie to me, boy. You know I can't stand my
brother and don't trust Silas or his boy."

"You could ask my grandmother."

"If she couldn't stop her husband from disinherit-
ing her own daughter, she couldn't protect Emily."

"You could hire someone."

"And have him sell out to Silas."

Bret had expected to have a difficult time convincing
Sam to trust him, but he seemed to be gaining ground.
It would probably be better if he kept quiet now, but
there was one fact he felt he couldn't withhold.

"This may not help my case," Bret said, "but I feel I
have to tell you I find your daughter very attractive."

Sam grinned suddenly. "I'd think something was
wrong with you if you didn't."

"What I'm trying to say is that although I am attracted to her, I have no intention of deepening our
relationship beyond trying to gain her friendship and
trust. That will be necessary if she's to pay attention
to any advice I might give her."

"That's obvious, so why are you telling me this?"

"Because you have to trust me. If anything
changes, I'll tell you."

"Are you always so straightforward?"

He shrugged. "I try to be. The couple who adopted me insisted I never keep anything from them, even when I knew it was something they wouldn't like and didn't want to hear."

Sam chuckled. "I can see why you and Silas don't get along."

"It has nothing to do with that. Silas just doesn't think I'm good enough for him."

"Then I know Silas better than you do." Sam leaned back in his chair, subjected Bret to a look that was so long and hard, Bret had to check the impulse to squirm in his chair. "I'm going to have to trust you. First, because I don't trust anybody by the name of Abbott or Abercrombie. Second, I don't really have another choice. Third, I like the way you present yourself, no pretending you can pull off a miracle. But if you betray me, I'll make you wish you'd never been born."

Bret was sure his smile was ironic. "You'll have to find a better threat than that. A small crowd of people have done that already, and I'm still here."

A slow smile gradually lit Sam's hazel eyes. "I like you, boy. I kinda wish you were interested in marrying Emily."

"It wouldn't do any good. She doesn't think I'm quite as useless as she did three days ago, but her opinion hasn't improved much."

A door opened and closed upstairs. "Unless my ears deceive me," Sam said, "that's Emily come to carry me off to bed. We'll talk again, but I accept your offer, on conditions."

"What offer and what conditions?" Emily asked as she came into the dining room where they still occupied the same chairs they'd used during dinner. She had apparently changed into her bedclothes, because her body was engulfed in a housecoat with only her hands and head visible. Elsewhere she had disappeared in a cloud of pale blue material that billowed around her when she moved. The most striking change was her hair. She'd unpinned it and allowed it to fall on her shoulders, framing her face in a cascade of soft brown brightened by blond highlights. It made her look more feminine, much more vulnerable. Bret had to remind himself he was here to do a job, not get emotionally involved with Emily.

"It's a secret," Sam said to his daughter. "We men don't tell women everything, you know."

"You should," Emily said. "That way we could keep you out of trouble."

"I don't want to be kept out of trouble. That's half the fun in life."

Bret wasn't at all sure he could agree to that sentiment, but he could see how a man like Sam would feel that way. He was certain Emily felt the same. She might end up staying in Texas, unmarried, and running her ranch. But if she did marry, her husband was in for a bumpy ride.

"I know you and Bret have spent the last hour plotting against me."

"It's for your own good," Sam said.

Emily took her father's hand and helped him out of his chair. "Time for bed. You can dream about having a dutiful daughter who does everything you want."

"Sounds very boring," Sam said as he allowed Emily to lead him to his bedroom on the main floor. "I prefer a filly with spirit."

"Tell Bret good night. It's way past your bedtime."

"Stay in bed late," Sam warned Bret. "She's got so much energy in the morning it makes me tired to be around her. We can see her at lunch after she's had time to slow down."

"Don't listen to him," Emily said. "He'd be in the saddle ahead of me if I'd let him."

Bret remained at the table to finish his brandy. He could hear Emily and her father teasing each other, scolding, showing their love for each other. He found himself thinking of Jake and Isabelle. They teased and scolded each other from the time they got up until they went to bed, yet he'd never seen two people who were more devoted. They'd laid down rules for the orphans and made demands they expected them to fulfill, but no one ever doubted it was all done out of love.

Until he listened to Emily and her father, Bret had forgotten what it was like—and how much he missed such loving banter. Being part of the Maxwell clan had never been comfortable. There were too many strong-minded people who didn't want to trust, didn't want to belong, didn't want to feel they owed anybody anything. Yet somehow Isabelle had woven a web of love around all of them that was stronger than their distrust, their suffering, even their fear—a web so strong they finally began to feel like a family.

That was what he saw in Sam and Emily, a father and daughter who were such close friends they sometimes could switch roles without destroying the fabric of their relationship. He had nothing like that in Boston, and he never would. For the first time, he asked himself if what he hoped to gain could possibly compensate for what he'd given up.

He didn't like the answer.

Chapter Seven

"What were you and Bret plotting?" Emily asked when she'd finally settled her father in his enormous four-poster bed. "Don't bother denying it. I can see the guilt in your eyes."

Her father's eyes twinkled. "I like that young man. I think you ought to listen to what he says."

"I'm not sure we can trust him."

"Why?"

Emily pulled a letter from her pocket. "This is from Joseph. He warned me Bret was sent here to bring me back to Boston, nothing more."

"Has Bret implied he has something else in mind?"

"No, but Joseph said he might try to make me fall in love with him. He said Bret has been trying to force his way into the family ever since he arrived in Boston."

"Since the boy is Joseph's cousin and Silas's nephew, I shouldn't think any *forcing* would be necessary."

"Read it for yourself." Emily held the letter out to her father, but he pushed it away.

"I distrust Joseph and his father only a little less than I distrust my brother. I agree we have to be cautious with Bret, but you can't believe everything Joseph says. I hate to say this, but your twenty-five percent of Abbott and Abercrombie is probably more attractive to him than you are. And that doesn't take into consideration the rest of your inheritance."

Emily hated to think of herself as a commodity, but she'd been the only child of a wealthy man too long not to understand the importance of her inheritance to potential husbands. It was part of the reason she wanted to stay in Texas and run the ranch herself. It was part of the reason she tended to trust Joseph. He was already wealthy and socially prominent. He didn't need her inheritance.

"My inheritance would be even more attractive to Bret," she said.

"Probably, but he was spared the influence of the Abbotts for the first twenty-one years of his life. He might actually be a decent member of that snobbish family instead of rotten to the core like the others."

"If you dislike them so much, why do you want me to go to them?"

Her father took her hand and squeezed it. She hated to see him look so weak and pale. He used to be a vibrant man who could work longer and harder than any other man on the place. He'd loved nothing better than to be in the saddle riding over his land. Now he leaned back against his pillows, exhausted from his evening with Bret.

"I don't want to send you to them, but I haven't made a very good job of my life. I have lots of enemies and no friends. I'm forced to fall back on family."

"I'd rather fall back on Lonnie and the boys."

Her father's grip tightened, his eyes narrowed, and

the stern look she remembered so well from past years rammed into her like a fist. "Are you thinking about marrying Lonnie after I'm dead?"

Angered, Emily pulled her hand from her father's grasp and glared at him. "I would if I loved him."

"Don't get your back up." He reached out and pulled her back down next to him. "I'm just worried about you."

"Ida said Lonnie's been in love with me for years." She settled down on the bed again. "I didn't mean to do anything to mislead him."

"You haven't done anything wrong, but we've got to put our heads together and figure out what's best for you after I die."

"Bret seems like a nice man, but we don't know him."

"After being with him for two whole days, you've gotten to know him better than I do."

Emily sighed. "If it weren't for Joseph's letter, I'd be ready to trust him with just about anything. I know he's kind, because he went out of his way to help an orphan boy in Fort Worth."

He leaned away to peer at her. "You didn't tell me about that."

"I didn't tell you Charlie's boys took to him immediately, either. They swear he can judge the quality of a horse at a hundred paces. Charlie says Bret knows everything about ranches, and Ida says he's probably as dangerous as he is handsome."

Her father chuckled. "And what do you think?"

Emily didn't know whether it was wise to tell her father what she thought, but they'd never kept secrets from each other. "I think he's the most intriguing man I've ever met. Except for being out of sorts when he got off the train, he's been kind, thoughtful, and courteous. He rides a horse like he was born on one, but he wears a suit and sits at a table like he was born and bred in Boston."

Her father studied her closely. "Sounds to me like you're in love with him."

Emily laughed. "I could easily become infatuated with him, but there's too much about him I don't know. He seems very open and straightforward, but I get the feeling some very strong passions flow well below the surface, passions that are possibly more important than even he knows."

"Are you sure you're not infatuated already?"

"No, but I'm captivated," she teased. "By the time he leaves for Boston, I intend to know everything about him."

"Be careful he doesn't know everything about you as well."

"I'm not worried about that. I have nothing to hide."

But having said that, she realized it wasn't quite the truth. She was hiding that she didn't quite trust him. He was a handsome man who apparently had very few resources. What could be more to his advantage than to marry a wealthy woman who just happened to own a large portion of the company he worked for? In one fell swoop, he would gain financial security, influence in the company, and a secure place in his family. It would be difficult for an ambitious man *not* to consider such a plan, and she had no doubt that Bret Nolan was a very determined as well as an ambitious man.

"He told me he was an orphan on the streets for two years," her father said.

"That's all the more reason to wonder if I can trust him."

"What would you do if you decided you could?"

"We'll have to wait and see about that."

But Emily already knew the answer. If she decided she could trust him, it would be nearly impossible not to fall in love with him.

Emily was shocked to find Bret in the kitchen drinking coffee when she came down the next morning. She was even more surprised to see Bertie talking to him like he was an old friend. Bertie didn't encourage men to invade her kitchen.

"After your long ride, I thought you'd be sleeping late," Emily said to Bret. "You didn't have to get up."

Bret stood and held her chair while she seated herself. Emily could tell from Bertie's smile of approval their cook had already succumbed to Bret's charm, something she would have never thought possible. She continued to underestimate this man.

"If I'd stayed in bed, it would have reinforced your opinion of me," he said.

"And just what *is* my opinion of you?" She was curious to know what he thought, but she wondered if he would tell her the truth or try to get away with some clever answer that didn't mean anything. "Got any fresh coffee left?" she asked Bertie. "Ida never could make it like yours."

"I just finished making this for Mr. Nolan," Bertie said as she took a cup and poured coffee from the pot on the stove.

Emily accepted the coffee and settled across the small kitchen table from Bret. "You should have had time to think up a good answer by now."

"I won't have no carrying on in my kitchen," Bertie announced.

Emily laughed, but she felt slightly annoyed, too. "I was just asking for his opinion on me as a person, Bertie, not a declaration of love."

Bertie didn't back down. "Could be the same thing."

"I'm sure it's not."

"It's probably best if I save it for later," Bret said with one of those smiles that thoroughly confused her. "It'll give me time to perfect my answer."

She felt certain he had a ready answer on the tip of his tongue, but she was perfectly happy to play his game. That implied he meant to spend at least part of the day with her. Though she didn't want him or Bertie to know it, she was anxious to spend some time alone with him.

"What do you want for breakfast?" Bertie asked.

"A couple of eggs with—"

"I was asking our guest," Bertie said. "He comes first."

Bret tried, but he didn't dip his head fast enough to hide his smile. As soon as she got him away from the house, Emily meant to ask him what he'd done to charm Bertie. Not even her father got that kind of treatment.

"I'll have whatever Emily usually has," Bret said.

Bertie gave Emily the evil eye. "You don't have to be afraid of her. You can have whatever you want."

There was no question about it now. His eyes positively danced with amusement. "I'm not afraid. I've got to talk her into doing something she's dead set against, so I'm trying to get on her right side."

Emily had never seen anything like it. He could tell a disagreeable truth and everybody loved him all the more for it.

"Ain't nobody ever made her be sensible when she's set her mind against it. Now what do you want to eat? I'm not sweating over this hot stove because I like it."

"Would some eggs with ham and hot biscuits be too much to ask for?"

"Eating like that won't put any meat on your bones. I got potatoes and gravy, some pork chops, canned peaches, and stewed tomatoes. The hands like to know they got something in their stomach."

"I'll eat whatever you fix," Bret said.

"Now that's a gentleman," Bertie said to Emily. "You'd do good to listen to what he says." Then she turned her back on the two of them and addressed herself to her cooking.

"Talk is cheap," Emily said.

"Not around here," Bertie muttered.

"You might as well stop trying to hide your grin," Emily said to Bret, beginning to feel annoyed. "I know you're laughing at me."

"I wouldn't be a gentleman if I didn't try to hide it," Bret said.

"I'm beginning to wonder if you're a gentleman at all. You show up and suddenly everybody's questioning everything I do."

"We've always been questioning it," Bertie said without turning around. "You just ain't been listening."

"I'm not listening to him either," she said to Bertie's broad back.

"I didn't expect you to. Anyhow, I'm too old to start fainting."

Emily considered going back to her room until Bertie called her for breakfast, but that would mean admitting defeat.

"What did you have in mind for me today?" Bret asked.

"I always work with my horses in the morning, but I thought I could show you some of the ranch this afternoon."

"What are you doing with your horses? Maybe I could help."

"I train horses to be cow ponies. Right now I'm teaching them to cut a cow from the herd."

"How many are you working with?"

"Eleven. I had twelve, but a piebald gelding can't seem to get the idea, so I'm sending him back to his owner. It's a shame, because he's a very nice horse."

"Maybe I could give him a try. I did spend nine years on a ranch."

"If you want."

She didn't know what he'd done when he was on that ranch. It was one thing to make sure your horse hadn't picked up any stones or that the packsaddle wasn't rubbing any sores. It was another to know how to convince a stubborn horse to cut a cow from a herd. The horse had to be intelligent, cooperative, and want to do his job. Emily wasn't sure the piebald was any of those.

"If you want her to go to Boston," Bertie said, "you're going to have to take those horses with you." She harrumphed. "She don't care about anything else."

"That's my work," Emily said.

"You ought to get married and let your husband worry about all that. You need to be having babies. Your papa ought to see one grandson before he's put in his grave."

The part about getting married and having babies simply annoyed Emily, but the part about her father dying without seeing any grandchildren hurt. She glanced at Bret to see his reaction, but his face was expressionless. Emily was relieved when Bertie sat a bowl of peaches and a plate of potatoes and gravy on the table. Those were followed quickly by a platter of ham and eggs.

"Take what you want now," Bertie said. "I've got to

feed the boys before they come in here wondering if I've dropped dead in front of the stove."

Neither Bertie nor Emily missed Bret's look of surprise.

"The men prefer to eat by themselves," Bertie said. "Mr. Abercrombie makes them nervous, and Emily makes them choke on their food."

"If you don't stop telling him stories, he's going to think we're the worst people in Texas," Emily complained to Bertie.

"I can't help it if you don't like the truth."

"I'm not afraid of the truth. It just sounds different when you tell it."

"Imagine that," Bertie said and turned back to her stove.

Emily decided that eating her breakfast in silence might be the safest way to get through the next few minutes. Bret had come knowing she was dead set against her father's wishes. Now he probably thought she was spoiled and self-centered. She *was* used to getting her way, but not because she was spoiled. She'd been given the responsibility to make decisions. It wasn't her fault if people didn't like all of them.

She watched Bret out of the corner of her eye. He'd looked mighty handsome in his suit, but there was something different about him in a tan shirt, denim jeans, and boots. He looked more virile, more exciting, more . . . *masculine*. His suit coat had emphasized the breadth of his shoulders, but his shirt allowed her to see the ridges of bone, the swell of muscle, the movement of sinew as he ate his breakfast. She'd been around men all her life, but she felt as if she'd never really seen one before now.

She hadn't realized she'd practically ignored her

breakfast until Bret wiped his mouth and put his napkin next to his plate.

"That was an excellent breakfast," he said to Bertie. "A worthy companion to last night's dinner."

"Don't you go trying to get around me with your pretty smiles," Bertie said, trying unsuccessfully to hide her pleasure at his words. "This ain't nothing compared to what you have all the time in a fancy place like Boston."

"I spent more than half my life in Texas. You make me feel like I've come home."

Emily didn't know Bret well yet, but she was developing a feel for the times when something touched a part of him he couldn't hide. A couple of times she'd sensed that things were slipping past his guard, getting around his defenses, reminding him of something he had tried to forget—or had refused to remember.

"Eleven kids around the table couldn't be anything like this morning," Emily said.

"It's the food, the air, the warmth of the breeze." He chuckled. "It's the hot biscuits with jam and butter. You can't know how many memories that brings back. Isabelle turned into a good cook, and she made fabulous biscuits."

"Better than mine?" Bertie asked.

Emily held her breath. Anybody who dared criticize Bertie's cooking took his life in his hands.

"I dreamed about that beef you served at dinner last night, but nobody can make a better biscuit than Isabelle."

Bertie took a moment to digest that. "Everybody has to be especially good at something. You wait until you taste my stuffed fillet of veal or my pecan pie."

"You can make a pecan pie?" Bret asked, his eyes growing excited.

Emily could have punched him. If he'd spent one year in Texas, he knew pecans grew wild and every woman knew how to make a pecan pie. And Bertie, the tyrant of the kitchen for as long as Emily could remember, was acting like a girl with her first crush.

"We'll have fresh peaches, too, if you hang around for a few weeks. Mrs. Abercrombie had Mr. Sam plant a fruit orchard, build a grape arbor, and set out rows of berries. We have to water them in summer and protect them against the cold in winter, but the hands think it's worth it when I start making pies."

Emily's father said he sometimes thought the hands worried more about his fruits and berries than they did about his cows.

"Maybe I'll move here from Boston," Bret said, giving Emily one of his innocent looks.

Refusing to rise to the bait, Emily took one last swallow of coffee. "It's time to go to work. If you're serious about seeing what you can do with that piebald, meet me out by the corrals in half an hour. I have to make sure Dad's awake and okay."

Emily was too irritated at herself for feeling jealous of the attention he was showing Bertie to wait around for his answer. She knew he was flirting with Bertie and that neither of them took it seriously, but that didn't seem to make any difference. She told herself she didn't want his attention, but she couldn't make herself believe it.

Maybe she was infatuated. She certainly wasn't acting like herself. Maybe it was normal to think about him all the time. His attention was going to be focused on her, so naturally hers would be focused on him. What she hadn't expected was for him to pay attention to other people. There was the orphan in Fort Worth, Ida's boys, her father, and now Bertie. It was like he was making a place for himself when she knew he had no intention of staying in Texas. The most obvious explanation would be that everything he did was part of his plan to convince her to change her mind about Boston, but she couldn't see how flattering their cook would help.

Then there was the possibility he was doing this so she would marry him. She wished she could talk to Joseph. She didn't know if she could trust everything he said, but he had to know his cousin better than she did. She liked Bret very much. In fact, the more she saw of him, the more she liked him. She didn't think she could stand it if his charm was all a pretense.

Bret was impressed by the size and complexity of Sam's ranch. In addition to a larger-than-usual ranch house and the expected bunkhouse and corrals, Sam had built a barn for equipment, another shared by cows, pigs, and chickens, and a small house which must have been where Ida and Charlie had lived. The orchard had been placed on the side of a small hill not far from the house, with the garden at the bottom. A shallow dam had been built to collect water for the garden as well as protect it from being washed out during a storm. A windmill provided plenty of cold, fresh water from a deep well.

Bret heard a door slam and turned toward the house, but it was only Bertie tossing out the dishwater. Apparently, Emily was still with her father. Bret wasn't sure it was wise to spend the morning working with her, but he didn't really have a choice. Changing her mind about leaving Texas wasn't going to be an easy job. But that wasn't what was bothering him.

His attraction to her was getting stronger by the hour, despite the fact that she'd only grudgingly decided he wasn't a green tenderfoot who would get into serious trouble if left to his own devices. Worse, she didn't appear to be happy about losing her preconceived notions. Maybe that was what he liked about her. She was a strong woman, determined to hold on to what she thought was right regardless of what other people thought. That was so much like Isabelle, it made him laugh.

It would have been impossible not to be attracted to Emily. Even Ida's boys talked about how pretty she was, and they hadn't reached puberty. He'd passed that stage long ago and discovered what it meant. Sexual desire was something that had never been a problem before, but he had a feeling that was about to change. He had to keep their relationship on a business footing. He couldn't forget his goal. Let Emily think he was interested in her that way, and she'd never believe anything he said.

And if he achieved that goal, he would then be faced with the problem of making sure Emily found a suitable husband. Except for Rupert, he didn't know a single man who deserved a woman like Emily, but Rupert was already married. It wasn't likely that Joseph or Uncle Silas would pay any attention to him on that subject. He had no reason to think Emily would, either. But if he accepted Sam's offer to let him vote the stock, he had to deliver on his promise.

He sighed. That wasn't his only problem. Returning to Texas had brought home two very unpalatable truths. He missed Texas and everything about his life on Jake's ranch. And no matter what he did, he would never receive the acceptance from his blood family that his adopted family had given him. He didn't understand why he was only now figuring that out.

"Didn't expect to see you up this early."

Bret turned to see Lonnie approaching him, making no attempt to hide his unfriendly scowl. He really didn't expect Lonnie to like him. His presence threatened the man's livelihood as well as his interest in Emily. Lonnie was dressed for work, but his jeans were clean, his shirt had been ironed, and his boots cleaned. Clearly he was out to make a good impression.

"I'm used to getting up early," Bret said. "Clerks don't have the advantage of being able to sleep late."

"Not even when they're related to the boss?" Lonnie was clearly skeptical.

"Especially not then." He didn't want to talk about himself to Lonnie. He knew the type—capable foreman with plans to move up in the world. Since his plan included marrying the boss's daughter, he could pose a serious problem to Bret's mission. He would have to keep an eye on the fellow. "Mr. Abercrombie has a very impressive complex here."

"He's a farseeing man. He's fenced in some of his land so he can improve the quality of his herds."

Jake had started doing that before Bret left for Boston. He'd spent a part of his profits each year buying quality bulls.

"Does Emily take a hand in the breeding?"

"*Miss Abercrombie* takes a hand in every part of the ranch, but her real love is her horses."

"I've offered to see if I can help her."

"What can you do?"

"Don't know yet, but she said I could try my hand at a piebald that seems reluctant to learn his lessons. Is that him over there?" Six horses occupied one of the large corrals. A piebald, larger by several inches than the others, was grazing a little away from the others.

"Yep," Lonnie said.

"Show me where you keep the saddles."

Lonnie reluctantly took Bret into the nearest barn,

where Bret chose a saddle from the half dozen there. He also picked out a rope.

"What's the rope for?" Lonnie asked.

"Unless he comes when called, I have to rope him before I can saddle him."

"You really going to ride him?" Jem asked as he came into the barn. In contrast to Lonnie, he wore badly scuffed boots, threadbare jeans, a plaid shirt that had been patched twice, and a hat with a ragged brim.

"I can't do anything with him if I don't," Bret told him.

"He bucks first thing in the morning."

"Most range-bred horses do."

"You'd better let Jem get him for you," Lonnie said. "I wouldn't want you to fall off and break something."

Bret was getting tired of everybody thinking he couldn't get out of his own way. Any kid growing up on a ranch in Texas knew how to rope and ride a horse. Nobody had to know he'd been afraid of horses, had never ridden one until he was twelve. Neither did they have to know how hard he'd worked to make up for that deficit.

"I'll take my chances." He put the rope over his shoulder and picked up the saddle.

"I could carry that for you," Jem offered.

"I already got it," Bret said. "You can bring the bridle and saddle cloth."

Lonnie and Jem followed Bret as he headed toward the corral. Two cowhands were there ahead of them. A couple more emerged from the bunkhouse. Bret balanced the saddle on one of the corral poles while Jem draped the saddle cloth beside it.

"You sure you don't want me to help you?" Jem asked. "He can be right ornery some mornings."

"So can I," Bret said but almost immediately cautioned himself to relax before the horses caught his mood. "Be ready with the bridle." Bret liked Jem. The boy didn't appear to resent him the way Lonnie did. "Do you help Emily when she trains her horses?"

"She don't let nobody help her," Jem said. "Not even Lonnie." Their boots stirred up dust as they walked across the corral.

"I expect he's too busy with the rest of the ranch work to have that kind of time."

"He'd make time," Jem said.

The horses had stopped grazing, all of them watching Bret and Jem. Bret glanced back to see that three more men had climbed the corral fence. "I see everybody's gathered around."

Jem laughed. "They're expecting a show."

"You mean they're expecting the piebald to grind me into the ground."

Jem laughed. "Something like that."

"Let's see if we can entertain them."

Chapter Eight

"What's Bret doing in the corral with Jem?" Emily asked Lonnie.

"He says he's going to ride the piebald."

"Did you tell him he bucks?"

"Yeah," said one of the cowhands perched on the rough, hand-hewn timbers of the fence. "I've got two bits he misses his first throw."

"And his second," another cowhand said.

The men had to shade their eyes against the sun, which was still low in the east. Dew glistened on the few blades of grass the horses hadn't eaten or trampled underfoot.

"I've got two bits that says the piebald chases him out of the corral," a third guy said. All the men laughed.

"I've got two bits that says he makes his first throw and stays on." The words were out of Emily's mouth before she had time to realize what she was saying.

"Who're you kidding?" one of the hands asked.

"He grew up on a ranch," Emily said, trying to figure out why she was going out on a limb for Bret. "He's got to know a good bit about horses."

"Bertie grew up on a ranch, too," the cowhand said, "and she's scared of horses."

"She's not scared of you," Emily replied.

"Or anything else on two feet," a cowhand added dryly.

Emily paid no attention to the jokes about Bertie. The men were a little afraid of her—they scattered like chickens before an attacking hawk when she got angry—but they adored her. Emily focused her attention on Bret as he approached the piebald. The horse had stopped grazing and started shaking his head from side to side. Bret had formed a loop and was slowly twirling the rope.

"Maybe he's a show cowboy," a cowhand said. "He twirls that rope real good."

"He'd better be more than show if he expects to lasso that piebald. He's not going to stick his head in the noose."

The piebald moved away, but not far. When Bret continued to walk toward him at a steady pace, the piebald ducked his head, turned, and trotted away.

"He's spooked him," a cowhand said. "He'll never catch him now."

The words were hardly out of his mouth before Bret raised the rope over his head and let it sail through the air. It settled easily over the piebald's head.

"Well, I'll be a polecat's daddy," one exclaimed.

"It had to be luck. How many times have any of us made a perfect throw when the horse was running away?" The cowhand turned to Emily. "You think he can handle the piebald?"

Emily tried to pretend she wasn't nearly as impressed as the cowhands, but she couldn't repress a smile. "I think we're about to find out."

Even though it was obvious that Bret knew how to handle a rope, Emily was inclined to think that toss had been a bit lucky. It had been too perfect. The piebald backed away as Bret approached. He was usually a difficult horse to handle until he'd worked the kinks out.

"Did you tell Bret the piebald is likely to strike out with his forefoot?" Emily asked Lonnie.

"He didn't give me a chance to tell him anything," Lonnie replied, his tone indicating he was in a bad mood. "Didn't act like he thought there was anything he needed to hear."

Emily was afraid Lonnie hadn't tried too hard to prepare Bret for dealing with the piebald. She hoped Jem had.

Bret approached the piebald slowly. He was too far away for Emily to hear what he was saying, but he talked constantly.

"Maybe he's hoping to hypnotize him."

"Or talk him to death."

Emily watched as Bret approached the horse, his hand outstretched.

"He's about to lose those fingers."

"Hell, he's gonna lose his whole hand."

But the piebald allowed Bret to rub the black streak resembling a lightning bolt that ran the length of his forehead.

"I'll be damned. He *did* hypnotize him."

The piebald backed up a few steps when Bret showed him the bridle. But instead of trying to slip it over his head immediately, Bret rubbed it against his neck, his shoulders, his jaw, finally across his nose so he could smell it.

"What's he doing?"

"Asking permission to bridle him," one hand said, chuckling. But his laugh stopped abruptly when Bret

111

slipped the bridle over the piebald's head without any resistance.

"Well, I'll be a polecat's daddy."

"You already said that. How about a skunk's brother?"

Bret slipped the noose from around the piebald's neck, snapped on the lead shank, and started toward the corral fence where he'd left the saddle. The piebald followed as docile as a lapdog. Emily knew it was silly of her, but she felt proud of Bret. He looked so confident.

"Think he can ride the piebald?" a cowhand asked.

"I'm not sure he can get a saddle on him," another said. "Some mornings he takes a disliking even to the blanket."

Bret wasted no time in dispelling any mystery about whether he could saddle the piebald. He handed the lead shank to Jem, then patted the piebald on the neck. He put the blanket on the horse's back, making sure there were no creases in it. He gave the horse a couple more pats, then settled the saddle easily on his back. The piebald sidestepped nervously a moment but calmed down when Bret talked to him.

"Let's get closer so we can hear what he's saying."

Bret adjusted the saddle, then tightened the straps. Again the piebald sidestepped and again he calmed down when Bret patted his neck and talked to him.

"I'm going to ask Jem what he said."

"You think it's some kind of spell?"

"Can't tell until I know what he's saying."

"Stop yammering. He's about to mount up."

Emily could feel the tension between her shoulders. Bret had taken care of his horses all during the trip, but being able to stay on the back of a bucking horse was something altogether different. Letting

Jem hold the bridle, Bret took hold of the reins, put his foot into the stirrup, and swung into the saddle.

The piebald went to bucking.

The piebald wasn't wild and he wasn't mean, but he had to be convinced each day to let someone stay on his back. He fishtailed, switched ends, ran a few steps, then stopped abruptly, trying to throw Bret over his lowered head, but Bret stayed firmly in the saddle. After about fifteen more seconds of bucking, he suddenly stopped. Standing spraddle-legged, he lowered his head between his forelegs and threw his rear end into the air. Bret leaned back until his head was nearly on the piebald's haunches, but he stayed in the saddle.

"Damn," one of the hands said. "I thought he was a goner for sure."

The piebald bucked some more, but it was clear his heart wasn't in it. A few halfhearted kicks with his hind legs, and he came to a halt. Bret dug his heels into the horse's sides, and he trotted around the corral.

"I never thought he'd do it."

"The piebald didn't put up much of a fuss."

"It was enough to plant your face in the dirt."

"Each of you owes me two bits," Emily said, grinning in spite of herself.

"We don't have any money until payday," one man said.

"Then I'll take it out in food. No dessert for a week."

The chorus of objections caused Emily's grin to broaden. "Forget it," she said. "I already knew he was good with horses."

"The real test will be to see if he can teach that dumb beast what to do with a cow," Lonnie said.

That didn't bother Emily. Bret had already proved he knew how to handle a horse.

"He done good, didn't he?" Jem said when he reached Emily. He turned to watch as Bret rode the piebald around the corral, getting him used to responding to commands. "I never seen the piebald act so gentle."

"He wasn't too gentle when Bret got on his back," Emily pointed out.

A few minutes later, Bret rode up to the fence and brought the piebald to a stop in front of Emily. "Where are those cows? It's time to send this bad boy to school."

"I brought some in off the range yesterday," one of the men said. "They're in the far corral."

"I want you to saddle your best horse," Bret said, turning to Emily.

"What are you planning?" she asked.

"I thought we might try showing the piebald what to do so he can copy it."

Emily hadn't thought of that, but then, she'd always worked alone. "It's worth a try. I'll meet you at the corral in ten minutes."

Emily chose a short-coupled paint that seemed to have a natural instinct for working cows. All the ranch hands were still at the corral when she got back.

"Don't you have any work for the boys to do?" she asked Lonnie when he lowered the bars for her to enter the corral.

"They want to see what he can do." Lonnie was clearly unhappy with Bret's success. His hangdog expression implied he didn't expect Bret to fail this time, either.

"Even the best horses don't learn how to cut a cow from a herd in one lesson," she said.

"I'm sure Mr. Nolan believes today will be an exception."

If Emily hadn't been so unhappy over Lonnie's attachment to her, his jealousy would have been amusing. She'd known Lonnie for more than ten years and thought she understood him perfectly. Now Bret was forcing her to question whether she knew men at all.

"I appreciate his willingness to help," Emily said.

"I'd be glad to help," Lonnie said. "So would any of the boys."

"Thanks, but you've got your own work to do." She knew enough about men to know that spending large amounts of time alone with any one of them would cause jealousy and threaten their camaraderie.

"How long is he going to stay?" Lonnie asked.

Emily laughed. "He's threatened to stay a year if it takes that long to change my mind, but I doubt he'll be here more than a couple of weeks."

"That'll be a couple of weeks too long."

Letting that comment go unanswered, she rode toward where Bret waited in the center of the corral. Six cows had bunched themselves into a tight group, moving nervously along the far side of the corral, their apprehensive gazes focused on Bret and the piebald. When she rode up, they started milling about.

"They seem skittish," Bret said. "Have they been pestered for any reason?"

"I doubt they've seen a horse and rider since spring."

"I heard Lonnie talking about rustlers. Maybe they've been chased."

"You'll have to ask Lonnie. I've been too worried about Dad to have time for much of anything but my horses."

Longhorns were essentially wild animals, but they had little to fear from a man on horseback. Except for roundups and doctoring for screw worms, they rarely saw a cowhand.

"What do you want to do first?" Emily asked Bret.

Bret glanced at the men hanging on the corral fence. "I'd like you to send them all about their work, but I realize they're trying to figure out what kind of man I am. They're jealous and contemptuous of me at the same time."

Emily couldn't suppress a laugh. "How do you figure that?"

"They're jealous of me because I'm from a big city, I wear fancy clothes, and I'm a guest they have to treat with courtesy. They're contemptuous of me for the same reason."

"Our boys aren't like that."

"Of course they are. My brothers and I would have felt the same way. Besides, they dislike me."

"They don't even know you."

"They don't have to. Whether I want to marry you or just convince you to move to Boston, I'm trying to steal you away. To make matters worse, I'm an outsider."

"I don't believe they feel like that."

Bret shrugged. "I want you to pick out a cow you want to cut from the herd and have your horse focus on it. Then I'll try to get the piebald to do the same thing. If that works, we'll go to the next step."

Emily selected the most distinctive cow in the group, one with a lot of longhorn blood and a white coat with large splotches of black. She moved toward it until the paint and the cow made eye contact. She could feel the paint tremble with excitement. He knew what he was supposed to do and was anxious to do it. She hated to pull him back.

"Your turn," she called to Bret.

He spurred the piebald forward until he was close to the cow, but the piebald seemed to take no interest in it or any other cow.

"Try again," Bret said.

They repeated the maneuver two more times before the piebald finally directed his attention to the longhorn cow. By now the cows were so worked up, they scattered each time one of the horses approached them.

"Let's give them a moment to calm down," Bret said.

"Do you think the piebald has made any real progress?" Emily asked when they came together in the center of the corral.

"A little." Bret looked around at the cowhands still hanging on the fence.

"I thought some of them would get bored and leave," Emily said.

"This is a competition," Bret said. "Nobody is leaving until the winner is decided."

Emily was relieved when the cows finally settled down.

"Let the paint cut the cow out of the herd," Bret said.

Emily gave the paint his head, and he went to work eagerly, focusing on the longhorn, pursuing it as it moved back and forth trying to evade the horse. After five minutes, the paint had isolated the cow. Emily reined him in and rode back to where Bret waited.

"Was he paying attention?"

"We'll find out in a minute."

The piebald did focus his attention on the harried longhorn, but Bret had to work hard to get him to attempt to cut the longhorn off when it tried to escape. After ten minutes, Bret turned the piebald and rode back to where Emily waited.

"Try it again using the same cow."

"It's thoroughly spooked by now."

Bret patted the piebald's neck. "I don't want to change until he figures out what he's supposed to do."

Emily was proud of the way the paint went to work. In a matter of minutes, he had the longhorn isolated once more. Emily turned him away and rode back to Bret.

The piebald seemed to have a better idea of what Bret wanted him to do, but he was slow to respond to Bret's commands and didn't keep his eyes on the longhorn. Emily began to despair of ever turning him into a cutting horse. He was quick and strong, but he didn't have either the motivation or the intelligence.

The same couldn't be said of Bret. Emily didn't mind that the piebald was taking a long time to learn his lessons—she was enjoying watching Bret. She was still amazed at how handsome he was, how wonderful he looked in the saddle. For a long time she hadn't been able to decide whether she preferred a well-dressed man or a capable cowboy. In Bret's case it didn't matter. He was perfect as either.

But it was the person inside that impressive physique that most interested Emily. She didn't know how long it would take him to teach the piebald to cut a cow from a herd, but she was certain he would keep at it until the horse learned. While that was fine for the horse, she wasn't all that thrilled about Bret's directing his determination at her. It made her uneasy to know his future rested on getting her to Boston. He had every reason to be committed to his future—no reason to be committed to hers.

She couldn't believe there was anything truly evil about him, but she couldn't relax as long as their purposes were in direct conflict.

"He's not a stupid horse," Bret said as he rode up on the piebald, "but he is mighty lazy. I want to try it again, but I want you to change horses."

"Why?"

"I'm hoping it will embarrass him. You know, if all the other horses can do it, then he has to do it, too, or be at the bottom of the pecking order."

Emily took the paint back to the corral and returned shortly with a sorrel mare.

"Do you want to use the same cow?"

"Yes. He needs all the hints he can get. He won't master anything today. I'll be more than satisfied if I can just get the right idea through his head."

The mare was eager for her work and approached the harried longhorn with all the calm of a professional. Within moments, she had succeeded in isolating the cow.

"You're obviously a savvy trainer," Bret said when she returned to his side. "Your horses don't waste any time or movement."

Emily had accepted extravagant praise from grateful owners and equally sincere compliments from their cowhands, but she was surprised at the pleasure Bret's compliment gave her.

"I enjoy it," she said, hoping a blush didn't betray the heat in her face. "I've always liked horses."

"I used to hate them," Bret said. "I couldn't ride and was scared of them."

She couldn't believe that a man who rode a horse as well as Bret could ever have been afraid of horses. But what surprised her even more was that he would admit it. "How could you grow up in Texas without being able to ride?"

"My father had no use for the skills most men consider necessary. If it wasn't in a book, it wasn't worth knowing. The orphanage where I ended up didn't have money for horses. When Isabelle rescued me, it didn't take me long to realize I was very lucky to have landed on Jake's ranch. I decided I'd either learn to ride or die trying. Now, I'd better put this horse back to work before he forgets what little he knows."

Bret didn't have to work quite as hard this time to show the piebald what he was supposed to do, but

Emily had a hard time concentrating on the horse's progress. How could a man who'd never been on a horse until he was twelve, and had spent the last six years in Boston, ride so well? Why did he care about proving to Emily and the ranch hands that he was just as capable as they were?

And why had he admitted his weakness to her?

A Texan would rather die than be thought a coward. When Charlie was foreman, he used to say it was easier to take care of the ranch than it was to keep the young hands from stupid attempts to prove their manhood. Bret had just admitted having been afraid of the one thing a cowboy couldn't afford to be afraid of—his horse. She wasn't sure whether she admired him for his honesty or was simply too shocked to know what she felt. Joseph's admonition not to trust him, that Bret would do anything to achieve his ends, had stayed in the back of her head. She didn't believe that Bret did anything by accident, even confessing his fear of horses. Everything he did had to be part of his plan.

"You ready for the next horse?"

Surprised, she turned around to see Jem standing next to her with a brown gelding. She'd forgotten she was to ride a different horse each time. "Sorry. I wasn't paying attention."

"Lonnie says that piebald is just as useless as he was an hour ago," Jem said, "but it looks to me like he's going more kindly."

"It looks that way to me, too," Emily said. "Maybe I'll have to try this embarrassment theory the next time I get a horse like the piebald." Jem held both horses while Emily dismounted from the mare, then mounted the gelding.

Jem scrunched up his face in a puzzled expression. "You think it'll work?"

"It's worth a try. Nothing I did worked."

Jem shaded his eyes against the sun when he looked up at Emily. "Bret seems real nice. I don't know why Lonnie is against him."

Jem was a top hand, dependable as well as capable, but he was satisfied to be right where he was. He had no reason to be jealous of Bret.

"He's coming back," Jem said.

"How'd the piebald do this time?" Emily asked when Bret reached her.

"A little better. I can't decide whether he knows what he's supposed to do and doesn't want to do it, or if he simply hasn't figured it out." He paused, a thoughtful expression on his face. "That sounds like a description of some people I know. Even myself on occasion."

"I can't imagine you ever not knowing what you wanted to do or being reluctant to do it."

Bret looked away from Emily. "I've spent most of my life in that position." He patted the piebald's neck. "Maybe that's why I think I know what's going on in this big fella's head."

Emily decided she didn't know how many more revelations she could take in one morning. "Should Jem saddle another horse?"

"Let's keep going as long as the longhorn doesn't go completely crazy on us."

Emily told herself to concentrate on her work, but the gelding was as thoroughly trained as the mare. If the longhorn hadn't been about ready to jump the fence, she wouldn't have had anything to do but think of Bret's revelations.

From what she knew of him, it was nearly impossible to believe there'd ever been a time when he didn't know what he wanted to do or was reluctant to do it. He'd made his goals very clear from the moment they met. She didn't understand how what he was doing now would achieve that goal, but she had no doubt he had a plan. How, then, could he consider himself indecisive?

That brought her back to what she kept telling herself: She didn't know much about him. There was something about him that felt honest, straightforward, unwilling to lie or deal in subterfuge. Maybe he was telling her about some tough times in his life in order to gain her sympathy, but they weren't the kind of stories most men told about themselves. Rather than build himself up, the stories sometimes revealed weaknesses or faults. And the only people he appeared to like and admire—possibly love—were his adopted family in Texas.

If he liked his family in Texas so much and disliked his family in Boston, why had he never moved back to Texas?

Chapter Nine

"I don't see why we need to show him around the ranch," Lonnie said to Emily. "He's not going to stay here."

"It would be rude not to," Emily said. "He helped me with the piebald, after all."

"Just because he can make that stubborn horse look a cow in the eye doesn't mean he knows anything about a ranch."

"Charlie valued his opinion."

"Charlie doesn't have to put up with him."

They were waiting by the corral while Bret saddled his horse. Emily was certain that part of Lonnie's irritation was because Bret had picked out her best horse even though he'd never ridden any of them, a big mouse-gray gelding with a reputation for being hard to handle. Lonnie had warned him, but Bret said he'd like to try him anyway.

"He's a guest," Emily told Lonnie. "You will treat him with courtesy."

After his work with the piebald, the cowhands

were willing to accept Bret as an equal. That seemed to irk Lonnie even more.

"I hope he doesn't stay long," Lonnie said. "I've got too much to do to be mollycoddling some tenderfoot."

"You don't have to go with us," Emily said.

"You think I'd let you go traipsing all over the ranch alone with him?" Lonnie asked in amazement.

"What could happen?"

"No telling with a man like him."

In fact, Emily was wishing Bret wasn't quite so well-behaved. She didn't like being so strongly attracted to him, but she was even less happy that he didn't seem attracted to her. She was certain there were lots of more beautiful women in Boston, certainly more sophisticated and more knowledgeable, but she wasn't used to being ignored.

Bret emerged from the barn leading the gray.

"Wait until he gets in the saddle," Lonnie said.

"He handled the piebald," Emily reminded him. "I expect he'll do fine with the gray as well."

"I really appreciate your taking the time to show me around," Bret said to both of them when he came up beside them. "I know you have work you'd rather be doing."

"I plan on enjoying the ride," Emily said. "I haven't gotten away much since Dad got sick."

Lonnie moved quickly to help her into the saddle before Bret had a chance to offer. She was annoyed, because she'd enjoyed the experience of Bret lifting her into the saddle as though it were easy to do. She gathered the reins, settled into the saddle, and waited for Bret to mount the gray. Lonnie was waiting, too. Emily thought she could detect a smile in Bret's expression.

When Bret started to put his foot in the stirrup, the gray sidled away from him. When it happened a second time, Bret led the horse to the corral and positioned him next to the fence. The gray tried to bolt when Bret mounted up, but Bret quickly tightened the reins.

"Don't be so anxious," Bret said to the horse. "You'll have plenty of chances to show your stuff."

"He likes to make mounting him as difficult as possible," Emily said. "Most of the hands don't like riding him."

Bret patted the gray on the neck. The horse responded by throwing his head about, fighting for control. "You've been getting off easy," Bret said to the horse. "I'll see what I can do about that." And with a few more words, he got the gray to settle down and trot peacefully alongside Emily's mare.

Emily knew she shouldn't have been amused to see Lonnie forced to swallow his anger, but his dislike of Bret was unfair. Maybe Lonnie wasn't able to separate the messenger from the message. She disliked the thought of having to move to Boston, but it was impossible to dislike Bret.

"Dad controls well over a hundred thousand acres," Emily said as they rode away from the ranch buildings.

"It's closer to two hundred thousand," Lonnie said.

"That's a lot of land," Bret observed.

"Mr. Abercrombie is a very wealthy man," Lonnie said.

Once Lonnie got started talking about the ranch, he gradually forgot his dislike of Bret. Emily realized he was trying to impress Bret with her father's wealth; even she didn't know some of the things Lonnie was saying. She'd been so busy taking care of her father and training her horses, she hadn't fully understood the vastness of her inheritance or all the problems of safeguarding it.

"Are you having much trouble with rustlers?" Bret asked.

"When you have as many cows as Mr. Abercrombie, there'll always be somebody trying to steal a few," Lonnie said, making it seem as though it weren't a problem.

"Jake never liked it when he lost a single cow," Bret said. "He said if anybody wanted a cow, they had the right to work hard enough to own one."

"It's not worth the trouble trying to chase down every two-bit rustler," Lonnie said. "We don't have the men or the time."

They had been riding for over an hour and were well away from the ranch. Post oak, blackjack oak, elm, pecan, cottonwood, and ash bordered the creeks. The slopes of the flat-topped hills featured Spanish oak, live oak, and mountain juniper. The prairie was covered with a variety of grasses—big and little bluestem, Indian grass, Texas wintergrass, blue grama, and buffalo grass—that produced fat cows because her father refused to put more cows on the range than it could support. Emily could remember as a little girl riding through grass up to the belly of her horse.

"We've got the best grazing land in the area." Lonnie waved his arm in a half circle, indicating grass-covered prairie that stretched to the horizon.

"We've had several offers to buy the ranch," Emily said. "I'm not interested in selling, but folks seem to think I won't be able to hold on to it after Dad dies."

"I'd be more worried about the rustling," Bret said.

"We don't have much rustling, do we?" Emily asked Lonnie.

"More than I let on." Lonnie's eyes became hooded.

"Why didn't you tell me?" Emily demanded.

"You had your hands full with your dad. Taking care of the rustling was my job."

"What have you been doing about it?" she asked.

"I've got the boys on patrol." Lonnie sounded defensive. "We haven't seen any signs of rustling lately."

Emily wasn't satisfied with that answer, but she decided to wait until they got back to the ranch to question Lonnie further. She didn't like the idea of anyone stealing her father's cows.

Bret and Lonnie traded stories about rustling and what some ranchers had done to stop it. Emily was interested at first, but after a while it sounded like a game men played with each other. Her attention had begun to wander when Bret pulled up, his sentence unfinished.

"What's wrong?" she asked.

"Why isn't that calf wearing the same brand as the others?" Bret asked, pointing to a calf no more than three months old among a group of cows and calves. "I thought we were well within the limits of your father's land."

Emily was confused, but Lonnie seemed agitated. "Maybe he got lost from his mother," Lonnie said.

"There's one way to find out," Bret said. "Let me use your rope."

"What are you going to do?"

"Rope that calf. If its mother is anywhere around, she'll come running."

"I don't like anybody using my rope," Lonnie said.

"Fine. You rope him."

Lonnie hesitated, and Emily wondered if he was afraid he couldn't rope the calf. Usually the cowhands did that kind of work, not the foreman.

"Here, use my rope," Emily said, handing hers over to Bret. "Next time, bring one for yourself."

Bret built a loop quickly and efficiently. The calf had moved away and broke into a run when Bret rode toward it. Emily found it exciting to watch him ride after the calf, sitting high in the saddle, the rope making a perfect circle in the air above his head.

"He's just showing off," Lonnie said. "He's probably never roped a calf before in his life."

Before Emily could remind Lonnie that Bret had spent nine years on a ranch, the rope settled over the calf's head, and Bret brought his horse to an abrupt stop.

"Then I guess he's doubly lucky today." Emily was so anxious to reach Bret, she didn't bother to look back to see if Lonnie was following her. By the time she dismounted, Bret had wrestled the calf to the ground and was examining its brand.

"This definitely isn't the same brand as its mother is wearing."

"How can you tell?" Lonnie asked as he joined them.

"Because the only cow that didn't disappear over the rise is wearing the Abercrombie brand. This calf isn't. How long ago did you brand your calves?"

"More than a month," Emily said.

"I'd say this brand is fresh."

Emily got down next to the calf. The brand was still surrounded by freshly burned hair.

"If you look really close," Bret said, "you'll see the brand is uneven. Someone has put this new brand on over the old one."

Emily had never looked at a brand in that way before, but it didn't take long before she could see exactly what Bret was talking about.

"Someone may be rustling your cows, but someone is also going through your herd rebranding calves."

"So they won't have to worry about where to hide them," Emily said. "Our hands will automatically separate them out when it comes time to choose the steers to sell. But that doesn't make sense. How can they claim the steers without being identified as rustlers?"

"Once the calf is weaned, you won't be able to tell it's a false brand without killing the steer and looking at the underside of the hide. Any one of your neighbors could register that brand, claim their cows had strayed on your land over the years, and there'd be nothing you could do about it. Do you recognize that brand?"

"No. Lonnie, do you know it?"

Lonnie looked white, shook his head. "I've never seen it before."

"What can we do about it?" Emily asked Bret.

"Several things, but we ought to talk to your father first. It's his ranch."

"Lonnie and I make most of the decisions now," Emily said. "We try to spare Dad as much as possible."

"This is something he'll want to know about. But before we say anything, we ought to see if we can find any more calves bearing this new brand."

It didn't take them long to find several others. But what disturbed Emily almost as much was finding the remains of a fire used to brand the calves.

"They've got plenty of nerve," Bret said. "They're branding your calves on your own land, right out in the open."

"It's impossible for us to watch all the grazing land all the time," Lonnie said.

"I'm sure Mr. Abercrombie would have expected you to have discovered this before now. From the numbers we've seen, it's been going on for at least a month."

"This isn't the farthest part of the ranch from the house," Emily said. "The boys should have been through this area at least a couple of times." Lonnie should have told her, but she felt guilty she hadn't made it her business to find out. She wasn't doing a very good job of running the ranch for her father.

"Knowing rustlers are out there has the boys a mite nervous," Lonnie said. "They don't like riding out except in pairs. That cuts down on the amount of ground we can cover."

"Why haven't you told me any of this?" Emily demanded.

"I didn't want to worry you, not with you already upset about your father. And now"—he glanced over at Bret, an angry look in his eyes—"having to put up with him trying to convince you to sell up and move to Boston."

"You should have told me," she said, angry that Lonnie had taken such a decision on himself. "This is my ranch—or it will be—and I have a right to know everything that happens on it."

"I was only trying to help."

"Next time, help by making sure you inform me of anything out of the ordinary. Do you think we ought to look for more evidence?" she asked Bret. She was aware that turning to Bret made Lonnie look bad, but she was too angry to care.

"I'd like to see if they're rebranding any older stock," Bret said.

They spent the rest of the afternoon riding over as much ground as possible but found that only spring calves had been branded.

"Calves are relatively easy to brand," Bret said. "Two men could do it by themselves."

"Do you think only two men are involved?" Emily asked.

"I'd say you have a conspirator on your crew, one

who tells the rustlers where the men are going to be at any given time."

"Are you accusing me?" Lonnie's face turned red, his mouth tight with anger.

"Of course not," Emily said. "Nobody would accuse you."

"I'm not accusing anyone," Bret said, "only making an educated guess."

Emily would have sworn all the cowhands were honest and trustworthy, but it was impossible to ignore Bret's reasoning. The rustlers *had* to know where the cowhands would be in order to have avoided notice for as much as a month. "I don't understand," she said, thinking aloud, "why none of the boys noticed those brands."

"They probably did," Lonnie said, "but cows get mixed up all the time. We worked at least a dozen different brands during roundup. Your father owns four himself."

"I know that," Emily said, "but cows don't accept the wrong calf."

Emily felt guilty she hadn't lived up to her responsibilities. She'd been telling her father not to worry, that she and Lonnie were taking care of everything. And it turns out that neither one of them had had any idea their calves were being rebranded. Worse yet, she had no idea who owned the brand or who was doing the branding.

Lonnie was uncharacteristically quiet, probably from embarrassment. He'd been very vocal in his opinion that Bret didn't know enough to get out of his own way. Yet it had been Bret who'd noticed that a cow and her calf had different brands—and that the second brand was an easy alteration of her father's brand.

"I hate to do this," she said to Lonnie, "but I want all the men in the saddle from dawn to dusk until we find out who's behind this. After we talk to Dad, I'll send one of them to Fort Worth to look for more help."

"I ought to do the hiring," Lonnie said.

"I need you here. You're the only one who knows the whole ranch as well as Charlie used to."

Emily felt a little guilty wishing Charlie were still their foreman, but she'd grown up depending on him and Ida. Nothing had felt the same since they'd left. She had to depend on herself now, but that wasn't as frightening as it had once been. And whether or not she wanted to admit it, Bret's being here was part of the reason. She couldn't let herself start to depend on him. He wouldn't be here very long.

But she was beginning to wish he would be.

"Do you want any more stew?" Bertie asked.

"If you don't stop stuffing me so full every time I sit down to the table, they'll have to carry me back to Fort Worth in a wagon," Bret said.

"Then you shouldn't be going to Fort Worth," Bertie said. "It's nasty and smelly. No place for a gentleman like you."

Bret was eating dinner in the kitchen. They'd arrived back at the ranch to find Sam so sick they postponed mentioning the false brands. Emily hadn't left her father's side all evening. Lonnie had called the men together to tell them what they'd found and to lay out a new schedule. Bret had suggested they work in pairs and take enough provisions to stay out for as much as a week. Lonnie hadn't liked his suggestion, but Emily had endorsed it immediately. According to Bertie, the hands had, too. They were angry that rebranding had been going on under their noses and were anxious to recover their self-respect by putting an end to it.

"I live in Boston, not Fort Worth," Bret told Bertie.

"A man like you has got no business in a place like that." Bertie was so busy removing bowls and platters from the table, Bret couldn't see her expression. "You ought to have a ranch of your own."

Bret nearly choked on his coffee. "What makes you think I want a ranch, or that I'd be able to manage one?"

"The cowhands haven't stopped talking about the way you handled that piebald," Bertie said, still too busy to look at him. "Now you're the one who discovered the rustling." She turned to face him. "Sounds to me like you know more than you're letting on." She turned away. "Besides, who wants to live in a place like Boston? It's full of nasty, pushy people."

Bret chuckled. "At least they don't wear guns and steal cows."

"They have lawyers who steal people's money."

Bret's smile vanished. "How do you know about Boston?"

"My father couldn't find work after the Yankees destroyed everything they could lay their hands on, so we moved there after the war. I didn't like it so I came back here. I was lucky Mr. Abercrombie was looking for a cook and housekeeper." She topped off Bret's coffee. "It was like breathing fresh air when I crossed into Texas. I knew I'd come home."

It chilled Bret to realize he'd felt exactly the same way. How could he feel like that when his future was committed to Abbott & Abercrombie? He'd devoted the last six years to making a place for himself in Boston, in the company, in the Abbott family. That future was what he'd always wanted. It was what had forced him out of Texas, caused him to leave a family that loved him, a family that accepted him whole-heartedly even though he'd tried to hold back, even though he'd kept telling himself it was only a substitute until he could go back to his *real* family.

The only thing was, the longer he was in Texas, the more he felt like he belonged here.

In the beginning, he'd hated everything about Jake's ranch: horses, cows, the dirt. He hated the guilt he felt because he didn't deserve the love Isabelle gave so freely, the acceptance Jake offered without question, the support the other boys gave him even when he was surly and mean-spirited. But most of all he hated the fact that he couldn't do anything as well as the other boys. Bitter anger and a fierce desire to prove he was just as good as anybody from Texas drove him to work doubly hard to learn to be a good cowhand. He hated the work, thought the job was de-meaning, but he was determined he was going to be as good as anybody else.

Of course he wasn't. Sean was bigger, Zeke was stronger, Hawk was a better rider, Luke was better with a gun, Chet was . . . in the end it didn't matter. He accepted he couldn't be the best at everything when he realized he was good enough at everything necessary to his job. He'd enjoyed his competency, the faith Jake and the other boys put in him, the re-spect everyone gave him. Before he left, everyone said he'd earned his place. Even more important, he knew it himself.

He'd conquered Texas. He would conquer Boston and Abbott & Abercrombie, too.

"Miss Emily could use some help from a man like you right about now."

Bertie's voice jerked him out of his brown study. "If

she needs more than her father and Lonnie, I'm sure Charlie and Ida would be glad to help."

"It was a sad day when they left," Bertie said. "A huge mistake, too. Big ranchers don't like little ranchers setting up in the middle of their land. Whenever there's rustling, it's the little ranchers they think are doing it."

Bret had seen it before. The small rancher was threatened or beaten, his property burned or torn down, herds scattered or butchered, water holes poisoned, dams destroyed, families terrorized. He hoped nothing like that would happen to Charlie's family.

"Has there been much rustling?" Bret asked.

"There's always rustling. The Yankees don't have a lock on thieves."

"That's all the more reason for Emily to sell the ranch and move to Boston. Her money will be safer in a bank."

Bertie shook a big wooden spoon at him. "Neither Miss Emily nor her money will be safe unless you marry her."

Bret choked, spraying coffee all over the table. Bertie wiped it up without batting an eyelash.

"No point in acting surprised," she said. "I know you like her. I can see it in the way you look at her."

Bret struggled to recover his composure. "Emily doesn't like me and refuses to move to Boston. Seems to me that puts it out of the question."

Bertie put her hands on her hips and gave him the kind of look she'd give a particularly dumb child. "Anybody with one eye and half sense can see she likes you just as much. And she needs a man who won't take advantage of her."

"I'm sure she can find—"

"How's she going to find anybody stuck out here in the middle of nowhere?"

"That's just why she should go to Boston."

Bertie harrumphed and favored Bret with a frown. "You belong in Texas, and Miss Emily needs a husband to take care of her. Seems to me like that would make everybody happy."

Feeling more than a little stunned, Bret laughed and said, "My Uncle Silas and Cousin Joseph wouldn't agree with that at all."

"Is he the same Joseph who's always writing Miss Emily?"

"Does he write often?" Bret knew that Joseph and Emily had exchanged a few letters over the years, but nothing that would qualify as *always writing*. He wondered how much his uncle had been keeping from him.

"This last year there's been a letter from him every time the mail comes from Fort Worth. Miss Emily brought one back this time, too."

Emily hadn't mentioned that. Bret was certain Joseph had told her why he was coming. Since that wasn't a secret, why hadn't she said anything about the letter?

"I don't like that man." Bertie shook an accusing finger at Bret. "Miss Emily read me some of his letters. He's encouraging her to do what she wants, not to be swayed by other people's arguments. Since her father and his father both want Emily to go to Boston, that doesn't sound right to me. He told her not to trust you, either."

Bret would have assumed that if Joseph was writing Emily, it would be to encourage her to come to Boston. He'd also be doing everything he could to look good in her eyes. It was possible that Bertie had misunderstood what Joseph wrote, but he doubted it.

From his limited experience, Bertie was a smart woman who saw right to the heart of things.

"Do you think I'm trustworthy?" Bret asked.

Bertie favored him with another of those hands-on-hips, you-poor-dumb-thing looks. "Do you think I'd be encouraging you to make up to Emily if I didn't?"

"Is that what you're doing?"

"You're acting like a lawyer who's afraid to say anything for fear somebody will expect him to mean it. I wouldn't have said anything if I didn't know you and Emily liked each other. And I wouldn't have said anything even then if her pa wasn't so close to dying. With the rustling and rebranding going on, it's as clear as the nose on your face she's got to marry somebody. I don't know as much about you as I'd like, but you've got to be better than Lonnie or that cousin of yours." She favored Bret with a fierce glare. "And if you weren't, I'd make sure you changed your ways or was awful sorry you hadn't."

"I wouldn't be living up to that trust if I tried to take advantage of Emily while she was in a difficult situation."

"How is telling a woman you love her taking advantage?"

Good question.

"Telling Emily I love her would be a lie. I do like her, but I barely know her. If I were to decide I wanted to marry her, I would be subverting the reason my uncle sent me here. I'd have to let everybody know my goals had changed."

"Would you do that if you loved her?"

Chapter Ten

Bret studied the night sky glittering with thousands of stars. After so many years in Boston, it was easy to forget the Texas sky seemed endless, especially at night. Sam Abercrombie had built his house on a flat-topped hill, and the sky seemed to enclose Bret on all sides. The coolness of the night air helped to dissipate some of the heat Bertie's comments had generated. He'd managed to avoid answering her last question, but he couldn't avoid answering it for himself.

He wasn't in love with Emily. He was attracted to her and liked her, but that wasn't love. Any man who married her would have to love her enough to be very patient and understanding. Emily was a lot like Isabelle—she had a mind of her own. Even though Isabelle and Jake squabbled, they shared the same vision. Emily's vision could hardly have been further from what Bret wanted, what he'd worked so hard for the last six years to attain. It wasn't out of the question that he could love Emily. It was just that he didn't. Considering everything, that was for the best.

Which brought him to the problem of how he felt about being in Texas again. He'd never wanted to stay in Texas. All of his plans had been built around his life in Boston. Yet the moment he'd entered Texas a few days ago, everything felt different.

And nothing had changed since.

He felt comfortable on a horse, pleasantly surprised that all the skills, the little bits of knowledge required to know how to ride really well, came back without any effort. He'd enjoyed working with the piebald. The rope had felt good in his hands; he'd relished wrestling the calf to the ground. He hadn't used his body that way in years, and it almost ached with pleasure. Even the clothes felt more comfortable than the suits he wore every day. He felt as if his life had been turned upside down without his knowing how or why.

Maybe he was simply tired and frustrated—tired because he'd worked so hard and frustrated because his uncle still hadn't looked at his recommendations—but this feeling of dissatisfaction had more than that behind it. Now that he thought back on it, it had started before he reached Texas. It had started when he finished his plan. It was as if it had taken all his energy, leaving him with nothing more to give.

After working late every night for more than a year, buoyed by the excitement of what he was doing, he'd suffered an emotional letdown when it was done. Having his uncle shove his plan aside just made the dissatisfaction worse. Only Rupert and his grandmother's support had kept him from tearing the whole thing up. But if he really had to pin his reaction down to one thing, it would be his uncle's parting comment.

What if I can't bring her back?
Then don't come back yourself.

Everything he'd done had been for naught. He was still where he had been six years ago.

Okay, so Boston wasn't going to be the big success he'd hoped for, but did that mean he wanted to move back to Texas? He had enough experience to get another job up North. Some of his uncle's competition would be thrilled to get their hands on his recommendations. In the cutthroat world of business, people would pay well for information like that.

But he had developed the plan in order to gain recognition and acceptance for his contribution. No wonder he'd been terribly disappointed when it didn't come. But that still didn't explain why he felt as if he'd come home when he reached Texas.

Could he fall in love with Emily? What would he do if he did? For as long as he could remember, he'd been focused on returning to Boston and convincing his family to accept him as an equal. That hadn't happened yet, so his plan for his life hadn't developed beyond that point. He'd always wanted a wife and family, but those pleasures had been put off until he achieved his primary goal.

Now he had to face the possibility that he'd never reach it. That thought should have crushed him, because it meant he was a failure. He was frustrated, annoyed, even angry, but he didn't feel like a failure. Why not?

He could have understood it if he had an alternate plan, a second goal, but he didn't. Everything depended on his success in convincing Emily to move to Boston, on convincing his uncle to implement his plan. What happened if he couldn't do either? He'd never allowed himself to consider the possibility of failure before. Did the way he felt now mean he'd changed, that failure wouldn't be the end of the world? And if that were true, what had brought about the change?

Fortunately, he didn't have to go back to Boston right away. By sending him to Texas, his uncle had unknowingly given him the opportunity to find the answers he needed in order to discover what he wanted to do with the rest of his life.

"Dad had a restless night," Emily told Bret at breakfast the next morning. "I don't think he's any better than he was yesterday."

She didn't look like she'd slept at all. Bret had offered to help with her father, but he wasn't surprised when she'd refused.

"When do you plan to take him to Fort Worth to see a doctor?"

"Mr. Abercrombie won't have anything to do with doctors," Bertie said from her position at the stove. Because of her father's illness, Emily was eating in the kitchen with Bret.

"Mama was in a lot of pain before she died," Emily explained. "Dad never forgave the doctors for not being able to help her."

"Doctors aren't miracle workers," Bret said, "but they might be able to help your father."

"I know," Emily said, "but Dad's stubborn. Besides, I don't think he'd survive the trip to Fort Worth in a wagon. He can't ride, and I'd have to tie him to his seat if we took a buggy."

"Mr. Abercrombie would rather die than put up with that," Bertie declared.

Emily managed a weak smile, tilted her head in Bertie's direction. "Mama used to say Bertie and Dad were cut out of the same block of wood."

"An oak doesn't blow over in the wind," Bertie

said. "Its roots go straight down and take a real good hold."

Bret was no expert on the root structure of trees, but he did know Sam's hold on life was loosening. That made it all the more imperative that Emily come to some decision about her future. But the very fact of her father's illness made it inappropriate for him to push for that decision just now. Once Emily was forced to make decisions about the future, maybe she'd be more willing to listen.

"Are you going to work with your horses this morning?" he asked.

"I'm afraid to leave Dad. I'm thinking I ought to send them back to their owners. I don't know when I'll be able to get back to them."

"Would you trust me to work with them?"

It was clear from her expression that Bret's question had caught her unprepared. He couldn't decide whether she looked surprised, shocked, or upset. When she didn't give him an answer right away, he figured she was looking for a polite way to refuse him.

"Sounds like a good idea to me." Bertie had moved from the stove to stand next to the table. "If he can handle that piebald, he can handle the rest of them."

"That's okay, Bertie," Bret said. "If she feels uncomfortable—"

"No, no, that's not it." Emily's guilty smile confused him further. "I've been trying to think of a way to ask you to do that without sounding like I was taking advantage of you."

"A woman's supposed to take advantage of a man." Bertie moved back to her stove. "What else are they good for?"

Bret could think of several answers but decided to keep them to himself. He liked having Bertie on his side.

"I'm a little rusty, but I think things will come back," Bret said. "I can't sit around all day doing nothing."

"But you need help with the piebald."

"Maybe you can let me have Jem for the day. I want to ride over some more of the ranch this afternoon, and I need somebody to show me around."

"What are you looking for?"

"It's unusual for someone to simply rebrand calves. Most of the time they want steers ready for market so they can sell them quickly. Whoever is doing this will have to come forward to claim the calves when they're ready for market in three or four years."

"Dad said he didn't understand that, either," Emily said. "He wanted me to send Lonnie out to see what he could find."

"I didn't mean to be taking over Lonnie's work," Bret said.

"I'd like for you to do it," Emily said. "With Tom gone to hire more hands, we're short right now."

Tom had ridden out last night with authorization to hire four more hands. Just before he left, Bret had given him a telegram to send to his adopted brothers, Hawk and Zeke. He had a feeling he was going to need someone he could depend on to be on his side.

Emily took a bite of sausage, washed it down with coffee, and got to her feet. "I'd better go back to Dad."

Bertie blocked Emily's path. "You haven't finished your breakfast."

"I've been away from Dad too long."

"Then take your breakfast with you." Bertie pointed to Emily's plate. "I won't have you looking like death warmed over. And that plate had better be clean when I come after it."

"Just in case you think I run the house, you've just seen proof I don't," Emily said with a wan smile at Bret.

Bertie gave Emily a stern look. "Don't you go wearing yourself out. If he takes a nap, you take one, too."

Emily agreed to all Bertie's strictures, picked up her plate, and left.

"She's no more going to listen to me than if I was talking to the chickens," Bertie fumed.

"I'd like to help with Mr. Abercrombie," Bret said.

Bertie turned her grim gaze on him. "Then make Miss Emily forget her worries for a few hours each day."

"How am I supposed to do that?"

"If you can't figure that out with all your looks, then you're not half as smart as that piebald."

Bret couldn't suppress a smile. "I don't think she's in the mood for romance just now."

Bertie looked at him like he was so dumb that talking to him was a waste of her time. "Every woman's got time for a good-looking man if he has a little sense and can think of something besides horses and whiskey."

It was impossible for Bret to ignore the irony of the situation. His uncle had given him strict instructions to stay away from Emily romantically. Now Bertie was ordering him to do just the opposite.

"I don't think she'll leave her father's side," Bret said.

"I'll get her out of that room. You just make sure she doesn't come back for an hour or two. Do you think you can manage that?" Bertie acted as if she were talking to a troublesome child.

"I'll try. Now, before you think of something else to get me into trouble, I'd better get started with the horses."

"How can entertaining Miss Emily for a few hours get you into trouble?"

"Just talking to a woman can get you into trouble.

Making her think you like her is the same as putting a noose around your neck."

"Or shackles on your legs?" Bertie said and grinned.

"That, too." Bret decided to escape while he could. Being around Bertie was not good for his health.

"What are we looking for?" Jem asked Bret.

"I'm not sure. I don't see the logic in what we've found so far. There must be something we're missing."

"I guess we should have been riding out every day," Jem said.

"You haven't been?"

"Lonnie said we could take it easy for a little while. We'd just been over the whole place branding calves. He said there wasn't nothing likely to go wrong this quick."

Bret didn't agree with that, but he could understand the reasoning. The men and horses must have been tired after the work of branding the new calves and cutting out and road branding the steers to be sent to market. Most ranchers depended on their cows to take care of themselves for much of the year. Some even dismissed their crews entirely during the winter months.

"We did ride out some to keep an eye on things," Jem said, "but there's not much to do in the summer."

They had spent the last several hours checking along the creek bottoms and anywhere else trees grew close enough together to offer shade. It was a hot day and most of the cows had sought out shady spots to chew their cuds and wait for the cool of evening before venturing out to graze again. Because the cows weren't in plain sight, it was difficult to tell if the count was down or to gauge how many calves had been rebranded.

Whoever was rebranding the calves only did it in one part of the ranch, the part that hadn't been ridden over since the roundup. It had to be an inside job. And what really worried Bret was the knowledge that it would have been easiest for the foreman to arrange everything and escape suspicion.

"Was there any problem with rustling right after your boss got sick?" Bret asked.

"Not that I know of," Jem said. "There was some people in here at first wanting to buy the place, but most of them stopped coming when Miss Emily told 'em she meant to run the place herself."

"Who kept coming back?"

"Old man Dockery. He's been wanting this place for years, but he's already got most of three counties. He wouldn't steal Mr. Abercrombie's cows. He hates rustlers something awful. He hanged two just this past winter. Some people say he's too quick to hang a fella, but he says a fella shouldn't be where he don't belong if he likes his neck the way it is."

"Looks like another fire," Jem said, pointing to a blackened circle in the prairie.

Bret dismounted when they reached the spot. The circle was less than two feet in diameter, a small fire. From the look of the torn-up grass, the rustlers had branded several calves within the last couple of days. Clearly the rustlers hadn't stopped.

"I think we've seen enough," Bret said as he mounted up.

"What are you going to do?" Jem asked.

"Talk to Sam. He'd got to know."

"You think it's one of us, don't you?" Jem said.

Jem was so quiet and self-effacing, it was hard to tell what was going on in his mind. Bret didn't think Jem was dumb, just that his mind seemed unengaged a lot of the time. Still, he had a feeling that Jem saw and understood more than anyone guessed. Bret turned in the saddle to face him.

"What do you think?"

Jem's eyes clouded. "I think someone is telling the rustlers where we're going to be riding." He shook his head. "They shouldn't do that."

"Don't say anything," Bret said. "I could be wrong."

They had ridden in silence for a while when Jem asked, "Is Emily going to Boston when Mr. Abercrombie dies?"

"She says she intends to run the ranch by herself."

"She's gonna need a husband to do that."

"Why?"

"Men don't like taking orders from a woman. It makes them feel they aren't men. I don't expect many of the boys will stay after Mr. Abercrombie dies."

"What about Lonnie?"

"He loves Miss Emily. He's hoping she'll marry him and he can run the ranch."

Apparently, Lonnie's aspirations were an open secret. Bret wondered if Emily knew.

"Will he stay if she doesn't marry him?" Bret asked.

"As long as she doesn't marry anybody else, he'll keep hoping she'll marry him."

"I thought Emily had made it clear she didn't intend to marry."

"When a woman gets scared or lonely, she's apt to change her mind."

And a woman left by herself in virtually empty country to deal with rustlers and cutthroat competition would probably change her mind fairly quickly given the right provocation. And who would be in a better position than her foreman to provide the provocation as well as benefit by it?

"Miss Emily ought to get married or go to Boston," Jem said. "It's not right for a woman like her to be by herself."

Bret doubted that Emily would be swayed by Jem's opinion, but she would be up against a group of wily wolves who probably wouldn't hesitate to take advantage of her. If she lost her crew, she'd be helpless to do anything about it. He would have to talk to Sam tonight.

"I can't believe you'd accuse Lonnie of rustling." Emily was so angry, she couldn't sit still. She had paced around her father's bedroom, firing off rounds of rebuttal for everything Bret said. "He'd never betray us."

"I didn't say he *was* behind the rustling," Bret said. "I only said he's the person in the best position to give the rustlers the information they need. I still don't understand why they don't just steal what they want rather than wait three or four years to claim those cows."

"They know I'll be dead by then," Sam pointed out, "and they think they can do anything they want and Emily won't be able to stop them."

"That doesn't sound like Lonnie," Emily said, an angry smile of satisfaction on her face.

"Whoever it is has access to inside information," Bret said.

"None of the boys would do this," Emily insisted. "They've all worked for us for years. They're fanatically loyal."

"There's always the lure of money." Sam propped himself up on his pillows. "We don't pay cowhands very much."

"I can't believe you're siding with Bret." Emily

turned angrily to her father. "You know the men even better than I do."

"Which is why I know Bret must be right. What other explanation could there be?"

"I don't know, but Bret and Jem must have missed something," Emily insisted. "I won't believe it's one of our men until I see the evidence for myself." She turned to Bret. "*All* the evidence."

"Show her everything you found," Sam said. "She'll fret me to death if you don't."

"I want Jem to go with me."

"Go with Bret," her father said. "He found the evidence. He's also the only one who doesn't have anything to hide."

Bret and Emily had ridden over half the ranch, but she'd barely spoken to him all day. They had more ground to cover tomorrow, but it was already clear the rustlers knew which parts of the ranch to avoid.

"The coffee's ready."

Emily had wandered a little distance from the campsite while Bret prepared their supper of beef stew with dried vegetables and coffee. She'd kept her back to him for the last several minutes, but when she approached the fire, her face seemed more open. She seemed less withdrawn.

"I guess I've been pretty stubborn," she said as she accepted the cup of steaming coffee. "Not even I can argue with the evidence of my own eyes."

"It's not easy to accept that a person we trust has betrayed us," Bret said. "It makes us feel stupid to have been so gullible, and it also hurts. It hurts even more because it makes it harder to believe that anyone can actually like us for ourselves instead of what we can do for them."

"Is that some more of what you learned from Isabelle?"

Bret poured his own coffee and settled on the ground to watch his stew. "I've spent a lot of time alone. I had more than enough time to think."

"How could you be alone in such a big family?"

Emily had always felt enveloped by her small family. She couldn't understand how it was possible to feel alone in a family of fourteen.

"I was a very angry boy when Isabelle and Jake adopted me. I was furious at the way life had treated me. Knowing I had a rich family in Boston, I looked down on anyone from Texas. At the same time, I was jealous and embarrassed that the other boys could do so many things I couldn't. Since I didn't *want* to feel I belonged to their family, I was more than willing to be the one who went out alone."

"Is that when you learned to cook over an open fire?"

"I had to eat. Being self-sufficient bolstered my feeling of superiority. Of course I was wrong, but it took me a while to figure that out. By the time I did, I was so embarrassed at my past behavior, I still took every chance to go out alone. I never felt like an equal member of the family until right before I left for Boston."

While he talked, Emily had come over to the fire, settling on the ground next to him. The glow from the embers lent a burnished orange cast to her face. Her light brown hair looked nearly black, her brows and lashes inky. She stared deep into the fire, as if she were thinking of something entirely removed from what he was saying. All during the day he'd watched her confidence wane and then disappear. He was certain that her decision to run the ranch alone after her father died had been founded on her absolute trust in the loyalty of the cowhands. It had to shake her to the core to find her trust had been violated.

"Is that why you went to Boston?" she asked.

"You can't imagine what it's like to have absolutely nothing, and know you have a family that's so rich they wouldn't miss the few dollars it would take to pay for your pitiful meals or flea-infested lodgings. I had to prove to them they were wrong about me."

Bret stopped himself. He didn't want to talk about this. He didn't even want to think about it. "We've got a full day of riding tomorrow. We'd better eat and get some sleep." He got to his feet, reached for a bowl, and ladled stew into it, then handed it to Emily.

"It smells good," Emily said, but she didn't taste it. "Will we see anything different tomorrow?"

"No."

She didn't speak again until she'd finished her stew. By that time, Bret had finished his meal, and washed the pot in a nearby creek. He banked the fire but left the coffee on to keep it warm.

"You realize the rustling means you can't stay here after your father's death unless you get married."

She didn't reply.

"Your husband will have to be able to command the respect of his crew, to work alongside them if necessary. Men won't respect a boss who can't defend his own property."

"I don't want to get married."

"Then you'd better sell up and move to Boston. You'll have enough money to live on your own."

"I don't want to go to Boston, but I can't find a husband like that out here."

"Move to Fort Worth or Dallas. You could even go to San Antonio." Bret laughed. "I've got a few unmarried brothers. Luke would be more than a match for any batch of rustlers, and he's one of the best-looking men I've ever seen."

"I wouldn't know what to do." Emily sounded as if the spirit had gone out of her. She turned away from Bret. A moment later she added, "I've never been courted. Never even been kissed."

Chapter Eleven

Bret didn't know why Emily would tell him something as personal as that, but his reaction was immediate and strong. His mouth felt dry, his tongue too big. He took a swallow of coffee, but it tasted bitter.

He wanted very badly to kiss Emily. Of course, that was the worst possible thing he could do. Even if she liked him—and she'd given him no reason to think she did—she wasn't happy with him right now.

Then there was the two-edged sword of kissing her when he was trying to convince her to go to Boston. She might think he really liked her, and make her decision based on the assumption of some future relationship. When that didn't happen, she'd be so furious—and humiliated—she'd probably head straight back to Texas . . . but not before giving his Uncle Silas a full account of his actions. That would effectively end his career in Abbott & Abercrombie as well as obliterate any chance of being accepted into the family.

On the other hand, she might believe he was trying

to seduce her purely for the purpose of convincing her to go to Boston. She'd be so angry, she would tell her father, who'd probably have his cowhands chase him all the way to Fort Worth with thundering shotguns.

Then there was the matter of Emily herself. Despite having had a lot of freedom and responsibility since her mother's death, she was inexperienced with men. He had no idea how she would react to being kissed. A first kiss was a momentous event. It assumed enormous importance because it ushered a woman into a whole new relationship with a man. It might be such an emotional experience, she'd start to believe she had feelings that only time and experience would show her were an illusion. He couldn't do that to Emily.

"What's Luke like?"

Bret had been so lost in his thoughts, her question made no sense. "What are you talking about?"

"You said I needed a husband who can handle the ranch and take on rustlers. You said Luke was more than a match for them, so I want to know what he's like. If I'm going to have to find a husband, I need to know what to look for."

Bret had the feeling his tongue and brain weren't connected. He could think of no other reason why he had said something like that. "I shouldn't have mentioned Luke. He's a gunman. You'd be more suited to Chet, but he got married last year."

"Do you have any brothers who aren't married?"

This was a ridiculous conversation, but at least it forced him to think of something other than kissing Emily. "Yes."

"What are they like?"

There was no harm in answering her. She'd never see anyone except maybe Zeke and Hawk—if they got his telegram, if they were free to come. "Pete's a nice enough guy, but he'll never settle down. Matt and Will Haskins are the two best-looking men you'll ever see, but Matt is a confirmed loner and Will is totally irresponsible. Zeke was a slave and Hawk is half Comanche. I haven't seen them in years, but I don't think they're the marrying kind either."

"Is there anybody else?"

"Only me."

"I'm sure a man like you wouldn't be interested in a woman who's never been kissed."

Bret threw away his coffee, which had gone cold. He turned and stared at her for a moment before he spoke. "Something would be wrong with any man who wasn't attracted to you, but you wouldn't want a man like me."

"Why not? You seem to know all about ranching. Even Charlie was impressed with you. Are you afraid of using a gun?"

Bret stared into the fire. Where to begin? What to tell her? Answering that question would be like trying to put together a puzzle with half the pieces missing. Until he'd crossed into Texas a few days ago, he'd thought he had his life all figured out. Now he wasn't sure, and discovering that he was strongly attracted to Emily was only part of the problem. "There's a lot more to being the kind of man you should marry than knowing how to use a gun."

"I'm not talking about marrying me, just being interested in me. No man has ever tried to kiss me."

"I'm sure Lonnie would like to." Though Bret was certain he was correct, he had no right to start guessing what might be in the man's head or heart. He certainly had no right to mention it to Emily.

"Lonnie wants to marry me. That's not the same thing."

Bret was surprised that Emily could make the distinction. She understood a great deal more about men than most of the women he knew. "Why would you say that?"

"Being a husband is a job. There are lots of things about it you don't necessarily like but you do them anyway."

"I'm sure some men don't kiss their wives just because they consider it part of their job."

"But wouldn't it be different? I mean, wouldn't a kiss that a man considered his duty be different from a kiss a man gave because he liked the woman?"

Bret's laugh was shallow, forced. "I don't know. I'm not a woman."

She got a little angry. "You're just trying to avoid answering the question. You've kissed a lot of women. They couldn't have all been the same."

Bret felt heat begin to rise from his neck to his face. He couldn't explain it, but her words seemed like an accusation rather than an acknowledgment of experience. He hadn't kissed all that many women, he hadn't taken advantage of any of them, and he'd been very careful to give Emily no reason to think he wanted to kiss her. "What makes you think I've kissed a lot of women?"

"You have a job, your family is wealthy, and you live in a city where there must be lots of women who'd be attracted to a handsome man. Bertie said she bet you had to beat them off with a stick."

Bret didn't find Bertie's comment amusing. He hadn't been respectful of men or women when Isabelle and Jake adopted him, but Isabelle had taught all the orphans to respect women. She gave them a lot of freedom in many ways, but on that she was unyielding. "Boston women may be willing to flirt with a man they find attractive, but they know that a man rarely marries a woman with a reputation for being too free with her affection."

"But you have kissed a woman, haven't you?"

"Yes."

"More than one?"

"Yes." His answer was reluctantly given.

She sighed. "How does a woman learn the difference between a casual kiss and a real kiss if she can't kiss anybody without being considered fast?"

"She doesn't," Bret says. "When she marries her husband, he'll teach her all she needs to know about kissing."

"I don't think that's fair."

Bret wished he could think of a good way to end this conversation. The more Emily talked, the more uncomfortable he became. Thinking about what he wanted to do but couldn't was irritating.

"We need to go to bed."

"I'm not sleepy."

"You will be once you get into your bedroll."

"What would Isabelle say about a woman kissing a man who wasn't her husband?"

Bret got up, emptied the pot of the remaining coffee, and kicked dirt over the coals. If this conversation didn't come to an end soon, he was going to end up doing something he'd probably regret until his dying day. "I'm sure she'd say a woman should never kiss a man who wasn't her husband."

"I thought you said she was a strong-minded woman."

"She is."

"Then why would she be afraid to kiss a man she liked?"

"She wouldn't be afraid. She just wouldn't do it."

"How do you know?"

She was relentless and ungoverned by social conventions, just like her father. "I don't really," he said. "I just got the feeling she never trusted a man before she met Jake." He laughed. "And she didn't trust him for a long time after that."

"I trust you."

"I'm glad. It'll make it easier to accept my advice about—"

"Could you kiss me without it being a terrible thing?"

Bret was certain he would choke on the strength of the desire welling up inside him. "I wouldn't do that."

"Why not? You said you thought I was attractive."

He wondered if she had any idea of the strain she was putting on him. It was difficult to see her expression in the light of the half moon, but he didn't think she was teasing him. "Why do you want me to kiss you? If your father found out, he'd probably come after me with a gun."

"Any man who wants to marry me is going to have to kiss me first. I want to be able to tell if he likes me or just my ranch."

"Before your engagement, a real gentleman would only kiss your hand."

"Are you talking about a Boston gentleman or a Texas gentleman?"

She had him there. His Cousin Joseph would undoubtedly refrain from kissing his future wife until after their official engagement, but he knew that wasn't true for his brothers. They weren't the kind of men to scatter their kisses recklessly, but neither were they likely to be reserved once they became interested in a woman. Even Isabelle had confessed to kissing Jake quite a few times before she agreed to marry him. She joked that she had to try him out to make sure he wasn't the terrible beast she thought him at first. Unfortunately, that excuse wouldn't work for Bret.

"Even in Boston, lots of couples kiss without having to be engaged. Only men in families like yours and mine are that formal," he said.

"Dad kissed Mama before they were engaged. It scandalized her family, but he did it anyway. Mama said she liked it. I remember them kissing a lot before she got sick."

Jake and Isabelle kissed, too. It used to embarrass him, maybe even upset him a little. There was the natural impulse of boys to avoid anything like a public display of affection, but that wasn't the reason for his discomfort. At first he told himself it wasn't proper for adults to behave this way in front of their kids. Later he realized he was jealous that no one loved him enough to kiss him. It took him years to realize that every time he saw Jake and Isabelle kiss, it increased his determination to go back to Boston.

"Jake and Isabelle kiss a lot," Bret said. "It made us boys uncomfortable, but my sister Drew thought it was wonderful."

"Do you think kissing is wonderful?"

"Yes. It's the perfect way for married people to show they love each other."

"I don't mean for other people. I mean for you."

He liked it fine, but it had never been something he couldn't resist. He had a feeling that wouldn't be true with Emily. "I've never been in love."

"I'm not talking about that. Ida told me men like holding hands, dancing, going for long walks, and kissing a girl even when they don't want to marry her. Do you?"

"Yes." He hadn't done those things all that often,

because he rarely had the time or money, but he had enjoyed them.

"Then you could like kissing me."

He didn't know why Emily was asking these questions. He'd expected her to stay so angry she'd hardly speak to him. What had he missed that could account for the change? "Why would you want me to kiss you?"

"I already told you."

"Then ask somebody you know."

"I can't ask Lonnie or any of the cowhands."

"But why me?"

"Because you don't like me. Even if you did, you'll be going back to Boston, and I'll never see you again."

"I do like you." Bret knew he shouldn't have said that, but he couldn't stop himself.

"I didn't know that." She sounded surprised, even a little embarrassed. "Why? I'm stubborn. I get angry and say things I shouldn't. I didn't treat you very well when I first met you. Why would you like somebody like me?"

Bret felt himself relax. "I'm also stubborn. I get angry and have to almost strangle myself to keep from saying things I shouldn't. I wasn't nice to you when we first met. And I'm trying to talk you into doing something you don't want to do."

"I'm trying to talk you into doing something you don't want to do, too."

"I never said I didn't want to kiss you." Damn! That was the last thing he should have said. Why was he losing his control?

"Then will you kiss me?"

He didn't know what had gotten into Emily, but he had two choices. He could either refuse to talk about this any longer and go to bed, or he could kiss her, get it out of her system, and they could both go to sleep.

The logical and safe answer was to go to bed and refuse even to talk about it any longer. Her father wouldn't like it if he knew. His uncle and cousin would run him out of Boston, and Lonnie would shoot him. He would be leaving before long, so a sensible person wouldn't do anything to cause trouble.

But he was tired of being sensible, of following the rules and getting nowhere. He *wanted* to kiss her. He'd been thinking about it almost from the time he first saw her. Forget that she was lovely. Or that she had the kind of body that would fit perfectly into a man's arms. He admired her courage if not her stubbornness, her ability if not her tendency to assume the worst about him. He also liked her loyalty, even though it was sometimes misplaced, her youthful innocence, and her sense of responsibility.

When all was said and done, he did want to kiss her.

"Okay, but you've got to agree to stop before we go too far."

"All I want is to know how to interpret different kisses. It's like a lesson in school."

Not in any school he'd ever attended! Heaving a fatalistic sigh, he got to his feet. "It'll be easier if we stand."

He reached out to help Emily, but she scrambled to her feet without waiting for him. He hoped it was nervousness, but he had a sinking feeling it was eagerness. Her attitude was flattering but a little frightening. And it made him want to kiss her all the more.

"The first one I'll show you is the formal kiss," Bret said. He took Emily's hand and kissed it.

"Why would a man do that?" Much to his shock and amusement, she wiped the back of her hand on her skirt. "It feels weird. Do men really do that?"

"Not everybody, but it's considered very elegant."

"Well, I don't like it. What's the next one?"

"The friendly kiss," Bret said. He hoped his voice didn't shake and betray his nervousness. "It's perfectly acceptable with relatives—cousins, uncles, grandfathers—but it's also acceptable with good friends. Depending upon circumstances, it can be acceptable during a courtship."

He leaned forward and kissed her lightly on the cheek. As kisses went, it was almost nothing, a mere brushing of his lips against her cheek, but shock waves rocked him and he felt like he might lose his balance.

"Have you kissed a lot of women like that?" Emily asked.

"I haven't kissed a lot of women," Bret said, wondering if he was being truthful because he wanted to be or because his brain couldn't control his tongue.

"Why not? Don't you like women?"

"I like women very much, but gentlemen don't go around kissing lots of women."

"It sounds rather boring to me."

It had been, but he'd been so focused on his work he hadn't had time to realize how bored and lonely he was. He'd certainly never met anyone like Emily.

"What's next?" Emily asked.

"Some variations on the friendly kiss." Bret leaned forward and planted a kiss on her forehead, then one on her nose.

"Ugh!" Emily rubbed her nose vigorously. "Do people really do that?"

Despite the tension building inside him, Bret laughed. "The kiss on the nose is usually for children or close cousins, but the kiss on the forehead is quite popular, especially with older relatives."

"My cousins or older relatives don't count," Emily said, dismissing the Abercrombie family in a single gesture. Bret wondered if he shouldn't do the same with the Abbotts. "I want to know what a man who likes a woman does."

"The rest of the kisses are more personal," Bret said. "They're placed on the mouth."

"I know. I saw my mother and father kiss. I even saw Ida and Charlie on occasion. Ida said Charlie's not a good kisser. Are you a good kisser?"

Bret didn't know when he'd been in such a potentially dangerous situation where he was exercising so little control. "I'm only doing this to show you the different kinds of kisses, not demonstrate my ability."

"Well, it would be helpful to know if you're good. How will I be able to judge other men if I don't know how you measure up against them?"

Bret knew that if he had any sense, he'd put Emily on her horse and take her back to the ranch despite the dark. "Women don't go around judging men on how they kiss."

"Why not? We judge them on everything else. How tall, strong, attractive, nice, well-mannered, rich—"

"I get the point. Look, here's how a man will kiss a woman he likes but isn't yet ready to marry her."

Bret grasped Emily by the arms and kissed her lightly on the mouth. He pulled back, but she just stood there, lips puckered. A moment later she opened her eyes.

"Is that all?" she asked.

"Y-yes." Bret was stunned. No woman had ever responded like that before.

"That kiss wouldn't tell me whether he liked me better than his horse." She sounded thoroughly disgusted. "If that's the only kind of kissing men do, no wonder women don't like it much."

"Those are just the polite kisses. When a man kisses a woman and means it, it's something she'll never forget." Bret would never have done what he did next if his pride hadn't been wounded . . . and his manhood threatened. He put his arms around Emily, pulled her into an embrace, and kissed her on the mouth with passion.

The moment Bret's lips touched Emily's, any control he might have had went out the window. Mother Nature took over and rode him hard with whip and spur.

He was barely conscious of what he was doing, only of the effect that holding Emily in his arms had on him. The feel of her thighs pressed hard against his loins sent sexual energy thundering into that part of his body. Instinctively his arms tightened around her until her breasts pressed hard against his chest. The heat that flowed from her body was hot enough to scorch him.

But it was the feel of her lips on his that nearly undid him. He'd thought about kissing Emily. He'd even dreamed about it once, but he'd never expected it to happen. Not only had it happened now, but it was unlike anything he'd ever experienced. He wasn't merely kissing her. He felt joined with her; energy flowed between them with the violence of a spring flood. He'd been drawn into the kiss with such force, he felt helpless to do anything except follow where he was led. When her lips parted— probably in shock rather than in invitation—he didn't hesitate to invade her mouth with his tongue. He realized he'd never really kissed anyone before, never really tasted a woman, never really understood at a visceral level what it meant to hold one in his arms. The reality nearly drained him of all strength.

It wasn't until they had pulled far enough apart to look into each other's eyes that he realized the kiss had ended.

For a moment, neither of them spoke. A thousand

thoughts blazed through his mind, leaving no trace but the feeling that everything had changed. Emily looked stunned, as if she didn't know quite what to believe about what had just happened.

"That's the kind of kiss a man gives a woman he cares about." Bret's voice was so weak, he wasn't sure Emily could hear him. He realized he still had his arms around her, was holding her against his body. He slowly released her and stepped back. "You should never let a man kiss you like that unless he wants to marry you." He took a deep breath. "Even better, don't let him kiss you like that until after the wedding."

"Why did you kiss me like that?" Emily asked.

"You wanted me to show you what kisses were like. You said—"

"Was that all you were doing, teaching me a lesson?"

He wasn't sure what he was doing. He'd wanted to kiss her, but he hadn't expected anything like that. Either he had a thousand answers or none at all. "That's what you asked me to do."

"Can you kiss a woman like that anytime you want?"

He would have given practically everything he possessed to know what was going through her mind. Did she like the kiss? Was she horrified to have let him treat her like that? Did she believe he was a shallow man who would kiss any woman who let him, making promises he had no intention of keeping?

"I've never kissed anyone like that before."

He wondered if it was wise to tell her the truth. Hell, he wasn't sure it was smart for him to know it. He should have been putting the whole thing out of his mind, treating it like a bad experiment. He should have been remembering how he'd put the success of his errand as well as his future at Abbott & Abercrombie in jeopardy. He should have been thinking about how to convince Emily this whole thing was entirely meaningless to him. Knowing it wasn't cut the ground out from under him.

"Why did you kiss me like that?" she repeated.

"No man likes to be told his kisses are forgettable, not to say regrettable." It was a safe answer and had the virtue of being part of the truth.

"It didn't feel like a challenge. It felt like you liked it."

Hell and damnation! Emily never might have been kissed, but she'd seen right through him. Nothing now would serve but the truth.

"I did like it, but it's something we can never do again."

"Why not?"

Surely she knew the answer to that. Why did she insist on making him put it into words? "You're a wealthy young woman who's a member of a very important family. You deserve a husband who's your equal. You won't have that if you go around kissing men like me."

"*You're* part of an important family."

"I'm not rich, I'm not powerful, and my family would be delighted if I never came back from Texas. Now it's time for us to go to sleep. We have a lot of riding to do tomorrow. I'll take the horses down to the creek for a last drink of water."

He turned and left before she had the chance to ask him anything else. All he needed was half an excuse and he'd take her back in his arms and make sure she could never like another man's kisses, another man's arms. He kept walking because he knew if he did that, it could end up hurting Emily. That was something he never wanted to do.

He pulled the stakes tethering their mounts out of the ground and headed toward the shallow creek a hundred feet away. The horses followed, their shod feet sending muted metallic sounds into the night as their iron shoes encountered small stones. They waded into the stream, sank their muzzless into the water, and drank deeply.

It almost made him feel as if he were back at Jake's ranch, sleeping out by himself, watering his horse before turning in. The work had been hard and physically tiring. But no matter how drained he felt at the end of the day, there was something about being outside under the open sky that leached away the tension and enabled him to relax, sleep well, and be refreshed in the morning. He remembered looking forward to getting back to the ranch and being part of the rough-and-tumble family Jake and Isabelle had cobbled together.

He pulled the horses away from the water. But as he walked back to camp, he didn't feel that old sense of relaxation, the feeling of being at ease with the world. Emily was there. After that kiss, he knew she was the greatest danger he'd ever faced.

Chapter Twelve

Emily hurried to slip into her bedroll before Bret returned. She wanted him to believe she was asleep so she wouldn't have to say anything to him. She was embarrassed, confused, and excited, not a condition conducive to clear thoughts or the ability to express them in a way that would explain what had happened in the last half hour.

She didn't know what had gotten into her. She'd never done anything like that before. If he'd tried to kiss her without being asked, she'd have slapped him. Instead, when he'd been a perfect gentleman and tried to talk her out of this madness, she'd practically forced him to kiss her. She didn't know what Ida or her father would say, but she was glad neither of them would ever know. It was bad enough that *she* knew, and worse that Bret did.

She finished spreading the bedroll on the ground. It wouldn't be easy to sleep under the circumstances. If rocks didn't jab her in the back, grass clumps created bumps under her bedroll. She finally managed to find a place between clumps and settled in. She could hear the horses blowing through their nostrils, so she knew Bret was still down by the stream. She pulled the blanket over herself and turned away from where he'd dropped his bedroll.

Despite the enormity of her embarrassment, she had something more important to think about. She'd liked Bret's kiss so much she'd clung to him, kissing him back. Even the thought was shocking. She'd never wanted to kiss any man, never considered allowing a man to kiss her. Prior to tonight, she'd been mildly curious about kissing, but she'd been too busy with her horses and taking care of her father to think about it much. Over the last two years, she'd gradually begun to picture herself running the ranch alone. It wasn't that she didn't want to get married. She just didn't feel the need for a husband, and no one had come along to change her mind.

Now Bret was causing her to question all her assumptions.

If she'd been looking for a husband, she couldn't have found anyone who came closer to her ideal. He was handsome, charming, and intelligent. He could ride, rope, and seemed to know as much about ranches as Lonnie. And she liked him. It was no longer mere attraction.

And he liked her—she was certain of that. She was a novice when it came to kissing, but she could tell theirs hadn't been an ordinary kiss. The effect on him had been as much of a surprise to him as it had been to her. However, their attraction to each other was destined to end in frustration. He would be returning to Boston, and she was determined to remain in Texas.

Yet somewhere in the back of her mind lurked the wisp of an idea that he might regret having left Texas.

She supposed she understood why he'd gone to Boston, but she didn't understand why he stayed. From all he'd said, she believed he'd been happy living with his adopted family. He spoke of Jake with respect and of Isabelle with near reverence. His memories of his siblings and the work he did were all positive. He certainly didn't show any reluctance to get hot, sweaty, and dirty. Nor did he back away from the danger of rustling.

That thought brought Emily face to face with a hard fact. If she didn't do something about the rustling, she could lose her ranch. Then she'd have no choice but to go to Boston. She didn't believe that Lonnie was involved in the rustling, but she couldn't deny that somebody at the ranch was. That meant Bret was the only person she could trust to capture the rustlers and find a way to get her calves back.

Maybe by then he wouldn't want to return to Boston.

Emily's gaze didn't focus on the familiar landscape of flat prairies and low hills as she and Bret headed back to the ranch. All day long she'd been going over in her mind what to say to Bret, where to begin. Finally she simply came out with it.

"I'm not going to Boston, so you might as well give up on trying to change my mind."

Bret smiled. "You ought to know by now I never give up."

She wondered if Bret knew how seductive his smile was. "I didn't expect you would, though I don't know why you want to go back to people who treat you so poorly. I'd have thought you'd have gone back to your adopted family."

His smile disappeared, to be replaced by a hurt look. "My family's in Boston. That's where I belong."

"I think people belong where they can be happy. You haven't said anything to make me think your family makes you happy."

"We all have different goals in life."

"I can't understand why making yourself miserable should be one of them."

She feared she was taking the wrong approach. She was supposed to be convincing him to help her, not making him angry.

"Sorry," she said. "What you do with your life is none of my business, but I'd like to ask for your help. I've got to stop the rustling or I won't have a ranch to manage. Since I don't know whom I can trust, I want you to take on the job of finding out who's behind it."

Bret's surprise was evident. "I don't think that would be a good idea. Your crew will resent me."

"They'll be so busy patrolling, they won't have time to investigate. They'll bring you any information they find so they'll feel like they're part of it."

"Lonnie won't be fooled."

"The rustling has been going on for a month, and he didn't notice. I can't put much faith in his ability to find the rustlers."

"You still don't believe he's connected with the rustlers, do you?"

"No." Emily shook her head. "I've known Lonnie too long. He's too loyal."

"What will your father say?"

"I won't know until I ask him, but I'm sure he'll agree."

"And what are you offering? You know my uncle will be furious if I return without you."

"Dad said you had a plan to reorganize the company so it would make more money."

"I didn't realize he'd discussed that with you."

"Dad discusses everything with me."

Well, maybe not everything.

"I'll give you the right to vote my stock in Abbott and Abercrombie," Emily said.

Bret laughed without humor. "I've already promised your father that, in exchange for the right to vote his stock, I'd convince you to move to Boston and look after you until you got married. I can't please both of you."

Emily felt a little uneasy. She knew how much her father wanted her to go to Boston. She also knew that if he'd made a deal with Bret, he'd stick to it. There was only one solution. She had to convince her father to change his mind.

"We'll talk to Dad as soon as we get back," Emily said and urged her horse into a fast canter.

They were later getting back than she'd planned. After two days in the saddle, Emily wanted a bath. Bret was equally insistent that he clean up before he came to the table, but Bertie said they would eat supper while it was hot or she'd give it to the hogs. By the time they'd finished supper and Bertie had cleared the table, Emily was nearly boiling with impatience. Once her father had his brandy, Emily couldn't wait any longer.

"Bret tells me you made a deal with him," she said. "In exchange for convincing me to go to Boston, you'll let him vote your shares."

"That was a private conversation," Sam said, looking angrily at Bret.

"It would have remained so," Bret said, "but your daughter made a counter offer."

"What?" Sam asked Emily.

"I told Bret if he'd stay long enough to get rid of the rustlers, I'd let him vote my stock."

"You don't have any stock," her father reminded her. "I do."

"I don't wish to be premature," Bret said, "but I feel I should point out that the shares will belong to your daughter after you die."

"What are you trying to say?" Sam asked.

"It would be better for everybody—not just me—if you and your daughter could reach a compromise. The way things stand now, I have to follow your wishes. After you die, I'll have to follow your daughter's. I couldn't honor my understanding with you if I followed her wishes. That would compromise my integrity."

"I'm sure Dad would agree with me that getting rid of the rustlers comes first," Emily said.

"He may agree with you, but he wouldn't necessarily want me to be the one to do it," Bret said. "But there's something else you need to consider. Your father is deeply worried about your future. He might be willing to lose the ranch if he thought that would force you to go to Boston, where he thinks I could see you were safely married."

Emily was furious. "Dad would never do anything like that."

Sam chuckled. "You have a devious mind," he said to Bret. "That possibility *had* entered my thoughts."

Almost too shocked to speak, Emily turned to her father. "You wouldn't give up the ranch. You love it too much."

"I'd give up everything I have if I could be absolutely certain you'd be safe after my death," her father said.

"But I love this ranch. I love training my horses. I'd be miserable in Boston."

"It would be different if you were married," Sam said, "but you've never shown an interest in any of the young men you've met."

"That's because I haven't met anyone I could love." She avoided looking at Bret. "I know the way you and Mama loved each other. I want that, too."

"Then you have to move to someplace like Boston. You'll never find a husband stuck out here on this ranch."

She and her father argued—they'd covered the same ground so many times before—for several minutes without getting any closer to an agreement.

"Can I make a suggestion?" Bret said.

"Not if it involves me going to Boston or selling the ranch," Emily snapped.

"As far as I can see, you each have to give a little, or nothing will ever be decided."

"What is your suggestion?" Sam asked.

"First, we clear up the rustling."

"I agree," Emily said.

"I'm listening," Sam said.

"As you know," Bret said, turning to her father, "the shares in Abbott and Abercrombie have paid very little in the last few years. Emily needs the income from the ranch to support herself." He turned to Emily. "You're unlikely to find a man you'll want to marry if you stay here. Why don't you agree to spend the winter in Boston? It's too cold here to train horses anyway."

"I'd agree if you make that Fort Worth or Dallas," Emily said to her father. "How about Galveston? No man I meet in Boston is going to want to live on a ranch in Texas."

"Who's going to look after you?" Sam asked. "You can't go running all over Texas by yourself."

"Bret can go with me," Emily said. "I'd be safe with him."

"He can't be in two places at once," her father said. "The whole point of letting him vote our shares is so he can force Silas and my hateful brother to bring that company into the modern era. If they lose their money, they might have to come down here and live with us."

Emily was sure her father was speaking facetiously. She had only met the Abercrombies once, but she was certain they'd rather jump into Boston Harbor and drown than be forced to move to Texas.

"Why can't you spend the winter in Texas and the rest of the year in Boston?" Emily asked Bret.

"That seems like a good solution," Sam said. "You don't have to be in Boston all the time to get that company shipshape. Let your other cousin keep an eye on things while you're gone. Besides, one winter and Emily will have half the young men in Texas trailing after her."

"I won't marry anybody I don't love."

"I hear Galveston is growing by leaps and bounds," Sam said. "That means lots of young men going there to make their fortune. You ought to go this winter. If I'm feeling well enough, I'll go with you."

"Then I could stay in Boston," Bret said.

"No," Emily said. "The deal is that you get rid of the rustlers and spend the winters in Texas until I get married. In exchange, you get to vote the shares whether Dad or I hold them. Is that okay with you?" she asked her father.

"It's not quite what I wanted, but it seems a good compromise."

"How about you?" she said, turning to Bret.

Bret appeared to be undecided. She thought of several points she could use to advance her argument, but decided against voicing any of them. He understood the situation as well as she did. What he *couldn't* know—and she didn't intend to tell him—was that she believed she was beginning to fall in love with him. It was too soon to tell, because she really didn't know how it felt to be in love. There was no point in talking to Bertie, because she didn't like men. Emily would have to find time to visit Ida. She had to have an explanation for the confusion in her mind, for the unfamiliar feelings that assaulted her at odd times during the day. She was certain of only one thing. She had to find a way to keep Bret from going back to Boston until she figured out what she was feeling and what she wanted to do about it.

"It wouldn't be suitable for me to be the only chaperon of an unmarried woman," Bret said. "If your father isn't well enough to come with us, we'll have to find someone else."

"Bertie," Sam said.

"Ida," Emily suggested.

"I was thinking of Isabelle," Bret said. "She always spends part of the winter in San Antonio. Maybe I could convince her to go to Galveston instead."

"We can hire someone if Isabelle can't go." But Emily hoped she could. After all she'd heard, she wanted to meet the woman who could gather up a bunch of teenage orphan boys and head across Texas in a wagon.

Bret and her father took a few more minutes to hammer out a couple of details about handling the voting power of the stocks, but Emily didn't pay attention. She would keep the ranch and she wouldn't have to go to Boston. The only question remaining was: did she want Bret? And if she did, could she get him?

Bret enjoyed the solitude of the Texas night. He rarely walked at night in Boston because he was too tired or had work to do. He didn't enjoy walking down crowded streets with houses on each side pressed up against the sidewalk. He would occasionally walk through the Commons, but it was usually thronged with people trying to enjoy a little open space. He had nothing against children or babies, but screaming children and crying babies didn't contribute to the peaceful atmosphere he was looking for.

Out here on the seemingly endless Texas prairie, he could turn his back on the ranch buildings and feel he was the only man in the world. The night had its own sounds—the howl of a coyote, the call of a whippoorwill, the sound of a horse blowing through its nostrils, the whisper of the breeze over the waving grass—but these sounds comforted rather than distracted. They were part of Nature's plan for the night. They made Bret feel like he, too, was part of the plan.

The cool, dry breeze felt good against his skin. This was Texas, and he was tempted to take off his coat, loosen his tie, and open his shirt collar—he'd changed into a suit for dinner—but the habit acquired in Boston was strong. The struggle was brief, and Texas won. He removed his coat and tie and spread them over a mesquite bush. Walking down the trail that led to Fort Worth, he stopped on the edge of the flat-topped hill Sam had chosen for his ranch house. He stood with feet apart, arms crossed, face into the gentle breeze, wondering what the hell kind of mess he'd gotten himself into.

Every time he opened his mouth, he got more firmly enmeshed in Emily's life in a way guaranteed to complicate his life in Boston. Uncle Silas would be furious when he didn't bring Emily back with him, but that wouldn't compare to his rage when he learned Bret had been given the right to vote twenty-five percent of the company stock. Bret might be able to force his uncle to accept the proposed changes, but there was no way he would ever be accepted by his uncle outside of the office. Joseph would probably hate him as well. Working in Abbott & Abercrombie would be like fighting a perpetual war.

Bret hadn't realized until he had been at the ranch a few days that he was tired of fighting. His whole life had been a struggle of one kind or another. Except for the years spent on Jake's ranch, none of those struggles had ever ended up making him happy or feeling good about himself. He was constantly struggling to keep from losing everything he'd gained.

But what had he gained? After six years of working long hours, he was barely making enough money to pay his bills. He certainly couldn't afford the clothes, horses, carriages, fancy restaurants, parties, and balls of his cousin's social world. Yet because he was a member of the Abbott family, he was pretty much cut off from the social world he could afford. Professionally, the prospects were equally dismal. His work wasn't appreciated, his ideas were resented, and his uncle wished he'd never left Texas.

What was he trying to prove, and who would care whether he succeeded or failed?

"A penny for your thoughts."

Bret had heard a door close, but he hadn't been aware that Emily had followed him until she spoke.

"Not for a hundred dollars," he said, turning to look at her. "They're just a lot of questions."

"Can I help you find any answers?"

"I'm still trying to sort out the questions."

She couldn't help, because she was part of the problem. The more he got to know and like her, the more his life in Boston seemed a futile exercise in blind determination to achieve a goal he now wasn't sure he wanted. He'd started off wanting to be accepted as part of the family. He'd been accepted wholeheartedly by some and grudgingly by others. Yet he didn't *feel* accepted. He'd wanted to prove his ability. His work had gotten glowing praise from his boss, but his uncle's resentment denied him the feeling that he was respected. Who was he living for, himself or his uncle?

"Dad says you're a man with a lot of ghosts in your past."

Bret's laugh was harsh. "Not all of them are ghosts."

"Would it be easier if they were?"

"It might be even worse if they were ghosts. Then the problem could never be worked out."

As long as he could remember, he'd carried a pocket of boiling anger in the pit of his stomach. Even during the best times, his determination to go back to Boston had never weakened. It was the memory of his uncle's letter saying he didn't want him that had given him a reason to stay alive when he lived on the streets. It was the anger boiling in his gut that had kept him warm through two winters of sleeping in alleys—or barns when he could find an unlocked door.

"You don't look like a man with terrible problems."

Bret couldn't help smiling. "You look too pretty to have problems, either, but we both know you do."

"You're better at covering them up than I am."

Bret turned away, stared out over the prairie. "When you live from hand to mouth on the street, you learn never to let people see what you feel."

"What did you feel?"

It would be impossible to explain. Total rejection, total isolation had to be experienced to be understood. "Mostly anger at the people who'd hanged my father, and at my family for not wanting me."

"Then why did you go back?"

"To prove something."

"What?"

He turned toward her. "At one time I could list all

the reasons without stopping for breath. Now I'm not sure."

"Do you want to talk about it?"

He turned away again. "No."

He could hear her sigh. "Have you decided what you're going to do about the rustling?"

"Yes, but I don't want to talk about that, either."

"What do you want to talk about?"

"What you're going to do when you go to Galveston this winter. The parties—"

Her soft laughter caused him to turn to face her. "What's so funny?"

"You're worried about your job, rustlers, and me, and you want to talk about parties."

"Not parties. You. I need to know what you're looking for in a husband."

She sobered and walked a few steps away from him. "I've never thought much about a husband, but I guess I'd better start thinking."

"It's not likely you'll find a husband and get married right away. Even if you find somebody you like and who likes you, a few months' acquaintance probably won't be enough to base a marriage on. And you can't be sure he'll still be interested when you go back the next winter."

She turned around to face him. "Then he couldn't really love me, could he?"

Her head was tilted to the left, her expression akin to a young girl trying to accept bad news without showing it. Despite her father's wealth, she'd had her share of hurt. Her mother's early death, her father's illness, and now wondering if she could find a husband who would love her rather than her money.

"He might take your leaving Galveston to mean *you* didn't love *him*."

"He would know. I would have told him."

"Young ladies don't tell gentlemen they love them."

"Then how is he going to know?"

"If he really loved you, there'd be a feeling between you that didn't exist with anyone else."

"Have you ever had that feeling?"

"No."

"Then how do you know about it?"

"I saw it with Jake and Isabelle. It's like they're connected. She knows when he comes into a room even when she can't see him. Most of the time, she even knows he's riding up to the house."

He remembered times when Jake and Isabelle teased each other, times they held hands and kissed. He could even remember hearing sounds from their bedroom and squirming in his own bed because he knew what they were doing. But the memory that stuck with him most was when, while doing separate tasks, one would look up, catch the eye of the other, and smile in a way that let everybody know they were two halves of the same whole. In that look was all the love Bret had never had, the kind of love he feared he never would have.

"Maybe it was just them," Emily volunteered.

"I saw it between Ward and Marina, Buck and Hannah. Even Drew gets a funny look every time she claps eyes on Cole, and there's no female in the world who thinks less of men than Drew."

"I wish you didn't have to invite anybody to chaperon me. It makes me feel like you don't want to be around me."

"That's not the reason. I explained—"

"I know what you said, but I'm talking about how I feel."

She looked so young and helpless standing there with the moonlight on her hair and her face in partial shadow. She didn't appear dejected, but her body lacked its usual energy. Her shoulders seemed to have sagged a little. He didn't know whether she was weary of the weight of her responsibilities or suffering because she knew her father's condition was growing worse every day. He knew he shouldn't, but he couldn't stand there without offering support. He stepped forward to slip his arm around her waist in a comforting gesture. He wasn't prepared for her to throw her arms around him and collapse against his chest.

Chapter Thirteen

Emily didn't know what moved her to put her arms around Bret and cling to him as though her life depended on it, but she felt better for having done it. She supposed she'd finally faced up to the fact that her father was dying. After he died, she'd be alone in the world. It didn't matter that she had relatives in Boston. She barely knew them, and didn't like the little bit she did know. They thought everyone in Texas was a barbarian, and she thought they were monumental snobs. They were ashamed of her father and had no reason to like her any better. Except for Joseph, she didn't like anybody in Boston.

She had the additional problems of rustlers and knowing that somebody she'd trusted had betrayed her. Now she was faced with the problem of finding a husband—or at least pretending to look for one. She might be able to fool Bret, but from what he said, nobody fooled Isabelle for long. And though Emily was very curious about her and anxious to meet her, she didn't know if she'd like living with her for four months out of the year.

And what about the other eight months? Even after Bret got rid of the rustlers and uncovered the traitor, she'd be alone on the ranch. If one of the men could betray her, there was no reason others wouldn't. She'd never felt alone or overwhelmed before, but right now everything seemed to be weighing down on her all at once. And it didn't help that her father had spent thirty minutes right after Bret left telling her how worried he was about her. By the time she'd followed Bret to where he was standing on the hillside, she'd felt desperate to have something, *someone*, to hold onto.

Now here she was wrapped around Bret like a vine, feeling better than she had all day, yet wondering how she was going to explain her behavior to him. He'd been sent to convince her to move to Boston. Nothing had been said about his taking responsibility for her life.

She felt his arms go around her, hold her close, and she felt a little less desperate, a little less fearful that he would back away. She couldn't explain why she'd trusted this man almost from the first, but there was something about him that was strong and unbending, something inside him that was evident in everything he did, said, was. He seemed to have a lot of questions about his life, maybe even about himself, but as time passed, she had fewer and fewer doubts. The message grew stronger every day, every hour. This was a man a woman could depend on.

"Are you feeling a little shaken?" Bret asked.

She nodded her head against his chest.

"You don't have to worry that you'll be left alone."

"You'll go back to Boston as soon as you find the

rustlers. There's no reason for you to come back until it's time for me to go to Galveston."

"We don't have to worry about that yet. We can take things one day at a time."

She'd been doing that for a long time now. That was how she'd found herself pushed into a corner. She hadn't worried about her future until her father got sick and she found out that someone on the ranch was helping the rustlers. Yet she held on to Bret, didn't want to let go.

"Are you scared?"

"A little."

She'd never admitted that before, maybe never felt it except when her mother died. Though she missed her mother terribly, her death had affected her father more profoundly than it had her. Bertie and Ida had tried to console him, but her father turned to her when he missed his wife the most.

He used to tell Emily all the time how strong she was, and she was proud of her strength. Later she'd had to be strong to take over the household, to train the horses, to help run the ranch. She'd never known what it was to depend on anyone. Now she was older, wiser, and more knowledgeable. Yet tonight she felt more lost than ever.

"You don't have to be frightened," Bret said. "There are a lot of people who love you, who'll be happy to help you whenever you need them."

She knew that. Bertie would defend her with her pots and pans if necessary, but Bertie thought Emily ought to marry some nice man and let him take care of everything for her. Lonnie would have been more than happy to do that, but she didn't love Lonnie. She couldn't imagine being married to him, having him touch her, make love to her. Besides, she suspected Lonnie loved the ranch more than he loved her.

She knew Ida and Charlie would do anything they could for her, but they had their own ranch, their own family. It wouldn't be fair to expect them to jeopardize their future to help her. So where did that leave her?

Standing with her arms around Bret, she held on to him as if he were her rock in the middle of a stormy sea. She laughed at the silly image. She'd never even seen the ocean. She didn't know if it had rocks or not.

"It can't be so terrible if you can laugh," Bret said.

"I'm laughing at a stupid thought."

"Want to tell me what it was?"

"It's too embarrassing. You'll laugh."

"Friends laugh *with* friends, not at them."

She lifted her head until she could look up at his face. "You have no reason to be my friend."

"I have no reason not to be."

"You have plenty of reason. I'm forcing you to spend four months a year in Texas. That will cause trouble with your uncle and problems with your work. Now you have to try to persuade Isabelle to spend her winters in Galveston while you help me find a suitable husband. What more reason do you need to wish you'd never heard my name?"

"Things haven't turned out the way I'd hoped, but it's not a bad compromise."

Emily wondered if he included her clinging to him as part of what he hadn't planned . . . or wanted. "You don't want to be in Texas."

"I used to."

"Then why don't you stay here? You don't like Boston or your uncle. You were happier when you lived with Jake and Isabelle."

She could feel him tense up, his arms go slack

around her. She'd angered him, and he wanted to back off. But he didn't. A moment later his arms gradually tightened around her again. "Are you upset about something?"

He didn't answer right away. She wondered if she should pull away. Bertie would say it was stupid to stand around hugging a man for no reason at all. But she wasn't hugging as much as holding on, and she had more than enough reason. She wondered what he felt about it. He wouldn't say unless she asked. She wasn't sure she should. She'd already upset him.

"Lots of things haven't worked out like I expected," Bret said. "I'm having to rethink some of my goals, and I don't like some of the things I've learned."

"Now you know how I feel with Dad dying, somebody I trusted helping the rustlers, and being forced to go to Galveston to pick out a husband."

Bret pulled back until he could look into her eyes. "Getting married and settling down will be the best thing for you."

"Staying in Texas would have been the best thing for *you*, but you didn't do it. Why should you expect me to be any different?"

His arms fell away, and a moment later he stepped back and turned to stare out over the prairie.

"I shouldn't have said anything," she said. "What you do with your life is none of my business."

Bret spoke without turning to face her. "I still have the letter my uncle wrote saying he didn't want the Texas authorities to send me to Boston, that there must be a family here who'd like a kid."

Emily knew that not being wanted by his family had to hurt, but seeing the written words must have been like a knife in his heart. She couldn't imagine what it must be like to want desperately to be accepted and respected by people who, by every law of man and precept of Christianity, ought to love you but didn't. He must have felt the whole world was against him. Yet here she was selfishly depending on him for support in her troubles which, by comparison, weren't very troubling at all.

"I had no right to judge you," Emily said. "I can't know what you—"

"I had to go to Boston."

He still didn't face her. She wondered if he wasn't talking to himself more than to her.

"I had to confront them. I had to know why they turned their backs on my mother." He turned. "Do you know what my uncle said?"

Emily shook her head.

"He said she married out of her class. That was it."

"My father's family wouldn't have anything to do with him because he didn't behave the way they thought he should," she said.

"I couldn't understand why they didn't want me." Bret spoke as though he hadn't heard her. "I was a child. I hadn't done anything. My uncle hoped I was so far away I'd never find my way back."

"Then why did you stay?"

"Because I have to prove to him he was wrong." A wry smile briefly crossed his face. "They didn't know that Isabelle grew up rich. She made sure I knew how to behave in social occasions, how to handle myself at the table, and how to dress, but I was determined to be even better than the Abbotts. Within two years, I could dance better than Joseph, carry on a more interesting conversation, and flatter the ladies without being obvious. I couldn't afford to dress as well, but I compensated by staying in better shape physically."

Emily had wondered about that. No city man she'd ever met was strong enough to lift her into a saddle.

His broad shoulders, flat stomach, narrow hips, and muscular buttocks looked good no matter what he was wearing.

"At the office I worked harder and longer than anyone else. I made it my business to learn everything I could about the company so I could make a bigger contribution than the others. I didn't ask for more money or my own office. I just wanted to feel I was a part of the company, that I was contributing to the success of the family as much as anyone."

She found it hard to understand why he'd put himself through so much misery.

"I was a fool," Bret said, the words sharp and bitter. "I thought I was finally close to achieving my goal when Uncle Silas said he would talk to me and Rupert as soon as he'd had a chance to study my recommendations. It was only when he told me not to come back without you that I realized I was no closer to being accepted than the day I arrived at Abbott and Abercrombie and saw Uncle Silas's horrified expression when he realized who I was."

Emily reached out, took Bret's hand. "He was the fool."

Bret gave her hand a gentle squeeze. "You have no reason to like me any better than he does. I'm making you do things you hate."

"My father is doing that. You're just the man who's stuck making sure I live up to my promises."

She was glad Bret didn't release her hand. She liked being connected with him. It made her feel he was standing with her, that she didn't have to face her future alone. It was odd, when she thought about it. She was surrounded by people, but Bret was the only one who gave her that feeling of support she needed.

"I don't mind," Bret said. "It's a relief to know I'm

not the only one caught between a rock and a hard place."

"But men have more freedom to do something about it. All they ever say to a woman is 'Get married and let your husband worry about it.' "

"It's not bad advice."

"The only reason you say that is because no one ever told you to get married to solve all your problems."

"Actually, someone did. My uncle said there were plenty of wealthy women in Boston who'd be happy to have a husband like me."

Emily didn't try to hide her amazement. "I think you ought to forget about your uncle and never go back to Boston."

"What am I supposed to do?"

"You could stay here and work for my father." That was a stupid thing to say. Bret would never take a job as a common cowhand.

"I'm already working for your father, but I don't recall anyone offering to pay me."

His remark surprised her, but she realized immediately it was only fair that they pay him for stopping the rustling. It was embarrassing that neither she nor her father had thought of it.

"I'm sure my father has already considered that," she said, hoping it was true.

Bret pulled her back toward him and turned her around so she had to face him. "I was only joking. My uncle is paying me to be here."

"Still, we ought to—"

"If you're going to take a joke that seriously, I'll have to be careful what I say in the future."

"I've never known you to make a joke."

He frowned. "Not many people have."

"I thought you said you have learned to make interesting conversation."

"That's an act I put on when I go to parties. I'm a lot less fun when I'm around people I care about."

It took Emily a moment to digest that. She hoped she knew what he meant, but she was afraid to take too much for granted. "You care about me?"

"Does that surprise you?"

"A little," she admitted, but it thrilled her, too. "I haven't always been very nice to you."

"You've been nice enough."

She'd started by thinking he was a hopeless greenhorn. Then Joseph's letter had made her think he might be after her money for his own reasons. Then she had practically called him a liar when he said he believed someone on the ranch was helping the rustlers.

"*Nice enough* won't do," she said.

"You underestimate the power of a beautiful woman to cause a man to overlook all kinds of obstacles."

Bret's smile was wonderful, but there was something about it that wasn't quite right. It was like his words. They might be true, but they weren't the ones he wanted to say.

"I wouldn't have expected you to feel that way."

"Why not? I'm a man like every other man."

"You're not like every other man," she said. "I knew that almost from the beginning." That was what drew her to him. She didn't know exactly how he was different. Even though he'd told her a lot about his life, he hadn't told her a lot about himself. "I don't quite know who you are."

Bret's expression froze. His whole body was motionless. Only the breeze ruffled his hair.

"How am I different?" he asked.

"You're full of contradictions. As soon as I think I've learned one thing about you, something happens that makes me think the opposite."

"Experience has taught me many different lessons."

"Like what?"

"That it's necessary to be flexible."

If he didn't want to talk about himself, that was all right with her, but she wasn't going to let him think she didn't know he was dodging her question. "I wasn't asking you to tell me about yourself. I was just trying to explain why I feel I don't know who you are. I *do* know you're very inflexible in some ways."

"No fair knowing my secrets."

Bret was pretending to be amused, but she could feel him retreat from her. "I don't want to know your secrets. I just want to know that you like me and wouldn't betray me."

Despite the shadowy moonlight, she could feel his eyes bore into her. Even if she hadn't been holding his hand, she couldn't have been unaware of the heat traversing the space between them. Some place deep inside him had been exposed and an incredible energy had poured out and encompassed her. She felt both scorched and comforted.

"You can."

Emily started to speak, then motioned Bret to look in the direction of her pointing finger. About thirty yards ahead, in a place where the ground was almost bare of grass, a family of raccoons was crossing the trail. The mother and father came first, followed by three babies. The biggest raccoon—she assumed it was the father—stopped in the middle of the trail and looked at them, the mask around his eyes making him look like a fugitive fleeing in the middle of the night. The mother and babies hurried on across the road, their odd, bouncing stride making them look a little uncoordinated. After his family crossed, the father disappeared into the tall grass on the other side of the trail.

"They're going from one watering hole to another," Emily said. "The men see them all the time."

"I used to like to watch the white-tailed deer come out of the trees in the early morning," Bret said. "Even when they were frightened, they seemed to skim over the grass or melt soundlessly into the trees. I never could figure out how they did that. When cows or horses run, the ground seems to shake."

"I can't imagine you paying that much attention to deer."

"Have you ever watched a fawn?" Bret asked. "They look all around them, wide-eyed and nervous. The slightest threatening sound or movement and they're off like a shot. I know how they feel because that's how I used to feel."

Emily couldn't imagine the Bret she knew being afraid of anything, any more than she could imagine him being a ten-year-old boy living on the streets. "It must have been awful."

"It taught me how to survive."

Odd how she could go from feeling that she had to hold on to Bret in order to be safe, to wanting to protect *him*. She could sense that behind the strength, behind the knowledge, behind the confidence, was a vast emptiness Bret kept hidden from the world, a place where some part of him wandered ceaselessly, looking for something he couldn't name. She moved closer and slipped her arm around his waist. "You make me feel guilty for having had such an easy life."

"No life is easy. They're just hard in different ways."

She looked up at him. "You ought to know I admire you very much." He would have pulled away, but she didn't release him.

"I don't want to be admired. It makes me feel I have to live up to something. I just want you to like me."

"I do. I like you very much."

He slipped one arm around her. "Maybe you shouldn't. You don't know that I'm not trying to cheat you or find a way to use you to my advantage."

"You'd never do that to someone you liked."

"You take a lot for granted."

"That's because I can—with you."

Emily wasn't experienced with men, but Bret's look was odd by any standard. She couldn't decide whether he was surprised or upset. She seemed to be saying all the wrong things tonight. Maybe she should go inside and leave him to—

The feel of Bret's lips on hers snapped her thoughts like dry grass in a high wind. It was unexpected and unexplained, but that didn't keep her arms from tightening around him or her from returning his kiss. She was swept away by the unexpectedness of Bret's kiss as well as the wonder of it. It was hard to believe that anything as simple as a kiss could make her feel as if all her troubles had vanished . . . or make her unconcerned that they hadn't.

As abruptly as he'd begun, Bret broke the kiss and backed away. "I shouldn't have done that."

"Why did you?" She was so breathless she could hardly speak.

"I don't know. One minute I was standing here acting like a sane man, and the next I was kissing you like I never wanted to stop. I'm supposed to be protecting you, not trying to make you fall in love with me."

Bret looked like he was wound so tight he was about to explode, like he was on the verge of losing control. He stared at her with wild eyes, but she had the feeling that only part of him was seeing her, that something else was even more firmly implanted on his vision.

"You've only kissed me twice," she reminded him.

"That was two times too many."

"You said you liked me."

"I do, but that doesn't mean I can go around kissing you whenever I like. Or that you should let me." The implication that he had wanted to kiss her more often made her feel warm all over. "You said friends could kiss."

"I said *some* men could. I can't." He paced three or four steps before turning around and retracing his steps. "What would your father think? Or Bertie? Lonnie would probably want to shoot me." He stopped and faced her. "Hell, I *know* he would."

"I wouldn't mind."

He'd started to pace again, but spun around at her words. "You *should* mind," he nearly shouted. "You're not the kind of woman a man goes around kissing unless he's got marriage in mind."

"Have you ever had marriage in mind?"

"No, and it's a good thing I haven't. I can barely support myself. If I had a wife and children, we'd all starve."

"If a woman really loved you, maybe she wouldn't mind being poor."

"I'd mind." He was pacing again. "What kind of man would I be to do that to a woman I loved?" He came to a halt in front of her. "You've been so rich all your life you can't have any idea what it's like to be poor, to work as hard as you possibly can day after day and wake up each morning a little further behind. It changes people."

"But you're not that poor."

"Not yet." He went stiff, as if something had occurred to him all of a sudden. "I don't know what I'm doing talking to you like this. You must think I'm crazy. We'd better go in. It's time for both of us to be in bed."

She didn't want to go in. She had dozens of questions she wanted to ask, but she could tell it would be useless to try to learn anything further tonight. Still, she'd learned two important things.

First, he liked her so much he wanted to kiss her . . . often. He was fighting that urge so hard, she knew it had to be more than just a friendly kiss. A man would give a friendly kiss with a teasing smile and maybe a joke. Bret was so serious, he was upset.

She'd also learned he was very unsatisfied with his life in Boston. The question was would he become so dissatisfied he would make a change? And if so, would he consider returning to Texas?

Chapter Fourteen

Bret forced himself to go to his bedroom. Though he undressed, he didn't get into bed after he blew out the lamp. He stood at the window, staring out into the night, trying to figure out what had caused him to lose control so badly with Emily. It wasn't just the kiss, though that was serious enough. It was everything else—what he'd said, what he'd done, and what both implied.

Having failed to control himself tonight, it would be harder to do so in the future. Standing with Emily on the side of the hill, letting down the barriers enough to talk about things important to him, had been a heady experience, such as he hadn't had since leaving Jake's ranch. He felt that Emily understood him in a way the Abercrombies never could, even his grandmother and aunt. But her empathy just caused him to think of a future that could never be. Emily would never agree to go to Boston. It was best to put that dream out of his mind while he still could.

The worst part was, he might have set up expectations in Emily's mind he couldn't fulfill. He didn't know if she liked him enough to consider marrying him, but he wasn't the kind of husband she needed. She needed a Texan who was proud to be a Texan and didn't want to live anywhere else. She needed a man who loved ranching and would be happy to spend half his life on horseback. She needed a man who enjoyed exercising his body as much as his brain. And she needed a man who didn't come with a past he couldn't forget.

He sighed deeply, turned, and got into bed. He had a hard day ahead of him and needed his rest. He also had a lot of questions he needed to answer. The difficult part was that each question seemed to hinge on his response to a question for which he had no answer. His brain felt like a logjam. Until one important log broke free, all of them would stay locked together.

"He insisted on coming with me," Tom told Emily. "He said Mr. Nolan was expecting him."

Emily didn't know who surprised her more, the orphan she'd seen Bret talking to in Fort Worth or the Indian and the black man who were with him now on horseback.

Jinx had slipped off his horse and walked up to Emily, his hat in his hands, his threadbare clothes barely covering his body. He had some bruises she didn't remember seeing before.

"What I told your man wasn't exactly the truth," Jinx said, "but Mr. Nolan said he'd take care of me."

"He promised to do that when he got back to Fort Worth," Emily said.

"I couldn't wait. Mr. Nolan left some money for me with Frank at the hotel, and Lugo was hopping mad about it. He said a worthless scamp like me didn't deserve that much money, that *he* ought to have it for putting up with me."

From what Bret had told her about Jinx's boss, Emily didn't find that hard to believe. The man was a thief. From the looks of Jinx, Lugo was a bully as well.

"Lugo tried to get Frank to give him the money, but Frank said he couldn't do that, that Mr. Nolan had said he wasn't to give it to anybody but me. When I wouldn't give it to him, Lugo beat me. I tried to run away, but he chased me and beat me again. If these fellas hadn't found me, I'd probably be dead."

These fellas were the black man and the Indian.

"I appreciate your watching after Jinx," Emily said to the men, "but you didn't need to come with him. Tom would have made sure he got here safely."

"We weren't babysitting the kid," the Indian said. "We came because your man said you had rustlers and needed some extra hands."

"We've had a bit of experience with rustlers," the black man said. "Haven't come up against any we couldn't handle."

Emily had no doubt of that. She'd never seen two men who looked more capable of handling any kind of trouble that might come their way. The Indian wore a dull yellow shirt with a brown vest and jeans, a typical cowhand outfit. It was the feather hanging down the back of his neck that was the jarring note. The black man wore only a vest and jeans. His skin gleamed with sweat over his heavily muscled body.

"I'm not the one who decides if you get the job," she said. "My foreman—"

"We don't mind waiting," the black man said.

Emily turned to Tom, who looked rather anxious.

"I know I was to bring four cowhands," he said,

"but there weren't nobody else around these two trusted."

"We're careful who we work with," the black man said.

"Especially when we're chasing rustlers," the Indian added.

"I'm sure . . . You see . . . What are your names?" she asked in frustration.

"I'm Zeke Maxwell," the black man said.

"Hawk Maxwell," the Indian said. Emily was sure it was her confused look that caused him to add, "We were adopted."

Emily didn't know exactly what to do. She couldn't invite them into the house, because her father wasn't well enough for visitors. She didn't want to send them off to the bunkhouse before Lonnie had had a chance to decide if he wanted to hire them. Then there was the problem of what to do with Jinx. She had just about decided to turn him over to Bertie when he yelled, *"Mr. Nolan!"* and took off running. She turned to see Bret coming around the side of the house from the direction of the corrals.

Jinx practically threw himself at Bret, talking a mile a minute. Bret made him stand back so he could look at the bruises. Even at a distance, Emily could tell he was angry. When Jinx pointed back at the two strangers, Emily was surprised at the look that came over Bret's face. He looked shocked. Then a smile slowly spread over his face. Jinx was still talking a mile a minute, but Bret was walking toward the men, his gaze fixed so firmly on them, Emily doubted he knew she was present.

"Zeke beat the stuffing out of Lugo," Jinx was saying. "If Hawk hadn't stopped him, he might have killed him. I wish he had."

"Never wish anybody dead," Bret said to Jinx without taking his eyes off the men.

"You didn't think we'd come, did you?" Zeke asked Bret.

"I knew you'd come if you could."

"We had to see what you're like now you're a rich man," Hawk said.

"You know these men?" Emily asked Bret.

"Yeah. Jake and Isabelle adopted all three of us."

"You mean they're your brothers?" Jinx asked.

"Yes. That's what I mean."

"Jumping Jehoshaphat!" Jinx exclaimed. "I never heard of anything like that."

Neither had Emily. She was only just beginning to realize she didn't know much about the years Bret had spent in what must have been an extraordinary family.

"Is your mother the lady you said might take me in?" Jinx asked.

"That's the one," Bret said, "but what am I going to do with you until then?"

"Hawk and Zeke said they're going to catch rustlers. Can I help?"

"What do you boys say?" Bret asked his brothers.

"I say he'd make a damned fine scarecrow," Hawk said.

"If we stuck some straw out of his ears, the crows would never know he wasn't real," Zeke said.

"You wouldn't let them do that, would you?" Jinx asked Bret anxiously.

"Not if you behave yourself. I think you ought to introduce yourself to Miss Abercrombie and ask very nicely if she'll let you stay."

Jinx didn't look at all happy about it, but he mustered his courage and walked over to Emily.

"I'm Jinx, ma'am," he said. "I don't have no last name. Nobody knows where I come from. Jinx is not even a real name. One of the ladies who took care of me when I was a baby used to say I was a jinx, that after she took me in she had nothing but trouble. I guess everybody agreed, because the name stuck."

Emily had been trying to make up her mind what to do with Jinx, but hearing how he got his name— knowing how it must hurt every time he heard it— convinced her to let him stay. She didn't know what to do with an eight-year-old boy, but Bertie would.

"I know you don't want nobody like me hanging around," Jinx said, "but I can slop hogs, feed chickens, fetch water and wood, just about anything you want."

"I'll be glad to have you," Emily said.

"Get down," Bret said to Zeke and Hawk. They'd remained in the saddle during the conversation.

"The lady hasn't asked us yet," Hawk said.

"I'm sorry," Emily said, mortified she'd been so nonplused she'd completely forgotten her manners. "Please, get down and come in."

"Let me take them to the bunkhouse first," Bret said. "They need to meet Lonnie." He looked at Jinx and grinned. "You'll have your hands full with him."

"I ain't no trouble," Jinx insisted.

"You wouldn't have been if you'd stayed in Fort Worth until I got back," Bret said.

"I was telling the lady here—"

"Save it," Bret said. "You can tell me later."

"You're not going to forget about me, are you?" Jinx asked, glancing nervously in Emily's direction.

"I couldn't if I wanted to," Bret said. "Now behave yourself and do exactly what Miss Abercrombie tells you."

Emily watched Bret and his brothers lead their

horses toward the corrals and the bunkhouse. It was hard to imagine three such different people growing up in the same family, but it was obvious that a strong bond connected them even if they did seem a little stiff with each other. She had a feeling Zeke and Hawk hadn't shown up by accident; Bret must have written to them. But Lonnie disliked Bret so much, he wasn't likely to want two of his brothers working for him. She also had the feeling Zeke and Hawk wouldn't work for anybody but Bret. If Lonnie figured that out, things could get difficult.

But right now she had to decide what to do with Jinx. "Come on in the house," she said. "I want you to meet Bertie."

"Who's he?" Jinx asked.

"*She* is the cook. And you have to be good to her or your life won't be worth a sack of oats."

"She's going to hate me," Jinx mumbled. "All women hate me."

"I don't."

"You're a girl," Jinx said.

That made her smile. "I'd forgotten that."

"How can you forget you're a girl?"

"Someday I'll tell you. For now, wipe your feet, push your hair out of your eyes, and be on your best behavior. Don't think you can impress Bertie with your poor-little-orphan-boy act. The only person I've ever seen get around her is Bret, and I still haven't figured out how he did it."

"That guy would have run us off if he could have figured how to do it," Zeke said to Bret. "Why does he dislike you so much?"

"Lonnie wants to marry Emily and run the ranch. That makes me a threat."

"How about the rest of the cowhands?" Hawk asked.

"They know one of them is helping the rustlers, and that hasn't gone down well. The crew is loyal to the brand. I think Lonnie is the culprit, but Emily and her father insist they won't believe me until I produce proof. The evidence points to him, but he's so crazy about Emily, I can't see why he would do something like that."

"I don't understand why the rustlers are branding calves rather than running them off," Zeke said.

"Neither do I," Bret said, "but I think that's the clue to the whole thing."

"Any theories?"

"Maybe."

They were leaning on the fence of the big corral. Each man had a booted foot resting on the bottom rail as they watched Hawk and Zeke's horses roll in the dust. Rather than trust their lives to unknown ranch ponies, they had brought their own mounts, a big Appaloosa and a heavily muscled steeldust gelding.

"I think Lonnie is doing it because he wants to make Emily believe she's in danger of losing the ranch," Bret explained. "If she's scared enough and believes he can save it for her, he thinks she'll marry him. That's why I think the calves are being branded rather than rustled."

"That sounds crazy," Zeke said, "but it covers all the points except one. What will happen when it comes time to sell the cows and they're wearing the wrong brand?"

"By then he may have thought of a way to sell them without her knowing. If he has to confess, maybe he hopes she'll love him enough to stick with him."

"I can just hear what Isabelle or Drew would say if somebody tried to pull a trick like that on them," Hawk said.

All three men laughed.

Bret had forgotten how good it felt to laugh. He'd also forgotten how good it made him feel to have two of his brothers at his side. He'd had a difficult time adjusting to being part of the Maxwell clan, and even longer to get over his prejudices against Hawk and Zeke. At first he didn't like Hawk because he was a "savage." He didn't like Zeke because Bret's father had been hanged for attempting to free slaves. But years of working together—and occasionally fighting—had taught him that Hawk and Zeke had far more to forgive and forget than he did. When they managed to do it, it became a point of pride for Bret to do the same.

"How is Isabelle?" Bret asked.

"The same as ever," Zeke said. "She'd like to see you."

Bret knew she would, and that made him feel guilty. He knew she felt all of the orphans were as much her children as her daughter, Eden.

"I'd like to see her, too, but there are some things I have to do first."

All three were silent for a few minutes.

"How do you want us to set about finding these rustlers?" Zeke asked. "If it's one of the cowhands, he's not going to do anything while we're here."

"I've been thinking about having Sam say he doesn't want you to work for him," Bret said. "That way you could disappear, I could make myself scarce for a few days, and the informer would think the coast was clear to start again."

"Do you think Sam would agree to that?"

"He'll agree to anything he thinks will make things safe for his daughter."

"And how do we find out if Sam has confidence in us?" Zeke asked.

"We'll talk to him tonight. Maybe you should hang

out with the rest of the crew. Make yourselves unpopular without going too far. That will give Lonnie a reason to tell Sam not to hire you."

"We can do that easy enough," Zeke said, looking at Hawk. "Just get him started acting like an Indian."

"You mean you expect me to put up with something like that in my kitchen?" Bertie said to Emily as she looked at Jinx as if he were some kind of rodent that had invaded her domain. "He's not even clean."

"I can wash up," Jinx said.

"He won't be here for long," Emily said. "Bret plans to take him to his parents' ranch when he goes back to Fort Worth."

"What would a respectable woman want with a creature like that?" Bertie demanded.

Emily had been afraid Bertie wouldn't be happy. She stood over her stove like she was protecting it from attack and glared at Jinx. "If you want him so much, you take him," Bertie said. "He ought to fit right into the stables."

"He's too young to work with the men." Emily was so stunned by Bertie's reaction, she was tempted to say something very sharp until she noticed that neither Bertie nor Jinx was looking at her. They were glaring at each other.

"You're a mean old woman," Jinx said.

"You're a dirty varmint," Bertie replied.

"I wouldn't tote your wood if you was to beg me."

"You'd keep the wood box filled or I'd take the skin off your backside."

"You'd never catch me."

Emily watched in amazement as they traded insults. It took a few minutes before she realized they weren't getting ready to kill each other. Instead, in a manner that was totally foreign to her, they were setting up the parameters of their relationship.

"You're too skinny to be worth anything," Bertie said.

"I don't have to be bigger than a market steer to tote wood."

Bertie wasn't fat, but she was big-boned and taller than every man on the ranch except Bret. Apparently, size didn't impress Jinx.

"It'd be a waste of food to feed a scoundrel like you," Bertie said.

"How do I know anything you cook is decent enough to eat?"

"You won't see nobody pushing away anything I cook."

"I'll leave you two to settle things between you," Emily said.

She had no idea how such an exchange could be the start of a working relationship, but it was obvious Bertie was beginning to unbend toward Jinx. She had stopped waving her big knife, and Jinx no longer stood with the table between them. The volume of their shouting had diminished to a growl; their gazes were no longer locked in mortal combat. Emily figured if she left them to it, they would manage to work something out. She was still shaking her head when Bret entered the house.

"Are your brothers settled in the bunkhouse?" she asked.

"Not yet. I've been thinking about the best way to find the rustlers, and I think I need to change my plans."

"How?"

He explained his reason for her father saying he didn't want Zeke and Hawk to work for him.

"Do you think the rustlers will believe it?"

"I don't know, but we have to catch them in the act."

When they went to his office to speak to him about it, Sam understood almost immediately. "All you want out of me is an acting job?"

"You can act as querulous and ill-tempered as you want," Bret said.

"Do I get to meet your brothers?"

"Have Lonnie bring them. It'll be better if I'm not in the room. That way I won't have to pretend to defend them."

Later that evening, an angry Zeke and Hawk stormed out of Sam's office, followed by a confused Lonnie.

"Sam doesn't want them to work for him," Lonnie said to Bret. "He's not having a black man or an Indian on his crew."

"They're my brothers," Bret said. "I can vouch for them."

"Sam said they were to leave first thing in the morning. He said if any cows were missing after they left, he'd hunt them down."

Bret wished he could have been in the room. Apparently, Sam had put on quite an act.

"I've got to go," Lonnie said. "Sam said I wasn't to let them out of my sight."

Bret waited until Lonnie had left the house before going into Sam's office. "It looks like you should have been an actor." Bret's feeling of satisfaction at the way his plan was going turned to concern when he saw Sam. The old man looked faded and lethargic.

"I guess all that blustering was too much for him," Emily said, looking worried. "As soon as Lonnie left, he seemed to collapse."

"I'm just tired," Sam said.

He was leaning against a bank of pillows, his full head of dark brown hair in stark contrast to the white pillowcases. The lack of gray in his hair accentuated his pallor. Even his lips had lost their color.

"Let me help you lie down," Bret said.

It took only a few minutes for Bret and Emily to make him comfortable, but Bret could tell that Sam's condition was getting worse each day. He wouldn't last much longer. Even after he relaxed, he still struggled to get his breath.

"They look like good men, those brothers of yours," Sam said.

"They are. I was lucky they were free to come."

"I can't imagine the three of you growing up together. Must have had some interesting times."

"A few," Bret said. "But our parents taught us to believe our differences were less important than the things we had in common."

"You make sure those boys have everything they need before they leave tomorrow. I told Lonnie to give them enough supplies to get off my land without having to stop, so you won't have any trouble with him."

Sam's eyes had closed before he finished his last sentence. Bret waited while Emily adjusted the bedspread, and then they left the room together. "I wouldn't have asked him to do this if I'd known it would take so much out of him."

"I tried to get him to let me do it, but he said as long as he owned the ranch, he'd be the one to make the decisions." Emily looked so worried, Bret put his arm around her shoulder to comfort her. She leaned against him. "It makes him feel better to have some part in running the ranch. Being confined to bed is hard on him."

"It's hard on you, too."

A wan smile was all Emily could muster. "Having you here has made it easier."

"How?" He would have expected her to feel he was in the way.

"I wouldn't have known what to do about the rustlers. And you worked out a compromise about Galveston I think both of us can live with."

Bret dropped a kiss on her forehead, wished he'd kissed her lips instead.

"Of course, I may not forgive you for setting Jinx on me." She told him about the unaccountable exchange between Bertie and Jinx. "When she let Jinx help her bring the food to the table, I knew she'd taken a liking to him. It's your doing, of course."

"How do you figure that?"

"She adores you. You could have brought a monster in here, and she'd have taken him in."

"I never figured Jinx would follow me across half of Texas," Bret said, laughing.

"He believes in you. It seems a lot of people do."

That stopped him in his tracks. Nobody had ever said that to him.

She pulled him down so she could give him a light kiss on his mouth. "I really don't know what I'd have done without you."

Bret would have liked nothing better than to continue doing what Emily had started. Her kiss was stretching the limits of his control to the danger point. He really wanted to make love to her. It had taken him a while to admit it, but he knew that was exactly what he wanted to do. And he knew it was the one thing he absolutely could not do.

"I'd love to stay here and listen to how wonderful I am," he said, trying to achieve a lightness he didn't feel, "but I have to confer with my brothers."

"I'm sorry I won't get a chance to get to know them."

Bret wasn't. He'd already seen the question in their eyes about his relationship with Emily. He didn't have an answer for himself. What could he possibly say to them?

Chapter Fifteen

"Once you've found a place to camp, let me know," Bret told his brothers in an undertone. "We need to keep in touch with each other."

They were standing by the corral again, a safe distance from the bunkhouse and anyone who might be listening. The way Sam had acted, the things he'd said, had caused the cowhands to feel a little sorry for Zeke and Hawk. Lonnie had been so sympathetic, he made no objection when Bret offered to see to their supplies.

"What do we do when we catch them?" Hawk asked.

"Bring them here. I'll let Sam decide what he wants to do."

"Surely he wants them to hang," Zeke said.

"If it's Lonnie, he's not really planning to steal any cows. You boys take care of yourselves. Isabelle would never forgive me if I got you hurt."

Zeke looked at him like he'd lost his mind. "You're

the one who's been sitting behind a desk for six years. We ought to be making sure *you* don't get hurt."

"I'm not sure anybody cares too much what happens to me."

"Either those people in Boston taught you to lie or you've gone stupid," Hawk growled. "I might not worry about your snotty ass, but you know Isabelle does."

Bret had been sorry the moment the words left his mouth. He knew the feelings of his adopted family for each other hadn't changed. Otherwise he wouldn't have felt he could call on Zeke and Hawk to help him. And they wouldn't have come.

"I didn't mean that," Bret said. "I've got some big decisions to make. I think I know what I *want* to do. The only problem is, I can't."

"It's not like you to give up," Zeke said.

Hawk nodded toward the ranch house. "Has it got anything to do with a certain young woman?"

"Yes," Bret admitted with an embarrassed grin, "but she's off limits."

"Who says?" Hawk asked.

"I do."

"Good," Hawk said, his intent expression relaxing. "Then you won't have any trouble changing your mind when you get the rest figured out."

"It's like a half dozen dominoes all set to fall," Bret explained. "Everything depends on which domino falls first and how it affects the rest of them. The number of possible outcomes are astronomical."

"Leave it to a businessman to turn everything into a bunch of numbers," Zeke said shaking his head. "It isn't that complicated. Decide what you want to do, then everything will fall into place."

"Has it for you?"

"We haven't decided what we want to do," Hawk said.

"So you're running around catching crooks and putting off the decision."

"Something like that," Zeke admitted.

"You're as bad as I am."

"Not yet," Hawk said. "We haven't fallen in love and are afraid to take the plunge and see if we pass."

"You don't understand," Bret said. "The problem is, I'm afraid I *do* pass."

Hawk and Zeke looked at each other. "It's time for us to go to bed," Zeke said. "This conversation is making no sense."

"Now you know how I feel," Bret said.

"Thank goodness I don't," Hawk said. "Being half Comanche and half white is problem enough."

Bret watched the two men head over to the bunkhouse. He envied the close friendship that had developed between Hawk and Zeke over the years. He was sure that when they married—if they ever did—their relationship would remain just as strong as ever.

He wondered why he'd never been able to form such a friendship. Was he too unlikable, or had he been too focused on his goal to take the time to get to know the people around him and let them know him? He supposed it didn't matter right now. He had a lot to do before he had to be back in Galveston for the winter. He hated to think of leaving Boston before the changes to the company were firmly in place, but at least staying there until December ought to give him time to get over Emily.

He hadn't meant to fall in love with her.

He didn't know when it had happened, but he knew when he'd first realized it: when she practically forced him to kiss her. He knew he was making a mistake, but not until it was too late did he realize just how monumental his mistake was. He had another chance to pull back the night she joined him on the hillside, but he'd only gotten in deeper by kissing her again. Now every time he saw her, he wanted to touch her hand, put his arms around her, kiss her.

He'd spent his whole life on the outside trying to get in. Why hadn't the acceptance of the family Jake and Isabelle had cobbled together made him feel like he belonged? Why had he thought the acceptance of his Boston family would be any different? Jake had told him a real family wasn't defined by blood, but he hadn't believed it. He was so obsessed with going back to Boston and *forcing* his family to accept him, *forcing* them to admit they'd made a mistake by disowning his mother and abandoning him, that he couldn't see anything else. He couldn't value what he had because it wasn't what he thought he wanted, what was *owed* him.

Now he could finally admit he'd been wrong. You may be able to force a person to *do* a particular thing, but you can't force him to *feel* a particular emotion. And whether he liked it or not, most of his blood family wanted nothing to do with him. Why couldn't he see what was real and what was just a fantasy? Without even thinking, he'd promised Jinx that Jake and Isabelle would give him a home. Without hesitation, he'd turned to Hawk and Zeke when he needed someone he could trust. His first thought when he realized Emily would need a chaperon in Galveston had been to ask Isabelle. His *real* family was right here in Texas, and he'd been too stupid to see it. He'd written several letters to Isabelle over the years, but letters were a poor exchange for what he'd been given by her and Jake. He didn't like his Abbott relatives, yet he'd spent six years trying to make them accept him. What a fool he'd been!

He would have to visit the Broken Circle. It would be difficult to swallow his pride and admit he'd been blind and ungrateful, but it was the least he could do before he headed back to Boston. He'd lost his enthusiasm for the changes he wanted to make there, but he knew they were important to the future of the Abbotts.

Emily was another reason he had to return to Boston: It was the only way he could forget her. Or at least get his feelings under control. It was also the only way he could forget how much he'd enjoyed being back in Texas, on a ranch, on horseback, doing the things he'd said he never wanted to do again.

He looked at the horses in the corral. A couple were lying down, but the rest had bunched along the far side of the corral, looking over the fence like they expected something to come from that direction. He wondered what they heard or smelled. Coyotes, foxes, maybe even a wolf? The piebald broke away from the group and ambled over to him, shoved his head between the rails. Bret obliged by rubbing his forehead. He would miss the cantankerous beast. Unexpectedly, he'd developed a real affection for the horse, who was turning into a good cow pony. Bret thought the piebald's strength and size made him an even better choice for a general mount. More than once, Bret had found himself thinking he'd like to buy the piebald, but it would be cruel to take such a horse to Boston.

Giving the piebald one last affectionate pat on the neck, Bret straightened away from the fence. He was beginning to find answers to his questions, but he didn't like any of them.

Emily couldn't decide where to direct her attention— to Bret, who was deep in thought over something, or to the incomprehensible relationship that had sprung up between Jinx and Bertie. While clearing up in the kitchen after breakfast, Bertie and Jinx were arguing over where he should sleep. Bertie had made up a temporary bed for him last night on the couch in the great room, but Jinx wanted to sleep in the bunkhouse with the cowhands. Emily sat quietly at the table and watched. Bret sat across from her, drinking coffee, a hint of amusement in his eyes.

"You're not sleeping in that dirty bunkhouse and then helping me in my kitchen," Bertie told Jinx.

"I can wash," Jinx protested.

"You could, but boys like you are allergic to soap and water."

"I'm not," Jinx announced with a show of outrage. "I worked in a bathhouse."

"Did *you* ever use your own soap and water?" Bertie asked.

"Lugo wouldn't let me," Jinx replied. "He said if I wanted to take a bath, I could use the horse trough."

Bertie harrumphed. "That's what the men in the bunkhouse use. Now you know why I don't let none of them set foot in my kitchen."

"But I can't sleep in the big house *and* work in the kitchen," Jinx wailed. "They'll think I'm a sissy."

"They'll think what I tell 'em to think," Bertie announced.

"He's right," Bret said. "You let a boy stay around a woman too much, and the hands will think he's gone soft."

"Yeah," Jinx said, beaming at Bret. "Mr. Nolan knows."

"That's men all over," Bertie complained. "They chase wild cows and hang around smelly horses and think that makes them a man. Not a one of them is smart enough to know that being a *real man* is something that doesn't come off with soap and water. Look at Mr. Nolan," Bertie said, pointing a finger that looked more like it was accusing Bret than complimenting him. "He takes a bath and sleeps in the big house. You don't see nobody saying he's not a real man."

"He's a gentleman," Jinx insisted. "Nobody would expect him to sleep in the bunkhouse."

"Do you want to be a gentleman like Mr. Nolan?" Bertie asked.

Jinx looked flabbergasted. He idolized Bret, but it was clear he didn't think the rules that applied to Bret could also apply to him.

"Isabelle made me sleep in the house, eat at a table with napkins, and wash and change my shirt before I came inside," Bret said. "But Jake taught me how to ride a horse, wrangle a fifteen-hundred-pound steer, and make my own camp and cook my own supper. As long as you *act* like a man, it won't matter where you sleep."

It took Jinx a few minutes to digest that. He looked from Bret to Bertie and back to Bret. "If you teach me how to do all those things and let me sleep in your room, nobody will think I'm a sissy for helping Bertie."

Emily had difficulty suppressing a smile. By giving a little, Jinx hoped to get what he really wanted—to be as close to Bret as possible.

"There's not but one bed in Mr. Nolan's room," Bertie pointed out.

"I could use your bedroll," Jinx said, giving Bret his most winning grin.

"If Bret will agree to let you share his room, I think we have a cot you can use," Emily said.

While Jinx asked Emily about the cot, the smile that had lightened Bret's expression vanished and he sank back into his earlier frowning silence. She wanted to know what was bothering him, but she was already asking more of him than he wanted to give. But not as much as she wanted from him.

She didn't know if it was love, infatuation, or just happiness at having the attention of a handsome, sophisticated man, but she couldn't get enough of his company. Now she found it hard to imagine how she could ever have thought he was a green tenderfoot. She should have sensed right away he was more than he let himself appear. There was an element of control, of competence, that rode easily on his shoulders.

"I wish Zeke and Hawk didn't have to leave," Jinx said. "They're a lot nicer than Lonnie," he said, turning to Emily.

"Lonnie doesn't know what to do with little boys," Emily said.

"I'm not a little boy!" Jinx exclaimed.

"How hard is it to know you treat a boy just like you would a man?" Bret asked Emily. "With respect."

She'd made that same mistake with Bret, but he hadn't held it against her.

"I'm going with you to see them off," Jinx said to Bret.

"You'll do your work for me before you go messing about with horses and cows," Bertie said, then turned to Bret. "And I'll not have you telling him otherwise."

She wagged her finger at him, but Emily could tell it didn't have the same emphasis she used when she talked to Lonnie or even her father. Bret had made a conquest of two female hearts without even trying.

"I wouldn't think of it," Bret said to Bertie, his smile reappearing. "Hurry up, scamp, or they'll leave without either one of us."

Emily was afraid Jinx would drop a bowl or break a plate in his haste, but he managed to clear the table without an accident. "I'll fill the woodbox and bring in fresh water as soon as they leave," he told Bertie. "Can I go now?"

"Don't mess about," Bertie said. "If Mr. Nolan is going to try to teach you to be a cowhand, he's going to need all the time he can come up with."

"I'll see he's back well before it's time to help with lunch," Bret said to Bertie.

"I don't know what that boy's going to do when Mr. Nolan goes back to Boston," Bertie said, sounding a little sad. She was looking out the window at Jinx as he practically danced alongside Bret. "It won't matter how wonderful those people are he's giving the boy to. They'll never take the place of Mr. Nolan in his eyes."

Emily wasn't sure what she was going to do, either. She'd promised to go to Galveston to look for a husband because it was the only way she could get out of having to go to Boston, but she knew she'd never find anyone she liked better than Bret. He insisted that people could kiss in friendship, but she was sure his kisses meant a lot more than that. Still, he was going back to Boston. He wanted his life there enough to face certain anger and increased antagonism.

She'd hoped to convince him to stay in Texas, but he hadn't done or said anything to lead her to believe he'd changed his mind.

She wasn't ready to give up. She wasn't sure she was in love with him yet—her feelings were new and confusing, but she wasn't going to let him get away until she decided exactly how she felt. And if she *was* in love—well, he didn't know the power of Texas loving if she thought he could just turn around and trot off to Boston.

Which presented still another problem. How could a woman keep a man where he didn't want to be?

And if she could, was it fair? That brought up still another question. If it was fair to her but unfair to him, which should she consider first? What if it was unfair to him now but good for him in the long run? She never would have guessed falling in love could be so complicated. Her parents always said they knew the moment they looked at each other. But Bret said Jake and Isabelle continued to argue even though they were crazy about each other. Ida and Charlie said they were in love, but she never saw them kiss or do any of the things she wanted to do with Bret.

As soon as she could be certain her father was comfortable, she'd ride over to see Ida. She didn't want to leave her father, but she needed to talk to somebody, and she needed to do it now. Bret was so busy looking for rustlers and taking care of Jinx, he wouldn't notice she was gone.

Bret grinned when Hawk materialized from the ground almost in front of his horse's hooves. "I'd forgotten how you could disappear before my eyes. If you hadn't stood up, I'd have ridden right over you. Where's Zeke?"

"At our camp in a mesquite-and-willow thicket by a trickle of water. He doesn't blend in as well as I do, but he's perfect for night work. Are you sure that foreman believes we're gone?"

"I heard him telling the hands that without you they would have to spend longer hours in the saddle, but I could tell he was relieved."

"He dislikes you that much?"

"Dislikes and distrusts me."

"She won't marry him."

Bret laughed. "When did you become an expert on women, especially one you only met for a few hours?"

"She's in love with you," Hawk said. "Why should she want to marry another man?"

Bret sobered, wished he could turn his horse and ride away. "I hope she's not in love with me," he said quietly. "That could only lead to unhappiness."

"Are you trying to tell me you aren't in love with her?" Hawk looked up at Bret with an expression he'd seen many times in the past, one that said white men were idiots who didn't deserve to rule such a beautiful country.

"It doesn't matter what either of us feels about the other," Bret said. "She can't live anywhere but Texas, and my life is in Boston."

Hawk broke off a long stem of grass and chewed on it. "Your life is where you decide to live it. And who you want to live it with. Texas and Boston are only excuses." Hawk spat out a piece of stem. "But I didn't come here to fix your love life," he said with a wicked grin, his black eyes shining cheerfully. "I'm much better with rustlers and bank robbers."

Bret was relieved to return the conversation to rustlers. "I've told Lonnie I'm spending the next few days riding over a part of the ranch about ten miles from here. Since this is where most of the branding has taken place, the rustlers ought to feel free to get back to work."

"Do we have to bring them in alive? They'll be a lot easier to handle if they're full of holes."

"Don't let yourself get hurt," Bret said. "They're not worth it."

Hawk tilted his head, looked up at Bret out of half-closed eyes. "I never expected moving to Boston would turn you sentimental."

Bret grinned in spite of himself. "I'm not sentimental, you cross-grained half-breed. We both know Isabelle will have my hide if either one of you gets hurt."

Hawk grinned back. "I wouldn't want Isabelle scaring our little Yankee boy, so I'll be sure to take good care of Zeke. Now you'd better go before the big bad rustlers run up behind you and yell *'Boo!'*"

With that, Hawk melted back into the grass. Bret turned his mount and rode away, thinking of the many times they'd traded insults. He hadn't always liked those exchanges with Hawk. Now they felt like warm memories to wrap around himself to keep off the chill when he returned to Boston.

"I wondered how soon we'd be having this conversation the minute I clapped eyes on your Mr. Nolan," Ida said with a smile that made Emily blush.

"Was I that obvious?"

"No, but Mr. Nolan was that impressive."

Emily had gotten up early and ridden hard all day. She'd helped Ida fix supper and clean up afterwards. Charlie was doing some work in the barn, and the children were in bed. The women had taken their coffee outside and were sitting on a bench under a post oak. The heat from the day still radiated up from the ground, keeping their feet warm despite the cooling night air.

"I know I like him a lot," Emily said, "but I'm not sure if my feelings are merely infatuation, excitement that a handsome man has shown an interest in me, or if it's more serious than that."

"What kind of *interest* has he shown?" Ida asked.

Emily shifted uneasily. "That's hard to say."

"Why? Either a man shows it or he doesn't. Men aren't subtle."

Emily looked down at her hands. She'd never expected to be embarrassed to tell her friend anything she'd done. "I made him kiss me," she said, looking up at Ida.

Ida sat forward, her body erect, her eyes searching Emily's face despite the lengthening shadows. "You need to explain that."

Emily had always admired Ida for her practical wisdom; she saw in her the kind of woman she wanted to become. Ida wasn't beautiful, but she had an attractiveness that was ageless. Her simple, practical clothes never detracted from her femininity. Though she had been married for more than a dozen years, her husband's eyes always warmed when he looked at her. Emily hoped her own husband would feel the same about her after a dozen years and five children.

"I'd never been kissed," Emily confessed, "so I asked him what it was like. I kept after him until he kissed me. He explained it was okay," she said hurriedly, "that a man could give a woman a friendship kiss, but it was more than that for me. I think it was for him, too."

"Exactly how much more?"

Emily shrugged. "It was my first kiss. I can't be sure."

"Did he kiss you on the lips?"

"Yes."

"Did he put his tongue in your mouth?"

"Was that wrong?"

Ida seemed to shudder. "Was that your only *friendship* kiss?"

"He kissed me a few days later, but I'd been holding on to his hand. I think he might not have otherwise."

Ida let out a long, noisy breath and leaned back. "I always knew you were a strong-minded woman, but I hadn't expected anything quite like this."

"Did I do something terribly wrong?"

Ida released another breath. "I wouldn't say it was wrong, but it certainly isn't the usual way a woman approaches a man she likes. I'm surprised he didn't mount the fastest horse on the ranch and head back East after that first kiss."

"He said it was okay."

"I'm sure he *said* that, but I doubt he believed it. Especially since he kissed you a second time. Did you encourage him that time, too?"

"No. I just held his hand and put my arms around him."

"I consider that encouragement," Ida said dryly.

"He didn't have to kiss me," Emily protested. "I didn't ask him that time."

"You don't understand about men. When a pretty woman wraps herself around a man, he can't help himself. They'll kiss you even if five minutes earlier they were saying you were the last woman alive they wanted anything to do with."

"That doesn't make any sense."

"Men don't make sense. You just have to know how their minds work, though sometimes I doubt it's their minds that are working."

"What do you mean?"

"Let's save that for the next lesson," Ida said. "Right now we need to figure out your feelings. From what you've told me, you're incredibly naive, a flirt, or you're in love and don't know it."

"I'm not a flirt," Emily protested. She stopped for a moment. "I guess I was naive, but it's probably more accurate to say I was stupid. I wasn't thinking about what I was doing, just what I wanted."

"I think subconsciously you knew exactly what you were doing. I doubt you could have talked Bret into kissing you any other way."

"That makes me sound like a flirt."

"He couldn't have been too upset about it if he kissed you again. How did you feel about it that time?"

She dropped her gaze. "I wanted him to do it yet again."

"Did he?"

"No." She remembered her disappointment. "He said he wasn't trying to make me fall in love with him, that he wasn't in a position to marry anyone."

"Do you want to marry him?"

"I don't know. I'm trying to figure out how to keep him from going back to Boston until I can decide." She explained the compromise she'd worked out with her father. "He's promised to come back to take me to Galveston, but I have the feeling it'll be too late then."

"You realize you'd have to live in Boston if you marry him," Ida said.

"That's something else I don't understand. His family doesn't like him. He's miserable in Boston, and he seems happy in Texas. You ought to hear him talk about living on Jake and Isabelle's ranch. He seemed so happy there, I can't figure out why he ever left. I think he'd like to go back, but he thinks he's got to prove something to his family in Boston. I'm not sure he realizes they're going to like him even less after he proves it."

"It sounds like he's got a lot of questions of his own that need answering before he can decide what he wants to do with the rest of his life. I think you could have a big influence on that decision. But before you do anything, you have to be absolutely certain you love him and you'd be willing to do anything to make him happy, even if it means living in Boston."

"I could never live in Boston."

"Then you don't love him. That being the case, you

should be careful not to be alone with him. If it does happen, you have to leave as quickly as possible."

"But what if he decides to stay in Texas?"

"You don't make your love for a man conditional on where he lives. What would your father have done if your mother had refused to marry him unless he stayed in Virginia?"

Emily knew her mother hadn't wanted to leave Virginia and her family, but she'd loved her husband so much, she'd followed him. She'd never liked Colorado and didn't like Texas much better, but she was happy as long as she was with Sam Abercrombie.

"He always says he would have stayed in Virginia, but Mama told me it would have made him miserable. She never regretted moving for a minute; she said that seeing Dad's happiness made all the discomforts worthwhile."

"Until you feel the same way, you're not in love with Bret." Ida stood. "I hate to bring your visit to an end, but we both have to get up early in the morning."

"I think I'll stay here a few minutes longer," Emily said.

"Okay, but give me a call if you want anything."

Emily wasn't sure exactly what she wanted, but she was certain she couldn't live in Boston. Just the thought of doing so caused her to feel a sense of panic. It wasn't simply that she disliked her Abercrombie relatives. Except for Joseph, she didn't like Bret's Abbott family, either. On top of that, she wouldn't have her horses or the freedom to do what she wanted. She'd be expected to conform to a rigid standard of behavior that seemed to Emily to have been formulated to take every bit of fun out of life. Her sole job would be to manage Bret's home and bear his children.

If he stayed in Texas, she knew Bret wouldn't have

any objection to her working with her horses. Nor would he lay down a lot of rules. She could imagine him grinning when she told him she wanted to do something a little bit unexpected. Rather than refuse, he'd probably insist she let him go along. Any man who would take on the responsibility of an orphan like Jinx must have a sense of adventure, a willingness to take risks. Anybody who could have Joey and Buddy eating out of his hands within half an hour had to be innately good.

Why wouldn't she be in love with a man like that?

There wasn't anything she didn't like about him. The only problem was, everything fell apart when it came to the issue of living in Boston. If that was the ultimate test, then she failed.

Emily got up to go into the house. It was pointless to keep going over the same ground. Still, she couldn't stop feeling she'd missed something important. The only problem was, she had no idea what it could be.

Chapter Sixteen

"She rode out before daylight," Bertie told Bret. "She said she had to talk to Ida about something."

"Are you sure she didn't take anybody with her?" Bret asked.

Bertie turned away from her enormous black cast iron stove and settled her hands on her hips. "I saw her with my own eyes. You suggesting I'm blind?"

"Of course not." Bret didn't know whether to be amused or irritated. "I was just hoping you'd missed seeing Lonnie or Jem ride out to join her."

Mollified, Bertie turned back to her stove. "They came in for breakfast with the rest of the boys."

"Ladies shouldn't go riding about by themselves," Jinx said. He was eating his breakfast standing next to the stove. Bertie said she'd allow him to eat in the kitchen, but despite Bret and Emily's objections, she refused to let him sit at the table with either of them.

"Are you certain she's coming back tomorrow?" Bret asked.

"That's what she said," Bertie said without turning

around, "but she's missed Ida since she moved away. She might decide to stay a day or two."

Bret was a little surprised that Emily would leave her father, but he was more concerned about what could have driven her to make such a long and tiring ride. She hadn't told him about anything that was bothering her. He wasn't her confidant, but she had become more and more willing to discuss things with him.

This is what you get for thinking she might be in love with you.

He had tried to convince himself that whatever Emily might be feeling for him, it was no more than an attraction for a new and exciting man. There'd be dozens of men in Galveston who would be newer, more exciting, far better looking, who wanted to stay in Texas. Despite the reservations he'd expressed to her, she'd probably be engaged before the end of the first winter.

"Emily wants you to exercise her horses."

Bertie's voice brought Bret out of his distraction. "Did she say that?"

"You think I'm making it up?" Bertie was glaring at him again.

"No. I'm just surprised she'd trust anybody with her horses."

"She never has before," Bertie said as though clinching an argument Bret didn't know they were having.

"It'll take me all morning," Bret said. "I was hoping to spend the day in the saddle."

"I'll help," Jinx offered.

"What do you know about horses?" Bertie demanded.

"Which end bites and which end kicks," Jinx said with a gap-toothed grin.

"If I want sass, I'll go talk to one of those good-for-nothing cowhands," Bertie snapped.

"I know how to saddle and unsaddle a horse," Jinx said in a more subdued voice. "I can ride a little bit, too."

"Miss Emily wouldn't allow anybody who can ride just *a little bit* up on one of her horses," Bertie announced. Jinx wilted like a cut flower.

"It would help a lot to have someone get the horses ready and unsaddle them when I'm done," Bret said.

Jinx's recovery was instantaneous. He opened his mouth, but Bret cut in before he could speak. "You'll have to settle with Bertie about your work first."

Jinx turned to Bertie, his eyes wide and hopeful.

"Don't you go making big eyes at me," Bertie said. "I'm not soft like Mr. Nolan."

"I want to be a real cowboy like Mr. Nolan," Jinx said, his lower lip protruding. "A real cowboy rides horses; he doesn't wash dishes."

"Well, you're not a real cowboy, are you?" Bertie snapped. "You're still a little boy, and little boys do what they're told. Once you've done your work, you can help Mr. Nolan with the horses, but not before. And don't you go egging him on behind my back," she said, turning to Bret. "Things haven't been right ever since you got here. What with rustlers in the bunkhouse, Miss Emily riding all over creation like she was a boy, and you shoving orphans off on me, I don't know that I can put up with things much longer."

"You can't leave Emily and her father," Bret said. "They couldn't get along without you."

Bertie didn't say anything, but her sniff was not reassuring.

"Jinx and I will leave as soon as I catch the rustlers," Bret said.

"Your leaving is not going to fix things," Bertie said. "Not even taking that troublesome brat with you." She cast Jinx a look that wasn't nearly as severe as her words before turning back to Bret. "Nor will catching the rustlers. Mr. Sam is going to die and Miss Emily will be left by herself. She thinks she can run this place alone, but she can't. Besides, messing around with dirty cows and mixing company with cowhands who don't have the morals of a coyote is not a fit life for a lady."

"I'm sure she'll meet some nice man in Galveston and fall in love with him."

"There's just as many skunks in Galveston as anywhere else," Bertie said. "What she needs is somebody like you to take care of her."

"You think Mr. Nolan ought to *marry* her?" Jinx asked, flabbergasted.

"Why not?" Bertie asked, being careful to look at Jinx rather than Bret. "He's not married, he's handsome enough for any woman, and he knows how to run a ranch."

"If you marry her, can I stay here with you?" Jinx asked Bret.

"That would be for Miss Emily to say," Bertie said.

"With Mr. Nolan teaching me, I'll soon be a real cowboy. Then I won't have to work in the kitchen no more," he concluded triumphantly.

"Don't be counting your chickens before the eggs is laid," Bertie cautioned.

Bret felt like he was being swept away by a flash flood. He and Emily didn't want the same things, didn't even want to live in the same place. The fact that Emily would run off without even speaking to him was proof they weren't in love. Besides, if two people wanted different things, not even love could keep them together.

"I'm happy to do what I can to help Emily and her father," Bret said, "but we're not getting married."

"Why not?" Jinx asked. "I could stay here then."

"We're not in love with each other," Bret said. "Giving you a home isn't sufficient reason for two people to get married."

"You like her enough not to see her get hurt, don't you?" Bertie asked.

"Yes," Bret said, "but liking isn't enough. I'll do what I can to make sure she's safe, but her life is here. Mine is in Boston."

"Your life is where you decide you want it to be," Bertie stated flatly. "Now you'd better go see Mr. Sam and get to the horses before Jinx worries himself into a fever."

"I've never been sick," Jinx declared proudly.

Bret had never been sick, either, but right now he felt terrible. Bertie had used almost the same words as Hawk. But they didn't understand. The Abbotts had rejected his parents and him as being inferior. It wasn't about being exiled to Texas. It wasn't even about being left an orphan. It was about rejection. He'd waited his whole life to prove to them they'd been wrong. He couldn't quit now. He had to go back.

He was too conflicted about too many things to know if he loved Emily. He was relatively certain she didn't love him. But that didn't really matter. He was in no position to marry her. He wasn't what she needed, but was she what *he* needed?

Was she what he wanted?

"If you're going to sit there staring off into space, maybe you ought to let one of the hands exercise the horses. From the looks of you, one could run off with you and you'd be none the wiser."

Bertie's caustic tone jerked Bret out of his thoughts. "I was just thinking."

"Now's time for doing," Bertie said. "You can think when you've done your work."

Bret laughed. That sounded so much like Jake, he could almost imagine he was back at the Broken Circle. "Remind me never to work for you, Bertie. I'd be whittled down to a nubbin in no time."

"Is she going to whittle me down to a nubbin?" Jinx asked, not certain what a nubbin was.

"I might if you turn out to be less helpful than a broomstick leaning against the wall," Bertie said, not totally successful in hiding her smile. "If you stop gabbing and get to work, you might be done by the time Mr. Nolan is through visiting with Mr. Sam."

Bret left Jinx darting around the kitchen at Bertie's orders. He was strongly tempted to postpone his visit with Sam, but he knew he'd only spend the time thinking about Emily and how much more relaxed he'd been since he returned to Texas. He'd been over all of that before, so there was no reason to go over it again. The answers kept coming up the same.

When Bret rode in the next day, he knew immediately Emily was back. The sorrel hammerhead with black markings on its legs was in the corral. He was surprised that Jinx didn't come busting out of the house to pummel him with questions about what he'd done and seen. Sometimes he tired of answering the boy's questions, but he never tired of Jinx. It was impossible to get bored with a child who seemed to have boundless energy, inexhaustible enthusiasm, and perpetual optimism despite the vicissitudes of his life. He was hardly ever without a smile on his face.

Emily didn't come to meet him, either.

Bret unsaddled his horse and started to rub him down. Emily was usually too anxious to know what he'd done and seen to wait for him to come up to the house. Just more proof she wasn't thinking about building her life around his. He finished rubbing down his horse and turned him into the corral. Less than a minute later, the horse was rolling in the dust. Turning, Bret started toward the house.

He climbed the steps and entered the great room. The silence was nearly complete. Not even the sunlight filtering through heavy curtains relieved the gloom, the sense that all life had been removed from the room. He walked through to the kitchen, certain he'd find Bertie and Jinx, but the kitchen was also silent and empty; no preparations were being made for supper. He returned to the great room and was about to call out when Jinx erupted from the direction of Sam's bedroom.

"Where is everybody?" Bret asked.

"Got to get some more cold water," Jinx said without stopping. "Mr. Sam took a bad turn."

Bret hurried down the short hall to Sam's bedroom. He opened the door to find Emily sitting next to her father and Bertie hovering over both of them. Sam was leaning back against a mound of pillows, his skin colorless, while Emily swabbed his sweating brow with water from a pan on the bed. Bertie turned. A tired smile relieved her deep frown.

"What happened?" Bret asked.

"It's his heart," Bertie said. "He was in a lot of pain earlier, but it seems to be letting up now."

"He called for both of us." Emily didn't take her eyes off her father as she spoke. "Neither one of us was here."

"You couldn't know he was going to take a bad turn," Bertie said.

"I knew he was sick." Emily looked pale and frightened. "I had no business leaving him."

"He wouldn't want you to stop living just because he's sick."

"I should have been here."

"Do you want me to do that for a while?" Bret pointed to the damp cloths she was using to remove the perspiration from Sam's brow.

Emily shook her head. "I'd never forgive myself if I left him now."

Jinx arrived with the fresh water, but from the little bit left in the basin, Bret guessed he'd left a trail of water all the way from the pump.

"Let me have that before you spill it all over Mr. Sam," Bertie said. She took the basin and exchanged it for the one in Emily's lap. "Now that Mr. Nolan's here, we'd better set about getting supper ready," she said to Jinx. "Sickness don't mean the cowhands won't be hungry. What do you want to eat?" she asked Emily.

"I'm not hungry."

"You've got to eat to keep your strength up. It won't help your pa none to have you in bed, too."

"Bring her supper in here," Bret said. "I'll see if I can coax her into eating something."

Bertie nodded and dragged Jinx away, her hand over his mouth to keep him from volunteering to stay as well.

"How is your father doing?" Bret asked.

For the first time since he'd arrived, Emily turned her tear-strained face toward him. "Better than when I got back."

"You can stop talking about me like I'm not here," Sam said, his voice a mere thread that was difficult to understand.

"Don't talk," Emily said. "You've got to save your strength."

"For what?" Sam asked. "So I can die feeling stronger?"

"So you can live longer," Emily said, fresh tears streaming down her face. "You're all I've got."

"Then you'd better start listening to that young man, because you won't have me for much longer."

Bret wished Sam wouldn't talk about that, but it was time to make Emily aware she had to start thinking seriously about her future.

"And you can take that wet rag off my face," Sam said. "I feel like I'm wringing wet."

"You sweated through your clothes and bedsheets," Emily said. "I'll have to change you."

"You'll do no such thing," Sam declared. "I'll lie in my sweat until it dries before I'll have my daughter see me naked. Bret can help me."

Bret had expected Sam would want Lonnie or somebody he was more comfortable with to help him. "I'll be glad to help," he said, hoping Emily didn't feel hurt that her father had pushed her aside.

Emily used the damp cloths to wipe the tears from her cheeks. Bret stopped his hand in time to keep from reaching out to do it for her. He hated to see Emily cry. He hated even more that there was nothing he could do to stop her tears.

"Mama said men always stick together." Emily got to her feet. "Since Bret is here to help you, I'll go see about fixing something for you to eat."

"Don't give me any more colored water," Sam grumbled. "Even a sick man needs food in his stomach."

"You'll get what I fix, and you'll eat it, too," Emily announced, then left the room.

"That means colored water," Sam moaned. "I might as well be dead already."

He didn't look good, but he seemed to be recovering from his attack. Emily had looked hurt that her father had wanted Bret to take care of him. He'd have to try to explain to her about a man's need for privacy. And his need not to feel completely helpless in front of the child he was supposed to protect and defend.

Looking at him now, Bret knew Sam wouldn't live until December. Who would take care of Emily then?

Bret didn't think he would ever get used to Hawk materializing out of nowhere.

"We found the rustlers," Hawk said. "I left Zeke to watch them while I looked for you. Where have you been? I figured you'd want to be in on the capture."

"Emily's father nearly died two days ago. I couldn't leave her until he was feeling better."

During the last two days, either Emily or Bret had been with Sam almost constantly. They'd shared meals and concern for Sam, but that was all. Emily was so preoccupied with her father's failing health, it wasn't an appropriate time for kisses or anything else. Emily felt so guilty about having been away when he'd had his attack, she wouldn't leave the house even to exercise her horses. Bret only left to work with the horses and give Jinx his daily lessons. If it hadn't been for the boy's smiles and endless supply of energy and optimism, it would have been a dreary household. Even Emily cheered up when he was around.

"We'd better get going if we want to catch the rustlers before dark," Hawk said. "How good are you at ambushes? Crawled on your stomach lately?"

"About all I'm good for is riding in hell-for-leather and shouting at them to put their hands up."

Bret had forgotten that Hawk's belly laugh sounded as if he were laughing into a drum. It wasn't something anyone had heard often recently.

"They're in a depression between two low hills and

screened by a blackjack and live oak thicket," Hawk said as he and Bret set out on their horses. "They don't seem worried about being caught. We'd have heard the bawling calves if we hadn't spotted the smoke from their fire first."

"I don't understand," Bret said. "They're either very stupid or certain they won't get caught."

"If we can come up on them before they go for their guns, it'll be the easiest job we've ever had."

Bret saw the smoke and heard the calves. "I swear they're trying to get caught," Hawk said.

What followed was the most bizarre situation Bret had ever taken part in. The two men didn't attempt to hide or go for their guns when Bret rode up with Hawk. Zeke came up behind the men, but they didn't stop what they were doing until they'd finished branding the calf they held on the ground. They released the calf, which went off bawling for its mother. Only then did one of the men turn to Bret and ask, "Who are you? Did Lonnie send you?"

Bret had been certain that Lonnie was behind the rustling, but he'd never expected to have one of the men blurt it out like that. "No. We represent Sam Abercrombie. We're taking you in for rustling."

The man looked confused rather than worried or angry. "We ain't rustling. We're just doing what Lonnie told us."

"Did he explain why putting another man's brand on Abercrombie cattle wasn't going to cause you to end up with your head in a noose?"

"He said the ranch was changing its brand. He said he didn't have enough hands to spare, so he hired us to do it."

"Who is that brand registered to?" Bret asked.

"Lonnie said it belonged to the ranch."

"Unfortunately for you, Mr. Abercrombie is *not*

changing his brand. You'll have to come with us until we get this straightened out."

"You don't have to take our guns," the man said when Zeke collected their rifles from their horses. "We're not going to try to run away. Lonnie will explain everything."

But Lonnie wasn't at the ranch when they got there.

"He ain't come in yet," Jem said. "I don't know where he is. He's never this late."

Unsure of what to do next, Bret took the men to Sam. Sam thought their story was just as unbelievable as Bret did.

"Lock them up in the barn," Sam said. "They'll keep until I hear what Lonnie has to say."

"He'll tell you we ain't no rustlers," the talkative man said as Hawk and Zeke pushed the two out of the room. The other man never did speak.

"I don't believe a word of it," Emily said after the door closed behind the four men. "Lonnie would never do anything like that."

"You heard what they said," Bret reminded her. "They didn't try to hide what they'd been doing."

"There's got to be another explanation," Emily insisted.

"You bring Lonnie to me the minute he gets back," Sam said.

But Lonnie hadn't returned by the time the men finished their dinner. Nor had he returned by the time they went to bed.

"I want you to keep your brothers here," Sam said to Bret while Emily was getting him ready for bed. "We're short of hands, and they seem like good men."

"The best you'll find," Bret assured him, "but what will they do?"

"I'll decide tomorrow. I'm tired now."

"Then I'll say good night," Bret said.

Emily put her hand on his arm. "I want to talk to you before you go to bed," Emily said.

"I'm going to check on the piebald. He seemed to be favoring his left foreleg."

Outside, the temperature had dropped and the air felt damp. Bret hoped they were in for a little rain before the dry months of summer set in. The piebald was standing at the edge of the corral. He didn't move away when Bret climbed through the bars. "Gotten used to me, have you?" he said to the big horse. The piebald butted him with his head. "I love you, too, you big ugly mutt, but try not to knock to me down. I just want to check your leg."

"If you have to make love to a horse, you're in worse shape than I thought."

Bret looked up to see Hawk leaning against the corral. He wasn't surprised he hadn't heard him come up. Hawk could move like a shadow when he wanted to.

"Not all of us have your success with the ladies."

Hawk made a noise that sounded like he was clearing his throat. "Hell, even my horse doesn't like me. What's wrong with his leg?"

"I can't find anything, but he seemed to be favoring it this morning. You have a look."

Hawk climbed through the bars, ran his hand up and down the piebald's leg. "It's a little warm. Might be a good idea to give him a couple days off." He stood and patted the piebald's neck. "He looks like a good, strong horse."

"His owner wants to make him a cutting horse, but Emily and I think he's perfect for all-around ranch work."

"You two working together?"

"Yeah." Bret laughed. "I had to prove to her I

241

wasn't a greenhorn. For my reward she gave me the only horse she couldn't train."

"How's he doing?"

"He's stubborn, but he figures it out."

"There seems to be a lot of stubbornness around here."

Bret laughed again, but not with as much humor. The sound of a closing door caused the two men to glance back at the house in time to see Emily starting toward them. "I think it's time I got some shut-eye," Hawk said. "I'm so sleepy I can barely hold my head up."

"Coward," Bret said.

"I'm just leaving the field to you. She's a lot prettier than the piebald."

Hawk waved to Emily as he made his way to the bunkhouse. Giving the piebald one last pat, Bret climbed back through the bars.

"Is anything wrong with the piebald?" Emily asked when she came up.

"Hawk thinks maybe he strained a tendon. He was favoring his left foreleg when we finished up this morning, so I'll probably give him a couple of days off."

Emily leaned against the corral, looked at the piebald, then the other horses. "I can't believe I thought you were a complete greenhorn."

"You had no reason to think otherwise."

"I should have been fair enough to wait until I got to know you before I made up my mind."

"You weren't angry at me, just at what I'd been sent to do."

"I was a little angry at you for agreeing to do it."

"And I wasn't exactly happy with your attitude toward me or my errand."

Emily laughed, a little nervously, Bret thought.

"I'm glad we both got a chance to change our minds," Emily said. After a pause, she added, "You *did* change your mind about me, didn't you?"

"Nope. I thought you were a beautiful, high-spirited woman when I first met you, and I think the same thing now."

He couldn't be sure in the pale light of the moon, but he thought she blushed.

"I'm not sure I ever thanked you for working out a compromise that keeps me from having to go to Boston. You know Dad only agreed because you said you'd come back."

Bret nodded.

"Why did *you* agree?"

"You got what you wanted, and I got what I wanted."

"You had already made an agreement with Dad about the stock. He could have sold the ranch, forced me to go to Boston. You would have got what you wanted without having to spend four months in a place you dislike helping me find a husband."

"I don't dislike Texas," Bret said. "It's just not my home anymore."

"Could it be again?"

Bret felt himself tense. "What do you mean?"

"When are you leaving?"

"I can't leave with your father so ill." That sounded like a weak excuse; there was nothing he could do to help her father. "And we still haven't caught Lonnie."

"The boys can take care of Lonnie, and we both know my father's not going to get any better."

"Are you trying to get rid of me?"

"No. I'm trying to find out why you're staying."

There it was, the question he'd been hoping to avoid. The question others had all been asking him in one way or another. "I don't want to leave you alone when you've got so much on your hands." That was only a small part of the reason he wanted to stay. "I'd feel better if Ida and Charlie were here." But even then, he still wouldn't want to leave.

"I can take care of myself. And if I need Charlie or Ida, I only have to send for them."

"But that'd take two days. Anything could happen in that time." It still wasn't what he wanted to say. They stood there, looking at each other—moonlight making it difficult to read expressions, impossible to see into eyes.

"Do you like me?"

Emily's question sent shock waves ricocheting through Bret's body. He turned away, looked at the horses on the far side of the corral. "Of course I like you."

"Look at me," Emily said. "Do you like me?" she repeated when he faced her. "I don't mean like a friend. I mean like somebody special, somebody you'd like to see a lot, someone you wouldn't want to leave."

She'd put the question to him squarely. He could refuse to answer, or he could lie, but there was no way he could equivocate. She had rested her arm on the top corral pole. Bret reached over to cover her hand with his. "Yes, I do like you in all those ways, but it's something I've told myself I can't have."

"What if I felt the same way about you?"

He felt his hand close around her fingers. "I hope you don't. It's not much fun to want something you can't have."

"Why can't I have it—*we* have it?"

"Because your life is here, and mine is in Boston."

"But you like Texas. You like being on a ranch again. You look happy when you talk about the time you spent on Jake's ranch. You like the people who made up your adopted family. Every time you need help, you think of them first. You look grim and determined whenever you talk about going back to Boston." She took his hand in both of hers. "You're not happy there, but you could be happy here."

Bret took her hand in both of his. "I don't expect you to understand this—Jake and Isabelle never did—but my uncle turned his back on my mother, my father, and me in succession, and he forced the family to do the same. That's been eating at me ever since I was seven. For twenty years it's been like gorge in my throat, always threatening to choke me. It doesn't matter whether I'm happy or not. Proving he was wrong is something I have to do."

"Why do you care what he thinks?"

Isabelle had asked him that question in one of her letters. It had bothered him a lot until he finally realized the problem was in his own head. He couldn't *feel* worthy until acceptance came from his uncle because his uncle had been the one to reject him. "It's just the way I feel. I know it's stupid, but nothing has been able to change it."

"Maybe this can."

Emily withdrew her hands from his grasp, took his face in her hands, and kissed him gently on the mouth. Bret tried to resist, but it was futile. In less than a second, his arms pulled Emily into a crushing embrace. All the passion he'd been holding back, all the desire, all the hope, came spilling from the broken dam and drowned his resistance. He'd never known that anything could feel so good, so right. It was as if they'd been made to fit with each other. He knew that what he was doing was foolish, but he didn't care. He'd worry about that later. Right now he held Emily in his arms.

Somewhere in the back of his head, he thought he

heard a horse approach the ranch house, but he had no thoughts to spare for anyone but the woman in his arms.

"That didn't feel exactly like a friendship kiss," Bret said once they'd broken their kiss and he'd been able to get his breath.

Emily slipped her arms around his waist and leaned against him. "It's a special kind of friendship. I can't stand to think of you going back to Boston and being miserable."

He'd been thinking it meant something a little different.

Their second kiss was more lingering, less impassioned. As they kissed searchingly, Bret realized they were both looking for answers, both looking for a level of interest, passion, desire, *need*, that neither of them had been able or willing to put into words. The sound of running feet caused them to break apart.

"You gotta come right now," Jinx called out even before he reached them. "Some man named Joseph has just come up to the house. He says he's got to talk to you right away."

Chapter Seventeen

Joseph Abbott's unexpected appearance at the ranch sent Emily's feelings into a tailspin. She'd forgotten how much she liked him. She *hadn't* forgotten he'd warned her against Bret. If she had, the tension between them would have reminded her. She and Bret had arrived back at the house to find Joseph standing in the middle of the great room looking as if he were afraid to sit down. She knew their ranch house was rustic compared to houses in Boston, but it was comfortable nonetheless.

"What are you doing here?" she asked. "I mean, why didn't you tell me you were coming?"

Joseph stepped forward, took her hand, and kissed it. She couldn't resist throwing an amused glance at Bret, who looked far from amused.

"I couldn't stop worrying about you all alone with your father so ill," Joseph said. "I decided to see if I could be of any help. I remember you very fondly from your visit several years ago, but I'm sure you know that from the letters I've written."

It was obvious from Bret's frown that he hadn't known anything about the letters. "I've enjoyed your letters," Emily said, "but they haven't made me like my Abercrombie family any better."

"I'm sure it takes a while for someone who's grown up in Texas to get used to our ways," Joseph said. "Everything is so new and *rough* down here, while Boston is more than two hundred and fifty years old. I'm sure Bret would tell you we're set in our ways."

"He's been too busy helping me with my horses and finding a couple of rustlers to have much time to talk. Sit down. You must be tired after your journey. I'm surprised you didn't stop somewhere and ride in tomorrow."

"After spending one night in a household of boisterous children, I'd have ridden 'til morning before being subjected to the same again." He turned to Bret. "Apparently, you got along fine with all the children."

"You must have stayed with Ida and Charlie Wren," Emily exclaimed. "He used to be our foreman."

"I can see why you replaced him," Joseph said as he eased himself reluctantly into a chair covered by a buffalo hide. "The man is thoroughly unpleasant."

"We didn't *replace* him." Joseph's criticism annoyed Emily. "He left to start his own ranch."

"I'm sure I wish him luck." Joseph turned a jaundiced eye to Bret. "So you've been playing the cowboy? You can take the man out of Texas, but you can't take Texas out of the man."

Emily liked Joseph, but she didn't like the way he said that. It was clear he thought the association with Texas lowered Bret's status. "With Dad being sick and our foreman helping the rustlers, I don't know what I would have done without him."

Joseph's reaction was so abrupt, so startled, Emily

would have thought it was *his* cows that were being rebranded. "I can't believe your foreman was helping the rustlers."

"I couldn't, either, but the rustlers said he hired them. We've got them locked up in the barn waiting for Lonnie to show up."

"You didn't catch Lonnie?"

"He disappeared. None of the boys knows where he could have gone."

Joseph's concern was evident. "I'm more glad than ever I decided to come. It must have been terrible to find you had a traitor in your midst."

"I am anxious to ask Lonnie why he did it."

"I don't imagine you'll ever see him again," Joseph said. "Why would he come back when he knows you'd arrest him?"

"Everything he owns is here."

"He will probably come get his belongings at night," Bret said. "I expect the hands will look the other way. Texans like to give people a second chance. That's what coming West is all about. It's why your father left Boston."

"Sam Abercrombie left Boston because—" Joseph broke off as suddenly as he'd started. His gaze swung from Bret to Emily, who was looking at him with narrowed eyes. "He left because he wanted excitement," Joseph finished up.

"Dad says he left Boston because it was full of dull, narrow-minded people who preferred living in the past and punishing anybody who didn't agree with them," Emily said. "He said his relatives were the most dull and narrow-minded of all."

"Bostonians are proud of their past," Joseph said. "At least we don't have savage Indians roaming around. I thought I saw one when I rode up."

"It was probably Hawk," Bret said. "He's one of my adopted brothers."

Joseph looked stunned. "He was talking to a black man."

"Zeke. He's another of my brothers," Bret explained.

"I didn't know you had such an interesting family," Joseph said.

"You mean Bret's been in Boston for six years and you didn't know about his brothers? I knew in a week."

Joseph looked a little uncomfortable. "Bret and I don't see that much of each other. We work in different parts of the company."

"But you're cousins. You must see him all the time outside of work."

"I work late a lot," Bret said. "Besides, I can't afford to do the things Joseph and his friends do."

"Surely he takes you along."

Joseph squirmed in his chair, looking more uncomfortable than ever.

Bret turned to him. "You must be tired. It's a long ride from Charlie's ranch."

"I'm sorry," Emily said, getting up. "Let me show you to a room."

"I can do that," Bret said. "I'm sure you want to check on your father."

"Thanks," Emily said. "I'll see you in the morning," she said to Joseph. "You can sleep as late as you want. Just tell Bertie what you'd like for breakfast. Now you can satisfy your curiosity about how exciting it is to live on a ranch in Texas."

Her father seemed to be sleeping peacefully when she checked on him, but she didn't like the way he looked. His skin was almost gray and his breath was shallow and labored. The trouble with his heart must have been more serious than either of them had thought. She'd make sure he got as much rest as possible for the next day or so.

She sat down in the chair next to his bed, took his hand in hers. This change in their roles seemed strange and uncomfortable to her. Until a few months ago he was the strong, invincible man who'd always been the center of her life. He'd taught her to ride, to love being outside, to love Texas. Her mother had said she should have been a boy. Neither Emily nor her father saw anything strange in a girl loving to ride, training horses, being happy to live on a ranch a two-day ride from the nearest city. They'd camped out, helped with roundups, branding, and doctoring. She'd even helped deliver a foal once.

All of this had made her father's insistence that she go to Boston a surprise. After all the years he'd spent instilling in her his love of freedom from Eastern society's rules and regulations, why would he think she'd leave the ranch? She knew he'd only agreed to the compromise of Galveston because Bret had promised to go with her.

She wished she could tell him how she felt about Bret. Maybe her father could tell her how to convince him to stay in Texas. She knew that no matter why he felt he had to go back, he wasn't happy in Boston. She didn't need words to know that Joseph didn't think of Bret as an equal. Bret *did* like being at the ranch. This was where he belonged. She just didn't know how to make him see that.

She sighed, placed her father's hand by his side, and stood. She kissed him on the forehead. Maybe she would talk to him when he started to feel stronger. He'd lived in the same two worlds as Bret and had never regretted turning his back on Boston. Maybe he could help her find a way to convince Bret he was making a mistake.

* * *

"I never knew you expected to find living on a ranch exciting," Bret said to Joseph after Emily had left them. "Nor did I know you'd been writing Emily."

"I can't see why you should think you ought to be privy to my thoughts or actions." Joseph had dropped all pretense of politeness. Scorn practically dripped from his words.

"I don't. I just can't understand why, if you were so fond of Emily and she valued your opinion so much, your father would ask me to talk her into moving to Boston instead of you."

Joseph laughed. "He thought it was too dangerous for me." He looked around in disgust. "With all of Sam Abercrombie's money, why would he choose to live in a place like this?"

"It's a working ranch. There's no need for velvet curtains, damask chair coverings, and Turkish carpets on the floor. They'd be cut to pieces in a few months. Ranch life is rough, and ranchers are rough men."

"You sound like you admire them."

"I've done their work. I know how hard it is."

"If you like it so much, maybe you ought to stay here."

"If I did, there'd be no need for Emily to move to Boston."

Joseph's body went rigid and he sat forward in his chair. "My father told you not to try to insinuate yourself into Emily's affections. If you've led that poor girl to believe you'd make a suitable husband—"

"I've made it quite clear I'd be just the opposite." Bret couldn't understand why Joseph and his father thought everybody would do whatever they demanded. He supposed it came from a lifetime of ruling other people's lives. "I'm going back to Boston any day now. Your father promised he'd look over some suggestions I had for changes to the company."

"You can forget about any insignificant ideas you might have had," Joseph said, his sneer back in place. "Father has come up with a brilliant plan to move Abbott and Abercrombie to the forefront of the industry for the next fifty years." Then, to Bret's shock and dismay, Joseph proceeded to outline the very plan Bret had presented to his uncle.

Uncle Silas was claiming Bret's plan as his own.

"Those are my ideas," Bret said. "I gave them to Uncle Silas months ago. Just before I left for Texas, he told me he hadn't had a chance to look at them."

If it was possible, Joseph's look became even more contemptuous. "You might have fooled Emily and her father into thinking you know a lot about the shipping business, but don't try that on me. Father hasn't kept you in a clerking position because he thinks you're brilliant."

"He's kept me in a clerking position because he doesn't want anything to do with me," Bret snapped. "Any more than you do. That's fine with me—I don't care about that anymore—but I won't sit silently by and let him steal my ideas."

"Assuming they were your ideas, what are you going to do about it?"

Bret opened his mouth to tell Joseph exactly what he intended to do, then thought better of it. If his uncle was willing to take the risk of claiming somebody else's work, he must have already planned how to make it look like Bret was lying.

"I thought so," Joseph said, a malignant smile on his face. "Father always said you were a bad seed. I didn't know you were a liar as well."

Bret stood. "I'm neither. Now I'd better show you to your room. I have work to do tomorrow, so I'll be up at dawn."

"You really are working on this miserable place?"

"Emily said you thought you'd find it exciting."

"I'd never seen a cattle ranch before," Joseph said evasively. "How was I to know what it was really like?"

"You could have asked me," Bret said, knowing that Joseph would never have done such a thing. "I could have spared you the trip."

"I didn't come to look at the ranch." Joseph had gotten to his feet. He looked at his suitcase, then at Bret.

"Out here you carry your own suitcase," Bret said. "It's part of what makes this a miserable place."

Joseph's look of anger did little to improve Bret's mood. He had to get a telegram off to Rupert quickly. Picking up the lamp on the table between them, he led Joseph to his room.

"Is this the best room they have?" he asked, clearly stunned. The room was barely larger than the bed. The only other furniture was a ladder-back chair and a small chest of drawers. The walls were unadorned, and the window had no curtains. A basin and a pitcher of water sat on the chair. Bret assumed Jinx had brought the water in.

"It's the only room left."

"What about your room?"

"I'll be happy to exchange, but you'll have to share it with Jinx."

"You mean that dirty boy I saw earlier? I couldn't get a wink of sleep with him in the room." He looked around in dismay. "I hope Emily's room is better than this."

"I can't say. I've never seen it."

"I'd be shocked if you had."

"I'll leave you the light," Bret said.

"Won't you need it?"

"I know the house well enough to find my room without it. Good night."

Bret closed the door and headed to his room. Joseph was going to be in for a surprise when he discovered that Emily and her father didn't share Joseph's opinion of Bret. He was going to be even more surprised when he learned that Emily was going to Galveston rather than Boston, and that Bret would be going with her. But he was going to be horrified when he learned that Bret had been given the right to vote Sam's stock in Abbott & Abercrombie.

But probably no more shocked than Bret had been at his uncle's intended theft of his ideas. It was almost more than he could comprehend. He'd barely been able to contain his shock and rage. For a moment he'd thought he might explode. It wasn't merely caution that had prompted him to control his outburst. Something had snapped inside. He didn't know what it was. It was as though some tension had finally let go, some restraint had finally been removed.

Maybe he was ready to confront his uncle without any of the respect or deference he'd shown him in the past. Maybe he was ready to pull out records showing how his uncle was bleeding the company. He wouldn't rest until he found a way to expose his uncle.

So what had changed? Why did he feel as if he'd been given a reprieve?

"Bertie said Joseph could eat what she fixed or he could go hungry," Jinx was telling Bret and Emily. "She said if her cooking wasn't good enough for him, he could head straight back to Boston. She said she never invited him to come sticking his nose in where it wasn't wanted."

Bret and Emily had finished working with the horses. Jinx had come out for his lessons, but he was so excited, he hadn't said anything about saddling up.

"I guess I'd better go up to the house," Emily said. "Bertie can take an unaccountable dislike to some people."

Bret thought Bertie was a genius for divining Joseph's true character so quickly.

"Bertie said you wasn't to bother your head about him," Jinx told Emily. "Mr. Sam wants to see him."

"Dad's not strong enough to be seeing people." Emily pulled off her gloves and tossed them on a shelf that held her riding equipment.

"You said he was looking a lot better this morning," Bret reminded her.

"Not well enough to have an argument."

"What makes you think he'll argue with Joseph? He's the one who thinks you ought to go to Boston."

"If Bertie has taken a dislike to him, I expect Dad will as well."

An idea popped into Bret's head. It was a gamble, but at this point he was willing to take a chance. If Sam disliked Joseph, he would be anxious to give Bret all the weapons he could to prevent Emily from marrying Joseph, something Bret would have felt honor bound to do even without Sam's help. Bret reached out to take Emily's arm. He released it as soon as she turned back. "I think you ought to wait."

"Why?"

"When your father decided you ought to move to Boston after his death, he contacted my uncle, *not* his own brother. I have a feeling he thought Joseph might be the perfect husband for you. Since you've been getting letters from him for years, I gather you have a liking for each other."

"Joseph was the only who was nice to me when Dad took Mama to Boston to consult those fancy doctors."

"If your father decides he's not the perfect husband

for you, he'll be a lot happier about your going to Galveston. You realize he's not happy about that compromise."

"Dad liked Joseph. He said he seemed to be the only decent member of the Abbott family."

Maybe he had been as a teenager anxious to please, but in the intervening ten years Joseph had assumed all the prejudices and arrogance of his father. Bret was certain Sam would see through him within five minutes.

"I'll wait a few minutes," Emily said, "but no longer."

"You can watch me," Jinx said.

"Watch you do what?" Emily said, smiling at the boy.

"Saddle my horse and mount up. Mr. Nolan taught me."

Emily patiently watched Jinx and complimented him on what he'd learned, but Bret could see she was anxious about her father. "That's enough for today," he said when the boy had shown Emily he could guide his horse by pressure from his knees without having to yank on the reins. "I'm taking you on a long ride."

Jinx bubbled over with excitement, and Bret resigned himself to the endless chatter of an eight-year-old while his mind would be busy wondering about the outcome of Joseph's conversation with Sam. Not only did his future depend on it. So did Emily's.

"Dad asked me to send Zeke and Hawk to him as soon as they finished lunch," Emily said to Joseph. "They've been in there with him half the afternoon."

"I can't imagine what he has to say to men like that," Joseph said.

"They found the rustlers," Emily said. "He wants to thank them."

"That should have been handled by your foreman."

"He can't do that when he's missing," Bertie pointed out.

Bertie had taken a profound dislike to Joseph. She usually worked in the kitchen most of the day, taking care of her cleaning in the morning and other chores during the afternoon. Today she'd busied herself wherever Joseph happened to be. While he seemed to be oblivious to her in the beginning, her gaze rarely left him. After she'd delivered several unexpected barbs, he began to cast caustic glances in her direction. That only encouraged Bertie. After she yanked him up out of a chair to dust cushions that hadn't been touched in months, he made sure to stay out of her way.

Emily was grateful to Hawk and Zeke for stopping the rustling so quickly, and she was pleased her father had wanted to thank them personally, but she didn't understand why he had kept them with him so long. He'd said he was feeling better, but he hadn't looked good. He needed plenty of rest. She would have interrupted them long ago, but her father had made it clear he didn't want to be interrupted, even by his daughter.

"What did you and Dad talk about this morning?" Emily asked Joseph.

"He asked me what Boston was like these days. He hasn't lived there in more than thirty years. It's changed a lot since the war."

She hoped Joseph was perceptive enough to realize that talking about the war was a treacherous subject best avoided. Though her mother's family had never owned slaves, the war had ruined them. She had lost her parents, a brother, two cousins, and several friends.

"Your father hasn't lived in a city populated by so-

phisticated people in so long, I assured him he'd forgotten what civilized life was like. I told him I didn't
know why he hadn't come back to Boston after he
made his fortune."

"What did he say?"

"He said if he'd gone anywhere, he'd have moved
to Virginia to be near his wife's family. I asked him
why he'd want to have anything to do with traitors.
He said he didn't see it that way."

Emily was beginning to wish she'd stayed with her
father and had let Bret take care of her horses.

"He also asked me what I thought you ought to
do," Joseph added.

"What did you tell him?"

"You should have said it was none of your business
what she did," Bertie interjected. She was dusting a
table she'd dusted at least a half dozen times already.
Emily expected to see her set up her ironing at any
minute.

"Exactly what I've told you," Joseph said. "I'm sure
you're capable of managing this ranch by yourself. Of
course, that would only be suitable if you had a husband to handle the more unpleasant tasks such as
dealing with your hands and riding about to see what
your cows are doing."

"I like dealing with the cowhands and riding over
the ranch," Emily said.

"That's exactly why I think Texas is bad for you. A
young lady from Boston would never think of doing
anything like that."

"Scared of cows, are they?" Bertie asked.

Joseph ignored her. "I would prefer that you move
to Boston," he said to Emily. "Since the war, Texas has
turned into a haven for liars, thieves, and murderers. I
told your father that my father would be happy to offer you a home with us as long as you want. Besides,

you'll need someone to oversee your financial affairs. My father will be happy to do that for you, too."

"She's got Mr. Nolan to do that for her," Bertie said.

Emily barely managed to keep from turning around to gape at Bertie. Neither she nor her father had made any such arrangement with Bret, and Bertie knew it. Bertie's statement surprised Joseph, and he didn't make any attempt to disguise his reaction.

"You can't do that," he declared. "He's nothing but a clerk."

"I thought it was clerks that added up the numbers to make sure everything came out right," Bertie said.

"Adding and subtracting is all they're good for," Joseph said. "I'm talking about knowing where to invest your inheritance, how to vote your stock in Abbott and Abercrombie."

"After working so closely with you and your father, I'm sure Mr. Nolan knows all about that." Bertie had stopped polishing the table and moved where she could face Joseph. She towered over him like a bull over a calf.

"Bret doesn't have any concept of how Abbott and Abercrombie is run," Joseph stated. "He wouldn't even have a job if my grandmother hadn't thrown a fit when my father said he didn't want to hire another poor relation."

"That brings up something I've wanted to know," Emily said, turning to look directly at Joseph. "What possible excuse could your father have had for not taking in his seven-year-old nephew after his father died?"

Bertie planted her hands on her hips. "I'd like to know that, too."

Chapter Eighteen

Rattled, Joseph couldn't stop his gaze from swinging to encompass Bertie before turning back to Emily. "The war was just starting, and travel from Texas was impossible. There were blockades all along the coast. My father was certain Bret would be safe until the end of the war."

"Why didn't he go after him then?" Emily asked.

"He didn't know where he had gone."

"And he didn't look?" Bertie asked, her disapproval emphasized by gathered eyebrows and compressed mouth.

"Things were very dangerous in Texas. The army had to be called in to keep order."

"The army was called in to help liars and thieves steal from honest Texans," Bertie said. "My father lost his land to one of your Yankee carpetbaggers."

The temperature in the room would probably have risen several more degrees if Jinx and Bret hadn't entered at that moment.

"I lassoed a calf," Jinx announced. "And I did it all by myself."

Bertie swung her attention to Jinx. "And I suppose Mr. Nolan was back at the barn with his feet up chewing on a straw."

"He was helping me," Jinx said, incensed that Bertie would malign his hero. "He chased the calf close so I could lasso it."

"You didn't let him ride a horse, did you?" Bertie said, turning to Bret.

"Yeah," Jinx said, bursting with pride. "But he made me let go of the rope as soon as I got it over the calf's head. He said I didn't know how to wrap the rope around the saddle horn without losing a finger."

"Thank God for small favors." Bertie glanced significantly at Joseph. "Now that Mr. Nolan's here, I can start supper. And you," she said, taking Jinx by the ear, "have to clean up before I'll let you set a foot in my kitchen."

"Why do you put up with that woman?" Joseph asked when she'd left. "My mother wouldn't keep her a week."

"Then your mother would be making a big mistake." Bret turned from Joseph to Emily. "How is your father?"

Emily couldn't help comparing Bret with Joseph. Both men were tall and attractive, but while Joseph was dressed in a black three-piece suit with white shirt, tie, and black shoes, Bret wore form-fitting jeans, a dun-colored shirt, and a brown vest, his dusty boots making dull thumps on the board floor when he walked. While Joseph's style of dress drew attention to his clothes, Bret's attire unerringly drew Emily's gaze to his body. He was so superior physically, he made Joseph's body seem unappealing. Emily began to feel a little warm as she noticed the way the jeans hugged Bret's thighs and bottom or the way his shirt was stretched across his broad shoulders. And she loved the fact that though he shaved every morning, by the evening he looked like he could use another. There was something about that slightly untidy appearance that made him seem more masculine, more attractive, more virile.

"I don't know how Dad's doing," she said, pulling her thoughts back from Bret's body and hoping she wasn't blushing. "Your brothers have been locked away with him ever since lunch."

Bret glanced in the direction of her father's room, then back. "You should have chased them out."

"Dad said I couldn't disturb him for any reason."

Bret's brow furrowed. "That's odd. I wonder if I should see what's happening."

"If Mr. Abercrombie doesn't want his own daughter to disturb him, I'm sure he wouldn't want you bursting in on him."

"I wish you would," Emily said to Bret, ignoring Joseph. "I'm worried he'll exhaust himself."

"I'll be right back," Bret said and headed toward her father's room.

"I can't understand why you would let Bret interrupt your father when you won't."

"He told me not to disturb him, but he didn't tell Bret. Besides, he and Bret like each other."

"I can't understand what a man with your father's breeding can see in a man like Bret."

Emily had had about all of Joseph's snobbery she could stand. "Since Bret has *your* breeding, I would think that was obvious."

"His mother was a disappointment to the family.

As for his father, no one could understand why she married him."

"*My* father was a disappointment to his family who could never understand why he married *my* mother."

"You're different," Joseph hastened to assure her. "You—"

Emily wasn't listening to him. The door to her father's room had opened and Zeke and Hawk came out. She jumped up to meet them. "What have you been doing all afternoon? Is Dad all right?"

"He's fine," Zeke said. "He asked us to act as foremen until he gets things straightened out."

"I can't imagine why Mr. Abercrombie would ask men like you to—" Joseph started.

"He asked if we'd take the job permanently," Hawk said, ignoring Joseph, "but we told him we like to keep moving. But with Bret leaving soon, we agreed to stay until things are straightened out here."

Emily had known that Bret would be leaving eventually, but the realization it could be any day now came as an unpleasant shock.

"We need to talk to the hands before supper," Hawk said to Emily. "Some of them aren't going to be too pleased."

"I wouldn't be surprised if they all quit," Joseph said.

"We won't be that rough on them," Hawk said. "They seem like decent boys."

"But you're an Indian and he's black," Joseph said, pointing to Zeke.

"We know. We got mirrors," Hawk said to Joseph before turning back to Emily. "Anything you want to tell me?"

Emily shook her head. Right now all she could think about was that Bret might leave before she had

a chance to make him realize he belonged in Texas—
with her.

"In that case, we'll be going."

"I can't believe your father would trust those men,"
Joseph said when they left.

"Why not? They're Bret's brothers."

"I don't care who they are," Joseph declared. "Your
father shouldn't trust men like them."

"They've proved perfectly trustworthy. I don't—"
Bret emerged from her father's room and she turned
to him. "How is Dad?"

"He is a little tired, but you can see him now."

Making a mental note to ask Bret later why he
looked so worried, Emily practically raced to his
room. Her father was lying back against the pillows,
his face drained of color. His breathing was slow and
labored. She tried to keep from showing how
shocked she was at his appearance.

"How are you feeling?" she asked as she took a seat
next to his bed.

"Tired," he said without turning his head to look at
her, "but relieved."

"Relieved about what?"

"Just a couple of things I've figured out." He turned
to look at her. "You're worried about me, aren't you?"

"Of course I am. You've been very sick, yet you
spent your morning talking to Joseph and the afternoon behind closed doors with Zeke and Hawk."

"They're good men. I'm glad Bret asked them to
come."

"I'm glad, too, but I'm not happy to see you looking so tired. As soon as you have your dinner, you're
going to sleep."

Her father's smile was slow in coming. He reached
for her hand. "You're a mighty fierce little girl when it
comes to taking care of your dad."

"You're the only one I've got. I'm going to hang on to you as long as I can."

"It's time to look for someone to take my place. A good man, one you can depend on to take care of you, one who'll love you as I loved your mother."

"I'm not sure there's another man like that."

"Of course there is. You just have to open your eyes. Now I am a little tired. I'd like to take a nap before supper."

Emily squeezed her father's hand. "I'll stay here until you fall asleep."

"I'd like that."

Her father's eyes closed before he finished speaking. Emily sat there, staring at him, trying to understand how the father who'd been bigger than life could be reduced to the frail man who lay in the bed, laboring to breathe, without the strength to sit up. She was going to lose him soon. Even though she'd faced that truth weeks ago, she hadn't fully accepted it. She couldn't imagine life without him. Why had Zeke and Hawk stayed so long? They knew he was sick and very weak. She was angry at them, even though she knew they'd stayed with her father because he wanted it.

He was breathing a little more easily now. If she made sure no one bothered him for the next couple of days, maybe he'd get back some color. One thing was certain. She wasn't going to let Joseph near him. Maybe she'd take Joseph on a ride around the ranch tomorrow. That would give him a chance to see what Texas was like.

Satisfied that her father would sleep soundly until suppertime, Emily got up and quietly left the room.

"I don't see why you want to stay in Texas," Joseph said to Emily. "There's nothing here."

They had been riding for two hours. Even though Emily was worried about her father—he seemed better today—it felt good to get out of the house and back in the saddle.

"There's plenty here," Emily said. "It's just not what you're used to. You'd be more comfortable in a town like Fort Worth."

"I don't call that place a town," Joseph said. "It's more like a collection of saloons and houses of ill repute."

Emily tried hard not to laugh. Only someone like Joseph would call a whorehouse a house of ill repute.

"Why did Bret have to bring that kid along?" Joseph complained. "I can't understand how he puts up with him."

Bret had managed to sweet-talk Bertie into letting Jinx out of his chores so he could ride with them. He'd tossed a loop at every clump of mesquite or juniper within reach. Emily and Joseph had had to give him a wide berth to keep from being struck by the rope he was constantly swinging over his head.

"Jinx was being mistreated when Bret found him," Emily said. "He plans to take him to live with Jake and Isabelle."

"Then why doesn't he leave? Now that I'm here, there's no need for him to stay."

Emily was thoroughly tired of Joseph's company. He'd done little but criticize or belittle everything he saw. He thought the sea of waving grass made for poor graze because it wasn't thick and green like grass in Massachusetts. He said the trees were nothing more than big bushes because they weren't the towering elms he'd known since childhood. His most severe criticism was leveled at the cows. He told her why the breeds favored in Massachusetts were better in every way than longhorns. He told her that if he were in charge of the ranch, he'd fence the range with the recently invented barbed wire.

"I'm sure ranchers will do that in the future," Emily said, hoping to shut him up, "but all this land belonged to the Indians until about ten years ago. Most of West Texas hasn't even been settled yet."

"That's all the more reason you ought to move to Boston and let someone manage this place for you."

Joseph was off again telling her how to arrange her life. He didn't seem to understand it was painful for her to hear, because all his suggestions were meant to be implemented after her father's death.

"We'd better get Bret and Jinx and head back to the house," she said, "or Bertie will have to keep supper warm for us."

"She's your cook," Joseph said. "It's her duty to have dinner ready when you wish."

"She also cooks for the hands and takes care of the house. We're lucky to have her."

Joseph looked ready to argue, but Jinx rode up, followed closely by Bret.

"Did you see me?" Jinx asked Emily. "Mr. Nolan says I can rope another calf tomorrow."

"Better not let Bertie hear that," Emily teased. "She thinks all cowboys are a little bit crazy."

"Mr. Nolan's a cowboy, and he's not crazy," Jinx said.

"Not everybody agrees with you," Bret said with a laugh.

Jinx looked up at Bret with pure adoration in his eyes. Emily didn't understand why Joseph and his father couldn't see that Bret was a wonderful man.

"Can you rope a cow?" Jinx asked Joseph.

"No, and I don't want to."

"I can show you."

"You ought to coil that rope before your horse steps on it and stumbles."

"Mr. Nolan says I handle a rope real good."

"I'm sure *Mr. Nolan* knows all about ropes, but I have better things to do with my time."

"What?" As far as Jinx was concerned, there was nothing more important than learning to be a cowboy.

"I work for a very important company," Joseph informed him. "We make a great deal of money."

"Mr. Nolan has a lot of money, too," Jinx said. "He paid for two baths. Then he left some money for me with Frank at the hotel. Lugo said it was too much money for a bastard like me. He tried to steal it from me. That's why I came here."

"You've got to stop telling people your life history," Bret said to Jinx.

"Why?"

"If they listen to yours, then you have to listen to theirs."

"You can tell me your life history," Jinx said to Joseph. "I'd like to learn how to make a lot of money. Then I could have a house of my own and nobody would have to take care of me."

"You don't need a house of your own," Emily said before Joseph could make a remark she was certain would be rude. "You can stay in my house as long as you want."

"That's okay. Mr. Nolan is going to give me to some very nice people. I wanted to stay with him, but he says he has to go back to Boston. He says I wouldn't like it there."

"No, you would not," Joseph said. "And the people in Boston wouldn't like you if you went around lassoing their bushes."

"Mr. Nolan says there's no cowboys in Boston. He says I'd have to take baths every day, learn not to speak until I'm spoken to, and go to school. I wouldn't like that."

The description didn't appeal to Emily, either.

"When do you plan to head back to Boston?" Joseph asked Bret.

"I haven't decided," Bret said, meeting his cousin's gaze. "There's still the question of Lonnie's disappearance."

"He's gone. How is that a problem?"

"Well, I don't *know* he's gone. There are several things about this whole rustling deal I don't understand. I need to talk to Lonnie and get some answers."

"I'm here now. You don't need to stay for that," Joseph said.

"I'd have thought you'd be headed back to Boston before me."

Emily had known there was no love lost between the cousins, but she was starting to feel like the prize in a game of tug-of-war.

"I don't want him to leave," Jinx said to Joseph. "Neither does Bertie. She wants him to marry Miss Emily."

Jinx could hardly have created more of a sensation if he'd said there was a herd of stampeding cows headed their way. Emily felt her face turn warm with embarrassment. Bret looked like he'd seen a ghost, and Joseph was apparently stunned.

"I don't think Bertie wanted you to tell that," Emily said to Jinx.

"Why? I heard her say it to Mr. Sam. She said—"

"And you most certainly shouldn't repeat what she said to my father."

Jinx looked thoughtful. "I guess I shouldn't tell you what Mr. Sam said, either."

"No, you shouldn't."

"You should get rid of that woman," Joseph said to Emily.

"Bertie has a right to her opinion."

"No servant has a right to an opinion about her employer's private affairs," Joseph declared.

"When will you understand that Texas isn't Boston?" Bret asked. "What's more, it doesn't want to be. We have our own ways of doing things down here."

Emily's breath caught in her throat. Bret had said *we*. He might not realize it, but he identified with Texas rather than Boston. Now she just had to figure out a way to get him to accept it.

"That's fine for people who want to live in Texas," Joseph said, "but Emily is in a class above that."

"I want to live here," Emily said.

"Even if you do, you don't have to be ruled by the conventions and habits of people who aren't your equal."

"Having lived your whole life in Boston, I'm surprised you don't know your history better," Bret said to Joseph.

"What do you mean?"

"The Declaration of Independence. It states that all men are created equal with certain inalienable rights. I think that means nobody's opinion is better than anyone else's."

"No wonder you're still circling on the fringes of Boston society," Joseph snarled.

"Does that mean my opinion is as good as anybody else's?" Jinx asked Bret.

"You need to learn a bit more, but that's exactly what it means."

"He's an orphan!" Joseph exclaimed.

"So was I," Bret said. "You can't expect me to hold that against him."

"You had family. You knew who your parents were."

Bret's expression hardened. "I didn't have a family. In case you've forgotten, they left me in Texas."

"You know what I mean," Joseph said angrily.

"Unfortunately, I know *exactly* what you mean. I've spent the last six years being taught that lesson very well."

"Did you have to go to school for six years?" Jinx asked.

It took Emily a moment to figure out what the boy meant. Bret seemed to know immediately.

"I went to school for more than six years," Bret told Jinx. "There's a lot of stuff a man needs to know when he grows up."

"I don't think I can learn that much," Jinx said.

"You don't have to learn it all at once. Just a little bit at a time, like you've been learning to be a cowboy."

Jinx brightened immediately. "I can learn a lot faster. Let me rope a calf and I'll show you."

Emily decided she was going to miss Jinx. He had a way of brightening her day.

"You'll have to ask Miss Emily. They're her calves. But don't ask her now," Bret said, stalling the question on Jinx's lips.

Jinx spent the rest of the ride back to the ranch pummeling Bret with questions about what he was going to teach him tomorrow. Emily had thought Bret might become impatient, but he seemed amused.

Just watching them made something go soft inside Emily. Joseph looked smart in his formal riding clothes, his white pants spotless, his black boots perfectly polished, but just looking at Bret in his worn jeans and shirt caused heat to pool in her belly. The memory of being in his arms, of his kisses, caused her to feel warm all over.

"Are you feeling all right?" Joseph asked.

She'd forgotten him. "I'm fine. Why do you ask?"

"You look a little flushed. I was worried the heat might have been too much for you."

She'd better keep her gaze away from Bret until they reached the house. She turned to Joseph, determined to listen to him, no matter how boring he was. It was harder than she'd thought it would be. Joseph talked about her plans after her father died.

"Since you want nothing to do with your Abercrombie relations, you'll have to stay with my family."

Thinking about that started her worrying about her father. He'd encouraged her to show Joseph the ranch. And though she hadn't wanted to leave him for so long, she knew he'd rest better if there was no one in the house.

They met Zeke when they were about fifteen minutes from the house and rode in together.

Jinx was still talking when they rode up to the corrals, and everyone dismounted. Bret coached Jinx through unsaddling his horse. The boy was too small to lift the saddle by himself, but he did his best to do everything Bret did. They were taking their saddles to the barn when Emily realized Joseph had walked off, leaving his horse still saddled.

"Where did he go?" Emily asked.

"To the house, I expect," Bret said. "I'm sure he's never had to unsaddle a horse in his life. It probably never crossed his mind he would be expected to do it now."

"Then it's time he learned," Emily said.

"I'll take care of his horse," Bret said. "It'll be easier than trying to make him understand why it's something he needs to do."

"If he was to get stranded away from the ranch, he'd understand quick enough," Zeke said.

"He was telling me last night of some of the changes his father is proposing to make in the company," Bret said. "Everything he said came out of the recommendations I made to Uncle Silas in writing over six months ago. He told me he hadn't looked at them, that he was sending me to Texas because I was the only one who knew how to handle people like me. Now it seems he was only trying to get me out of the way so he could take credit for all the work I did. Then he sent Joseph down here to make sure I didn't do anything to keep him from getting control of Emily's interest in the company."

"You can't let him steal your ideas," Zeke said.

"I don't intend to. I've sent a telegram to Rupert. I discussed the plans with him and my grandmother. They'll look out for my interests until I get back."

Bands of tension circled Emily's chest. How could she possibly convince Bret to stay in Texas when everything he'd worked for was in jeopardy? As Joseph said, Bret didn't need to stay now that he was here.

But Emily didn't want Joseph to stay. She was rapidly starting to dislike him. She intended to ask Bret to handle her inheritance, but how could he do that from Boston?

She didn't know what she could do, but right now she had to check on her father. Once she was certain he was resting comfortably, she'd bend her mind to figuring out how to make Bret stay in Texas. Or at least come back.

Chapter Nineteen

Emily stared into the night sky, hoping it would somehow provide answers to the questions that buzzed about in her head. Bret had gone to talk to his brothers, Bertie and Jinx were in bed, and Joseph had gone to his room. Her father had been asleep for more than an hour, but she was too stirred up to sleep, too restless to remain inside. She'd hoped being outside would restore her calm, that the cooling night air might make her sleep, but she was too aware of the sound of the wind in the tall grass, the faint rustle of trees down by the tiny creek, and occasional sounds from the horses in the corral behind the barn. The night seemed too alive, too filled with movement, with sound.

She couldn't shake the feeling of foreboding that had settled over her. Her father looked better and was more cheerful after his long afternoon of rest. He'd eaten a good dinner and been in a genial mood. He'd even laughed at some of Jinx's more ingenuous remarks. The boy stood in awe of Mr. Sam. The wealth and power of a man who owned a big house and a ranch had assumed almost mythic proportions in his mind.

Joseph had been on his best behavior. Emily had been very tactful when she explained to him that he was responsible for his own horse whenever he went riding. He'd promised to remember and even thanked Bret. He'd been charming during dinner and made a point of complimenting Bertie.

Bertie's sniff had indicated she wasn't impressed.

Jinx had bubbled over with high spirits until Bertie sent him off to bed with visions of himself becoming a legend in Texas for his skill with a rope.

Bret hadn't acted like himself. He'd spoken when spoken to, even laughed at Jinx, but Emily could tell his mind was elsewhere. She supposed he was thinking about his uncle trying to take credit for his ideas, and trying to decide just how soon he could leave. She was certain he'd wanted to leave the moment he heard what his uncle was trying to do, but he probably didn't want to leave while Joseph was here. Bret didn't trust his cousin. The right to vote her twenty-five percent was vital to his success, and he wouldn't do anything to jeopardize his deal with her and her father. Besides, Joseph had been making an open play to have his father handle Emily's inheritance.

She sighed inwardly. She'd have to reassure Bret that even if he left now, she wouldn't go back on her promise. Even though she felt guilty about his staying, she couldn't force herself to let him go. Not before she told him she was in love with him. Not before she made him understand his real home and family were in Texas. Would he believe her? He'd spent virtually his whole life planning what he'd do when he went back to Boston. She couldn't expect him to turn his back on all of that now.

If he wouldn't stay in Texas, would she go to Boston? She didn't see how she could endure that. She could have a horse, but she'd have no reason to train it, or thousands of unfenced acres to ride over. She couldn't imagine living in a place where the streets were paved with cobblestones, where iron horseshoes and iron-rimmed wagon wheels made horrendous noise all day, and the voices of thousands of people echoed through the night. She couldn't imagine living where houses packed together crowded out the sunlight.

Nor could she imagine being hemmed in by the rules and customs of Boston society. Being relegated to a position where she had to defer to her husband on everything—even a husband like Bret—was something she couldn't endure. No, she couldn't go to Boston. It would kill her.

She was just as certain that Bret found it impossible to give up everything he'd worked toward his whole life. His desire to reach that goal was so strong, it had pulled him away from the only real family he'd ever had, the only place where he'd been happy. It was foolish to believe he'd give it up for a woman he didn't even love.

And he didn't love her. He'd held her in his arms, kissed her, but he'd never attempted to make love to her. Maybe she'd have to wait until he took her to Galveston. By then he might have succeeded in proving the ideas for modernizing Abbott & Abercrombie were his, might have achieved the respect and acceptance he wanted. Maybe then . . .

She was kidding herself. Success would be all the more reason for him to stay in Boston, all the less reason to be interested in a strong-willed woman with a ranch in the wilds of Texas. And once he'd succeeded, he wouldn't need the voting rights to her stock anymore. She'd have nothing to hold him but his promise to come back to Texas for four months every year until she found a husband.

She probably wouldn't hold him to that. It would be too difficult to see him after eight long months of waiting, knowing that at the end of winter he'd go back to Boston. It would be impossible if he married and brought his wife with him. And sooner or later he would marry. So it would be best to release him from his promise and never see him again.

Emily stopped at the spot where she and Bret had talked that evening not long ago, where they'd watched the raccoon family cross the trail—where they'd held hands and kissed. It was here, on the side of this hill, looking at a sky spangled with countless stars, that she'd begun to hope Bret would come to love her, that his kisses meant more than friendship, more even than liking. It was here she'd come to realize he belonged in Texas.

She sighed. She wondered if it would help if she contacted his family, told Isabelle he was miserable in Boston. If anyone could get him to change his mind, it would be Jake or Isabelle. Though he'd left their ranch, he had enormous respect and great affection for them.

She sighed again. She should be thinking about her horses, about the ranch, planning her future, not standing here staring at the sky. Bertie would say she was woolgathering, but she knew—

"A penny for your thoughts."

Emily nearly jumped a foot at the sound of Bret's voice behind her.

"Sorry. I didn't mean to sneak up on you."

"I guess I was so deep in thought I didn't hear you."

"Worried about your father?"

"Some."

"I checked on him before I came out. He seems to be sleeping peacefully."

How could she not fall in love with Bret when, in addition to looking like the man of her dreams, he had trained her horses, caught the rustlers, and worried about her father almost as much as she did? And that didn't count not trying to force her to go to Boston even though he knew it would make his uncle angry, or taking responsibility for Jinx because no one else would. She wondered what her father had said when Bertie told him she thought Emily ought to marry Bret.

"Did you have a good talk with Zeke and Hawk?"

"There wasn't a lot to talk about. They know more about ranches than I'll ever know."

They were only adopted brothers, but they'd do anything they could for Bret. She didn't understand why he didn't know that was so much better than any relationship he was likely to have with his uncle and cousin.

"I was hoping you'd be here to help me." She was tired of beating around the bush. She wanted Bret to know she liked him. "All of us have sort of gotten used to having you around. *I* have gotten used to it, and I like it."

Bret took both of her hands in his, looked down into her eyes. "You know I have to go back to Boston. That's where my life is, just as yours is in Texas."

"I think you're wrong." She was going to put it on the line. "I know why you feel you have to go back to Boston, but you're not happy there. You've admitted that your uncle is never going to accept you, and it's clear that Joseph feels the same way. You belong in Texas. Here, everybody likes you and is impressed by your abilities. But most of all, I know you miss your adopted family."

Bret tried to pull away but she wouldn't let him.

"Do you know how often you mention Jake or Isabelle? You love them as much as they love you. You feel the same way about your adopted brothers. When you needed help, you didn't hesitate to send for Zeke and Hawk. You've mentioned every other member of your adopted family with affection, usually a smile at some memory. They're your *real* family. You belong with them."

Bret closed his eyes and rolled his head back. "You don't understand."

"Then explain it to me so I can understand it, so I don't think you're making the biggest mistake of your life."

"Everything you've said is true. All of it."

"Then why—"

"What you can't see, what no one—including my adopted family—has ever been able to understand, is that there is a need inside that chews at me constantly. It never gives me a minute's peace. I know the Abbotts don't love me, that they're probably responsible for my parents' deaths. If they hadn't disowned her, my mother wouldn't have been alone and without a doctor when I was born. If they hadn't driven my father out of New England, he wouldn't have been hanged in Texas. If they hadn't refused to take me in after he died, I wouldn't have been forced to live on the streets, to beg and steal for food."

Bret's feelings were so intense, he was shaking. Emily could see the pain in his face. Even more clearly, she could see the anger he'd never allowed to show.

"I need—*I have to find*—some way of forcing them to realize they made a mistake." He stopped, took a deep breath, broke her hold on his hands, and stepped back. "I know that is not an admirable goal. I've tried, but I can't change it." He took a long, slow breath. "I don't want to destroy them. I don't even want to hurt them. I just want them to know they made a mistake."

"Do you think they will admit that?"

"No. I think I've learned to accept that, but I can't accept Uncle Silas stealing my plans. Can't you see? He's doing it all over again. I can't let him get away with it."

Emily was enough of a fighter to understand how Bret must feel, how much his uncle's betrayal must be hurting him. She wanted him to win, to feel he'd finally gotten a measure of satisfaction, but she doubted it would ever happen. Even if he succeeded in proving his uncle was a liar, the Abbotts would never accept him. That hurt would never heal until he realized he didn't need their acceptance. From the intensity with which he spoke, she doubted that would ever happen.

"When will you leave?"

"Soon. I have to take Jinx to Jake and Isabelle."

"He can stay here. Bertie has grown very fond of him, and I'd miss him."

"He's my responsibility, not yours."

"Well, I'm taking him on, so that's the end of it. Will you come back in December?"

"I don't go back on my promises."

She couldn't stand the distance separating them. She walked over to him, put her hand on his arm. "I know you don't. I was just trying to reassure myself."

He turned to her. "You shouldn't be worrying about me. You need to start thinking about finding a husband."

"I don't need to look for the man I want to be my husband. I've already found him."

Bret seemed to freeze in place. She couldn't tell what was in his mind because his face had become a mask, his eyes hooded and dark. Gradually he seemed to thaw, come back to life.

"You can't want me for a husband. I'd make you miserable. You know why I have to go back to Boston, and I understand why you could never live there. Besides, you're a wealthy woman. I have nothing. Your father wouldn't be doing his duty to you if he allowed me to marry you."

"My father thinks you're a fine man. Jinx thinks you practically walk on water, and you're the first man Bertie has ever really liked. And don't forget Ida's boys begging you to sleep out with them. Practically everybody you meet thinks you're a wonderful person."

Emily was prepared for an argument. She was prepared for him to walk away. She was not prepared for Bret taking her in his arms and kissing her so thoroughly her head was spinning. Just as abruptly, he broke the kiss and stepped away from her.

"I shouldn't have done that."

She had to catch her breath before she could say, "I liked it. It gives me hope you might like me as much as I like you."

"I have no right to like you, to love you," Bret said. "I should have gone back to Boston before I let any of this happen."

"You couldn't know I would fall in love with you."

Bret took a moment to absorb what she'd said. "No, but I did know *I* was in danger of falling in love with *you*."

She moved a step closer to him. Her heart felt too large for her chest, as if it were pushing out against her rib cage, demanding more room. She'd been so involved with her father's illness, the rustlers, Lonnie's betrayal, even Jinx and Joseph, she hadn't realized how much she'd come to depend on Bret, how deep her feelings were becoming, until she was already in love with him. She'd had no warning, no time to protect her heart, no time to reason away the feelings she'd first taken to be friendship.

But none of that changed the fact that Bret was exactly the man she wanted in her life. She hadn't wanted him to come to Texas, but she'd liked him almost from the first. She hadn't wanted him in her life, but she'd started to depend on him just as quickly. Now it was impossible to think of her days without him. He fitted into her life as though the space had been made to measure for him.

She wondered if she was a fool to let herself be drawn into the battle of emotions that ruled Bret's life. She'd seen enough of men to know that for some, the need to satisfy an inner goal was more powerful than love. They would sacrifice loyalties, friends, family, even their own lives for it. She didn't know if Bret felt that way. If he did, there was nothing she could do to change it.

"Do you love me?" Her voice was a thread.

Bret's mouth opened, but no words came out. He tried a second time, but still no sound. She could feel a cold chill begin to spread through her. He didn't love her, and he didn't know how to tell her. Was he choking on a lie, or on the words he knew would hurt her? It didn't matter. Either would be equally painful.

"I'm sorry," she said. "It was unfair of me to ask that question."

"You had every right." Bret kept his distance, seemed even more uncomfortable than before. "I haven't answered because I don't want to hurt you."

It was hard to swallow, but she managed without choking. "There's no rule that says you have to love someone just because they love you."

Bret stepped forward, took her hands in his. "That's not the problem. I *do* love you."

Emily had been jerked back from the edge of despair so abruptly that for a moment she felt dizzy, disoriented, but she understood enough to realize Bret had said he loved her.

"Hold me."

When Bret hesitated, she stepped forward and threw her arms around him. He resisted a moment longer before enfolding her in an embrace. She didn't have words to describe how wonderful it felt to have his arms around her, to know he loved her. She'd never believed a man was necessary to her life, to her happiness. No matter how handsome or strong, none had even made a dent in her feeling of self-sufficiency. She wasn't sure Bret was necessary, but she knew she wanted him, *needed* him.

"I shouldn't be doing this," he whispered against her hair.

"I want you to."

"It'll just make it harder when I have to leave."

"I don't want to think about that now."

"We have to."

"I don't," she murmured against his chest. "All I have to think about, all I *want* to think about, is that you love me. All I want you to do is hold me."

His arms tightened around her. "That's not all I want to do," he whispered. He withdrew one hand from her back, placed it under her chin, and tilted her head up until she could look into his eyes. Even in the shadowy darkness, they seemed to glisten. Pinpricks of light like tiny stars gleamed down at her. "I've wanted to do this for so long it hurts."

His kiss was slow and gentle. He seemed to be tasting her mouth, exploring it, consuming it, inviting her to do the same. She'd never kissed anybody other than Bret, but her response was automatic, instinctive. Maybe that was what happened when two people were in love. They were so attuned to each other, they didn't need words or past experience. They simply meshed.

He was just the right height to bend down and kiss her, her arms just the right length to encircle his neck. He had just the right strength to make her feel safe and secure. She had just the right need for his kisses.

She rested her head against his chest and sighed. "I was afraid you didn't love me."

"It would have been much easier if you didn't love me."

"I don't want to talk. I just want you to hold me, to make me feel safe and loved."

It was silly to think she could face the future alone. It wasn't enough that she had Bertie, even Ida and Charlie. They couldn't stand beside her, stand with her, the way Bret could. She wanted someone whose life would become so entwined with hers, their lives would become one, their needs and wants the same. She'd always thought of herself as independent of any need for a man. Bret had awakened a need in her she didn't know she had.

There would be difficulties to be faced tomorrow and the days after that, but she refused to think of anything except Bret's arms around her, the warmth of his body flowing into hers, the heat building up inside her so rapidly it threatened to spill over.

She couldn't get close enough to Bret. She wanted to crawl inside his clothes, inside his skin. It was an itch she couldn't scratch, because it was buried deep out of reach. Instinct told her that only Bret could relieve the tension.

Lifting her head from his chest, she looked up at him. He looked so troubled, she wanted to kiss his worries away. Nothing was so difficult that they couldn't figure it out together. If they loved each other enough, if they—

"Emily." It was Joseph's voice.

She didn't want to see Joseph, talk to him, even think about him. He was part of the problem that kept Bret from staying in Texas.

"Emily. Bret. Are you out there? Can you hear me?"

He sounded upset, but Emily and Bret kept their silence, hoping he would go away.

"Emily, you've got to come to the house immediately. Something is wrong with your father."

Emily's feet were flying before the last of Joseph's words left his mouth. Bret was beside her, her hand held tightly in his.

Emily's body couldn't cry anymore, but her soul was awash in tears. She had known her father was going to die, but the reality of it was more overwhelming than she could ever have believed. Even though Bret had never left her side, even though Bertie had held her in her arms and cried with her, she felt bereft and utterly alone.

Her father had apparently suffered a massive heart attack. By the time she reached the house, he was past suffering. His face was no longer creased with care or distorted by pain. His features had relaxed until he was the man she'd known all her life. Now he was gone. She felt that her support had been pulled out from under her.

"We can't keep on sitting here," Bertie said softly. "We've got to get your father ready for burial."

Emily had sat by her father's bedside all night. Jinx had tried to stay awake but had finally gone to sleep in a chair by the window. Joseph had stayed with her until he yawned so much, Bret sent him off to his bed. Bret hadn't spoken since.

"I don't want to let him go," Emily murmured.

"You can't hold on to him anymore," Bertie said. "It's time to let him be with your mother."

Her mother was buried in a plot between the ranch house and the small stream. Emily's father had put an iron fence around the gravesite with enough room for at least a dozen other members of his family to rest alongside him and his wife someday. She knew the men would prepare the grave today, but it was up to her to decide when her father would be buried.

Emily thought of Ida and Charlie. They'd want to pay their respects to Sam Abercrombie. They'd lived on the ranch for so many years, they felt like family. Then there were the ranchers who participated with him in the roundups, the people he knew in Fort Worth, friends elsewhere. Waiting for Ida's family would mean two more days, the ranchers another day after that. That was too long.

"We'll bury him this evening," she said to Bertie. "Will you get him ready?"

"I'll do it." Bret said.

"I couldn't ask you to do that," Emily said. "You—"

Bertie put a restraining hand on her shoulder. "I think Mr. Sam would like that."

Bertie was probably right. Her father had been a modest man.

"What do you want him to wear?" Bertie asked Emily.

How could she think of anything as unimportant as clothes when her father lay dead? It didn't matter what he wore. He was gone and was never coming back. She would never see him smile again, hear him call her name. He would—

Emily caught herself before she broke down again. She had to think. She had to make decisions. She'd have more than enough time to cry after the funeral.

"You decide," she said to Bertie. "Make it something nice, but not fancy."

"I've got a nice suit all pressed and ready," Bertie said. "A fresh white shirt, too."

Emily kissed Bertie's cheek. "I don't know what I'd do without you."

"Probably hire some flighty female who would burn the biscuits and serve the beef underdone." Bertie stood. "Come. You need to lie down for a while. You didn't sleep a wink all night."

"I don't want to lie down. I can't sleep."

"I know, but you need to rest. It won't be easy to bury your father."

Emily stood, turned to Bret. She didn't know how to say what was in her heart. His presence had meant so much. His offer to prepare her father's body for burial was as generous as it was unexpected. She reached for his hand. "One of these days I hope I'll be able to tell you what your being here has meant to me."

"There was no one to stand by me when they hanged my father," he said. "I think I know."

Every time she thought something truly terrible, something almost unbearable, was happening to her, she learned that something even worse had happened to Bret.

"You need some rest, too."

"There'll be plenty of time later."

He kissed her on the cheek, then glanced at Bertie, who took that as a signal to lead Emily out of her father's bedroom.

The morning sunlight poured in the windows facing the east, but the house was eerily quiet. There were no smells of breakfast, no aromas of bacon and coffee to start her mouth watering. No sounds of the cowhands downing their breakfast, talking amongst themselves about the day ahead. No Bertie bustling about the kitchen, and no Jinx dashing about with childlike energy. It seemed the whole world had stopped to show respect for her father.

"I think you are right to bury your father tonight," Bertie said. "If you want, you can do something with everybody else later."

"I don't know. I'll think about it."

She couldn't decide anything right now. She wanted to talk to Bret, to feel his arms around her. She wanted to lean on him and let his strength support her. She felt he was all she had left, and she didn't mean to let him go.

Chapter Twenty

Bret stood outside Emily's bedroom door unable to decide what to do. Everyone in the house had gone to bed and fallen into exhausted sleep, but Emily was awake and crying. His heart urged him to comfort her even if it meant entering her bedroom. His head warned him he could hardly do anything more dangerous.

It hadn't been a difficult task to ready Sam for burial. Jinx had insisted upon helping. Despite his youth, he seemed to understand the significance of what they were doing and was uncharacteristically quiet. For himself, Bret found it was surprisingly difficult. He hadn't realized how attached he'd become to the old man. His emotions had been very close to the surface all day.

"Is he really dead?" Jinx had asked.

"Yes."

"He doesn't look dead," Jinx had said. "He just looks like he's asleep."

Hawk had supervised the men who dug the grave.

The ground was hard and rocky. It had taken all of the men working in shifts to get it finished by late afternoon. Emily had decided she wanted to inter her father as the sun sank in the west.

They had stood in a solemn group around the grave and inside the iron fence. Emily had tried to lead the brief service, but her voice failed. It was seeing Joseph about to offer his help—and the withering glance from Bertie—that had spurred Bret to step forward.

Afterwards everyone had gone up to the house for supper. All the cowhands spoke to Emily before they returned to the bunkhouse. Bret hoped it would be a comfort to her to know her father was so well liked by the men who'd worked for him. Joseph had behaved well, seeming to be genuinely sorry that Sam had died. Emily appreciated his comfort, but Bertie continued to regard him as she might a coiled snake.

But it had been Jinx who'd offered her the greatest comfort. Bret was certain Jinx didn't know what he was doing, that he was looking for comfort more than giving it, but he'd stood next to Emily from the time she emerged from her bedroom until he was sent to bed. He'd held her hand. He'd put his arm around her. Maybe knowing he was in need of comfort had given her something to think about other than her own loss.

Things had been awkward when they all returned to the house. Everything had been said, but everybody seemed to feel it was wrong to just disappear. Finally, Emily had said she was tired and was going to her room. Ten minutes after she'd left, only Bertie, Joseph, and Bret remained.

"How long can you stay?" Bertie had asked Bret.

"I ought to leave in the morning," he replied.

"You have to stay for the reading of the will," Joseph had said.

"Why? Emily is his only heir."

"It may be a formality, but it's a necessary part of settling her father's affairs."

Bret was certain Joseph expected that his father would be designated to handle Emily's financial affairs. Since the voting rights to the shares in Abbott & Abercrombie was Joseph's and his father's real concern, Bret was certain there'd be a lot said that would make his return to Boston even more difficult.

But all of that would be taken care of tomorrow. He couldn't keep standing at Emily's door, undecided as to whether to go to his room or check on her. Unable to hear her crying and do nothing about it, Bret knocked softly on Emily's door.

"Who is it?" Her words were muffled, barely understandable.

"It's Bret. Are you all right?"

"I'm fine."

"You don't sound like it."

She started crying again. "I'm okay, really."

He couldn't stand it. He opened the door. Emily was sitting up in her bed, surrounded by a halo of light from the small oil lamp on the table next to her. Dark shadows shrouded the edges of the room, making it appear that the lighted area was detached from its surroundings, that she existed in a reality all her own.

He entered the room and eased the door closed behind him.

"I couldn't sleep knowing you were so unhappy," he said as he approached the bed.

"I knew Dad was going to die, but I didn't expect it to be so soon," Emily said through her tears. "I'll get used to it, but it'll take a while. He was all I had."

"You've still got Bertie," Bret said, drawing near the bed. "I'm sure Ida would come stay with you as long as you need her."

Emily lowered the handkerchief from her tear-filled eyes and looked up at Bret. "Do I still have you?"

Hoping he wasn't promising more than he could fulfill, he sat down on the edge of the bed and took Emily's hand in his. "You have me for as long as you need me."

Emily's hand gripped him hard. "What if I never stop needing you?"

Bret didn't know how to answer that question. Loving someone, he'd come to realize, didn't solve life's problems. In their case, it had just created more.

"It wouldn't be normal if you didn't feel lost, even abandoned, right now. But you'll start to feel stronger in a couple of days. Before long, you'll be raring to get back in the saddle, back to training your horses. You're a very strong woman."

"I don't feel strong."

The appeal in her eyes was so potent, the hurt so deep, all he wanted to do was take her in his arms and hold her until the sadness went away. He didn't because he was afraid if he did, he might never let her go. He'd thought he had his feelings under control, but that was before he was forced to watch Emily suffer. Dark circles around her eyes caused them to appear sunken into her head. They were slightly swollen from crying, but her tear-stained cheeks were still creamy without a single red blotch. She had let her hair down from its usual bun and allowed it to fall over her shoulders. Somehow it made her look more vulnerable. Even helpless.

"Do you want me to stay a little while?" he asked.

"I never want you to leave."

That was more than he'd bargained for, but his response to her plea was something else that would be left until tomorrow.

She came to him in a rush, her arms around his

neck, her head on his shoulder, as the tears started again. He didn't know it was possible for a person to cry so much without running dry. He'd been nearly overwhelmed by heartbreak and loneliness after his father died, but fear had locked his tears inside his heart. Years later, when it was at last safe to cry, the tears had been absorbed into his determination to return to Boston.

But Emily had no such ghosts, no such fears, no such loneliness. She was free to mourn. Later she would be free to take up her life where she'd left off. But for tonight she needed him. And though he didn't like to admit it, he needed her to need him, to want him, to look to him for comfort, for courage to face the days ahead.

Almost as a reflex, his arms tightened around her as he kissed the top of her head. Her hair felt soft against his cheek, against his lips. In the semidarkness, her hair looked almost black, the blond highlights barely noticeable. He'd never thought of Emily as delicate, but through the thin material of her nightgown, her body felt almost fragile. She was so soft, she fit so well against him, he had to close his mind to the thought she was meant to be in his arms. He reminded himself that the courses of their lives were too far apart ever to join.

He asked himself why he couldn't make himself stick with that thought. Did he have to go back to Boston? Was it possible to convince her to go with him? Could he be happy if she stayed in Texas?

The woman in his arms had caused him to question the nature of the drive that had imprisoned as well as supported him during the last twenty years.

"I'm soaking your clothes," Emily murmured.

He was wearing only a robe with nothing underneath. "I don't care." He wouldn't care if she drenched him as long as it made her feel less miserable.

"I'm sure you don't want to be here."

"I wouldn't have come if I didn't."

She gave him a gentle squeeze. "I don't know why your family doesn't adore you. I could give them a dozen reasons why you're the most wonderful man I know."

Bret chuckled, though he didn't know why. "You can put it all in a letter to my uncle."

"He doesn't deserve you."

Bret agreed. But the question in his mind at the moment was, what did he deserve, and could it possibly include Emily?

"Are you feeling better?" he asked.

"I am now that you're here."

"If you're better—" He started to release her, but her arms tightened around him.

"Don't leave yet."

He knew he shouldn't stay. Things he wanted to do, things he *longed* to do, crowded his mind. He told himself they were all inappropriate during this time of grief, but he couldn't stop himself. He held a beautiful woman in his arms, a woman who loved him, a woman he loved in return. It was impossible for a young man not to think of making love to her, just as it was impossible for a man of honor to take advantage of her at a time such as this. He would hold her and comfort her. He would stay with her as long as she needed him, but he would leave without dishonoring her or himself.

"Could you lie down with me?" Emily asked. "I'm sitting at an awkward angle."

Bret's heart nearly jumped into his throat. He couldn't stop his body from going rigid. She was asking him to do the one thing he couldn't do and remain in control of himself. "I'll keep you awake."

"I can't sleep, and I don't want to be alone."

"You've got a house full of people. You're not alone."

She pulled away. "If you don't want to stay with me—"

"It's not that," Bret said, desperate to think of something to say that wouldn't require him to explain she was pushing him to the edge of his self-control. "Bertie should be the one sitting with you."

"I don't want Bertie. I want you."

How could he leave after that? But how could he stay, knowing his body was stiff with desire? Emily moved to the other side of the double bed, making plenty of room for him. Maybe, if he could keep his distance, he could make it through the next half hour without losing his honor. Making sure to keep space between him and Emily, he swung his legs onto the bed and propped himself up against the headboard.

"Wouldn't you be more comfortable lying down?" Emily asked.

"I'm liable to go to sleep." That was absolutely impossible, but Emily didn't need to know it.

"That'll be okay."

His laugh was mirthless. "I don't want to think what Bertie would do if she came in and found me asleep in your bed." And if by some miracle Bertie didn't kill him, Hawk and Zeke would.

"You said it was okay for friends to kiss. Surely it's harmless to lie side by side in the same bed."

The last bit of his control snapped. "Are you trying to drive me crazy, or are you so naive you don't understand what you're saying? You said you loved me. I said I loved *you*. This is not a matter of friends lying down on a hillside to take a nap after lunch. We're in bed together. Even in the wilds of Texas, that means trouble."

"I don't want to drive you crazy. I just want to be next to you, to have you hold me."

"That's what I want, too." However, it wasn't *all* he wanted.

She looked at him, questioning, waiting for him to make the first move. Yielding to the inevitable, Bret put his arm around her shoulders. With a contented sigh, Emily moved over until their sides touched.

"You know I love you, don't you?" she asked.

"I know."

"I don't mean like a friend. I love you like someone I want to spend the rest of my life with."

"Emily, we've already been through this. Our lives are—"

"They don't have to remain separate." Emily sat up and turned so she could face him. "You don't like Boston, and your family doesn't like you. You're happy in Texas and you love your adopted family. You shouldn't go back to Boston. You should stay here."

If she had any idea how much he wished he could stay in Texas, wished he could spend his life with her, she'd never stop trying to convince him to change his mind. "I know you don't understand, but I've known my whole life what I have to do. I probably stayed in Texas longer than I should because I was leaving people who loved me for a family that had rejected me at every opportunity."

Emily had risen to her knees. "What about you, your life, the things you want? You can't live your whole life just to avenge an old injustice."

"You don't understand."

Emily thumped him on the shoulders with the heel of her palm. "I *do* understand. My father was disowned by his family. They wouldn't answer his letters, acknowledge his marriage or my birth. It hurt Dad, but he was determined to live his life for himself, not for someone else."

"Isabelle said practically the same thing. Jake warned me not to expect them to change, but I had to leave."

"Okay, so you don't care about yourself, but it's not fair to ruin my life because of something your stupid uncle did twenty years ago."

Bret opened his mouth, but nothing came out.

"You know I love you," Emily insisted. "I wouldn't have said anything if you didn't love me, too. If you were going to turn your back and go off to Boston never to return, you shouldn't have said anything. Teasing me with something I can't have is cruel."

"You knew I had to go back to Boston," Bret said, desperate to get out from under the weight of guilt. "I told you that from the beginning." He could see the tears pool in Emily's eyes, spill over and run down her cheeks.

"I thought falling in love with me would change that," Emily said through her tears.

He didn't know how to explain to her that the present couldn't change the past, didn't cancel out the terrible sense of injustice that wouldn't let him rest. He couldn't ignore it. He couldn't explain it away. All attempts to get around it had failed. Only by facing it could he free himself from this unbearable burden. "I have to go back to Boston," he said. "There are things I have to do there if I'm ever going to be happy."

"If you loved me like I love you, you wouldn't leave me." Emily's tears began to flow faster.

"Would you come to Boston with me?" He knew it wouldn't work, but he couldn't stop himself from asking.

"You know I hate Boston. Besides, my family doesn't want me any more than yours wants you. And Joseph only wants my share of Abbott and Abercrombie."

"Once I've finished what I set out to do, maybe I can come back," Bret said.

"You won't come back, because you don't really love me."

It would make it easier for her to forget him if she believed that, but he couldn't tell her that lie. A man could be expected to give up only so much, even for an old and grievous wound. Taking her by the shoulders, Bret pulled her to him. He leaned forward and kissed her hard on the mouth. "I never wanted to hurt you," he said. "I tried not to fall in love with you because I knew it wouldn't work, but I couldn't help myself."

"I don't believe you really love me."

"How can I prove it to you?"

"Make love to me."

If she'd asked him to marry Bertie, he couldn't have been more surprised. "I could never do that."

Emily shrugged his hands off her shoulders and moved back. "Then you don't love me."

"You don't know what you're asking."

"I know exactly what I'm asking." Despite her grief over her father's death, she looked determined and clear-eyed.

"When you fall in love and marry—"

"I'm not going to get married, because I'll never fall in love again."

"You can't know what. When you go to Galveston—"

"I'm not going to Galveston. You can still vote my shares, but there's no point."

"I don't give a damn about your shares. I promised your father—"

"My father is dead. I'm the one who's alive."

"You're too young and too lovely to give up on having a husband and family."

"My parents fell in love the first time they saw each other. Why do you think I'd be any different? I love you. I want to marry you, be your wife, have your children."

"Stop."

"Why? Because you want the same thing, or because you've been lying to me and your conscience is bothering you?"

Bret was going crazy from the conflicts inside him, but one thing he did understand. He had to convince Emily he loved her. Before he knew what he was doing, he'd pushed her down on the bed and was leaning over her. "I love you so much it's tearing me up inside. I didn't want to love you. I fought it as hard as I could, but I couldn't help myself."

Then he kissed her. It wasn't a gentle kiss. It wasn't even rough. It was brutal. Behind it was all his frustration and anger, driven by a need for her that gripped his guts and twisted until he wanted to scream. It was like a demon trapped inside him, fighting, struggling, ripping, and tearing.

Instead of being shocked by the force of Bret's kiss, Emily was thrilled. It showed she'd finally made a crack in that ironclad self-control Bret wrapped around himself. She knew that was the only way she'd ever get him to admit he wanted to stay in Texas, that loving her was more important than settling a score with his family. But she didn't want him to forget it altogether. She wanted them to face his family together.

She held him tight when he tried to pull away. She liked the feel of his body pressed hard against her, his arms resting on the bed on either side. She felt penned in, captured, safe, desired. She'd been desired before. She had seen it in the eyes of men when they looked at her, but their desire had left her untouched. It was flattering, but she didn't care about the flattery of strangers.

Everything was different with Bret. She wanted him to be so attracted to her that all other women ceased to exist for him. She wanted to inspire passion because for the first time she felt passionate about a man. That first kiss had been a revelation. Each succeeding kiss had reached deeper and deeper, until finally piercing a well of passion, of femininity, of the need that had been waiting untapped for the right man to come along. Once the reservoir had been uncapped, there was no possibility of containing it.

Nor did she want to contain it. For the first time in her life, she was in love. She wanted to enjoy every minute of it, experience every sensation, wallow in every dream, explore every errant thought. She didn't want anything to escape unnoticed, untried, undreamed of. Ida had said falling in love was wonderful, but nothing had prepared Emily for the sheer immensity of its wonderfulness. She'd been only half awake all her life, her body experiencing only half of what happened around her, her mind sleepwalking through life.

Now everything was in vivid color, exciting detail, and instantly burned into her memory forever. She wasn't young enough to think that everything would be perfect, but she was young enough to want to experience everything without restraint. She'd save self-control for later—if she ever wanted it at all. She'd seen what it had done to Bret, and she didn't like it.

"Mama once told me a person should never fight being in love," Emily said. "She said true love doesn't come along very often. She said when it does, that couple is truly blessed."

Bret held her in his arms, his head buried in her shoulder. "Your parents were very fortunate," he said. "Not every pair of lovers is so lucky."

Emily made him lift his head until she could look into his eyes. "You don't think we're lucky?" In response to her question, his expression was pained.

"Love is never about just two people. It spills over into everything and everybody in their lives."

"I don't want to think about anybody but us. Maybe that's selfish of me, but I don't care. I don't want our love ruined or diluted by my problems or yours. I want it to be perfect. I *need* it to be perfect, at least for a few hours."

"Are you sure?" Bret asked. "You know the world won't go away."

"We've only just faced the fact that we love each other. We tried to push it away before we even knew what it was like. We have to give our love a chance to be shared, to grow, to gain meaning before we can know whether it's infatuation or something strong enough to last a lifetime."

"Are you sure?" he repeated. He didn't sound like he was.

"Yes, I'm very sure."

For a moment Bret didn't move, just looked into her eyes as though he could find the answer there to some unspoken question. Finally, apparently having found the assurance he was looking for, his arms tightened around her body and he kissed her.

Chapter Twenty-one

Emily wondered why she'd never wanted to kiss a man before Bret, why she'd never suspected that kissing could be so wonderful. Maybe it wasn't just the kiss. Maybe it was that Bret held her in a strong embrace. Maybe it was the feel of a powerful, virile male body pressed up against her. Maybe it was knowing that Bret was so strongly attracted to her he couldn't stop himself. Maybe it didn't matter what it was. All that really mattered was that she loved Bret, he loved her, and she was in his arms.

She responded eagerly to his kiss, pulling him down to her until his weight rested on her body. She couldn't get enough of his nearness. She had begun a journey in which every step was new, filled with wonder and excitement, a journey in which she keenly anticipated each step in hopes it would link her life more inextricably with that of the man she loved.

Emily had thought Bret would break his kiss after a few seconds. Instead, his attentions grew more intense. She loved the feel of his arms around her, his hard chest pressing against her breasts, the weight of his powerful thigh against her hip. When his tongue pushed between her teeth and delved into her mouth, she was so shocked it took her a moment to respond, a moment during which her body—impatient with the brain's slowness—took over. Every muscle strained to push her harder against Bret as her tongue attempted to make its way past his tongue and into his mouth.

Success sent a chill all through her. Bret's tongue dueled with hers in a sinuous dance that caused her heart to beat faster and her breath to come in short gasps. When they finally broke apart, she felt exhausted.

Her senses were in such an uproar she didn't realize that Bret's hand had cupped her breast until he began to massage her nipple through the thin material of her nightgown. The jolt she felt caused her breath to catch in her throat. For a moment it was impossible to swallow. She thought she might pass out when her muscles relaxed enough for her to breathe and to swallow. A soft moan escaped her.

"Do you want me to stop?" Bret asked.

Incapable of speaking just then, she shook her head.

"Do you like this?" Bret asked.

Nodding, she reached up to cup the side of his face with one hand. She hadn't realized how rough his face became when he hadn't shaved. She liked it. He seemed like a man who spent his days in the open, on horseback, overseeing his domain, rather than one who spent his days inside an office adding and subtracting numbers.

She didn't object when he unbuttoned the top of her nightgown and slipped his hand inside. His palm felt rough against the softness of her breast. Her nipple was so sensitive that when the ridged skin of his fingertip rubbed across it, she nearly rose off the bed in sweet excitement, nearly every muscle in her body tensing. She hadn't known her body could feel like this. Now she knew she wanted more.

Bret undid a few more buttons. "Sit up so I can slip your nightgown down to your waist."

Emily was sure Bret knew what he was doing, but she was still nervous. This was a big step for her. She hesitated so long he drew back.

"If you want me to stop—"

"No." She raised herself into a sitting position.

She allowed Bret to push her nightgown off her shoulders, so that it pooled around her. Her body tensed, anticipating his touch, but when it came it wasn't what she expected. Bret leaned forward to drop kisses on her shoulder. It must have been instinct that caused her to tilt her head to one side so he could leave a trail of kisses along her neck. The tensed muscles let go, and she felt herself melting back onto the bed.

Bret devoured her with his eyes. "You're beautiful," he murmured, "more beautiful than I imagined."

She'd never thought of her breasts as beautiful, but then she'd never guessed they were capable of giving her such incredible pleasure. She certainly wouldn't have guessed Bret would look at her as if seeing a woman for the first time.

He looked for so long without moving to touch her, she was caught by surprise when she felt his hands gently cup each breast. A sharp intake of breath signaled her body's response to his touch, to the amazing sensations that radiated out from her breasts, causing small bursts of heat to scatter throughout her body. The sensations increased incrementally as Bret gently massaged her nipples. Then she went into orbit when he touched her nipple with his tongue. How could she have lived so long and still have no real knowledge of her body? It was as if something had been broken or unconnected. Whatever it was, Bret was putting it together, piece by piece.

When he took her nipple into his mouth and sucked gently, it was like throwing logs on a fire and watching the flames go a little higher each time. She wondered how high they could go before they consumed her. When he took her nipple between his teeth, she was convinced she was about to find out. She was certain the moan that burst from between her lips was loud enough to wake everyone in the house.

Bret's lips moved from her breasts and began to scatter kisses across her abdomen. Her body had barely come down from the screaming point when he moved his hand down her side, along her hip, and down her thigh. By the time he reached her knee, the tension was back.

She wasn't aware just how tense she'd become until Bret said, "I can stop now."

She didn't want him to stop, but she did want a minute to pull herself together. Her mind and body had been so overwhelmed, they weren't communicating with each other.

"I'd like to touch you." She moved her hand inside his robe until she found the silky mat of dark hair that covered his chest. She'd caught glimpses of the cowhands when they washed at the trough, but she didn't remember anyone with hair. It fascinated her. She tried to move her hand around, but the closed robe restricted her movement.

"Open your robe," she said.

"I can't," Bret said. "I'm not wearing anything under it."

"Can you pull it off your shoulders?"

Bret pulled his arms out of the sleeves and allowed the robe to slide off his shoulders, but not before Emily discovered he was completely aroused. Made slightly uncomfortable by the heat that suddenly suffused her body, she redirected her gaze to Bret's chest. His upper arms and shoulders were smooth, the hair in a diamond-shaped patch in the center of his chest. As it descended, it narrowed to a thin line, then disappeared beneath the robe bunched at his waist. She ran her hands over his chest, over his shoulders. She smiled when she touched his nipples and he flinched, but she was having a hard time concentrating on what she was doing. Bret had both her breasts in his hands, was kneading her nipples, kissing her shoulders and the side of her neck. Giving in to the lassitude gripping her—she didn't understand how she could feel so limp when moments before she'd been strung tight—she leaned against Bret, running her hands over his back, marveling at the power of his muscles. Bret's body was a newly discovered treasure that was hers alone to do with almost as she wished. Bret pulled her nightgown up enough to run his fingers lightly along the inside of her leg. She forgot her fascination with his body as she was overwhelmed by new senations.

"Open for me."

She wasn't sure what he meant. He must have sensed her confusion, for he laid her down on the bed, took hold of the gathered nightgown at her waist, and slipped it under and off her body.

She lay naked before him.

The suddenness of it was a shock, but she was determined not to flinch or draw back this time. This was what she'd wanted from the first. She admitted it frightened her a little. Giving herself to a man for the first time was an event of colossal importance in her life, a major milestone. If he was as big as she thought, she was afraid it would hurt.

"Relax," Bret said. "I won't hurt you."

Ida said men never thought about making love the way women did. She said it would be up to Emily to teach her husband to be considerate of her, but Ida had neglected to tell her in what ways a man would be inconsiderate and what she was supposed to do to change it. But Bret loved her. She believed him when he said he wouldn't hurt her. It wasn't easy, but she willed her body to relax.

Emily practically held her breath as Bret's hand gently stroked the inside of her thigh. He'd taken her nipple in his mouth again, dividing her attention. He was so successful, she almost missed it when his finger gently prodded her entrance.

"Don't tense," he whispered. "It won't hurt."

The anticipation was so great, she couldn't control her muscles. As Bret continued to stroke her, she relaxed enough to take a deep breath. At that moment, his fingers entered her.

It wasn't anything like she expected. It didn't hurt. She just felt slightly stretched. Then Bret touched something inside her and she nearly rose off the bed.

"What—" She tried to get out the rest of the sentence, but her throat wouldn't let the words pass. She swallowed once, twice, and then again. She didn't know what he was doing, but her body convulsed with feelings unlike anything she'd ever experienced. Her muscles, alternately tensing and relaxing, were beyond her control.

"Relax," Bret said. "It'll feel even better soon."

She didn't think she could stand any more. She tried to ask, how much better? Yet despite her moving lips, no sound came from between them. Bands of steel encased her body, but at the same time she felt she might explode. Heat that had pooled deep in her belly began to spread to the rest of her body, setting her afire. Her hands gripped the bedding on either side of her and dug in hard as the sweet agony gradually drove her to the edge of an unknown abyss. She didn't understand how anything could feel so wonderful and so terrifying at the same time. Surely Bret would explain it, but she'd passed beyond the point of being able to think coherently or utter any sound other than a groan or a moan.

Through the haze that surrounded her, she was vaguely conscious that Bret had stretched her a little more, but she had no thought for what he was doing except that he was torturing her body and she was unable to do the same thing to him. Ida had said men's bodies were very sensitive, but she'd failed to mention that women could be driven crazy by what a man did to them. Bret had to stop. She didn't think she could stand any more.

Yet the feelings grew even more intense, the pressure on her body increased until she felt she couldn't breathe. She could only lie there, writhing under the pressure of his hand, struggling to keep from crying aloud, wondering if it would ever stop, yet hoping it never would. Bret had leaned forward to place his cheek alongside hers. He was saying something in a soft, sing-song voice, but she was beyond understanding. She didn't understand why he should be so calm while she was nearly insane.

The movement of Bret's hand increased, and the tension shot up so rapidly she gasped. There couldn't be more. She couldn't stand it. She opened her mouth to scream, but the tension inside her exploded and cut off the scream as cleanly as a sharp knife. Her body shuddered violently, and she felt sensation after sensation flow through her, bringing an ecstasy she'd never known. One by one, the muscles in her body started to relax until she was able to take her first full breath in what seemed like hours. Finally, her body began to sink into the mattress.

Only then was she aware that Bret had let his robe drop to the floor. When he raised his body over her, his arousal looked larger than ever. She was sure she couldn't contain him.

"This won't hurt," Bret said. "You're ready for me."

She was certain he was wrong. She took a deep breath, gritted her teeth, and waited for the pain.

It never came. When Bret pushed against her entrance, she was certain he would tear her apart. Instead of pain, she was only aware of gradually being filled until she could hardly believe what was happening. Bret was moving within her, and the feelings were starting all over again. She couldn't believe this could happen twice, but it was. Only this time, Bret was being carried along with her.

As the sensations spiraled around her, they bound Bret ever closer to her until they started to merge. As their bodies moved together, their breathing fell into sync. Even their hearts beat in unison. It was better than what he'd done to her only minutes earlier because now they were together, their bodies joined in a conjugal dance that had been celebrated throughout the history of man. The oldest dance in the world, yet it had been created anew tonight just for them.

Emily had more thoughts to explore about how wonderful it was to be together as they were tonight, but she gradually lost all desire to think. She could only feel. That was more than enough.

This time she didn't fight against it, didn't worry about it, wasn't afraid. Instead, she welcomed it, rushed to meet it, jubilant that she and Bret would go together. She recognized the moans, but they were no longer hers alone. She could sense when Bret approached the edge. His body grew taut, his movements more and more uneven, his breathing as jagged as her own. Then he let out a guttural moan and she felt him spill inside her.

Her own waved crested, and they floated down the other side together.

Bret lay awake a long time after Emily had gone to sleep. He couldn't believe he'd allowed his feelings to run away with him so completely. It didn't matter that he had *made love* rather than simply taken advantage of a willing woman. But he *had* taken advantage of Emily, and he felt like the most rotten scoundrel in Texas. It didn't matter that he loved her and wished he could marry her. That was the excuse of someone who was weak-willed and lacking in honor. He knew how the world worked. Emily didn't. What was more, he knew how *he* worked. And though he didn't like it, he knew he couldn't change it. The need to settle accounts was too deeply burned into his soul. Maybe he could have turned his back on Boston if his uncle hadn't tried to take credit for his ideas. At that point, the die had been cast and his return to Boston was inevitable.

He rolled up on his elbow so he could look at her. The moonlight coming through the open window drained her complexion of color, making her look as though she were made of the purest mother of pearl. She looked so peaceful, so content—so happy. She thought she'd gained the world when she fell in love, but he was old enough to know that love was never the answer. More often than not, it was the problem.

He'd been a fool to come to Texas in the first place. He knew his uncle was hoping he'd fail, looking for a way to get rid of him. There was no other reason Silas would have subjected Joseph's priceless person to the dangers of this wild and lawless land. Bret should have known that the daughter of two people who'd fled the confinement of Eastern society in favor of the freedom of the West would never agree to go to Boston. He should also have known that coming to Texas would remind him of what he'd given up in his pursuit of redemption. He'd traded something wonderful for an empty dream, and now he was caught in its coils. The worst part was, he'd drawn Emily into its coils as well.

He had to leave as soon as possible even though he knew there was no way he could square his departure with his conscience . . . or with Bertie. He would leave Jinx here. He would write Jake and Isabelle and hope they would honor a commitment he'd made in their name. He didn't know what to say to Hawk and Zeke, either. They wouldn't know he'd made love to Emily, but they knew he and Emily loved each other. They wouldn't understand his turning his back on her and leaving. They'd come when he needed them. They wouldn't understand how he could leave Emily when she needed him.

Unable to remain still any longer, he eased out of the bed, picked up his robe and put it on. With one last look at Emily, he tiptoed out of the room.

The silence in the house was so deep it felt ominous, as if the whole world knew what he'd done and had turned its back on him. He made his way down the dark hall slowly and with extreme care. Bumping into a single chair, table, or painting on the wall could awake people. He couldn't think of a single explanation for his being out of bed that wouldn't cause suspicion, raise eyebrows at the very least.

He eased open the door to his room, entered, and

closed it silently behind him. Jinx was sound asleep in his cot, his arms and legs flung out, his breathing slow and even. The sleep of the innocent. How long had it been since Bret had felt innocent? Could he remember ever going to bed without bitterness in his heart?

He felt like the biggest piece of buffalo dung in the world, but the need was burned too deeply inside him. He could never give himself to anyone until he drove it out of his mind and heart. Then, if she would still have him, he would come back to Texas and see if he could build a life for them together.

Without pulling off his robe, he lay down on the bed. He'd talk to Emily tomorrow after the reading of the will. She wouldn't be happy, but he hoped she'd understand. She might even go with him as long as she knew they'd be coming back. He wouldn't let himself think that far ahead. One step at a time.

He didn't sleep. By the time he heard Bertie in the kitchen and Jinx stirring on his cot, he'd worked out his plan for dealing with his uncle. For the first time since he went to Boston, he felt hopeful about the future.

Other than being a little sore, Emily had never felt better in her life. She was disappointed that Bret seemed to be in poor spirits, but she couldn't wait for him to make love to her again. Yet she could tell it wouldn't be as easy to convince him to do it a second time.

"If it's okay," Bret said when she joined him and Joseph for breakfast, "we'll read the will as soon as we're done eating."

"It doesn't matter to me when we do it," Emily said. "I know what's in it."

"It doesn't seem right that we don't have a lawyer for the reading," Joseph said.

"Emily will have to go to Fort Worth to deal with the legal aspects, but there's no reason not to read it now."

"What is a will?" Jinx asked.

"It's a piece of paper that says who gets Mr. Sam's property," Bertie said.

"Can I read it?"

"I don't mind reading it if—" Joseph began.

"I think Mr. Nolan ought to read it," Bertie announced with such finality everyone turned to her.

"Emily ought to read it," Bret said. "There's no need to stand on ceremony."

"It's not proper for Emily to be telling herself what she gets," Bertie said. "Somebody else has to look at the will to make sure of what it says, so it might as well happen now."

"Fine. Bret will read it," Emily said. Changing the subject, she talked with Bret about which horses were ready to be returned to their owners.

"I think you ought to give up training horses," Joseph said. "It's not a suitable occupation for a wealthy woman."

"I'm a rancher," Emily said, pleased to hear herself say the words. "Nothing is more suitable than working with horses and cows."

Joseph tried to change her mind, but breakfast ended without his having any success.

"Let's read the will," Emily said. "I need to get to work."

A little while later they were all seated in her father's office. Emily felt a pang to be here without her father sitting behind his desk. She'd always assumed she'd take over running the ranch after her father died, but falling in love with Bret had changed things. It had taken only one night spent in his arms to know that what she really wanted was to be his wife and the mother of his children. The ranch came after that.

She'd been disappointed when she woke up to find that Bret had left her bed sometime during the night. She knew it was the sensible thing to do. Though she wouldn't have really cared, there would have been a big uproar if they'd been found together. Okay, what Bertie and Ida would have said would matter, but Emily wasn't sure what that would be. Both women were very impressed with Bret. Bertie wanted her to marry him, but Bertie also had very clear ideas of what was right and wrong. Emily suspected she would have thought last night was wrong.

But Emily was too happy to care right now. As soon as they finished with the will, she and Bret would work with the horses. After that, she intended to spend the rest of the day with him. By nightfall, he would have agreed to marry her and stay in Texas. He had a few scruples, but she would explain them away. Their love was all that mattered. It would take care of everything.

Emily pointed to a tall, narrow cubbyhole in her father's roll-top desk. "That's where he keeps the will and some other papers."

Bret pulled out a handful of papers, and Emily moved to her seat to wait for him to sort through them. Joseph was seated next to her. Bertie stood next to the door with Jinx.

Bret seemed to be taking a long time with the papers. He opened each one, cast it aside, then moved to the next one. "Do you need any help?" she asked.

"Not yet. Your father kept a lot of documents in that drawer."

"Mr. Sam kept all his important papers in the same place," Bertie said.

"I wish he'd put the will on top," Bret muttered.

Going on the assumption that his father would be named administrator of Emily's estate, Joseph was explaining what his father would do, why it would be so very helpful if Emily were in Boston. Emily was weary of the conversation and returned only half answers. She was more interested in the expression on Bret's face. Initially, it had been confusion. He'd set a couple of papers aside and looked through the rest before picking up the first two again. He opened one and glanced through it. From his smile and nodding head, he apparently had found what he'd expected. Then he picked up the second paper and opened it. Emily was about to turn back to Joseph when she saw Bret's expression change to shock and the color drain from his face.

"What's wrong?" she asked.

Dragging his attention from the document, Bret folded both papers and stood. "I have to speak to Hawk and Zeke."

"What business can they have with the will?" Joseph demanded.

"It won't take long. I'll be back in a few minutes."

"Bret, what's wrong?" Emily asked.

"I don't know. That's what I'm trying to find out."

Then he walked out without offering any further explanation.

"He stole the will!" Joseph exclaimed.

"Don't be a fool," Bertie said. "Mr. Nolan doesn't steal."

"Mr. Nolan beat up Lugo because he was trying to steal from me," Jinx said.

"You don't know him like I do," Joseph insisted. "I could tell you things—"

"Don't," Emily said. "I don't know why Bret left like that, but I'm sure he has a good reason."

But as the minutes stretched from a few to a lot, she became impatient and began to wonder. Not that she doubted Bret's honesty for one minute. It had to do with the second document. She'd seen her father's will. It was a simple document on a single sheet of paper. She couldn't imagine what the second document contained or how it could possibly affect the will, but Bret would explain it all when he came back.

When he did return, Hawk and Zeke entered the room with him.

"What are they doing here?" Joseph demanded.

"You'll see," Bret said.

He moved to the desk and practically dropped into the chair. He looked very unhappy. His expression didn't change when he turned his gaze to Emily. He was deeply troubled.

"Well, get on with it," Joseph said. "No need to keep these men from their work any longer than necessary."

"You're right," Bret said. He looked down at the paper in his hand before he began to read.

The will was exactly as Emily remembered. Everything went to her after her father's death. A simple and straightforward statement. Without looking up, Bret picked up the second document, then raised his gaze to Emily. "The day before his death, your father made a second will, changing some of the provisions of the first."

"Why would he do that?" Joseph asked.

"If you'll stop interrupting long enough for Mr. Nolan to read the will, you'll find out," Bertie said.

Emily was in a state of shock. What changes could her father have made, and why hadn't he told her about them?

"Read the damned will, then, and get it over," Joseph said ill-naturedly.

Bret glanced at Emily, seemed to take a deep breath, and began to read.

"'When I made my will after my wife's death, I thought that would be the only will I'd ever have to make. Having only one child, it was a simple document. Everything would go to my daughter, Emily Abercrombie, without reservation. But the situation has altered, and I find myself compelled to make significant changes.'"

"I don't understand," Joseph said. "Why would he make significant changes without discussing it with me or my father?"

"I guess because it didn't concern you," Bertie said.

Emily wished Bertie wasn't so eager to cut Joseph down, but he brought it on himself with his pompous self-importance.

"'The voting rights to my shares in Abbott and Abercrombie go to Bret Nolan as long as he feels he needs them.'"

"No!" Joseph's exclamation was practically a scream. "The voting rights have to go to my father."

"Let him finish," Hawk said.

"This is a mistake," Joseph insisted. "Bret must have told Sam lies about my father. I won't let him get away with this."

"Either shut up or I'll throw you out," Hawk ordered.

"Be quiet, Joseph," Emily said. "I knew about that."

"But—"

Hawk grabbed Joseph by his collar and lifted him out of his seat. In an effortless display of strength, he hauled Joseph through the door Zeke held open and pushed him out of the room. "Now you can finish," he said when he turned back to Bret.

The pounding on the door made that impossible until Zeke left the room. Joseph's protests easily penetrated the walls before they gradually grew less distinct. Finally, they stopped altogether.

"Go on," Bertie said to Bret, a definite twinkle in her eye.

" 'Bret Nolan and his brothers rendered me a significant service when they put an end to the rustling. In light of that I have asked Hawk and Zeke Maxwell to act as foremen until Bret and Emily can find someone for the job.

" 'I'm very unhappy that my daughter has insisted upon remaining in Texas. I have complete confidence in her ability to run the ranch. However, a single woman is not safe in Texas. In light of that, I'm giving Bret Nolan the administration of my daughter's estate until she marries or reaches the age of twenty-five, whichever comes first.

" 'For Bret's contribution, I will to him one half of the ranch with the exception of the ranch house and its contents. That and the other half of the land will remain the sole possession of my daughter.' "

Chapter Twenty-two

Emily couldn't breathe. Her brain was in such a whirl she couldn't think. "That can't be right," she finally managed to say. "My father would never have made those changes without telling me. That can't be a true will."

"Yes, it is," Bret said. "I asked Zeke and Hawk to be here because they witnessed it. Here." He held the document out to her. "Read it for yourself."

Emily lurched to her feet and reached for the will. She read the short document twice, but the words never changed. She had no doubt it was genuine. The whole was written in her father's hand. The signature was his. Below, both Zeke and Hawk had signed and dated it. That had to have been what her father was doing when he spent so much time closeted with Zeke and Hawk the day before he died.

"Did you know about this?" she asked Bret.

"Not until just now when I read that second will."

"But you were with him after Zeke and Hawk left. He must have said something to you."

"He never said a word about the will."

She turned to Hawk. "What did you say to him to make him change his mind?"

"I tried to talk him out of it, but he wouldn't listen," Hawk said.

Joseph burst into the room. "What was in that will?" he asked. When Emily told him, he turned to Bret, pointed a finger at him, and shouted, "You always were a liar and a thief. Now you're trying to steal Emily's inheritance."

"Want me to throw him out again?" Zeke had returned with Joseph and was eyeing him with a complete lack of friendliness.

"That's what everybody's going to think when they hear about this," Bret said. "I own half the ranch, have control of Emily's inheritance, and my brothers are the foremen. That puts me in a position to rob her blind if I wanted."

"Which is exactly what you intend to do," Joseph shouted.

"If you don't learn to talk without shouting, I *am* going to throw you out again," Zeke said.

"He's just angry because he thinks Mr. Nolan beat him to stealing Emily's money," Bertie said.

"My father is far too wealthy to consider such a paltry sum as what this ranch is worth."

"I noticed you didn't say anything about your father having too much integrity or honor," Bertie pointed out before turning to Jinx. "Come with me. There's things likely to be said here that won't be good for your ears."

"How can words hurt my ears?" Jinx asked.

"If I have to take hold of one to drag you out of this room, you'll find out," Bertie snapped.

"I don't think it's fair," Jinx said as he headed for the door. "I'm always being bossed around."

"Be glad somebody cares enough about you to bother." Bertie didn't sound the least bit sympathetic.

"He bewitched your father," Joseph said.

"I didn't ask for this responsibility, and I don't want it," Bret said.

Emily swung her gaze to Hawk and Zeke, but they shrugged their shoulders. "We really did try to talk him out of it, but he was determined," Zeke said.

"I warned you not to trust Bret," Joseph said. "I warned you even before he got here."

Joseph *had* warned her, but Bret wasn't anything like the man she'd expected. From the very first, he'd chipped away at her preconceived notions until it wasn't long before nothing of them remained. In their place was a man she'd fallen in love with, a man Bertie liked, a man her father apparently had trusted. A man Jinx adored.

"Mr. Abercrombie thought a long time before he made up his mind to change his will," Hawk said. "He had to do some pretty sharp talking to convince Zeke and me to sign it."

"What did he say?" Emily asked.

"It all boiled down to him thinking Bret was the man best able to see you and your interests protected," Zeke said.

"Bret is no more than a fancy clerk," Joseph said.

"There's more than one person ready to step in if he needs help," Hawk said.

"Who? His pitiful family of orphans?" Joseph sneered.

"For a man nobody likes, you sure do have a mouth on you," Zeke said. "You might consider keeping it shut."

"Are you threatening me?" Joseph demanded.

"You're damned right," Zeke shot back.

"You heard him," Joseph said to Emily. "The three

of them are in league to cheat you. And they're willing to murder me to get away with it."

"Don't be stupid," Emily snapped at Joseph. "Nobody's going to murder you."

"Don't go speaking for me," Zeke said. "I've got nothing against spilling a little blood from time to time."

Bret took Emily's hands, met her gaze squarely. "I didn't ask for this, and I don't want it. I'll find someone else to handle your inheritance, and I'll give you back my half of the ranch as soon as I can."

"I don't think you ought to do that," Hawk said.

"See, I told you they were trying to cheat you," Joseph said, pointing to Hawk and Zeke. "You should never have trusted men like them."

Everyone ignored Joseph.

"Why not?" Bret asked Hawk.

"Because it's what Mr. Abercrombie wanted, for one thing," Zeke said. "He had a lot of good reasons. If he hadn't, we wouldn't have agreed to witness the will."

Emily turned to Zeke, hopeful he could unravel this mystery for her. "What reasons?"

"Hawk already told you. He thinks Bret is the best man for the job."

"But that doesn't explain why he'd give away half my ranch," Emily said. "Did he tell you why?"

"He made us promise not to tell you," Hawk said.

"Why?" Emily looked from Hawk to Zeke to Bret. "My father never kept things from me. Why would he tell you something he wouldn't tell me?"

"Because he thought it was best," Hawk said.

Emily couldn't accept that. She liked Zeke and Hawk, and she loved Bret. He had said he would give her back his half of the ranch, but that wasn't what was bothering her. Why had it been given to him in the first place? What had been said and done that she didn't know about?

As much as she wanted to trust Bret, everything pointed to him. The dramatic change in the will benefited him to the exclusion of anyone else. Even herself.

Bret's hold on her hands tightened. "You don't believe I did something to cause your father to change his will, do you?"

Emily couldn't answer. She didn't know what she believed.

"I will give back my half of the ranch. It would be impossible for me to run it from Boston."

"You don't need to be here," Joseph said. "You've already made sure your *brothers* are in control."

Even after swearing he loved her, after having made love to her, Bret didn't love her enough to stay in Texas. He figured he could handle her financial affairs from Boston, and his brothers would run the ranch.

"I don't know what I think, and I don't know what I want to do," Emily said, addressing all four men. "This has come as a complete shock."

"I can tell you exactly—" Joseph began.

"You *won't* tell me exactly what to do," Emily nearly shouted. "*Nobody* is going to tell me what to do." She had to get away. She had to get her feelings under control so she could think clearly. The man she loved didn't want to marry her, and her father hadn't trusted her. The two most important men in her life had let her down, and she had to figure out what she was going to do about it. She wanted to talk to Bertie, but Bertie thought Bret was perfect. "I'm going to visit Ida for a couple of days," she announced. "I'm not running away," she said when Bret started to speak. "I just need some time to think, and I need it without you being so close."

"I'll go with you," Joseph said.

"I'm going alone." She turned to Hawk and Zeke. "I've got to try to figure out what Dad was thinking." She turned back to Bret. "I don't understand. I thought you loved me."

"I do love you."

"Then why are you leaving?"

"I told you why. But I thought of a way to—"

"I don't want to hear it," she said, stopping him. She pulled her hands from his grasp. "I'll leave as soon as I can pack a few things and saddle my horse."

"You have to go after her," Hawk said to Bret as Emily was leaving the room.

"No. If she can't find a reason to trust me by herself, nothing I say will make any difference."

"She'll never trust any of you again if I have anything to say about it," Joseph said.

"Leave her alone," Bret said.

"You can't tell me what to do," Joseph spat at him. "I'm not a clerk."

"If we tie you to a fence post, nobody will have to tell you anything," Hawk said.

"Right now she's more hurt about her father doing this without telling her than she is about anything else," Bret said.

"You're a fool if you think she's more worried about that than about the money," Joseph said.

"I think I just may have been a fool," Bret said, "but it has nothing to do with money."

"Amen," Hawk and Zeke said together.

Two hours in the saddle under the hot summer sun had done a lot to take the steam out of Emily's anger, but it hadn't altered any of the facts. Bret didn't love her, and somehow he'd been responsible for her father changing his will. How could she work with the man she loved, knowing he didn't love her? It didn't matter that he'd be a thousand miles away. She'd have to communicate with him about how to handle her inheritance. They would have to develop a plan for the management of the ranch. He would insist upon taking her to Galveston. He would be woven into the very fabric of her life.

Maybe he thought *she* didn't love *him*. She'd refused to go to Boston with him before he'd refused to stay in Texas for her. It probably didn't matter that she thought he had more reason to move to Texas than she did to move to Boston. It was all a matter of perspective. They each saw their position as unalterable.

Emily glanced over her shoulder. She knew someone was following her, and she was certain neither Bret nor his brothers would let Joseph out of their sight. Bret distrusted him. Hawk and Zeke distrusted *and* disliked him.

At first, she'd thought Bret was trying to catch up with her, but after a while she realized he was only following. Knowing he was trying to make sure she reached Ida's safely made it hard to stay angry at him, but she had some serious issues to face, some hard decisions to make. What she decided in the next few days would determine the course of the rest of her life. She couldn't afford to let her decisions be clouded by sentiment or anger.

The landscape didn't offer much to distract her. The various kinds of grama grass, along with buffalo and Indian grass, were tall and green from the spring rains, but they would turn yellow during the course of the summer. She passed fat, healthy cows grazing in grass up to their bellies, their calves either hidden by the tall grass or struggling to fight their way through. As the day progressed, it would become so hot the cows would seek shade in the scattered stands of oak or the willows and cottonwoods found along a water course.

She'd only seen one white-tailed deer, but several small herds of pronghorn antelope had eyed her uneasily as she rode past. Most ranchers wanted to get rid of them because they competed with the cows for grass.

She wondered if Bret would want to eliminate the antelope. They weren't pretty—their convex faces and blunt noses made them look almost comical—but she liked the little animals.

She realized she could hear the hooves of the horse behind her. Though she was relieved that Bret wanted to make sure she reached Ida's safely, she was angry that he hadn't respected her need to be away from him for a few days.

Damn! Being in love was hell.

After hanging back for a time, it was clear that Bret meant to catch up with her. Emily held her horse at a steady pace, practicing the things she'd say. When his horse reached the flank of her horse, she slowed her mount and turned, words ready to tumble off her lips. When she realized she was looking at Lonnie instead of Bret, the words died stillborn.

"Are you surprised to see me?" Lonnie asked.

"What are you doing here? Where have you been?" She was so surprised she didn't even think about the rustling.

"Waiting for a chance to talk to you."

"What about?"

"To ask you to marry me."

With all that had happened during the last few days, Emily had forgotten that Lonnie was in love with her. Her father was dead, Bret didn't love her, and now the man who'd tried to steal her cattle wanted to marry her. She couldn't take much more. "Don't be ridiculous," she snapped before she realized how hurtful that sounded. "I don't love you," she said in a milder tone. "And if I had, my love certainly would have ended when you betrayed me and tried to steal my cows."

"I didn't betray you or try to steal from you."

"Hawk and Zeke have two men locked up in the barn who swear you hired them to brand my calves."

"I did that because I love you. When we get married I'll explain everything."

"I'm not going to marry you. I'm on my way to stay with Ida for a few days. If you're smart, you'll leave Texas as fast as you can."

"I can't leave you. I love you. Everything will be fine once we're married."

Emily was in no mood to explain that things had gone too far ever to be fine again. "If Bret or his brothers find you, you'll hang."

"I'm sorry we have to do it this way."

Lonnie had always been extremely deferential to Emily, so she was utterly unprepared for him to grab her, pull her arms behind her back, and tie her wrists with rawhide. "What are you doing?" she demanded.

"Taking you to find a preacher to marry us."

Grasping her horse's bridle, he turned off the trail and headed cross-country.

"I thought you said Emily needed time alone," Hawk said as he watched Bret saddle his horse.

"I'm not going to stop her," Bret said. "I'm not even going to talk to her, but I can't let her ride all the way to Charlie and Ida's ranch by herself. It's a full day's trip. If anything were to happen to her, she could die before anyone found out."

"I insist that you let me go, too," Joseph said.

"Shut up, little man," Zeke said. "I'm tired of listening to you."

Joseph was the shortest of the four men, but at

close to six feet, he was used to being referred to as tall and imposing.

"You can't keep me from riding out whenever I want," Joseph said, his volume rising along with his temper.

"I can't think with him interrupting all the time," Hawk said to Zeke. "Why don't you take him outside until I'm done talking to Bret."

In a movement that was so fast Bret could hardly follow it, Zeke had both of Joseph's arms behind his back at an angle that would make it extremely painful if he struggled.

"I don't know why you insist on making things hard for yourself," Zeke said as he propelled Joseph out of the barn. "We're just looking out for you. If you tried to follow Emily by yourself, you might get lost."

"Are you sure you don't want to do more than just follow her?" Hawk asked Bret.

"Of course I want to do more," Bret exploded. "I want to convince her I love her more than anyone on earth, that I don't want to go a day without seeing her, holding her, making love to her."

"That doesn't sound all that hard to do. I've got a notion it's what she'd like for you to do."

"She would, but she doesn't understand why I have to go back to Boston."

"Hell, Bret, nobody understands why you went there in the first place."

"I realize the Abbotts are never going to be my family. That's what I wanted to tell Emily. I was going to ask her to wait while I went to Boston to finish some business. Then I'm coming back to Texas." Bret grinned in spite of himself. "If Jake will let me, I'll take up that land he offered me before I left." Bret's smile faded. "I don't know about that now. Emily doesn't trust me anymore."

"Sure she does. She's just upset."

Bret smiled again. "It's obvious you've never been in love."

"You think I'm too ugly for a woman to love?" Hawk asked.

"You'd probably scare them half to death with that damned feather you insist on wearing. What I'm trying to say is, once you fall in love with someone, you're connected in a way that lets you know what they're feeling, even what they're thinking sometimes. Right now she doesn't trust me, and your making a secret of what her father said didn't help any."

"Hell, I'll tell her if it'll make a difference."

"She's got to decide on her own whether she can trust me. After she does, maybe you can tell her what he said."

"Why are you making things so hard on yourself? Go after her. Talk to her. Make love to her until she can't think of anybody but you."

"You don't know how much I want to do just that. But sooner or later you have to stop making love and face the real world. I want to know that after she does that, she'll still want me to make love to her." Bret tightened the cinch on his saddle. "I'm playing for keeps this time."

"When should we look for you?" Hawk asked. Bertie had packed him some food, and he had his bedroll.

"I don't know. I may need a little time alone myself."

"You sure won't get it here with your cousin yelling at you and Jinx dogging your heels like a puppy. Why did you adopt him?"

Bret grinned as he swung into the saddle. "I didn't. He adopted me. Keep an eye on him. He reminds me of a cross between Will and Pete when they were his age."

"God help us! We ought to smother him while we can," Hawk said, following as Bret walked his horse out of the barn.

"I was going to take him to Jake and Isabelle," Bret said, "But if Emily still wants me, I think I'll keep him with us."

"What is it with this family? Matt just took in guaranteed trouble in some kid called Toby, and Drew and Cole keep adding to their gang with more orphans even though Drew is pregnant again."

"Blame it on Jake and Isabelle. I've got to go. I shouldn't have waited this long."

"Don't give up on her. Any woman who can get you away from those bastards in Boston is worth all the trouble it takes to keep her."

"I know, but it's up to her now."

"You can't make me marry you," Emily said to Lonnie.

"After spending several days alone with me, you'll have to marry me to preserve your reputation."

"Maybe no decent man will want me, but I still won't marry you."

"Why not?" Lonnie asked. "You know I love you."

Lonnie had brought Emily to his hiding place in a dense grove of trees on the far side of the ranch. The deep ashes inside a circle of stones indicated the site was well used. The open area inside the grove was about twenty-five feet in diameter, but the surrounding trees formed such a dense barrier, Emily doubted Lonnie's campfire could be seen even at night. The limbs overhead—so thick Emily could see only tiny patches of sky—dispersed the smoke, making it nearly impossible for a rider to know he was passing by a campsite.

Emily was sorry Lonnie had fallen in love with her. She wondered if she had done anything to encourage the attraction, if she could have done anything to help him get over it. She was sure it was just infatuation, or the fact that she was the only single woman of marriageable age within fifty miles.

Lonnie had hidden her horse in a mesquite thicket. She was seated on a blanket on the ground, her hands tied behind her back. She guessed it was close to noon. Lonnie had made coffee and was heating some antelope stew. Two quarters of antelope covered with a sheet to keep the flies off hung from tree branches. A sack of potatoes, a side of bacon, coffee, even cans of tomatoes and peaches indicated the site had been stocked over a period of time and was well used.

"How did you get all this stuff here?" Emily asked. "Bertie knows everything in her larder down to the last coffee bean."

"This is where the two men I had working for me stayed. They'd just stocked up again before your friends caught them."

"Why did you try to steal our calves?" Emily asked. "Dad and I trusted you."

Lonnie looked up from stirring the stew. "I didn't try to steal anything."

"You were putting your brand on our calves so all you had to do was wait until they were old enough to be sold; then you could claim the brand and the cows and no one would know you were stealing them."

Lonnie's gaze became more intense. "I wasn't stealing. I registered the brand in your name."

At first Emily didn't believe him. It didn't make any sense to take that kind of risk. But when Lonnie's gaze didn't waver, when his expression remained open and lacking in any trace of guilt or anger, she started to wonder.

"You'll have to offer a better explanation than that if you expect me to believe you."

"All you have to do is ask that man staying at the ranch."

The bottom fell out of Emily's stomach. For a moment she thought she was going to be physically sick. How could Bret have done such a thing? *Why* would he have done it? Every plan, hope, and dream came tumbling down around her like the skeleton of a building after a single, devastating lightning strike.

"What are you talking about?" she asked when she was finally able to get the words past the constriction in her throat.

"He wrote me from Boston. He said you were dead set against going there after your father died and wanted to know what would make you change your mind. I didn't know what he had in mind, but I said losing the ranch would probably do it. That's when he hired me to rustle your herd."

"He paid you money to steal from me? We trusted you, Lonnie. We liked you. How could you do that?"

"I didn't steal from you. I just made it look that way. He didn't really want you to go to Boston. He just wanted control of your father's piece of his company. I knew you didn't love me, but I figured if you thought you were losing the ranch, you would turn to me to save it for you. It would be only natural for us to get married after I stopped the rustling. He'd have what he wanted—I didn't think it would be hard to convince you to turn that part of your inheritance over to him—and I'd have what I wanted. You and the ranch."

It all made sense. She'd wondered why Bret had agreed to the compromise so readily when his uncle had told him not to return without her. From the beginning, he'd wanted just one thing—control of her shares in Abbott & Abercrombie—and both she and her father had been willing to hand it over. Bret probably wouldn't be at the ranch when she returned.

Dozens of questions hurtled through her mind, each more terrible than the one before it. Bret had organized an incredibly elaborate plot and had carried through every part of it with aplomb. Everybody believed him. Everybody liked him. And she'd fallen in love with him. What was she going to do now?

Feeling overwhelmed, she broke down and started crying.

Bret forced himself to keep his horse at a fast canter by constantly reminding himself he didn't want to catch up with Emily, just make certain she reached Ida's safely. Only he *did* want to catch up to her. He wanted to hold her, to kiss her, to make love to her until she couldn't think of anything except being with him for the rest of their lives. Until she could forget she'd ever thought he could betray her.

He tried to keep from dwelling on those thoughts. He knew she was upset by the will, both by its contents and the fact that her father had changed it without talking to her. He knew that having so many people she barely knew invade her life was bound to cause confusion, especially with the rustling and her father's death. Yet none of the things he told himself could ease the hurt, the pain of knowing she didn't trust him.

He tried to force himself to concentrate on following her trail, but that didn't take one-tenth of his concentration. The hoofprints of her horse were clear—and so were those of another horse. He wondered why one of the cowhands would be using this trail, but since the hoofprints were practically on top of each other, it was clear that the two riders hadn't been riding together. Bret could also tell from the prints that the horses were traveling at a slow canter. Emily should come into sight well before mid-morning.

He hadn't decided what to do once he knew she'd arrived at Ida's. He needed to return to Boston as quickly as possible, but he couldn't leave without seeing Emily once more. He also needed to see Jake and Isabelle, but he didn't want to do that until he had left Boston for good. He didn't want to go back to the ranch today. He had nothing to say to Joseph and didn't want to hear what Zeke and Hawk would say to him. Maybe he'd camp out along the trail and wait for Emily to return.

He'd noticed that the footprints of the second horse had changed paths, but he didn't attach any importance to the change until he noticed that both horses had stopped. When the trail of both horses turned sharply to the right and headed cross-country, Bret became concerned. Why would Emily leave the trail, even if she was riding with one of her hands? She'd been late starting. She wouldn't reach Ida's until dusk as it was.

Bret turned his horse and followed. Curiosity turned to concern and then fear as their trail led toward the northern limits of the ranch. Bret could think of no reason for Emily to ride this far from her intended destination unless she was being forced.

Lonnie.

He was in love with Emily. He'd taken a tremendous risk when he organized the rustling in hopes of getting her to marry him. He wouldn't have wanted to leave without a chance to see her one more time. Bret was certain Emily wouldn't have gone with him willingly. She had been kidnapped. Bret didn't believe Lonnie would hurt Emily, but he knew how desperate a man in love could be. He had to find them, and soon.

If Bret hadn't been looking for it, he might have missed the barely noticeable trail of smoke rising out of a large thicket of trees and visible against the pure white of a cloud low on the horizon. He rode to where the land fell off toward a small stream. He dismounted and ran along the bottom of the ridge, hoping Lonnie didn't happen to be looking in his direction. Thickets of willow tangled by berry canes and wild grape vines provided cover until he reached the edge of the trees. Hoping he wouldn't disturb any birds or small mammals and give himself away, Bret carefully parted some oak branches.

A small fire burned inside a circle of stones. He could make out Emily seated on the ground, her hands tied behind her, but he didn't see Lonnie. Certain he was somewhere close, Bret gradually worked his way through the thicket until he was close enough to Emily to whisper, "This is Bret. I'm right behind you. Where is Lonnie?" He was prepared for Emily to be startled, but not for the anger of her pinched mouth or the hurt in her eyes when she twisted around to face him.

"Why are you trying to sneak in?" she demanded. "I'm sure Lonnie's been expecting you."

Confused by her attitude and her words, Bret looked around, expecting to see Lonnie pointing a rifle at him. "Keep your voice down," he whispered urgently. "Where is Lonnie? How soon will he be back? It won't take but a minute to untie you."

"Lonnie!" Emily called out. "Your partner is looking for you."

"What the hell are you talking about?" Bret said, frantically looking around.

"I know all about your scheme, so you can stop pretending. There's coffee on the fire. Help yourself while you wait for Lonnie."

"I don't know what's gotten into your head," Bret said as he crawled toward Emily, intent on untying her and getting away before Lonnie returned, "but we can figure it out later. Right now we have to—"

"Right now you have to stop where you are."

Bret turned to see Lonnie standing not ten feet away, his rifle pointed at him.

"It's Bret," Emily said. "Surely you were expecting your partner."

"Joseph Abbott is the man who wrote me," Lonnie said. "He warned me this man would try to make you fall in love with him so he could steal your ranch."

Chapter Twenty-three

Emily swallowed hard. She didn't need any more proof than the expression on Bret's face to know she'd leaped to the wrong conclusion. "But you said . . . I thought—"

"You thought I'd pay your own foreman to steal your cows and kidnap you," Bret said.

"Lonnie wasn't stealing my cows," Emily said. She felt so shocked, so mortified, *so stupid*, she could hardly think. "He was only pretending to so I'd beg him to save my ranch and then marry him out of gratitude. Joseph didn't want me to go to Boston. He just wanted control of my shares in Abbott and Abercrombie."

Bret's expression didn't change. "It doesn't matter what he was *really* doing. What matters is that you thought I'd have any part in it."

"I didn't want to, but when he said he was hired by that man at my house—"

"You automatically thought of me," Bret finished for her.

"I haven't thought of anybody but you in days," Emily threw at him. "Why should it be any different now?"

She didn't know why she'd never thought of Joseph as being capable of doing anything like this. Maybe because she'd met him years ago and liked him. Maybe because he seemed more like an annoyance than a danger. With Bret, Hawk, and Zeke around, who would think of Joseph as posing a problem? Still, she should have believed in Bret. She should have believed in herself enough to know she couldn't love a man who would do what Joseph had done.

"I'd never have believed any of this about you if it hadn't been for the will," she said.

"What about the will?" Lonnie asked. Neither he nor Bret had moved.

"Dad left control of my inheritance and half of the ranch to Bret," Emily said.

"I saw the will myself," Lonnie said. "Everything goes to you."

"He made a new will just before he died," Bret said. "If you don't believe us, you can ask your *boss*. He was there when I read the will."

"Did you see it?" Lonnie asked Emily.

"Yes. There's no question Dad wrote it."

"I'll bet you witnessed it," Lonnie said, waving his rifle at Bret.

"He didn't know anything about it," Emily said. "Zeke and Hawk witnessed it."

"His own brothers," Lonnie said with a sneer. "How can you believe he didn't know anything about it? I bet he planned it."

"It was Sam's decision," Bret said before turning to Emily.

"You can't believe anything he says," Lonnie protested.

"Then who is she supposed to believe?" Bret asked. "You've already admitted to plotting against her with Joseph. I was honest with Emily and her father from the beginning."

"It doesn't make any difference," Lonnie protested.

"Maybe not, but the plan you hatched with Joseph is useless now," Emily said. "Bret has control of the stock, half the ranch, and all my money. There's no point in your marrying me now."

"But I love you," Lonnie said.

"I'm never going to marry you, so you might as well let us go," Emily told him.

"He'll try to get me hanged," he said, pointing to Bret.

"You'll certainly hang if you kidnap Emily or kill me," Bret said.

Emily could tell that Lonnie was undecided, but he kept his rifle on Bret.

"I'm going to untie Emily," Bret said, moving toward her as he spoke. "Point that rifle somewhere else."

"You'll get away."

"That would be better than you shooting Emily by mistake," Bret said. He wasted no time in untying Emily and helping her to her feet. "Now put the rifle down," he said as he moved away from her. "Don't make things any worse." He had moved around the opening in the trees until Lonnie was between him and Emily, making it impossible for Lonnie to keep his eye on both of them at the same time.

"Put the rifle away, Lonnie," Emily said. "If you don't, I'll take it from you."

The moment Lonnie half turned toward Emily, Bret launched himself at Lonnie. The rifle went off and both men went down in a tangle. Emily held her breath until she was certain both men were fighting much too hard to have been injured. She was afraid that Lonnie was stronger than Bret. She picked up the rifle, intending to hit Lonnie over the head with it. To her surprise, when she looked up, Bret was pounding Lonnie with such rapid and powerful jabs her ex-foreman was reeling. One last blow to the jaw sent Lonnie tumbling to the ground.

"That last one was for Emily," Bret said. "If you ever touch her again, I'll break every bone in your body."

Emily thought that was one of the nicest things Bret had ever said.

"Pack your things and leave this house immediately," Emily said to Joseph. "I don't want to see you ever again. After all the letters we've exchanged, I can't believe you'd lie to me."

"I never lied to you," Joseph protested. "I still don't trust Bret. Lonnie wasn't trying to steal your cows, only scare you into being sensible and coming to Boston where my father could take care of your inheritance and my mother could take care of you."

"You didn't want me, just my shares in the company."

"The situation would have been advantageous to everybody. Handing everything over to Bret was a horrible mistake. It'll be a disaster. You just wait and see."

It was pointless to talk to Joseph. Nothing anybody could say had been able to convince him he'd done anything wrong. On the contrary, he acted as though he were the one who'd been mistreated.

"I'll take my chances," Emily said. "I can't believe I didn't see through you."

"People like Joseph only show their true colors when something important is at stake," Bret said. "In this case it was control of the family firm."

"I don't want to have to think of Abbott and Abercrombie ever again," Emily said to Bret. "I'm glad Dad left control of the shares to you. I'd much rather think about my ranch—at least my half of it."

"How many times do I have to say I'm leaving control of my half to you? I'll be happy with anything the three of you decide."

"Thanks for the vote of confidence," Hawk said with a grin.

"Everybody knows you two know more about ranches than I do."

"You could change that," Zeke said.

"First things first," Bret said. "Emily wants to talk to you about finding a new foreman."

"One of us can stay here, and one of us can leave with Bret for Fort Worth," Hawk said. "We ought to be able to find somebody there or in Dallas. You sure you don't want to prosecute Lonnie?" he asked Emily.

"I'm sure. He'd never have thought of trying to force me to marry him if it hadn't been for Joseph."

"What about the two who were doing the branding?"

"Let them go."

"I guess that's all we need to know," Zeke said.

"Which one of you is going with me in the morning?" Bret asked.

Zeke and Hawk each pointed at the other and said, "He is."

Bret laughed. "You two fight it out between you. In the meantime, I need to talk to Emily."

Emily's heart seemed to jump into her throat. She followed Bret outside, and he led her to the spot on the side of the hill where he'd kissed her. The night seemed extraordinarily quiet. There was no wind to stir the trees or bend the grass. Stars filled the sky while clouds floated silently overhead. The usual sounds of the night were absent—not even a cow lowing softly to her calf. The whole world seemed to be waiting to hear what Bret would say. She didn't want to hear it.

He was leaving.

She didn't know how she was going to stand it. Maybe some women died of a broken heart, but she was certain she wouldn't be so fortunate. Fifty years from now she'd probably be standing on this hill, remembering how he'd held her in his arms, how he'd kissed her, how she'd thought the rest of her life would be perfect because he would be at her side.

"I love this spot." Bret waved his arm to indicate the wide expanse of Texas prairie spreading out before them. "It's the one place on this ranch that reminds me of Jake and Isabelle's spread."

"You were truly happy there, weren't you?"

"Yes, but I was too eaten up by bitterness to understand what they were offering me. I couldn't forget what had happened to my parents, to me. I couldn't stop wanting to do something to even the score."

"Will you be able to even the score when you go back?"

He turned to look at her. "I've finally realized that's impossible. I can't undo what was done, and nothing else would make any difference."

She warned herself not to leap to any conclusions, but his words offered hope. "Then why are you going back?"

"I have some unfinished business."

"Then I'm going with you."

Bret looked startled. "Why?"

"If you won't stay in Texas, I have to go to Boston. I don't want to leave the ranch, but I'll follow you wherever you go."

His expression was odd. She'd wanted to see deliri-
ous happiness. She'd hoped for a smile that would
start in his eyes and gradually transform his face. At
the very least, she'd expected surprise. It looked
more like pain.

"I'd never let you move to Boston. You'd hate it
there."

"I'll hate it here without you."

The pain seemed to deepen. That was when she
knew his plans didn't include her. The truth hit her
like a fist, brutally and without warning.

"After I've finished what I need to do," Bret said,
"I'm leaving."

"How long will that take?"

"I don't know."

"What will you do when you're finished?"

"Come back to Texas."

Emily thought her chest would explode with happiness. After being certain she'd lost him, he was
coming back.

"But not here," Bret said.

The bottom fell out of her world. "Where are you
going?"

"Home."

Emily had to swallow a couple of times before she
could speak. She was relieved he'd decided he belonged in Texas, but she'd hoped he'd want to be with
her enough to learn to think of her ranch as home.
She could almost dislike Jake and Isabelle because he
loved them more than he loved her. "What are you
going to do about your half of the ranch?"

"I'll have that deeded to you as soon as I get to Fort
Worth. I never wanted it, and I don't intend to keep it.
Your father may have thought it was a way to keep us
together, but I won't take what's yours or force you to

work with me. That's no way to convince two people they ought to marry."

Hawk had told them her father had named Bret to handle her inheritance because getting to know Joseph had convinced him he couldn't trust Joseph or Silas. Furthermore, he'd wanted Bret to marry Emily and hoped that by forcing them to share the ranch, they'd have time to fall in love.

"I want to work with you," Emily said. "I want to marry you."

Bret didn't answer, but he didn't have to. She knew what stood between them. She was sure he'd tried, but he couldn't forgive her for thinking he'd lied and tried to steal from her. What was worse she'd believed Joseph, the man who *had* lied and tried to cheat her. She'd explained that she'd only believed it because she was upset and confused about the will, but it hadn't made a difference.

"What are you going to do?" she asked.

"Jake has been spending nearly every penny he makes buying up land so all of us can have ranches close to each other. He must own a whole county by now. Zeke says Isabelle's house is slowly being overrun by grandchildren at Christmas. I've missed so much of that. I don't want to miss any more. It's a perfect place for Jinx to grow up. Ward has a couple of boys close to his age."

Emily could feel the shadow of loneliness settle over her. Despite Bertie's efforts, Christmas had been a sad season since her mother's death. It would be even worse this year without her father. Now she would not have Jinx or Bret, either. Even though they'd been at the ranch only a short time, she felt like that they belonged there. It was nearly impossible to think of the future without them.

"What about me?" Emily asked. "You know I love you, and I know you love me. Don't you want me to be part of your future?"

"More than you'll ever know, but—"

"There is no *but*. I told you I was too upset to think clearly. You must remember how you felt when your father died."

"I remember all too well. That's what has driven me every day since then. It's what I *allowed* to lead me in the wrong direction. Coming back to Texas was the best thing that ever happened to me, but I need time to adjust. I think I know what I want, but I've got to take a little time to make sure."

"I don't need any time. I know what I want."

"Your life has changed just as dramatically. You need time to think as well. I know I have to return to the hill country. This ranch can never be my home. I want you to go with me as my wife."

Emily was so shocked she couldn't move. *Bret wanted her to be his wife!* She'd been thinking he was going to leave her. Instead, he wanted to marry her and take her with him. Her heart beat so wildly she could hardly breathe. It was all she could do to keep from throwing herself at him.

"You need time to decide if that's what you want. You'll be stepping into my world, into my family." He smiled suddenly, and she could tell he was reliving some cherished memory. "Believe me when I say it can be a little overwhelming."

He had to be crazy to think exchanging one ranch for another would stop her from wanting to be his wife. How did men get these weird ideas? She'd finally learned that if a woman loved a man, it didn't matter where they lived, only that they lived there together. "What do you want me to do?"

"I'll write and tell you when I'm coming back. If

you decide you love me enough to trust me with the rest of your life, meet me in San Antonio. If you're not there when I get back, I'll know you decided I asked too much."

If he only had any idea what she'd do for him. But she wouldn't tell him now. Maybe never. It wasn't good to spoil a man too much.

"Now I want to spend the rest of the evening kissing you," Bret said. "I want to leave you something to remember me by."

Emily didn't need any reminders, but she wasn't going to tell him.

Two months later

"Are you sure Will can find Bret?" Emily asked Isabelle. "He didn't look like he wanted to go."

"Will never likes to do anything when he can get away with doing nothing," Isabelle said. "But if he agrees to do something, nobody will do it better."

Emily had been at the Broken Circle for a week, and she still couldn't see Will Haskins without a little gasp of astonishment. She knew her love for Bret was deep and solid when Will's incredibly handsome face never once dislodged Bret's image from her thoughts or her dreams.

She'd had an unbelievably busy two months since Bret left. Even before she got the deed transferring Bret's half of the ranch to her, she started looking for a buyer. She hated to leave. It was the only home she could remember, but she would have given up even more to be with Bret. Before he left Fort Worth for Boston, Bret had helped Hawk find her a foreman. The foreman had introduced her to a man interested in buying her ranch. She had signed the papers before she left.

Jinx and Bertie had accompanied her to the Broken

Circle. Isabelle had been shocked, then delighted when she heard Bret was coming home. Bertie had immediately made herself at home in the kitchen—much to Isabelle's amusement—and Jinx acted as if Christmas and every other holiday had come at once. He finally had a real home and real playmates. Almost as good, he was surrounded by real cowboys who were willing to teach him anything he wanted to know. Today, however, he was waiting just as anxiously as Emily for Bret. He had gone with Will. Isabelle had said that was okay. They both acted the same age.

"I know you've told me at least three times everything that happened," Isabelle said, "but I still find it hard to believe. I never thought we'd see Bret again." She took Emily's hand and gave it a squeeze. "If it hadn't been for you, I'm sure we never would have."

Emily squeezed back. "It was a close call. I nearly ruined it."

When Emily first met Isabelle, she found it hard to believe that a woman as young, beautiful, and feminine as Isabelle could have corralled a houseful of men. A week later she knew it was the love Isabelle had for these men that made them willing to move heaven and earth for her. A little jealously, she wondered if Bret would ever feel that way about her.

They had been seated in chairs on the front porch of Isabelle's large and comfortable home, but Emily was too anxious to remain seated. She stood at the railing, peering at the spot along the trail where Will and Jinx would reappear after they sighted Bret. She'd wanted to go with Will herself, but Isabelle had held her back. She said it wasn't a good idea for a woman to throw herself at a man's feet. It gave him an exaggerated opinion of himself. But after watching Jake and Isabelle together, Emily decided Isabelle wasn't very good at following her own advice.

"Are you sure you don't regret selling your ranch?" Isabelle asked.

"Not at all. I want us to do everything together, own everything together, build everything together. I don't want him ever to have a reason to believe I don't trust him implicitly."

"I can see you're going to spoil him," Isabelle said with a smile.

"I won't have a chance. Bertie will do it for me. She adores him."

"So does Jinx. You know he's going to want to live with you when you build a house, though I expect he'll be at Ward's place enough to give you a few moments alone." There were ten boys in the extended Maxwell clan, ranging in age from one to nineteen. Jinx still hadn't gotten over his excitement.

"Did Bret tell you what he was going to do in Boston?" Isabelle asked.

"No. I was more interested in what he was doing right then than what he was going to—"

Jinx suddenly rounded the bend in the trail, waving his arms frantically and running as fast as his legs would carry him. "He's coming," he shouted at them. "He's coming." Then he turned to run back down the trail to meet Bret.

It was instinct that made Emily reach for Isabelle's hand and grasp it hard. "Sometimes I was afraid this moment would never come. Now I'm so choked up, I'm about to cry."

"I think it's okay," Isabelle said. "I'm already crying. Another of my boys has come home."

Bret's pulse beat a little faster as the landmarks along the trail brought back memories of the years he'd spent riding through these hills. Almost every rocky outcropping, ridge, or stream tumbling down a hillside pulled him gently back into the world he'd loved, and away from the one he'd thought would be his future. At last he was absolutely certain of what he want. And most of all he wanted Emily to be his wife. He hoped she'd wanted to live with him here in the hill country, but he'd decided before he'd gone halfway to Fort Worth that he'd live anywhere to be with her.

Boston had been even more of a turning point than he'd expected.

Joseph had reached Boston before Bret, but Bret had already corresponded with his cousin Rupert through a series of long telegrams. By the time Bret reached Boston, the battle lines were drawn and the ramparts firmly in place. Uncle Silas had the most votes and seemed to have control of the situation. The first crack in his support came when Bret was able to prove that Silas had stolen his ideas. His uncle had steadfastly denied it, calling Bret and Rupert unconscionable liars. The roof had fallen in on his head when his own mother said Bret had explained his ideas to her more than six months earlier.

When Bret showed how much of the dwindling company profits Silas had been paying to himself and Joseph in salaries, he lost support from the Abercrombie side. In the end, he lost his position as head of the company as well. The family wanted Bret to take over but settled for Rupert when Bret said he was going back to Texas. His grandmother was mollified only when Bret promised to bring Emily to see her.

Emily hadn't been in San Antonio, but there had been a message from Isabelle, saying it was crucial for him to get to the Broken Circle immediately. He considered going to see Emily first anyway, but Isabelle wouldn't have left such a message if it wasn't important. He was worried that something had happened to Jake or somebody else in the family, but he couldn't stop wondering why Emily wasn't in San Antonio. He didn't know whether she hadn't gotten his telegram in time or if she'd changed her mind. He'd spend as little time as possible at the Broken Circle before he left to find Emily. He wouldn't make any conditions this time. Well, only one. She had to love and trust him. Everything else was immaterial.

He hadn't stopped thinking of her while he was in Boston. Everything that happened, nearly every word said, confirmed he had made the right decision. His parents were beyond help and he didn't need retribution. His future lay in Texas. He had returned to Boston to finish what he'd begun, not because he needed to prove anything to himself, but because he'd made promises to Rupert and his grandmother. And because improving the company's chances of remaining in business was part of taking care of Emily's inheritance. And that of the children he hoped they would have together.

He urged his tired mount into a canter. He wanted to see Isabelle and Jake, to make sure nothing was wrong with anyone in the family, but he wanted to head back to Emily as soon as possible. Thoughts of seeing her, holding her, and kissing her filled his dreams every night. Thoughts of making love to her were even now making him uncomfortable in the saddle. He had wasted too much time in his life. He was in a hurry to start making up for it.

He knew practically every rock and tree in the bend in the trail ahead. He'd ridden the trail more than a thousand times, always anticipating the view of the house when it came into view. Today that turn was more important than ever. It would mark the end of the first stage of his journey home.

It was hard to say what he noticed first. Certainly

he saw the house. It was impossible to miss anything that big. At first he was distracted by a child waving at him, shouting something he couldn't understand, and coming toward him in an odd stride that seemed to be a combination of running, jumping at random, and skipping from one side of the trail to the other. If he hadn't been so distracted by the boy, it wouldn't have taken him so long to notice the two women standing on the porch. In the same second that he realized the boy was Jinx, he recognized the woman standing next to Isabelle.

Emily.

With no regard for the condition of his tired mount, Bret urged him into a slow gallop. He didn't need words to know Emily's decision. Her presence—and Isabelle's note—told him that even though he'd made a questionable decision in leaving her as he had, things had come right in the end. If he kept trying, maybe he could get this right. Emily was not only his promise of a future, but she'd also freed him from the misery of his past.

As Jinx drew closer, Bret figured out the boy was trying to tell him everything that had happened since he'd arrived at the Broken Circle.

"—every night," he was saying. "I have my own bed in my own room."

Bret was anxious to reach Emily, but he stopped long enough to swing Jinx into the saddle behind him.

"Will took me with him to watch for you," Jinx said between gasping breaths. "I was way up on this big rock, and I wasn't even afraid."

Jinx wrapped his hands around Bret's waist and rattled on, but as Bret drew closer to the house, Bret's attention zeroed in on Emily. Her expression told him all he needed to know. She was smiling, leaning forward over the railing, wanting to see him as much as he wanted to see her. Will stepped forward when Bret brought his horse to a halt and lifted Jinx from the saddle.

"You'll get your turn in a minute," he said to the boy. "This is one of those times when kids should neither be seen nor heard."

Bret was barely aware of Will's laconic comment or that Isabelle had stepped away from Emily's side. He saw only Emily waiting for him in the home of his heart, her arms held out to him, her face wreathed in smiles. He was surprised to see her eyes swimming with tears, her lips trembling with emotion. Yes, she loved him. More than he'd ever imagined any woman could.

He bounded up the steps two at a time, ready to begin the first minute of the rest of his life.

The Mavericks

LEIGH GREENWOOD

Hawk and Zeke have been inseparable ever since boyhood—two loners, outsiders, as free as the wild horses they chase across the Arizona desert. So when they join up with two misplaced dancehall girls on the trail, they react about the same way as unbroken mustangs to the saddle. Kicking and bucking at every step of the way, the bachelors are gentled by soft touches and warm caresses until each finds himself riding the range with a brand-new partner.

LEIGH GREENWOOD
The Independent Bride

Colorado Territory, 1868: It is about as rough and ready as the West can get, a place and time almost as dangerous as the men who left civilization behind, driven by a desire for land, gold . . . a new life.

Fort Lookout: It is a rugged outpost where soldiers, cattlemen and Indians live on the edge of open warfare, the last place any woman in her right mind would choose to settle.

Abby: She is everything a man should avoid—with a face of beauty and an expression of stubborn determination. Colonel Bryce McGregor knows there is no room for such a woman at his fort or in his heart. Yet as she receives proposal after proposal from his troops, Bryce realizes the only man he can allow her to marry is himself.

LEIGH GREENWOOD

The Reluctant Bride

Colorado Territory, 1872: A rough-and-tumble place and time almost as dangerous as the men who left civilization behind, driven by a desire for a new life. In a false-fronted town where the only way to find a decent woman is to send away for her, Tanzy first catches sight of the man she came west to marry galloping after a gang of bandits. Russ Tibbolt is a far cry from the husband she expected when she agreed to become a mail-order bride. He is much too compelling for any woman's peace of mind. With his cobalt-blue eyes and his body's magic, how can she hope to win the battle of wills between them?

his right, Gabriel stood *shevirse*, a combination of groomsman and bodyguard. He carried Jonmarc's sword as well as a sword of his own, although they both knew that Gabriel himself was the deadliest weapon.

Jonmarc and Carina had already made their offerings to the Lady at sunset in Dark Haven's chapel. Now all that remained was the ceremony. Like most things in Dark Haven, the ritual differed here from what they had seen in Margolan or elsewhere, following more ancient sacred ways.

"It's time." Gabriel said solemnly, and leaned forward to open the doors. A crowd awaited, and voices buzzed as the guests turned to watch them enter. Jonmarc took a deep breath and squared his shoulders. He flashed an impudent grin at Carina before sobering and taking his place beside her as they walked to where Taru stood.

Taru wore the brown robes that marked her as one of the Sisterhood mages. In her right hand, she held an oak staff, and she wore a stole of evergreen twigs plaited with strips of oak bark. Together, the icons of immortality and ancient magic were powerful symbols. At Taru's feet was a circle of braided cloth, and in its center, a mat of oak leaves. The mage had requested that Jonmarc and Carina each give her a garment they had recently worn to make the strips that became the braid, making the magic highly personal. Jonmarc had no magic of his own, but he felt a shiver go down his spine as he and Carina stepped into the circle and knelt facing each other.

Chanting in a language Jonmarc did not recognize, Taru struck her staff on the floor behind him, and then turned it in her hands to strike the floor behind Carina with the opposite end. Jonmarc felt a sudden wind sweep along the ground, and by the way Carina's eyes widened, he suspected that her magic gave her the power to see something more dramatic. Turning the staff as she chanted, Taru marked four corners of the warding, one for each of the Light Aspects. When she had returned to her original position, she laid the staff aside and lifted an oaken chalice adorned with a band of silver that wound from the lip to the base. She filled the chalice with red wine, and lifted it to the four corners.

"Blessed be the elements. Wine from the soil." She swirled the cup, and a flame flickered over the chalice. "Fire from the sun." Drops of water fell from her cupped palm into the chalice. "Waters of the oceans." The air over the cup stirred, descending into the wine to form a vortex. "Winds of the sky."

"Do you consent to be bound in life, in death and in the dark places between life and death, joined in body and soul?"

Jonmarc's gaze locked with Carina's. "We do."

Taru took Jonmarc's left hand, turning it palm up. She withdrew a dagger with a moonstone hilt and an obsidian blade from her belt. In one smooth motion, she opened a thin cut to form half of the Lady's symbol on Jonmarc's palm, and flicked droplets of the blood into the chalice. She took Carina's hand and made a cut in the shape of the symbol's matching half, adding her blood to the chalice. Then she pressed their hands together so that their blood combined to form the Lady's mark, and took the mantle from around her neck, wrapping it four times around their wrists.

"Drink."

Jonmarc had spent enough time around mages to recognize the tingle of strong magic. He felt it sear through the joined blood between their palms, even as he felt Carina's presence slip against his mind. She smiled at the secret they shared, that she was a few days pregnant with his child. Then he felt the familiar burn of her magic healing the cut Taru had made, and Carina laced her fingers between his.

"Rejoice," Taru said. "You are joined in the law of the kingdoms and in the presence of the Lady, in life and in death—and beyond." She removed the stole from their wrists, and when they released their clasped hands, the cuts had healed into thin, white scars.

Behind them, the crowd began to clap and cheer as Jonmarc and Carina rose to their feet.

Jonmarc took Carina in his arms and kissed her. The ritual bond heightened his awareness of her, and it felt as if her thoughts and emotions flitted just beyond his grasp. He could only imagine the strength of the bond for those who shared magic as well as love.

"Congratulations." Gabriel handed Jonmarc his shirt as well as his swordbelt and weapons, which Jonmarc accepted with a sense of relief. "May the Lady in all Her Aspects bless you now and always."

The guests crowded around them to wish them well. Riqua and Rafe were present, as were Kolin and Tamaq. Vigulf, the *vyrkin* shaman, added his blessing. Laisren stood arm in arm with Lisette, looking none the worse for the injuries he had sustained in the battle against Malesh. Jonmarc felt the absence of Yestin and Eiria keenly, and although the days of mourning were completed, he knew it would take a long while for the feeling of loss to lessen. Near the wall, Raen swayed to the music with her eyes closed, singing silently. From the cold spots in the room and the inexplicable drafts of air, Jonmarc was certain Raen was not the only one of Dark Haven's ghosts that was present, although she alone was visible. The head of the wine guild and the other town dignitaries were present, along with the *vayash moru* and *vyrkin* who had fought alongside Jonmarc and Gabriel. Even Jonmarc's old friends Maynard

Linton and Jolie had managed to arrive in Dark Haven for the wedding. But as Jonmarc moved among his guests, more than once he heard the others whisper an unfamiliar word, and he turned finally to Gabriel.

"Who are the '*mogorifi*'?"

Gabriel looked at him. "You and Carina. It's an old word. It means 'the changed ones.' There are legends about a few who stand between the living and the undead, who are both and neither. In the legends, the *mogorifi* are guardians." He gave a pointed glance at the puncture scars on Jonmarc's neck. "You returned alive from making Istra's Bargain. Carina returned as a mortal from Malesh's attempt to turn her. Either one would be rare, to say the least. For the two of you together," he shrugged, "it's not unreasonable to view it as highly significant."

The implications of Gabriel's comments were more than Jonmarc wanted to think about.

"Oh, and just so you know," Gabriel continued, "the only ones who aren't aware that Carina is expecting are the mortals. The *vayash moru* and *vyrkin* can sense a shift in the life force like that." He smiled. "Congratulations, to both of you."

Jonmarc slipped his arm around Carina's shoulders as musicians began a round of lively tunes and drew her out on the dance floor for the circle dances, enjoying her laughter as they wove through the complicated steps.

As the dance concluded, a hush fell over the room. Jonmarc turned to see an unfamiliar *vayash moru* in the doorway. He tensed, unsure whether the newcomer was friend or foe.

"That's Alfarr," Gabriel said in a low voice just behind him. "He's the keeper of the torches in the Lady's chapel beneath the manor house. He's kept them lit for hundreds of years, but he rarely ventures out. This is highly unusual."

Had Alfarr been mortal, Jonmarc would have supposed him in his middle years, with dark black hair edged with gray at the temples. He moved with a dignified confidence, and something in his eyes hinted at a burden long carried. Alfarr stopped in front of Jonmarc and Carina and made a low bow.

"Peace and blessings to you both." His voice had an unusual accent, one Jonmarc could not place. Alfarr met Carina's eyes. "Now I can rest, because my vision has come true. Twin daughters will each bear a son. One will wear a crown, and the other will wield a sword, and together they will challenge the abyss."

Carina's eyes widened. "Twins," she whispered.

Daughters. Jonmarc caught his breath and tightened his grip on Carina's hand.

Before he could collect his thoughts to reply, Alfarr was gone.

"What do you suppose that means?" Carina asked, looking toward the empty doorway.

"Visions are strange things," Gabriel said. "They can mean a great deal, or nothing at all. Even if they come true, they can lead to an end that the seer never imagined." Jonmarc met his eyes, and knew that Gabriel's insight came from visions of his own.

Gabriel clapped a hand on Jonmarc's shoulder. "Let the future take care of itself, for once. There'll be time enough for visions. Today, we celebrate."

"That works for me. I'm a one-day-at-a-time kind of guy." Jonmarc pulled Carina into his arms and looked into her eyes. "Twin girls, huh? That'll take some getting used to."

She chuckled. "It's too late for second thoughts."

He kissed the thin pink scar on her palm. "Second thoughts? Never. But even if they're healers like you, expect me to teach them to use a sword."

"We'll see about that."

Jonmarc leaned down to kiss her. As he met her lips and drank in the scent of her hair, he realized that for the first time in half his life, the future was no longer a dark unknown. He heard the crowd around them clinking goblets and cheering for their kiss as Carina leaned against him and returned his kiss with fervor.

Visions be damned.

The Lord of Dark Haven had come home.

ABOUT THE AUTHOR

Gail Z. Martin discovered her passion
for science fiction, fantasy and ghost stories
in elementary school. The first story she
wrote—at age five—was about a vampire. Her
favorite TV show as a preschooler was Dark
Shadows. At age fourteen, she decided to become a
writer. She enjoys attending science fiction/fantasy
conventions, Renaissance fairs and living history
sites. She is married and has three children, a
Himalayan cat and a golden retriever.

You can visit Gail at:-

www.chroniclesofthenecromancer.com

Read her blog:-

blog.myspace.com/chronicleofthenecromancer

And follow her on twitter:-

twitter.com/gailzmartin

SOLARIS BOOKS

Founded in 2007 as an independent imprint, Solaris set out to publish a mix of innovative and traditional science fiction, fantasy and horror, by new and familiar authors alike, and to fill the gap between large-scale mass-market publishers and the small genre press. In two years, we've published gritty, hard-SF and high-octane adventure, creepy horror and swashbuckling fantasy. We've discovered new gems like the hugely successful Gail Z. Martin and snagged old favourites like Brian Lumley and Eric Brown. We've published seven anthologies, including new science fiction and fantasy, steampunk, and stories inspired by H. P. Lovecraft and Edgar Allan Poe, with contributions by some of the best-loved and most recognised names in science fiction. As of 2009, Solaris has been part of Rebellion, and are confident that they can only go from strength to strength in the future.

More than anything, Solaris exists to publish fantastic books by great authors, and to bring to your attention, as a reader, a plethora of exciting new stories and novels.

http://www.solarisbooks.com/

"Attractive characters and an imaginative setting combine in an excellent, fast-moving quest novel."
—— David Drake, author of the Lord of the Isles series

GAIL Z. MARTIN

THE SUMMONER

Book One of the
CHRONICLES OF THE NECROMANCER

UK ISBN: 978 1 844164 68 4 • US ISBN: 978 1 844164 68 4 • £7.99/$7.99

The world of Prince Martris Drayke is thrown into chaos when his brother murders their father and seizes the throne. Forced to flee with only a handful of loyal followers, Martris must seek retribution and restore his father's honour. If the living are arrayed against him, Martris must call on a different set of allies: the living dead.

 WWW.SOLARISBOOKS.COM

Follow us on Twitter! www.twitter.com/solarisbooks

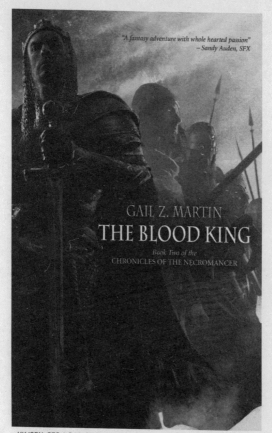

FALCONFAR

Dark Lord

"A master of fantasy world-building.
His magic and wizardry are wondrous
to all."—Margaret Weis, New York
Times best-selling author

ED GREENWOOD

BOOK ONE

UK ISBN: 978 1 844166 17 6 • US ISBN: 978 1 844165 84 1 • £7.99/$7.99

When he mysteriously finds himself drawn into a world of his own devising, bumbling
writer Rod Everlar is confronted by a shocking truth - he has lost control of his creation to
a brooding cabal of evil. In order to save his creation, he must seize control of Falconfar
and halt the spread of corruption before it is too late.

UK ISBN: 978 1 906735 63 0 • US ISBN: 978 1 844167 64 7 • £7.99/$7.99

Having been drawn into a fantasy world of his own creation, Rod Everlar continues his quest to defeat the corruption he has discovered within. With the ambitious Arlaghaun now dead, he sets off in pursuit of the dark wizard Malraun, only to find that he has raised an army of monsters and mercenaries in order to conquer the world...

 WWW.SOLARISBOOKS.COM

Follow us on Twitter! www.twitter.com/solarisbooks

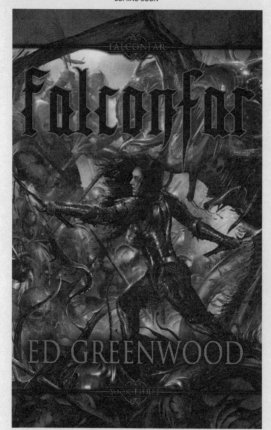

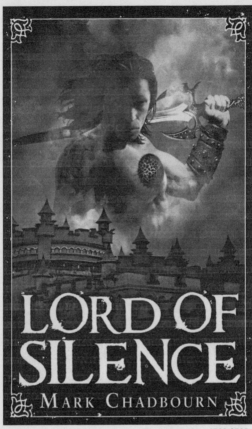

LORD OF SILENCE

MARK CHADBOURN

UK ISBN: 978 1 844167 52 4 • US ISBN: 978 1 844167 53 1 • £7.99/$7.99

When the great hero of Idriss is murdered, Vidar, the Lord of Silence, must take his place as chief defender against the terrors lurking in the forest beyond the walls. But Vidar is a man tormented – by his lost memories and by a life-draining jewel. With a killer loose within the city and a threat mounting without, he must solve an ancient mystery to unlock the secrets of his own past.

 WWW.SOLARISBOOKS.COM

Follow us on Twitter! www.twitter.com/solarisbooks

DEFIANT
BOBBI SMITH

Clint knows that although he stands reading his own epi-
taph, the words are true. Ever since the attack that killed his
entire family, he's been dead inside. Only one thing keeps him
going—the burning need to bring in the outlaws who did it.

Posing undercover to infiltrate the gang, Clint can let no
one know his true identity or the fact that he was once a Texas
Ranger. Not even the pretty daughter of a preacher man who
bursts into the Last Chance Saloon. As far as she knows, he's
a gunslinger who has no right to touch a good woman. But
sometimes a man's got to break all the rules, ignore common
sense to follow his heart, and get downright…*Defiant*.
